THE PYTHON PIT:
THE COMPLETE ADVENTURES OF
SINGAPORE SAMMY, VOLUME 2

George F. Worts

THE PYTHON PIT

THE COMPLETE ADVENTURES OF
SINGAPORE SAMMY, VOLUME 2

GEORGE F. WORTS

ILLUSTRATED BY

SAMUEL CAHAN

STEEGER BOOKS • 2020

PUBLISHING HISTORY

"Singapore Sammy" originally appeared in the December 12 and 19, 1931 issues of *Argosy* magazine (Vol. 226, Nos. 1 & 2). Copyright © 1931 by The Frank A. Munsey Company. Copyright renewed © 1959 and assigned to Steeger Properties, LLC. All rights reserved.

"The Python Pit" originally appeared in the May 6, 13, and 20, 1933 issues of *Argosy* magazine (Vol. 238, Nos. 2–4). Copyright © 1933 by The Frank A. Munsey Company. Copyright renewed © 1960 and assigned to Steeger Properties, LLC. All rights reserved.

"Isle of the Meteor" originally appeared in the August 19, 1933 issue of *Argosy* magazine (Vol. 240, No. 5). Copyright © 1933 by The Frank A. Munsey Company. Copyright renewed © 1960 and assigned to Steeger Properties, LLC. All rights reserved.

"Buddha's Whisker" originally appeared in the May 26, 1934 issue of *Argosy* magazine (Vol. 247, No. 2). Copyright © 1934 by The Frank A. Munsey Company. Copyright renewed © 1961 and assigned to Steeger Properties, LLC. All rights reserved.

"About the Author" originally appeared in the January 25, 1930 issue of *Argosy* magazine (Vol. 209, No. 5). Copyright © 1930 by The Frank A. Munsey Company. Copyright renewed © 1957 and assigned to Steeger Properties, LLC. All rights reserved.

Visit steegerbooks.com for more books like this.

TABLE OF CONTENTS

Singapore Sammy 1

The Python Pit 81

Isle of the Meteor 175

Buddha's Whisker 237

About the Author 300

SINGAPORE SAMMY

Seven years in the South Seas had made Sammy Shay
as hard as iron and as wise as sin—but the thieving
father he trailed knew a thousand vicious tricks

"Ah! A woman can destroy the world."—
Saying of the Shans inspired by the treachery
of Supayalat, Thebaw's queen.

CHAPTER I

THE BLUE FIRE-PEARL

IT WAS MIDNIGHT aboard the Laughing Lady, and the red-headed American was about to be stabbed and robbed. But the young man was happily in ignorance of this danger.

He lifted his brandy highball and said to the beautiful, dusky-eyed girl across the table from him:

"Here's a toast we used to say in Mexico, sister: 'Health, love and wealth—and a beautiful widow to enjoy them with!'"

"But I am not a widow," the girl said in her lazy musical voice.

"No? Well, I'm not wealthy."

"Ah! But you have health and—who knows?—the capacity to love," she said with a slow, soft smile, and lifted her liqueur glass to her red lips. "Here's looking at you!"

It would have been a happier choice if she had said "me" instead of "you." Since the little coasting steamer had crossed the Menam bar and steamed out into the Gulf of Siam, the red-headed American had been paying her the closest attention.

Her name was Dolores de Silva. Her beauty was of that rare type which blooms only where the East meets the West and sometimes mingles. She was unmistakably Eurasian—half white, half yellow. Such a combination often produces exceptional beauty. It is the same beauty which a man sometimes glimpses in the deep equatorial jungles; a ripe, strange, seductive beauty which it is generally safer to let alone.

Like all her kind, she was very slim, boneless, and exciting. She chanced to be remarkably beautiful. She was the most beau-

1

McCoy snatched up the dagger.

tiful Eurasian the red-headed American had seen in seven years in the Far East. Her appeal was that of a spiced wine. Her eyes were velvety brown, her skin was satiny olive, her red mouth was a lure, and her teeth were perfect pearls. Her black hair reminded the bewitched young man across from her of a starry midnight sky. He was intoxicated by the spiced perfume which it gave off. It suggested the tuberose on a moist, tropical night.

He suspected she was as dangerous as she was beautiful, but he didn't care. He sighed luxuriously.

"How come you're on this old tub, sister?"

"I am going to Chantaboun-town."

"That's what I call a break. So am I."

She was gazing at him obliquely, and this attitude brought out all the Oriental in her. Her smile was mysterious.

"It is such a desolate place," she said. "Nothing but Burmese and hideous land crabs. They look large enough to carry off a cow. Land crabs and filth and heat."

"And sapphires," the American said.

Her plucked eyebrows went up slightly. "You are a sapphire buyer?"

"Not me, sister. I am a T.T.T."

Her smile was amused. "I know—a typical tropical tramp. You deceived me. You look so vigorous. What can possibly interest you in Chantaboun?"

"I am looking for a man."

"You say that as if you intend to kill him when you find him."

"Well, not unless he tries to kill me. Now tell me why you're goin' to Chantaboun."

HER ANSWER was to withdraw her slim, olive left hand from her lap where it had been lying. A remarkable sapphire set in platinum glowed at him from her engagement finger.

His eyes sparkled with admiration, but his mouth dipped with disappointment.

"Is he in Chantaboun?"

"Yes. Are you curious? I will tell you all about him. He owns a sapphire mine upriver. He is Bruce McCoy, an American and very handsome."

"Young?"

"As young as you."

The red-headed American grunted. "You can send McCoy a wireless, sister, that you have met a better man than he is."

Dolores de Silva laughed. Her teeth flashed. When she laughed, she squinted her eyes and her lashes came down. They were long, black and so thick that they formed a mat.

He reached across the table for her hand, but she quickly dropped it into her lap. Her smile remained alluring.

"I have found," she said, "that red-haired men are very impulsive."

"Sister," he answered, "all the other red-headed men you met were asleep or doped."

Miss de Silva laughed again. "You are amazing. You haven't known me a half hour, and already you are boasting that you are going to take me away from the man I have promised to marry. Real love cannot happen so suddenly."

"A real war is going to happen to this guy McCoy!"

"How exciting!" she said, with a laugh. "And the survivor will carry me off to his cave. I think you are kidding me. I would rather hear about this man you may have to kill."

The American's mouth became grim and his eyes became hard. They were as blue as his hair was red. A faint tinge of yellow in the whites, from jungle fevers, made them seem bluer. He leaned toward Miss de Silva with a slightly undershot under lip.

"He's my old man," he said harshly. "When I was a kid two years old, he ran off and left my mother and me flat. He took all the money she had, and he took my grandfather's will, which left us between a half million and a million, gold. You want to hear the rest of it? He was an elephant man with a circus. He came out to the East because he's nuts about pearls and nuts about elephants.

"For seven years, since I hit seventeen, I've trailed him. I've used everything from ox-carts to airplanes. I've followed him from Peking to Rangoon, and from Ceylon to Rarotonga. I've been face to face with him three times, and each time he outfoxed me. Generally, he disguises himself as a begging priest. I heard in Singapore he is in on some sapphire deal in Chantaboun. That's why I'm headin' for Chantaboun. When I find him, I get that will back. He's done his damnedest to kill me—and I won't handle him with gloves this time. He won't get away this time."

Miss de Silva's large brown eyes were glowing with excitement—or something else.

"You know Chantaboun," he said grimly. "You know whether or not an old man who dresses in the yellow robes of a beggin' priest is there. Is he?"

The words of the question were like two bullets. The girl's eyelids fluttered at him. A vague look of fear flickered in her eyes for a moment, but he was intent on her lips and missed what happened in her eyes;

"I have been away from Chantaboun for six months," she told him breathlessly. "I don't know this old man, but I know you. They call you Singapore Sammy. I have heard of you for years. What I heard was that you cry into your beer because you cannot find your dear old father who is lost out here! But I've heard other things, too. You are a killer!"

"I have never killed a man except in self-defense."

The girl's eyes were as bright as a pair of gems.

"Your real name," she panted, "is Samuel Larkin Shay. I know something else about you, Mr. Shay! I know you have in your possession the most beautiful blue pearl in the Far East. I am dying to see that pearl. Show it to me."

Singapore Sammy looked at her, heavy-lidded.

"I never carry it on me, sister."

The suddenly hard, greedy look in her eyes might have warned him, but it did not. He was at that moment inhaling air scented with the heavy, spiced perfume she used in her hair. And his eyes were as hungry as hers.

Miss de Silva said softly: "You are a liar, Singapore Sammy. What is that copper wire around your neck?"

THE RED-HEADED man compressed his lips and grunted through his nose. Without removing his infatuated eyes from her red mouth, he reached up and hooked the copper loop with one thumb. The wire came up from his chest until a small chamois-skin bag dangled at his Adam's apple. With strong white teeth, he loosened the draw-string and decanted into his palm a blue pearl which gathered unto itself all the light in the Laughing Lady's smoking room.

"The blue fire-pearl!" Miss de Silva whispered, and her eyes gloated.

The blue pearl rolled about in the cupped palm of his hand, a bubble of magic flame. As blue as a Chantaboun sapphire, as big around as the end of its owner's forefinger, as full of fire as the eye of a charging leopard, the blue pearl was fit to grace the finger or the throat of a princess.

A soft throaty sound came from Miss de Silva's moist red lips. Her hand darted out with the swiftness of a striking snake; but with equal swiftness, Singapore Sammy tossed the blue pearl into the air and dexterously caught it on the bunched tips of his fingers.

"Where did you get that pearl?" the girl breathed.

"Malobar. I got in wrong up there, and they threw me in jail. The maharaja is a sport; he is hipped on box-fightin'. So he staged a ten-round bout between me and another American prisoner. The winner was to get this pearl. The loser was to go to the maharaja's pet black leopards for breakfast. I won the bout."

Dolores de Silva's eyes were dilated, catlike.

"Did the other man go to the leopards?"

"Nope. We both got down to the coast O.K."

The beautiful Eurasian sighed.

"How much is it worth?"

"I've refused twenty-five thousand gold."

"But you are a fool to carry it!"

"A lot of people have made the mistake of thinkin' that."

Her eyes narrowed, glowed again. She licked her lips with a dainty pink tongue.

"What are you going to do with it, Singapore Sammy?"

He regarded her, faintly smiling.

"Find its mate. I hear the chief of a Moosar hill tribe has it. Two of these matched would bring a cold hundred thousand in New York or Paris."

The famous Malobar pearl vanished into the palm of his hand. Singapore Sammy dropped it into the chamois-skin sack and returned the sack to his bosom.

"Or, the one you have there," Miss de Silva said in her lazy musical voice, "would be beautiful set in an engagement ring."

"To take the place of a sapphire?" he asked, heavy-lidded again.

She shrugged her lovely slim shoulders.

"Perhaps. Who knows? I think I like you very much already— perhaps too much."

With a grin, the red-headed American shot out a brown paw to capture her hand. But she was a little too quick for him. She had sprung up, and was smiling down into his eyes.

"Good night, Singapore Sammy," she said, giving him her mysterious, oblique look. "I am going to my room and to bed. It is late, and the captain says we will dock before dawn, because high water at the bar is at four. I will see you in the morning—perhaps?"

"You'll see me plenty, sister."

Dolores de Silva went out on deck with her hand caught to her heart. It was impossible to say whether it was the appealing feminine gesture of a slim, lovely girl, or the impulsive act of a woman whose madly thumping heart threatened to leap from her breast.

Singapore hardly observed it. He was watching the back of her neck, which was olive and rendered inviting by tendrils of spiced black hair.

CHAPTER II

A FINE BLADE

NOT A BREATH of wind moved except the sluggish current set up by the ship's passage. The night was hot and stuffy, and Singapore's stateroom was like an oven. He decided to sleep on the foredeck and to avail himself of such random breezes as might be adrift.

The foredeck was dark and deserted. Singapore carried one of the pillows and a blanket from his bunk. He stretched out the blanket on the deck; the pillow he propped against the forward wall of the cabin. In his travels he had learned that it was possible to sleep very comfortably in this fashion. He did not mind a teakwood mattress. He had slept on docks and decks for the past seven years.

Settling himself, he started a cigarette and thought of Dolores de Silva's alluring loveliness. He told himself that a guy could go off his nut over a girl like Dolores. He recalled a sea captain who had flung himself off the balcony of a Hongkong hotel to his death because of a Eurasian girl who could not hold a candle to Dolores de Silva. Singapore had never had much time for women, but he was going to make time for Dolores. Thinking of her luscious red mouth, he sighed.

He watched the greenish lines of phosphorescence streaming out in the waves which folded back from the blunt old bows of the Laughing Lady. Toward the eastern horizon, far off and ghostly, was a lifeless sail. Sam made out dimly a schooner rig. A schooner out there, hard by the nameless islands, was becalmed. Her sails hung limp in the light begrudged by a scimitar of chalky moon. Her starboard light beamed at him like a fabulous emerald.

Was she, by some prank of fate, the *Blue Goose?* The *Blue Goose* was owned by Singapore Sammy's closest friend, Lucifer—"Lucky"—Jones. Lucky had told him, when they parted, that he intended to go pearling in the bight of the Great Green Gulf. No one had had luck pearling in the bight, but Lucky Jones had dreamed a dream. He believed in dreams. And he believed in acting on them.

Singapore Sammy was homesick for that young buccaneer, and he was homesick for the *Blue Goose*. She was a fast little steel-blue schooner with lovable lines and a stout heart. Shipmates with Lucky Jones, Singapore Sammy had seen her ride through hurricanes and typhoons on the highroad to adventure. She would weather anything brewed by any sea. Since he had parted from Lucky Jones, in Java, to continue his quest for his father, Singapore had longed to be back aboard the *Blue Goose*, to have his hands on her wheel, to be lounging again on the poop in a Bombay chair under glittering tropical skies, swapping yarns with Lucky.

Thinking, dreaming of that pleasant and reckless life which he had deserted, Singapore Sammy fell asleep, to dream of precious stones. He had a passion for precious stones, and in his dreams he often saw them in great brass-studded caskets—mounds of sapphires, rubies, emeralds, diamonds, pearls.

HE WAS awakened by something damp and sticky trailing across his left cheek. Coming fully awake, he detected a heavy, pungent, oily smell. The fumes of it seemed to fill the air all around him.

The night was no longer aglow with moon or stars. The sky was overcast; a fine, warm drizzle was falling and making a faint hissing sound on the deck. Above that, he heard the labored clanking of the Laughing Lady's old tin teapot of an engine.

He braced himself and waited. The pungent, heavy smell became more pronounced. Then something that was damp and sticky touched his nose.

With a startled grunt, he struck it aside and, with it, the fingers of an invisible hand. Acutely aware of danger now, he made a lunge for the hand and trapped it, but it was snatched away. Another hand snatched at the copper wire about his neck. Singapore imprisoned the wrist attached to that hand, heard a panting and gasping close to his face, and tried to struggle to his feet.

He fell back. His free hand, groping, encountered metal—the long, thin blade of a knife. He grasped it and gave it a violent wrench.

Something, perhaps a foot, struck him sharply on the point of the chin; but he did not relinquish the knife. He gave it another wrench, and his invisible antagonist let the knife go.

There was another sharp blow on the point of Sammy's chin. The wrist he had captured was snatched out of his hand. Footsteps padded swiftly, softly, around the turn of the deck, on the starboard side, and Singapore Sammy scrambled to his feet.

He raced after the departing footsteps, but when he reached the lighted area of the deck it was, except for himself, deserted. He investigated the smoking room and the small reading room.

Both were empty. A rapid tour of the ship afforded him not the slightest satisfaction.

Singapore had been grasping the knife by the hilt all of this time. In the light of a dim, yellow deck Lamp he examined his souvenir. It proved to be one of the most beautiful daggers he had ever seen. Of native workmanship, the blade was long, straight and thin. The handle was a treasure. It was of soft gold so thickly crusted with sapphires that little of the yellow metal was visible.

Not a little pleased with his good fortune, Singapore placed the jeweled dagger in his pocket and returned to the foredeck.

Striking matches, he presently found a small lump of silk sponge. He picked it up and gingerly sniffed it. The piece of sponge was saturated with the pungent oily stuff he had smelled. It was some volatile drug the purpose of which was doubtless to make him sleep.

He lighted a cigarette and pondered that not very mysterious attack. Some one aboard who knew that he had in his possession the Malobar pearl had made a determined effort to relieve him of it. His suspicions centered on Dolores de Silva. He believed she was as dangerous as she was beautiful. Yet he could not believe that the intended robber was a girl. Those invisible hands had not been a girl's hands. They were too strong. And the more he pondered it, the more he was inclined to shift suspicion elsewhere. Miss de Silva was too clever, too smooth, to stoop to such crudity, even if she wanted the Malobar pearl badly enough to steal it.

If this logic were sound, then one of the other passengers had been the owner of this valuable dagger. He recalled the ten faces he had counted at dinner last night. All but Miss de Silva were men. Six were Siamese, two were Burmese, one was a tall, lean, and ugly-looking Cantonese. Any of them, or any one of the crew, might have been the thief.

It was likely that to-night's attempt on the Malobar pearl

would be added to previous attempts as one more unsolved mystery.

THE RED-HEADED American spent the remainder of the night in his stateroom with a gun under his pillow. He was wakened shortly before dawn by the shouts of a Tamil boy who was heaving the lead. When he awoke again, red sunlight was slanting in at his porthole. Looking out, he saw the sun just rising above the mangrove swamps which were moving slowly past; beyond them, he saw the damp green of the Siamese jungle. The Laughing Lady was making her way up the Chantaboun River.

Singapore Sammy dressed and went on deck. Up forward he found Dolores de Silva, slim and lovely, with one slender arm encircling a stanchion as she gazed over the jungle at the rising sun. She wore a crisp white linen suit and a pert little sun helmet; white silk stockings and trim white oxfords. Her olive skin and dark eyes, in contrast, made her romantic. When she saw him, her brown velvet eyes became lustrous, and she gave a delighted laugh.

"You are up early, Mr. Shay!"

"I hate to miss things," he said.

A sapphire-studded wrist watch of platinum twinkled at him from a wrist against the stanchion. The wrist was slim. It looked fragile. It looked as if a pair of fingers could snap it. Her hands were slim and small, but there was a capable look about them. Were these the hands which had tried to drug and stab him last night? She was dangerous; but was she dangerous enough to kill a man for a twenty-five thousand dollar pearl?

"YOU LOOK," she told him, in her lazy, musical voice, "as if you had got out of the wrong side of the bed. Why are men so surly the first thing in the morning?"

Singapore smiled wryly. His eyes remained blue marbles.

"It depends on what happened to them the night before, sister."

"Did something happen to you?"

"I had some funny dreams. I dreamed I was holding your hand,"

The girl gazed up at him with laughing eyes.

"What are you planning to do, if you please, to my *fiancé?*"

Singapore held out his two large brown hairy paws. He slowly encircled them about an imaginary something. This he shook violently, then made the gesture of tossing a limp, lifeless body, with contempt, overboard.

The beautiful Eurasian placed her back against the stanchion and looked up at him with brown eyes glowing with amusement. Then they dropped for a fraction of a second to the copper wire about his neck. It was hardly more than a flicker of a glance.

He said, lazily, "Isn't there anything about me, sister, you like?"

She quickly held up her left hand, so that the sunlight flashed on the velvety facets of the sapphire.

"You see this, my friend? It was the very first sapphire out of Bruce's mine."

"Does that mean you're in love with him?"

"I adore him!" she cried. "He is rich, handsome, romantic. Life to him is a romance and I am his great romance."

"He sounds like a sucker. Will he meet you on the dock?"

"Certainly!" She searched his face anxiously. "And you will start no brawls!"

Singapore removed a deck of greasy-old playing cards from his hip pocket. He effortlessly tore the entire pack in half, and tossed the pieces overboard.

"I will tear him apart like that—and throw the chunks to the land crabs. Where do you stay in Chantaboun?"

"With my father. I warn you, Mr. Shay, he is a very dangerous man."

"Will he be on the dock, too?"

"No."

"I am certainly anxious to meet this guy McCoy," Singapore said.

THEIR CONVERSATION was interrupted at this point by the appearance of a dining room steward, who announced that breakfast was being served. The red-head and the Eurasian went down to the little dining room, where further familiarities were impossible. And by the time breakfast was over, the Laughing Lady had creaked around the last snake-like bend in the river and was lying alongside the old rotting wharf at Chantaboun. The yells of river boys filled the air, and the torrid smells of a Siamese town crept in at the portholes.

Singapore did not see Miss de Silva again until he went down the gangplank with a battered suitcase in his hand. He saw her go into the arms of a fat, elderly, oily-looking man who wore loose-fitting white drill and a dirty and dented khaki sun helmet shaped like a mushroom.

Was this the young, romantic, handsome Mr. McCoy?

The first mate of the Laughing Lady was standing on the dock at the end of the gangplank.

"Who," Singapore asked him, "is that buzzard talking to the de Silva girl?"

The mate, an Australian, looked at Sammy curiously, then glanced to where the girl and the fat man in the mushroom sun helmet were standing.

"That's Roderigo de Silva."

"Her father?"

"Yes, sir."

"What's his racket?"

The mate's eyes took on a veiled look. He shrugged.

Singapore, with a grimace as if he had tasted something sour, made his way through the yelping coolies. He saw Dolores de Silva quickly speak to her father. The fat man turned and stared. His eyes were the color of wet slate. His face was as yellow and as oily as butter. The look he addressed to Singapore was hard, measuring.

Singapore, drawing nearer, revised his first estimate of Roderigo de Silva. De Silva was not a fat man. He was a big-barreled, beefy man—heavy and tough, but not fat. The butt of a heavy-caliber revolver protruded from the waistband of his loose, white drill trousers.

The red-headed American gave him a grin which was answered by nothing but a continuation of the hard, hostile stare. It was easy to guess that Roderigo de Silva was, for some reason, on the defensive. His eyes ran up and down Sammy suspiciously.

Singapore said affably, "Howdy, Mr. de Silva. Excuse me for buttin' in. But I'm lookin' for a man—a white man about fifty years old who is tourin' around these parts dressed up as a beggin' Buddhist priest. I heard in Buitenzorg he was here. His name is Bill Shay. He happens to be my father. Do you know him?"

Roderigo de Silva continued to stare at him. He placed his hand firmly on the butt of his revolver. Singapore saw that the butt plates were mother-of-pearl, and that large sapphires were mounted in them.

The slate-colored eyes were wary and suspicious. Ignoring the American's question, de Silva took Dolores by the arm and led her toward the inshore end of the dock.

Singapore, with a faint frown of wonder between his eyes, watched them start along a path leading along the river to the village. But they did not enter the village. They left the path and descended the river bank and got into a canoe which was hollowed out of a whole breadfruit log. It was manned by two natives with bamboo poles.

De Silva seated himself so that he commanded a view of the dock. His hand lingered on the mother-of-pearl-mounted gun.

Singapore wondered why de Silva had behaved so suspiciously. Either he possessed an extremely suspicious nature, or else he was up to his ears in some dirty work. If the latter were the case, he would naturally look upon any white man with distrust.

The red-head was convinced that Dolores, with all her loveliness and charm, was just as safe to play with as a queen cobra. One glimpse of her father was enough to convince him that he was equally reptilian.

Yet this interesting pair were, after all, of no consequence to Sammy; he would probably see neither of them again. His job was to find his father.

SINGAPORE SAMMY watched the canoe until it turned in toward the bank again, vanishing, presumably, into a *klong*, or native canal. Then he asked a half-naked brown man, who appeared to be the number-one man in the dock gang, if he had recently seen about Chantaboun an elderly white man who wore the yellow robes and carried the *dugot*, the *thinbaing* and the *thabeit* of the mendicant Buddhist priest.

He asked the question in Siamese and received a courteous answer.

"*Aie*, master!"

"Where is he?"

"Gone, master! He left last night on a fast elephant for Annam. He went to hunt tigers."

Singapore groaned. It never failed. His father had some sixth sense which warned him when Sammy was close on his trail. Like the yogis of India, he seemed able to foresee events.

"There is another white man here I want to see," Singapore told the dock foreman. "His name is Bruce McCoy."

The native's eyes shimmered and narrowed. A queer expression flitted over his brown face.

"*Aie*, master! He is here. I think you will find him in the Sapphire Sandal."

Singapore thanked him and went on into the village. He wondered why the dock foreman had made that queer grimace when McCoy's name was mentioned. He was curious to meet

McCoy. Doubtless, McCoy could give him some information about his father. And he wanted to see the sort of man Dolores de Silva had been working on. Unless he was mistaken, McCoy would prove to be just another sucker.

HE PASSED the mat-making stalls, the shops of the Burmese lapidaries, and the bazaars. The Sapphire Sandal, in spite of its pretentious name, was nothing more than a grog shop. It had been in existence since the days when American clippers sometimes put in on their voyages to India. The original structure had been burned. The present Sapphire Sandal, with its familiar faded blue sign studded with fragments of blue glass, had thatched *nipa* palm sides and a corrugated iron roof.

Its interior was dusky and cool-looking, smelling sourly of spilled liquor. A worn teak bar ran along one side. There were tables and benches in one corner. The floor was dirt. Behind the bar stood a brown man whose eyes and mouth might have been made with three quick, careless slashes with a knife. His lips were puffed and blackened from betel-chewing. He looked half asleep.

Somewhere in the semi-darkness, a man cursed in a low voice.

Singapore looked around. His eyes, adjusted to the tropical glare of the street, saw nothing at first but the purple darkness of the corner. But presently he made out the seated figure of a man in white.

The man cursed feebly in a thick voice. Singapore guessed that he was drunk. A further inspection disclosed riotous blond hair and a bronzed face which had not been shaved in about a week.

Fiery, bloodshot eyes were staring sightlessly at Singapore. Sharp lines of dissipation and the grim set to the man's jaw, taken with the fiery eyes, gave him a belligerent look. They were green eyes.

A square pale-green bottle and a half-filled glass sat on the table in front of this white man. It was trade gin, the raw liquor of the Far East.

As Singapore watched, the green-eyed man reached with an impulsive gesture into one of the side pockets of his coat. He fetched out a small round bottle. With a violently shaking hand he removed the cork and spilled some of the contents of the little bottle into the drink before him.

He lifted the drink toward his mouth with a hand so tremulous that some of the stuff splashed out onto his shirt.

Singapore clearly saw the skull-and-crossbones on the little bottle as it rolled across the table. He bounded across the room just as the glass reached the green-eyed man's mouth. With a sharp slap of his hand, Singapore sent the glass flying to the floor. It smashed.

He said steadily, "I guess you must be Mr. McCoy."

CHAPTER III

POISON

BRUCE McCOY STARED up at him dazedly, then got to his feet. His under lip was projecting. His green eyes were now small shining orifices in nests of packed muscle. He swung a fist wildly in Singapore's general direction. Singapore evaded the swing by merely tilting his head back a little, and gravely watched the infuriated young man spin about and fall in a heap beside the chair.

He picked him up with one hand grasping his collar, and sat him down in the chair again. Then he picked up the phial and read the label under the skull-and-crossbones. He had expected carbolic acid. It was cyanide of potassium.

The blond man was glaring up at him. He growled: "Who the hell invited you to this party?"

Singapore seated himself, picked up the gin bottle, read the label, and replaced it on the table. He took out a package of cigarettes, lighted one and sent a puff of smoke into the scorpion-infested rafters. He said nothing.

Bruce McCoy hit the table with his fist. The bottle of trade gin jumped.

"Who the hell asked you to horn in on my private affairs?"

"Keep your shirt on," Singapore advised him.

"I'll knock your dirty block off! If I wanna bump myself off, no red-headed gorilla is gonna stop me!"

He started to get up, with plans of violence. Singapore's hand shot out and dropped on his shoulder, forcing him back into the chair.

"I want to talk to you," Singapore said.

The intoxicated one began to curse. He cursed Singapore Sammy for being in existence. He cursed Chantaboun. He cursed the tropics. He cursed the bugs, the birds, the flowers, the land crabs, the jungle, the alligators, the food, the liquor, Siam, the Far East. He concluded his outburst by declaring, with purple trimmings, that nothing Singapore had to say interested him.

Singapore listened to it all gravely and attentively. A man, he reflected, must be badly bitten to take it so hard. Often enough he had felt that way himself about fate, life, and the rest of it. And the green-eyed blond man was well equipped with appropriate language for the occasion.

"It's about an old man I'm lookin' for," Singapore broke in presently.

"I'm not interested in any old man!"

"This old guy's name is Bill Shay, and he goes around made up like a Buddhist beggin' priest."

The results of this simple statement were startling. Mist cleared from the angry green eyes. They became so hard and bright that they seemed to scintillate.

"You're damned right I know him!" McCoy shouted. "He's the partner of the dirty crook who got my bank roll and made me what I am to-day. Take another good look, you red-headed gorilla! They cleaned me! They stole my rifle and my automatic, so I wouldn't shoot 'em! I haven't even the price of this drink!"

Singapore's brain went quickly to conclusions.

"Partner's name de Silva?" he asked.

"That's the guy!"

"Sapphires?"

"Who told you about it?"

"Listen, blondy; they have been takin' suckers for sapphire rides in these parts ever since Buddha was a pup. How did they rig you? Tell me about it."

"I don't want to talk about it. I want to forget it."

"Did they sell you a phony mine?"

"Never mind."

"They salted it on you, didn't they?"

"If you know all about it, why bother to ask questions?"

SINGAPORE STROKED his nose with the wet end of his cigarette. "I was thinkin' maybe we could get together on this. I just ran into de Silva on the dock. He looks to me like the kind of vulture who would snatch food away from a starvin' cripple. I know that Bill Shay is. He happens to be my old man. I have been huntin' him high and low over the East for seven years past. I know he's picked up a fortune along the way. Help me get him. If we grab him, I'll get you your money back."

The green eyes were staring at him suspiciously.

"What do you want to get him for?"

"I want to kill him. He's got a will, makin' me the heir of almost a million, gold. I want the will, and I'm gonna kill him for the way he ran out on my mother."

Bruce McCoy shook his head.

"You're a worse sucker than I am. He is smarter than a leopard. And he's gone. He pulled out last night on a fast elephant. He bought the fastest elephant in Chantaboun and blew. That lets you out."

"I'm sayin' we ought to team up on this."

The green-eyed man shook his head obstinately.

"Nobody can help me now. I've made a mess of my life. I'm a failure. I'm licked and I know it. I don't want any help."

"Don't think so fast, blondy. I've been knockin' around these parts for a long while. These guys haven't got a corner on all the tricks. I may look dumb, but once in a while I get an idea. Let's get together on this."

"No. I'm not gonna involve anybody else in this damned mess. They shook me down, and I'm through."

"How much did they ring up on your cash register?"

"All I had—ten thousand dollars and a hundred carats of sapphires."

"Tell me how they worked it."

"What's the use? They made a sucker out of me. I drifted in here about seven months ago. De Silva and his partner tried to interest me in this sapphire mine. They took me out and showed me the mine. It's just above town."

"In the river?"

"Sure! They're all in the river. They showed me all the sapphires they were getting. They had a sluice box rigged up on the bank, and they were using outrigger canoes to get the blue clay. The native boys sat in the canoes and brought up the blue clay in buckets. Then the sluice boys on shore ran the blue clay through the sluice box. They were getting sapphires by the handful. Every time they dumped a bucket of blue clay down the box and sluiced it with water, there were sapphires— plenty! It looked like money in the bank. So I bought the layout—mine, canoes, sluice box and all."

"How much?"

"The first hundred carats of sapphires—and thirty thousand ticals."

Singapore quickly estimated that thirty thousand ticals equaled approximately ten thousand dollars, gold. "The hundred carats," he guessed, "represented the exact amount of sapphires they salted your mine with. The sapphires were their investment, and they wanted their investment back."

McCoy growled: "The ten thousand wasn't my money. It was my father's—practically his entire savings. I thought it was a chance to put him on easy street. And he trusted me. I cabled him to cable me a draft for ten thousand on a Bangkok bank. When the draft came, I endorsed it to de Silva. About two months ago I turned over to him the last of the hundred carats of sapphires."

He picked up the gin bottle, put it to his mouth and took a swig, He set the bottle down and glared at the red-haired man.

"Call me a sucker!" he said defiantly. "Go on and call me a sucker!"

"I'M NOT callin' you anything," Sammy said. "After you came to the end of the hundred carats, what did you do?"

"For a long time I thought I had only exhausted a pocket and would strike another soon. That's what de Silva kept saying. I kept the boys working, but I gradually knew I had been trimmed. And there wasn't a damned thing to do about it."

"Did you watch these Burmese workin' their mines?"

"No. I was too busy workin' my own."

"Did you find all your hundred carats in the blue clay?"

"Yes. Why?"

"Didn't you know—didn't anybody tell you—that sapphires ain't found in the blue clay, but in the powdery white sand under the blue clay?"

McCoy stared at him resentfully. The new drink was taking hold swiftly. "All the sapphires I found were in blue clay. But what difference does it make now? It's all over. I'm licked. I haven't even got a gun. I guess you'd better roll your hoop."

"You mean," Singapore said grittily, "you're gonna let those two polecats get away with this?"

"What can I do? They outsmarted me. I'm through."

"Where you goin'?"

"I dunno."

"How you gonna get there?"

McCoy indignantly started to get up. Singapore pushed him back again, and said:

"The first thing you do is sober up. Lay off this trade gin. I sort of like your looks and I have a hunch we can work something out of this. What are you gonna do about Dolores?"

The green eyes flashed fire again. McCoy was drunker than ever.

"Where'd you meet Dolores?"

Singapore jerked his head in the general direction of the dock. "On the hooker. She seemed to expect to see you waitin' for her with a bouquet in your hand."

McCoy expelled a sigh which sounded like a sob.

"How could I meet her? I look like a bum! I've made such a failure of myself that I couldn't look her in the face. She won't have any respect for me when she finds what a fool I've been."

The last words were sobbed. Singapore feared that the young man's fighting jag was about to veer off into the crying variety. His guess was promptly upheld. Bruce McCoy started to sob. While tears gushed from his eyes, he roared with grief. He declared, between sobs, that he wasn't fit to be shot; that he had broken the heart of a little white flower of girlhood. Dolores trusted him! She believed in him! She was so little, so innocent, so easily hurt!

"Her old man is a dirty crook," McCoy said, "but he treats her like the princess she is. He loads her up with jewels. She has sapphire bracelets, anklets and necklaces. She even has a sapphire-mounted gun and a sapphire-mounted dagger."

SINGAPORE DROPPED his hand into the pocket where the sapphire dagger lay.

"Anything like this?" he sharply asked, and flipped the little dagger so that it stuck into the table-top, its handle vibrating in a blue blaze of sapphires.

The crying jag came to an abrupt end. "Where," the green-eyed man demanded, "did you get that?"

"Listen, blondy," Singapore said; "I grabbed this in the dark last night out of the hand of somebody who was tryin' to rob me of a very valuable pearl I carry. A couple of hours before, I had showed the pearl to Dolores. When you put all that together, what does it spell?"

McCoy leaped up. His face was unhealthily red and contorted with fury; his eyes were blazing.

"You dirty rat!" he cried. "What's your game? Why are you trying to drag an innocent girl into it?"

"So it *is* her dagger!" Sammy murmured.

McCoy snatched up the dagger. His apparent intentions were to carve Singapore's heart out. But the redheaded man was a split-second faster. His hand darted out and closed viselike on the blond man's wrist. He increased the pressure until McCoy, with an oath, dropped the knife.

Then the blond man seemed to wilt. He stared past Singapore at the doorway. His jaw sagged. He turned suddenly pale. He said, in a husky whisper:

"Dolores!"

Singapore supposed that this was only another phase of the young man's drunkenness. He heard no sound behind him; not a single footfall on the dirt floor. But he was suddenly aware of a familiar, spiced perfume.

A lazy, musical voice said, "I hope I'm not intruding."

THE AMERICAN swung around and looked at her, covering the fallen dagger with his hand as he did so. Dolores de Silva, with her little sun helmet tilted at a jaunty angle, gave him a look in which was expressed wistful sadness; then her velvety brown eyes traveled across the table to the tragic, unshaved face of Bruce McCoy.

The red-head waited expectantly. He was familiar enough

with her and her type to know just about what was coming. She said reproachfully:

"Bruce, why didn't you meet me?"

McCoy stared up at her. He struggled halfway out of the chair, then, with a gasp, fell back.

"Look at me!" he cried. "Just look at me!"

She said sternly: "You haven't shaved in a week. Your clothes are filthy. You look like a beach comber."

"That's the answer," McCoy said. "How could I meet you? I couldn't look you in the eye."

It all made Singapore Sammy feel pretty sick. In spite of his present alcoholic condition, McCoy was, Sammy was certain, a good egg—a clean-shooting kid. It hurt him to see a nice kid like this so infatuated with this beautiful young snake. She and her father and Bill Shay had taken the kid for a cleaning. Now, she was through with him. Cold-bloodedly, she was going to give him the air.

"I am disgusted with you," she was saying. "You have broken my heart."

"Dolores! Will you listen to me? I'm cleaned out. I'm flat broke. That's the only reason I didn't meet you. I was ashamed of myself. I couldn't look you in the eye."

"Do you suppose a girl who loves a man as I loved you cares if he loses his money?" she demanded. "It's the way you have let it make a drunkard and a fool out of yourself. I could have respected you if you had held your chin up. But no! You are just weak. And I could never respect a weakling."

Singapore felt sicker still when he saw how her clever little speech was affecting McCoy. The look in the boy's eyes he had seen in the eyes of an affectionate dog that had been unwarrantably kicked. McCoy was biting his lower lip; staring up at her with hopeless worship.

"You can't kick me aside like this, Dolores. You've got to give me another chance!"

HER ANSWER to that was to strip from her engagement finger the handsome sapphire ring. She placed it carefully on the table. Singapore could not help admiring her acting. She was as clever as she was crooked. Her next move, he was certain, would be a strong play for him—and that twenty-five-thousand-dollar pearl.

She was gazing up at him softly. "When I talked to you last night," she said, "if I could have dreamed that my life would work out so tragically! You must know how I feel, Mr. Shay."

"I know how you feel, sister."

"You don't blame me? You—you understand?"

"Sure! I understand."

"Well, so do I!" McCoy snarled, and staggered to his feet. He pointed a shaking finger at Singapore. "That guy," he declared hotly, "is trying to put something over, Dolores. He just got through telling me you tried to stab him last night and steal a pearl he carries." He glowered at Singapore. "If you deny saying that, you're a dirty liar! Show her that dagger you claim she tried to stab you with, you big gorilla!"

Singapore took his hand off the dagger, and watched the girl's face. She looked at the dagger with round, astonished eyes, then darted a glance at him. It was a soft glance. It could almost be described as a loving glance. The corners of her mouth dimpled.

"I'll knock his block off!" McCoy declared.

She ignored him. Her shining eyes remained uplifted to Singapore's face.

"We all make mistakes—don't we, Mr. Shay?"

"Sure, sister. We all make mistakes."

She quickly reached into the bosom of her dress and removed a small, cobalt-blue leather sheath. From this she extracted a dagger with a handle of gold thickly encrusted with sapphires. She tossed it on the table beside the other one.

"I didn't know," she said, "there was another dagger resembling mine in Chantaboun."

Singapore grinned his admiration. He examined the daggers.

They were not identical. Hers was smaller, slimmer, of more delicate workmanship, with finer sapphires in the handle.

With his hands on the table, bracing himself, McCoy jeered: "Now, what are you gonna say, you big gorilla? I'm gonna settle with you for this! I'm gonna—"

His hands on the wet table suddenly slipped. He sat down heavily in the chair, banging his head on the edge of the table. He looked at the treacherous table in astonishment.

Singapore picked up the two daggers, returned the small one to Dolores, and placed the one to which he had fallen heir last night in his pocket.

"You're right, sister," he said; "we all make mistakes."

"Don't apologize," she said softly. "All I want you to do is to believe in me. I like you so much, and I admire you so much. Last night, I felt that I had found a new friend—one whom I could depend on, one whom I could trust. To-day, with what has happened, I feel so alone; and my father is so cruel!"

"I know, sister. It's a tough world."

"I am so afraid. I am the only white woman in Chantaboun. Please don't go away and leave me here! I must go home now. Good-by!"

WITHOUT EVEN a glance in the direction of her rejected suitor, she walked to the doorway; vanished into the lush tropical afternoon.

Singapore sat down again. He said: "Look here, kid. Do you still think that dame is on the level?"

Bloodshot green eyes glared at him. "If you say one more word against her, I'll knock your block off!"

He reached for the bottle of *gin-bijt*. Whether he intended to take another drink or to use the bottle as an implement with which to bash in Singapore's head, Singapore did not know—or care. His hand reached the bottle first.

McCoy began to curse again. Singapore, with dark dents between his eyes, looked at him and heard nothing. He was trying to fit together in his mind the pieces of a jigsaw puzzle. Where were the hundred carats of sapphires and the thirty thousand ticals? Had the two old crooks split up the proceeds and gone their separate ways? It was unlike Bill Shay to leave profits behind. But, he reasoned, the sapphires must have belonged originally to Roderigo de Silva, They would have logically returned to him.

In short, where de Silva was, the sapphires were.

Sammy lighted a fresh cigarette and pondered. He wanted to put McCoy back on his feet, outfox de Silva and capture his father all at once.

The first move was to find de Silva—to grab him before he got away.

McCoy had stopped cursing; was glaring at him in menacing silence. He burst out, "Say! What's your game, anyhow?"

Singapore answered: "Blondy, we're goin' places and do things. We're gonna try to get your money back—and those sapphires. It can be done."

The green-eyed young man told him he was crazy.

"I'm gonna help you," Singapore said, "whether you like it or not; and you're gonna help me. I'm gonna help you catch your sapphires and your jack, and you're gonna help me catch my old man. First of all, we're goin' callin' on Roderigo de Silva. How do we get there?"

"In a canoe. But I'm not going. I don't trust you. I don't trust anybody."

Singapore took him firmly by the arm. Putting McCoy back on his feet looked now as if it might prove to be a long, hard and thankless job.

CHAPTER IV

WITH DRAWN GUNS

RODERIGO DE SILVA'S house occupied the summit of a grassy knoll above the river. Shaded by mahogany and tamarind trees, it was patterned after the other houses of the section, being constructed of thatched *nipa* palm, with bamboo legs to discourage the invasion of snakes, alligators, the hideous land crabs which infested the region, and thieves of all species.

A bamboo ladder ran from the ground to a platform beyond which was a dark doorway covered with gray mosquito bar.

The canoe ride up the river from the village had somewhat sobered Bruce McCoy. Throughout the ride he had stared at Singapore, his bloodshot eyes giving him a belligerent look; but Sammy suspected that he was no longer belligerent. The fresh air, clearing his brain, was sobering him and making him think. Ever since Singapore had given him his spare revolver to carry, he had been thoughtful.

When the canoe touched the river bank just below the de Silva house, McCoy said in a rational voice:

"What are you planning to do?"

"Put de Silva on a spot."

"You mean, kill him?"

"Sure—if he tries to kill me! He won't hesitate to shoot. Neither will I. Come on, kid!"

McCoy followed him. Singapore covered the distance to the bamboo ladder in long, catlike strides. Only once, he turned about to whisper:

"Have that gun ready—and don't hesitate to use it. Are you O.K.?"

"Yes."

Singapore went up the ladder with the agility and quietness

of an ape. He swung himself onto the platform and gripped his revolver firmly. He swept the mosquito bar aside and stepped quickly into a large darkened room.

A glance informed him that these premises had been hastily vacated. A grunt of disgust escaped him. Empty boxes were scattered about. Discarded clothing lay in careless heaps.

He called: "Come on up, blondy. They've blown!"

McCoy came into the room and stared about him with bewilderment.

"They must have packed up and got out in the last few minutes."

"Yeah," Singapore agreed. "The minute I laid my eyes on that girl, I knew she was as clever as she was good-lookin'. Why do you suppose she came down to that gin mill and wasted all that good time on us? So's her old man would have time to get things packed! Listen!"

In the silence of the jungle, he heard the Laughing Lady's whistle.

"You hear that, blondy?"

McCoy said grimly: "I'm gonna ask you for the last time to leave her out of this."

Singapore turned and glared at him. "I thought you were sober!"

"I'm sober enough to think straight. You've had your knife out for that girl all along. I'm telling you, she's not in on this. Her father is as crooked as a cobra track. She's on the level. Get that."

Singapore sighed. "O.K., kid," he said cheerfully. "We'll leave her out of it from now on. The fact remains that her old man has blown with the plunder. They are now standin' on the after deck of the Laughin' Lady, givin' you and me the laugh. I take it back, blondy! She ain't laughin'! She's standin' there with her little heart just breakin'. But the old man is laughin' at us for a couple of suckers. Let's go back to town. We aren't licked yet."

WHEN THE canoe reached the village, the Laughing Lady was gone. Far down the river, a smudge of black smoke indicated that she was proceeding at full speed in order to reach the bar at high tide.

The coasting steamer would put in at Paklan to-morrow morning and lie there most of the day. Singapore wondered if he could reach Paklan, over jungle trails, before she pulled out for Saigon, to-morrow night. Then, on the dock, he saw a large rattan-fibre crate containing a phonograph. It was addressed to Roderigo de Silva, Bangkok.

This puzzled Singapore. If de Silva and his daughter were going to Saigon, why was the phonograph going to Bangkok, which was in the opposite direction?

He found the dock foreman and asked him if de Silva had shipped anything on the Laughing Lady.

"No, master. There was no freight for the Laughing Lady, and there were no passengers."

"You mean," Sammy said, "no passengers except the de Silvas?"

"No, master. There were no passengers at all."

It took Singapore several minutes to be convinced that Roderigo de Silva and his daughter had not taken passage on the Laughing Lady. Then he returned excitedly to McCoy, who was seated dejectedly on a bale of rattan mats.

"They aren't," he announced, "on the Laughing Lady. Where are they?"

"I don't know. I wish I was dead. Maybe they took elephants."

"Let's take a look-see down at the caravansary."

The caravansary was on the other side of Chantaboun. An old Burmese from Terasserim, who tamed, trained and dealt in elephants, admitted, under persuasion, that he had rented a caravan of five elephants to Roderigo de Silva, with *mahouts*.

"I am anxious to join him," Singapore said, "I'll pay you well for an elephant fast enough to overtake him."

"Alas, master; I have no more elephants! I have a mule, but she is a lazy creature."

"No horses?"

"Not a horse, master! My last horse was devoured by the elephant leeches through the carelessness of a fool of a servant."

"Let's take a look at that mule. Where is she?"

"This way, master." The Burmese led the two young men into a small *kraal*. It contained a large, but flea-bitten and mangy-looking mule. One of her eyes was closed. Her ears drooped dejectedly.

A spirited dickering began. Sammy claimed that the mule would die of old age before she had gone ten *ri*. The Burmese, realizing that the shortage of four-footed carriers had placed a premium on any form of transportation, held out for a hundred ticals. Sammy, who thoroughly knew Burma and the Burmese, waxed eloquent. He got the mule finally for fifty ticals, with a worn-out Indian army saddle thrown in.

THEN HE took Bruce McCoy into the shade of a mango tree for a conference. The green-eyed man was now sober enough, but he remained stubborn and discouraged.

"What's the sense of it?" he inquired. "I know those elephants. They travel fast. The *mahouts* know the trails. You don't. They'll be five jumps ahead of you all the way into Bangkok. It's a wild goose chase. It's worse than that. You're licked before you start."

"When the mule gets tired, I can walk," Sammy argued. "I'll travel all night and catch up with them before they pull out in the mornin'. There's a moon, and I've been over these trails before."

McCoy remained unconvinced. "What do you do when you find them? Those *mahouts* will be armed. De Silva won't hesitate to shoot you."

"First off, I'll disguise myself. I'll disguise myself as a Burmese mat maker. I'm on my way to Bangkok, because times are slack here."

McCoy grunted skeptically. "You can't swing it. De Silva is too smart. Maybe he didn't even take the sapphires with him."

"I'm gamblin' that he did, blondy."

"If there's any shooting, you may hit Dolores!"

"I'm a better shot than that. If there's shootin', I'll guarantee to restrain myself and not hit Dolores."

"Then you are planning to shoot it out with them?"

"Blondy, when I get into a jam, I get ideas. I will have plenty of time to dope some out on the way. Now, look. While I am gone chasin' the wild geese, the best thing for you to do is to start workin' your mine again."

"Don't be ridiculous!"

"Let's get together on this," Singapore pleaded. "You are more obstinate than that mule looks. I am hatchin' a plan. Maybe there are sapphires in that mine. Because it was sold to you as a phony mine don't mean there aren't sapphires in it. I want you to work the mine."

"How can I pay for labor?"

"I'll attend to that. I'll leave you some jack."

"But what do you get out of it?"

"Blondy, you'll have to take my word that I ain't Santy Claus. The scheme I am cookin' up will, if I can put it over, bring my old man back to Chantaboun. That's all I ask out of this—to get my hooks into that old polecat. It means a million dollars in gold, and ten million dollars in personal satisfaction. You will just have to humor me. Take this money—and promise me you won't touch a drop of this nitro-solvent you were pourin' into yourself this mornin'. Is it a bet?"

"I'll lay off the liquor, and I'll open the mine, if you say so. But I still say you're shooting at the moon."

"Don't tell me," Sammy said, with a laugh, "it ain't a big target!"

McCOY WAS looking at him with puzzled but friendly eyes. His mouth suddenly dropped open, as if in alarm.

"Say!" he cried. "Is your name, by any chance, Samuel L. Shay?"

Singapore looked startled. "Yeah."

"I've been carrying around a letter for you for a week!"

He produced from his inner coat pocket a letter somewhat worn and soiled from handling. It bore a Malayan postage stamp and cancellation mark, and was addressed:

> Samuel L. Shay, in care of any American, Chantaboun, Siam. Please hold.

Singapore opened the envelope, extracted a single sheet of paper covered with scrawls in blue ink, and read:

> "You big bum:
>
> "I am going after pearls in the bight of the gulf, as stated. Expect to be stopping in at Chantaboun for water and supplies sooner or later. Don't leave there without seeing me, as have run into something red-hot and need you, or will knock your big block off at next meeting.
>
> "Don't let anybody slip a knife into your back, you big gorilla.
> "Lucky."

Singapore looked up from the letter with a broad grin.

"It's from my pal," he said. "It's from Lucifer Jones—the great big pirate! He owns the prettiest little schooner south of Shanghai. You ought to see that guy handle his mitts! You ought to see him when he gets good and mad! Did you hear what he said? He's comin' in here and he's got a deal on."

McCoy was looking at him curiously. He licked his lips, quickly shifted his eyes elsewhere, and muttered:

"Any guy would be playing in real luck to have a pal like you."

"Boloney!" Singapore grunted. "You don't know me, blondy. I am on the waitin' list of half the jails in China, India and Malaya. Now, listen. We've done enough palaverin'. I am pullin' out right now. Take this jack and use what you need. Keep it for me. I've got enough silver on me for current expenses."

He extracted a worn sharkskin bill fold and tossed it into the lap of the green-eyed man.

"If Lucky blows into port," he went on, "tell him to stick

around. We can use that bozo. He was born with a gun in each hand. When I come back, here's hopin' I have a hundred carats of sapphires in my kick. Where is this mine of yours?"

"Upriver a quarter of a mile above the de Silva house."

"O.K. I'll be seein' you there in a few days. Make your boys go down through the blue clay to the white sand."

He saw McCoy aboard the canoe, then returned to the village. He had some shopping to do. Dropping in at the Sapphire Sandal, he bought six bottles of blue Javanese *arrack*—a vile and potent drink beloved by the lower class of natives. From a drug merchant he purchased sufficient walnut dye to stain his face, neck, hands and arms. And from the Burmese elephant man at the caravansary he borrowed a *longyi* and an *engyi*—garments worn by Burmese. A worn and battered sun helmet, discovered in a harness room, would cover his flaming hair.

Singapore was preparing to change his clothing when a sweet, lazy voice behind him caused his heart to jump and begin to hammer. His brain, even before he spun about to face her, was extremely busy. Why had she stayed behind? Why wasn't she with her father on his flight to Bangkok?

CHAPTER V

"PLEASE DON'T GO!"

THE ANSWERS WERE easy. As he had guessed in the grog shop, Dolores had discarded McCoy for him. She, her father, and Sammy's father had cleaned McCoy. Now she was turning her talents loose on him. She wanted that blue pearl. If the three of them had worked so hard for McCoy's ten thousand, to what lengths wouldn't they go in an attempt at securing the Malabar pearl?

He turned around and looked into her eyes. They were as innocent as a little girl's.

"You're going away!" she cried.

"Yeah," he admitted.

"I thought you were staying in Chantaboun!" she wailed.

Singapore was visited at this moment by a distressing thought. Supposing her father had left the sapphires with her? Supposing his flight via elephant was nothing but a blind—part of some intricate scheme? Why not? White men in the Far East fell into Oriental ways; went in for intricate schemes. Certainly Sammy's scheme, still hardly hatched, was intricate enough.

"Sister," he said, "I gotta see a guy about a camel."

Her eyes were hurt and pleading.

"I depended on your staying here, Mr. Shay. I am afraid to stay in this horrible place alone. Please don't go."

"It's a tough break for both of us, sister."

She came a little closer. He could smell the delicious perfume she used in her hair. It intoxicated him a little, as it had last night.

"There is something you must know, Mr. Shay. Only to-day I discovered that your father and mine had deliberately sold Bruce McCoy that worthless mine. You can imagine how shocked I was."

"Sure. I can imagine."

The velvet-brown eyes were shining. "To learn that my father is nothing but an old crook!"

"Yeah. I know how you feel."

"Then you don't think wrong of me because of it?"

"Sister, why should I throw bricks at your glass house? I am nothin' but a chip of another tough old block."

Gazing up at him, she sighed. "Why do you leave me, Sammy? Stay here with me. Don't go. I know where you intend to go. You're going to follow my father! You will make a great mistake if you do. He knows you will try to follow him—"

"—so he left you behind to—"

"No, no! You must not even think such things. Why would a girl say that she likes a man as much as I like you? You see? It would kill me if you were even hurt. You must not go. He is well armed. He will kill you!"

"I'll take the chance, sister. And if luck is with me, I'll be seein' you in a couple of days."

Seeing that he was obdurate, she began to sob. She produced a wisp of handkerchief and held it to her eyes while her lovely slim shoulders shook.

It was hard to realize that she was a little snake; hard to realize that his only attraction for her was the Malobar pearl. It made him sick to know that a girl who was so beautiful and looked so innocent should be what she really was.

She whimpered, "Please don't leave me—Sammy!"

He looked at her a moment longer and sighed heavily, "So long, sister." He picked up the bundle of clothing and the mule's reins.

Across the caravansary compound, he turned and looked back. She was huddled against the bole of a palm tree. Her face was obscured by the jaunty little sun helmet. She seemed to have wilted.

Doubts assailed him as he went on. Did de Silva have the sapphires—or had he left them with Dolores? And he was worried on another score now. It had occurred to him that Dolores might discover that he had left his money with McCoy. And if she found that out, she would certainly get to work again on McCoy.

It was an open question whether he should follow de Silva or stay in Chantaboun. He suspected that his father would meet de Silva somewhere along the trail. It was absolutely essential to Singapore's plans that he obtain those sapphires. He was sure that, by means of those precious blue stones, he could not only help McCoy, but he could lure Bill Shay back to Chantaboun.

But who had the sapphires?

In a clearing on the other side of the village, Singapore teth- ered the mule and removed his clothing. He daubed the walnut stain over his face and such portions of his body as the *longyi* and the *engyi* would not cover, and got into his borrowed clothing. Then he mounted the mule and set off through the steaming jungle.

SINGAPORE SAMMY did not overtake Roderigo de Silva's caravan that first night, as he had hoped. He was dealing with forces beyond his control. The first was the mule; the second, the weather. The mule was old, weary, and reluctant. She balked frequently. By the time night came, he had covered no more than ten miles.

With the falling of night, he counted on the assistance of the moon. But with dusk, the sky became overcast. An hour later, rain was falling in torrents. Drenched, Singapore pressed on. The mule grew balkier. Her rests became longer and more frequent. And presently she strayed off the trail and doubled back toward Chantaboun and home.

Singapore discovered this when, through a break in the clouds, he saw, to his amazement, the moon shining in the wrong direction. He kicked the mule about and started back toward Bangkok. But the breaks were against him. Riding and leading the mule by turns, an hour before sun-up he reached the spot where de Silva had camped. The coals of the watch fires and cooking fires were almost cold.

He had brought no food, as he had planned to steal enough rations to sustain himself from de Silva's supplies. He was sleepy and disgusted. Even if he pressed on and overtook the caravan by daylight, the plans he vaguely had in mind would be useless.

Further to complicate matters, the mule now lay down and refused to rise. There was nothing for Singapore to do but to press on afoot. It was unwise, but necessary. And it was necessary, and also unwise, for him to eat such natural food as the jungle afforded. The safest food was bananas. So he breakfasted on bananas. He slung the bag of *arrack* over his shoulder and started down the trail. An hour later, he had such a violent attack of banana cramps that he could do nothing but lie on the ground, doubled up, and groan. He opened one of the bottles of *arrack* and took a dose of the vile blue stuff to cure the cramps. The result was prompt and violent nausea. But after half an hour the cramps had stopped, and he could go on.

It was slow and cruel going, through swamps and dense jungle. And it was fairly certain that when he returned, if he ever did return, jungle beasts would have finished off the mule, if elephant leeches hadn't.

The sun rose to its zenith, beat fiercely down on him when he crossed open spaces; then the afternoon heat set in. The jungle steamed. Sweat ran from him.

Dusk of that second day found him limping badly, as the result of stepping on a thorn. He had brought along no iodine. His leg began to swell. But he limped on.

IT WAS close to midnight when he saw, in a clearing ahead, the watch fires of de Silva's caravan. If he were called on now to defend his life with physical strength, he was whipped before he started.

He limped toward the encampment, with his revolver ready. Near him was a small sleeping tent, in darkness. Before it, a Siamese crouched with his knife across his knees. Near him, under a tarpaulin, was a pile of provisions. Beyond, the five elephants were picketed. Their *mahouts* squatted or lay asleep about the fire. A pair of them were smoking white Burmese cheroots and talking in low, sleepy voices. These two were evidently standing guard.

Singapore stealthily encircled the encampment, taking care that the bottles did not click together in the bag. His heart was racing with excitement. The slightest hitch now in his plans would mean his death. It wasn't a case of getting or not getting the sapphires. It was, for the time being, life or death.

A twig cracked under heel. It made a report which sounded, to Sammy, as loud as a pistol. He heard one of the elephants whistle through its trunk in alarm. He was counting on those elephants—but not yet!

The camp remained silent. The two *mahouts* continued to

smoke their cheroots and whisper. Sammy limped on. As he passed the elephants he concealed his revolver in the folds of his *longyi.*

He was, he was sure, past the danger zone now.

Boldly, with a smile at his lips, he approached the camp fire. There was something audacious in his bearing, despite the limp. He meant to play the role of a swaggerer, and to play it through.

To the *mahouts* he softly cried, in their native tongue:

"Heaven born! May the blessings of the Buddha of Kapili-vastu be upon you!"

ONE OF the *mahouts*, half dozing, sprang up with his *parang*—a long, wicked, carved knife—glittering in his hand. He and the other stared over the embers into the sweat-glistening brown face of the jeering intruder.

Snatching one of the bottles from the bag, Singapore said:

"A wayfarer along the lonely, twisting road salutes the friends of an evening! You have eaten your fill of iguana's eggs, fish paste from Gaung, pickled tea fresh from the Shan hills, and sweet purple rice. Now let us drink!"

The *mahouts* laughed at his audacity. The foods he had named were the choicest and rarest of Burma. They had eaten nothing but coolie rice for their evening meal.

One of them rolled sparkling black eyes at him and asked, in Siamese, *"Nai bai naidja?"* Whither goest thou?

And Singapore answered, *"Haigah!* Who knows? Who cares? We are here for to-day—to-morrow we are but a puff of ashes! I have a bag of stolen wine. The friendships of the night—"

"—are those of self-interest alone!" one of the *mahouts* finished the old Shan proverb for him.

"Ah! Wrong!" Singapore laughed. "Are drinking friendships!"

One asked, "Where did you steal the *arrack?*"

"In Lombak! I left there at dawn. But first I robbed the grog shop. It is good *arrack.*"

"You are a fine thief!" another *mahout* laughed. "Let us have a sip of that stuff!"

Sammy produced another bottle. And another. All the *mahouts* were now awake, eying him expectantly.

One asked, "Who are you?"

"A hunter."

They all laughed. An old man said: "You are a liar. You are from Teresserim, where they make mate. You are a rogue. What do you do here at this hour?"

"I drink and laugh and tell my story!" Sammy answered.

He had aroused enough curiosity so that they demanded his story.

SAMMY SPUN them the story—a saga pieced together from the famous sagas of the East; of adventure, of danger met and vanquished, of slim, golden dancing girls who pursued him for his love. It was a tale spun for the sole purpose of holding their attention, while he fetched more and more bottles from the bag.

It was finally empty. He waited results. He knew *arrack*. He knew its swift and certain effect upon the Eastern mind. One of the *mahouts* began to snore. The others began paying scant attention to Sammy's endless saga. A quarrel began between two of them. It ended suddenly in snores.

It took less than two hours. The moon had set when the last of them was asleep. The fire had subsided to darkling embers.

Singapore composed himself to wait. He reasoned that a man who drinks himself to sleep is drunker still when awakened half an hour later.

Assuring himself that his audience had slipped off to slumber to the last man, he arose from his haunches and picked up a faggot from the dying fire. One end glowed redly. In the dense black of the jungle night it would provide him with enough light to see by.

Cautiously he approached the picket line. One by one, he freed the elephants. A great bull ran its trunk exploringly over his neck and head, and uttered a trumpet of alarm. From the other end of the line came an answering call.

Sammy had not bargained on this. It was simply his good fortune. When he had freed the last elephant, he hurled the glowing fagot into the center of the line and raised his voice in an unholy shriek.

One of the elephants squealed in a panic. Others took up the shrill trumpeting. Then the two hostile bulls, staked out at opposite ends of the line, renewed what must have been a very old war indeed.

Singapore heard their roarings and angry squealings. He heard the remaining three elephants thunder off into the jungle.

His evening's work was well begun. Suddenly the slim silver beam of an electric flash light pierced the blackness near the tent. In the beam's diffusion Singapore saw a large, heavily built man in white come charging toward the *mahouts'* fire. He knew it must be Roderigo de Silva. De Silva was roaring curses in Burmese, English, Portuguese, with his revolver held ready for instant use. And his course was taking him straight for Singapore.

CHAPTER VI

A ONE-MAN RAID

A FIRE KINDLED into existence in front of the tent. The native who had been on guard there was on his hands and knees, blowing the embers with blasts from puffed-out cheeks.

Sammy, circling about to avoid de Silva's hasty progress, reached the provision pile under its tarpaulin. There were bags of rice, sheathed with straw, also cases of canned goods.

He seized several cans and tossed them to the base of a tamarind tree. He would recover these later. Then he applied flaming matches to the pile.

There was already confusion in abundance. But he wanted more. He heard de Silva roaring at the *mahouts*. He heard the two bull elephants trumpeting as they fought.

The man at the fire sprang up as Singapore limped toward him. His knife came up—not a *parang*, but a Siamese skinning knife.

Singapore knocked him over the head with the butt of his revolver as the knife came up. The man quietly seated himself, and quietly rolled over.

Listening a moment, Singapore plunged into the tent. He knew that de Silva might be carrying the sapphires. Yet he might not. Singapore hoped not. He did not relish a revolver duel with de Silva. He neither wished to kill nor to be killed. He had been a guest in Siamese jails, and he had no hankering to repeat the experience.

He found the stub of a candle on a packing box. He struck a match, held it to the wick, and began hastily but systematically to search. The angry roars of de Silva indicated that he was trying to arouse the drunken *mahouts*.

Singapore smashed the lock of a small iron trunk with the butt of his revolver. Far away, he heard the squeal of an elephant. Was it a wild one? Was a herd of wild elephants coming to add to the confusion of de Silva's encampment?

The red-head tossed the contents of the trunk on the ground. Clothing. Nothing of value. No sapphires. He heard the man he had knocked unconscious begin to groan. He smashed the lock of a leather trunk. Shotgun shells. Rifle cartridges. Pistol ammunition. No sapphires.

He ransacked a suitcase, a valise, a small red-lacquer box. Toilet articles. A set of Mah Jong. Oil, rags, cleaning rods.

He heard rapid footsteps approaching from the picket line. De Silva was returning!

A happy impulse sent Sammy to the cot on which Roderigo de Silva had recently been reposing. A folded soft blanket

Dolores shrank back at the sound.

served as a pillow. Singapore jerked at the corner of the blanket. It came snapping off, unfolding.

A buckskin bag tumbled onto the dirt. Singapore snatched it up, hooked two fingers into the throat and yanked.

The interior of the tent was faintly suffused with cool white light as the powerful beam of the flash light in de Silva's hand fell upon the canvas.

Singapore held the opened throat of the buckskin sack to the candle light; peered inside. A dull blue glow produced a pleased grunt from him. Sapphires! Uncut, assorted sapphires. Deep blue. Pale blue. Large fellows. Little fellows. Just about a hundred carats of uncut sapphires!

HE STUFFED the bag into a hip pocket. He blew out the candle. He picked up the empty leather trunk as fingers plucked at the tent flap. When a head showed, he hurled the trunk.

It collided with a hollow thump with de Silva's forehead. The flash light vanished. De Silva roared in pain and fury. A revolver went off. The bullet smashed through the roof pole past which Singapore, on his belly, was sliding snake-like under the tent.

He heard de Silva, still roaring with rage, plunge into the tent;

heard him stumble over the litter Sammy had scattered about on the floor, and fall headlong. The revolver went off again.

Singapore scuttled about to the front of the tent, picked up the still beaming flash light and clicked off the light. He now hastened to the tree where he had tossed the canned goods. These he stowed away in his *engyi*, then paused a moment. He needed iodine for that thorn wound in his foot. But he dared wait no longer. He heard the drunken shouts of the *mahouts* as they pursued the panic-stricken elephants. The provision pile was blazing merrily.

While men shouted and elephants trumpeted, the man who was sometimes described as the worst trouble-maker in the Far East slipped out of the encampment and limped down the trail which led back to Chantaboun.

Behind him, the uproar of the camp continued unabated. The provision pile was sending fat golden sparks higher than the tree tops. Singapore limped along. The blaze behind him dwindled. The drunken shouts grew fainter.

He flashed on the light at intervals. It presently fell upon an alarming mountain of gray which moved. Two pig eyes, glittering in the flash light, scrutinized him.

Sammy and the elephant, facing each other on the trail, came to a halt. The elephant made a sniffling sound.

The man spoke softly but urgently. In the *mahout's* tongue, he called the gray mountain a fragrant flower from the hills of Shan. He called it a wretch and a lazy pig, and bade it bow down in shame to the sovereign commands of its master.

Singapore was taking a very long chance. It might have been a wild elephant, pausing there a moment before it charged and trampled him to death.

But Singapore was filling straight flushes in the middle that night.

The gray mountain whimpered in its trunk and salaamed. When it got to its feet again, Sammy was astride its neck, poking it behind the ear with the butt of his revolver.

And so the return trip to Chantaboun was begun.

BRUCE McCOY'S bungalow occupied the center of a cleared space in the jungle at a point where the river bent like a crooked arm. Inland a hundred feet from the point of the elbow, the palm-thatch bungalow stood. The Chantaboun River moved past with the stately dignity of a gorged snake. McCoy's sapphire claim encompassed all of the bend on both sides and about five hundred yards up river and down river to boot.

When Singapore, yellow-eyed and burning with fever, returned and restored the elephant to its astonished and grateful owner, he proceeded at once by canoe to McCoy's property, to find that the young man had been acting most energetically upon his share of their bargain.

He had gone even farther than Singapore had hoped, for he had begun the construction of a stout teakwood dam at the narrowest point of the river, which would divert the sluggish water through a low swamp and thence, by a bayou, back into the river on the opposite side.

McCoy was smeared from head to foot with blue clay when Singapore arrived. His green eyes were glittering with the light to be seen in men's eyes who are on the happy side of a good fight. He was already master of the river. The dam would be done in a day or two. Boys could then go down into the blue muck; shovel down to the white sand and bring it up in large quantities. He had been studying the methods of the Burmese and had picked up the idea from a man who knew something about large-scale emerald mining.

He was so enthused over the development of his idea that he was scarcely interested in Sammy's buckskin bag of sapphires.

"I've got a hunch," he said. "I've got a hunch there's sapphires down there if we dig deep enough."

"The layout looks good," Singapore complimented him, but he was, in his heart, doubtful. "I'm goin' to bury these sapphires somewhere where Do—where de Silva, if he comes sneakin' back, won't find 'em."

"Suit yourself," the dam builder answered indifferently. "I'm gonna make that sack of sapphires look like a drop of water in an ocean."

"Go to it," Singapore said heartily. "Seen anything of Dolores?"

Some of the glow receded from the green eyes. McCoy's mouth hardened. "I've seen her about the village, but I haven't talked to her. What are you grinning about?"

Singapore swallowed the grin. McCoy stared at him coldly.

"Would you mind not bringing her name up?" he asked. "You know how I feel about her. You're convinced she's no good. I happen to think you're mistaken. I intend to marry her as soon as I've struck pay dirt. As long as we disagree about her, let's not discuss her—now or ever."

"O.K., blondy," Singapore said gravely, and went about his business which was, first of all, to heal his infected foot.

For the next week, he lounged about the bungalow or in the clearing, waiting for antiseptic-soaked bandages to draw the poisons from the wound.

When the swelling went down and he was able to travel about again, he went to the village and picked up what gossip he could. De Silva's *mahouts* had returned, with their elephants; but de Silva had vanished. Dolores, he learned, was living in her father's house. He did not want to see her for a while, and wondered what her next move would be. He was sure she had not stopped trying for the Malobar pearl.

His real interest, however, was in the murmurings among the Burmese lapidaries. They had heard, to be sure, of the salted sapphire mine. Now, as McCoy and his laborers got nearer possible pay dirt, the Burmese were beginning to display a lively interest in the operations. McCoy was already tapping the curious soft white sand below the blue-clay stratum.

Singapore continued to circulate. He made friends among the lapidaries, the mat makers. He wanted to be informed when his father and de Silva returned, if they should return.

He was certain de Silva would retaliate in some way for his invasion of the encampment and theft of the sapphires. What form would the blow take?

ONE AFTERNOON in the bazaar a lazy, musical voice beside him inquired:

"Why are you avoiding me, Singapore Sammy?"

He turned slowly and looked down into large, shining brown eyes. There were dark blobs under them, as if Dolores had been crying a great deal, or been ill. He was shocked at the change in her. She looked more fragile; and this fragility gave her an entirely new appeal.

He said, amiably: "Hello, sis! Was I avoiding you?"

"You have been back from your famous mule ride two weeks and you haven't made the slightest effort to see me."

"I didn't know you'd be speakin' to me after my famous mule ride."

"Then you are very foolish and do not understand women at all. I thought it was very audacious of you. I had heard that you often did such things, but when I heard of the way you threw my father's camp into such confusion, I laughed till I cried."

"Your old man tell you about this?"

She laughed at him. "You would like to know, wouldn't you, Sammy?"

He shrugged. "Maybe not so much, sister. I got what I went after. At least, I got some of what I went after."

"And do you think Mr. McCoy's mine will produce sapphires in paying quantities this time?"

"It would put you on a pretty mean spot if it did, wouldn't it, baby?"

"You mean, I would regret I hadn't married him? No, no, no. I wouldn't regret it. Even if he were suddenly worth millions, I wouldn't regret it. I don't want riches, necessarily. First of all, I want love."

"Yeah? Well, it takes all kinds of things to make the world go round, sister. Drop up and see the diggin's some day."

"Drop in and see me some day," she answered.

"Thanks, sister," he said.

He left her, wondering just what Dolores would do if McCoy did strike sapphires in paying quantities. He was sure she had flipped one fish off her line because a larger one was lurking. But he wished he was surer.

He was cleaning his revolver one morning in the bungalow when shouts from the river attracted him. He went down to find that McCoy had struck sapphires. There were only three of them, and they were not large—less than a carat each—but they were a rich reward for his faith and his hard work.

McCoy was standing in blue mud ankle deep, with mosquito bar shrouding his helmet to keep the flies and mosquitoes out of his eyes. A broiling hot sun was steaming the clay. A lazy wind from the Apple Green Gulf drifted up the valley, bearing the stench of the stewing marshes, the sickening odor of the mangrove swamps at low tide.

One of the Annamese coolies had clambered up the oozy wall to the sluiceway with a bucketful of the white moist powder at either end of a bamboo shoulder-pole. He had poured the sand into the trough and lifted the tiny dam from the crude culvert so that a yellow, foaming flood had run down.

When the sand had settled through the copper mesh and floated off down the tail race, three dark pebbles had remained.

McCoy had seized them with trembling fingers and polished them eagerly upon a cloth of raw silk. The color of the three pebbles had emerged—as blue as the dome of the sky!

HE HAD begun shouting, and these were the shouts which Singapore heard and to which he responded. He squinted at the little blue lumps cuddled in McCoy's palm. The boy slapped him boisterously on the back.

"Half of all the sapphires that come out of here are yours," he declared.

"Boloney," Singapore said.

"All right! Take charge of them and we'll argue about it afterward. Hide them somewhere. Cache them with the others."

"O.K., blondy."

The news traveled down the native grapevine telegraph to the village. Within two hours, the river about the bend was swarming with dugouts and a hundred brown men were staring down into the swampy pit below the dam.

And late in the afternoon, McCoy's coolies struck another pocket, a richer one this time. In a dozen buckets of sand, they found sixteen sapphires, ranging in size from a half carat to three carats.

Singapore was in the village when the news reached there. He hastened back to find McCoy so excited he could hardly talk. He showed Singapore the sapphires and cried:

"Sam, old-timer, we're going to be millionaires!"

"Listen, kid," Singapore said; "I don't wanna be a millionaire. All the millionaires I've met are so busy countin' their jack they don't get time to have any fun. All I want out of this is the fun. Don't forget: this is your old man's money."

"We'll settle up later," the boy said. "Will' you cache these with the others?"

"O.K."

"Where you hiding 'em?"

"I'm buryin' 'em when nobody's lookin'."

Next morning the river bottom below the dam disgorged further riches. By noon McCoy had taken out of the white sand and Singapore had weighed more than forty carats of the blue stones. Among them was one which weighed five carats.

Early in the afternoon Dolores de Silva came visiting. She said she wanted to be among the first to congratulate Bruce. She did it very prettily, Sammy thought, and he wondered just what was taking place in her clever little brain.

HE AND McCoy were in the bungalow when she came to

the door. McCoy turned white, then red, then white again. But Dolores was not rattled or, apparently, the least embarrassed. Singapore, in the background, looked and listened with cynical attention.

It was wonderful, she said, that Bruce was reëstablishing his lost fortune.

"I hear it's going to be one of the richest strikes on the Chantaboun," she said. "And I want you to know that it makes me terribly happy that your luck has changed."

McCoy said bluntly: "Dolores, I'm glad myself, for two reasons. I don't want my father to suffer, and I want to marry you. I'm making no bones about it: I'm crazy about you, and I want to prove to you that I'm worthy of you. I'm not saying that becoming rich through a lucky sapphire strike proves that; but you'll have to admit that I took my beating and came back."

She was looking up at Bruce in her familiar way, obliquely. Singapore awaited her answer, holding his breath. He wondered how she was going to handle this.

"Bruce," she said, "I admire you tremendously, but I can never marry you. It's simply that I do not love you."

"Do you love somebody else?"

"I do!"

"Who is he?"

"I won't tell you. People said I would have married you before because you were rich, and people said I broke things off with you because you went broke."

"Did I ever say that?" he demanded angrily.

"No, Bruce. I think people will realize now that I might have married you, not because you were rich, but because I thought I loved you. They were mistaken, and so was I. I hope you do become a millionaire. Good-by! Will you take me down to my boat, Sam?"

"O.K., sister."

The green-eyed man did not look at Singapore as he followed her out the door. On the path to the river she snuggled her arm through his, looked up at him and said: "Now, what do you think of me?"

"I can't make up my mind," Singapore admitted.

The truth was, he was completely bewildered. By all indications, McCoy would soon be a very rich young man. In comparison to his wealth, the Malobar pearl was worthless.

"I told you," Dolores said, "you don't understand women."

As her canoe went down the river, Singapore suddenly realized that she was much cleverer, much more dangerous, than he had hitherto given her credit for.

What he particularly wanted to know was, when would the presence of Roderigo de Silva and Bill Shay make itself felt?

CHAPTER VII

CASH FOR SAPPHIRES

SINGAPORE LEARNED VERY definitely the next day that Roderigo de Silva was back. He heard it in the bazaar, in the lapidary stalls, and in the Sapphire Sandal. De Silva had slipped home some time after midnight last night.

That afternoon Dolores paid another visit to the mine; a business visit: she was her father's emissary.

To the two young men she said:

"I won't beat about the bush. My father wants to buy this mine back."

"Listen, sister," Singapore said; "you run along home and tell daddy if he wants to talk business to us, to come and talk it in person."

"The mine isn't for sale," McCoy said curtly.

She smiled at both of them, but her eyes lingered on Singapore's face.

"My father is willing to pay cash and to pay generously.

He knows how many carats of sapphires, approximately, have come out of the mine so far. He is willing to take a chance that you have struck pockets and that your mine may peter out at any moment."

"You can tell him," McCoy repeated, "the mine isn't for sale. We've already taken out over a hundred and forty carats of sapphires. There isn't enough money in the world to buy this mine."

"If he wants the mine so bad," Singapore put in, "why won't he come up personally?"

"He is ill, and he realizes the feeling there is between you and him and between him and Bruce."

"Any feeling between him and me," Singapore said, "is all on his side."

"Of course it is!" she cried. "How would you feel if a man you wanted to do business with had stolen into your encampment, got all your *mahouts* drunk, burned up your food—"

Singapore laughed. "He must be a lot more sensitive than he looks, sister. Well, you can tell him the mine ain't for sale."

"He offers one hundred thousand ticals."

"He must be crazy," Bruce snorted. "This is the richest strike that's ever happened in this field. Tell him we're not interested in his proposition."

"Very well," Dolores murmured, and departed.

"If de Silva is on the job again," Singapore reflected aloud, when she had gone, "it's a cinch my old man ain't far away. And believe me, blondy, we'll know it when that old fox hits town!"

"How?"

"Hang around and see!"

The mine continued to be a sensational producer. Within a week McCoy had taken from the sluice and Singapore had weighed upward of three hundred carats of sapphires. And they continued to come in unabated abundance.

At the same time, strange and mysterious things began to

happen. Little things; trivial things. And you would have to know the tropics, and especially the Siamese tropics, to understand how maddening these trivialities could become.

There was, to begin with, the laundry. Chinese in the village did the laundry. It began coming back with buttons missing, holes in places. Holes likewise mysteriously began to appear in the mosquito bars which surrounded the two men's cots.

NOW, IN tropical Asia, a mosquito bar is not merely a protection against mosquitoes and similar insects. It is a white man's fortress against death in strange and terrible forms: not only Anopheles mosquitoes, but scorpions, tarantulas and the like.

More than one white man has packed up and left Siam when holes began appearing night after night in his mosquito bar. For any white man living long in such countries will read very important meanings in such trivialities.

Singapore listened to his companion's profane ravings; saw him get up each morning, more irritable, paler, with a little less energy to carry on the day's work. He knew what was going on, but he said nothing about it until the morning when McCoy awoke to find that, during the night, a log had become loose from the dam, and a day's mining would be lost while repairs were made.

Then he told McCoy what it meant.

"My old man's here," he said. "He's back of all this."

"But what the hell is the big idea?"

"Ain't it plain enough, kid? He and de Silva want this mine back."

"They won't get it back!"

"Well, this is their way of making it easy for you to make up your mind to sell."

"Can't we put a stop to it?"

"You're in Siam, blondy."

The petty persecutions continued. One morning the coolies did not put in an appearance. An entirely new crew had to be recruited. The drinking water went bad. An entire family of chickens, the pride of McCoy's native cook, died one night in their pen behind the bungalow.

Their cook vanished. They hired a new one. The fish he cooked for their evening meal tasted queer. An hour later, Singapore felt queer. He felt as if flies were buzzing inside his skull. He knew that the fish had been doped. He felt sleepy. He went into the kitchen; interrogated the cook until he was convinced of his guilt; kicked him down the ladder and told him he would shoot him the next time he saw him. The cook fled.

Singapore mixed mustard with warm water; drank the mess and forced McCoy to do likewise. For the next half hour, the two young men were heartily sick. But the emetic had not brought up all of the drug. What had previously entered their circulation was getting in its work. They grew sleepier. They drank brandy to stimulate their hearts; but the effects of the brandy wore off, and the effects of the drug became more pronounced.

They decided to walk about their compound. They tried to box. And their boxing was like a slow motion picture. They staggered and floundered about. They fell down, and when they did, found it difficult to prevent themselves from falling asleep where they lay.

"This," Singapore said presently, "is bad on our hearts. Supposin' we take turns sleepin'—an hour on and an hour off. You take your nap, and I'll take mine. Whatever you do, don't sit down when you're on watch. We don't trust anybody in the world to-night but ourselves."

HE AROUSED McCoy at the end of an hour; aroused him by slapping his face and dousing him with buckets of water.

It was during Singapore's hour of sleep that McCoy learned something of the truth about Dolores de Silva. At a few minutes before midnight, he was standing in the copper-screened window which overlooked the river. In the light of stars and a half moon he saw a canoe slip across the river from the opposite shore. He saw it come to rest at the clump of areca palms some distance below the sluiceway. He saw a slim figure emerge from it and walk swiftly toward the house.

When he perceived that this figure was Dolores de Silva, he slipped into a dark shadow and waited with a racing heart. He heard the faint scraping of her feet on the ladder. A moment later, he saw the silhouette of her slim body against the palely glowing sky.

She came into the room. Now she was invisible. A moment later he saw her pass the cot in which he always slept. The mosquito bar shrouding it would have made it impossible for her to see him, if he had been lying there.

He waited, with clenched fists and madly thumping heart.

He saw her go to Singapore's cot; saw her lift the mosquito bar slowly, an inch at a time. A small flash light beamed. Light fell on Singapore's face and flaming red hair. He was sleeping on his back with his mouth slightly ajar. He was softly snoring. His freckles stood out sharply.

The light glistened on the copper wire about his neck, at the bottom of which, McCoy knew, was the celebrated Malobar pearl.

He saw the girl's slim fingers reach to the copper wire and slowly begin to pull it up. It was undoubtedly the bitterest moment of McCoy's life—far bitterer than his discovery that he had lost his father's savings. He was incredulous still. He had had faith in Dolores, in spite of Singapore's frequent allusions to her.

If he had had a revolver in his hand at that moment, there is no question but that he would have shot her dead.

Instead, his voice shot from the darkness: "Get away from there, you slut, before I kill you! Get out of here!"

The flash light blinked off. He ran to her. Even in the face of discovery, the pressure of her eagerness made her desperately try to gain this thing that she coveted so.

She snatched at the wire in the darkness. McCoy heard Singapore grunt. The boy's groping hands found hers. She had the wire in her hand. It was broken. He snatched it away from her; made sure the chamois sack was still on the end of it; felt of the priceless round bubble inside.

"Get out of here before I kill you!"

He hardly heard her go. Singapore growled: "What the hell is goin' on here?" Then: "The blue pearl's gone!"

"I've got it," McCoy snapped. He struck a match and lighted candles. He extended the broken wire with the dangling sack to the red-haired man.

Singapore frantically opened the sack with his teeth, dumped out the fire pearl into his hand, and gave a deep grunt of relief.

"Come here," McCoy said at the window. "A thief got in."

"Dolores?"

McCoy did not answer for a long time.

"Yes," he said.

Singapore got up, yawning. "I guess we can both sleep now," he said. "We know who doped the fish."

"What a sucker I've been!"

"There's an old Siamese sayin'," Singapore grunted. " 'The more you know, the more luck you have.' "

THE TWO young men awoke late next morning to find that their new force of coolies had failed to appear for work, and that, some time during the night, the sluiceway had been carted away.

Contemplating the empty pit, Singapore said:

"Blondy, I've got to talk to you like a Dutch uncle. I have spent seven years in these nutty countries, and I know something about the way the Oriental mind works. I also know something about the way the mind of a white man works who has spent a lot of time out here. You are gonna be licked. You might as well sell out and blow."

McCoy turned on him fiercely. "It isn't like you to make that kind of a crack, Sam. I've never heard you say quit yet. I'm going to keep on scrapping—damn their rotten hides!"

"It's like this," Sam explained. "Did you ever hear about the time Napoleon tried to lick Russia? Did he get by with it? Listen! What you are up against is what Napoleon was up against in Russia. He went bargin' in there with a big army, expectin' to meet a big army and lick it, like he always did. That's where the Rooshans put over a fast one on him. He didn't meet any army. All that happened was a lot of little pesky things. It wore him down. The harder he hit, the less it got him. It was like havin' a fight with a python. The python don't fight you. All he does is hang on and squeeze a little harder. And before long, the python has you inside, digestin'."

McCoy nodded. "I see what you mean, but we can't quit now. We're right on the verge of real money."

"We'll quit, but we'll put on that we ain't quittin'," Sammy compromised. "We'll repair the dam, and build a new sluiceway, and hire us a new gang of coolies. We'll put up a bluff. But you'll sell. How you fixed for jack?"

"The roll you left me when you went to follow de Silva is just about gone. We'll have to sell some of the sapphires."

They cooked their own breakfast. And while they were solemnly eating it, Dolores came.

Pale, haggard, and with hollow, frightened eyes, she came up the ladder and into the kitchen.

IN SURPRISED silence the two men stared at her. Then McCoy sprang up and sent his chair spinning on one leg into a corner. Singapore looked up at her and grinned.

He said amiably: "Hello, sister! Walk right in and have a cuppa coffee. Honest to God, there ain't a drop of dope in it!"

She had caught her hands to her slim breast. "You must think I am a fool to come here," she gasped, "after last night. But I had to come!"

"Sister," Singapore answered, "you don't have to apologize for anything. You are always welcome. Sit down!"

"My father made me come here."

She was wearing a white silk shirt, trim white breeches, snake boots. In her hand was a large bulking canvas bag.

Singapore flipped a freckled hand toward the bag.

"What you got there, kid—dynamite?"

"Money."

"Well, that's just dandy. How much money you got there?"

"Two hundred thousand ticals! It isn't all in ticals; but at current rates of exchange, it amounts to that. There is Hongkong money, Singapore money, Siamese—"

"Then it must be my old man's bank roll," Singapore interrupted her. "He always carries a lot of mixed currency."

Dolores said tensely: "My father wants to buy this mine."

"It is not for sale," McCoy said harshly.

She flicked an oblique look at him; returned her glittering, frightened eyes to Singapore.

"I can't argue. I'm too nervous. But I will tell you that what has happened here in the past few days is only a sample of what may happen."

"Trot some more tricks out of your bag!" McCoy jeered.

"Sam," she said in a broken voice, "I don't have to argue with you. You know I'm not lying or exaggerating. You know what those two men can do to you. You and Bruce are strangers here. They'll kill you if you don't get out."

"Boloney," McCoy growled.

"No," Singapore contradicted, "it ain't boloney, blondy. Go on, Dolores."

"They could kill you, but they would rather not. They would rather pay a fair price for the mine. Two hundred thousand ticals is a fair price. It's more than sixty thousand dollars, gold. Perhaps this mine is worth more. Perhaps it's worth less. You know, Sam. You talk to him."

"I'll tell you what, sister," Sammy replied. "You go back to my old man and tell him he can have the mine for sixty thousand, gold, if he comes here personally."

"You know he won't come here!" she cried.

Sammy knew it. He had scouted industriously about the environs of Chantaboun since the petty persecutions started, trying to find some trace of his father. But Bill Shay was too foxy. It was beginning to look as though half of Sammy's plan would succeed, and the other half would fail. He would send McCoy back home, a rich man; but he would not succeed in capturing his father. However, he would keep on trying.

"Just what," he asked Dolores, "is your proposition?"

"Two hundred thousand ticals for this property. A bill of sale signed by Mr. McCoy."

"Not a chance," said the stubborn young man.

"When do we clear out?" Singapore asked.

"By noon," Dolores replied.

"No," said McCoy. "We stick and we fight."

"Supposing," Dolores suggested, "you reason with him, Sam."

"There's a trick in it somewhere," McCoy said. "They tricked me before—or thought they did. They'll try it again."

"What she said a minute ago," Singapore argued, "is true. We're strangers in a strange place. They know the natives. They've got the natives behind them. If we don' take this offer, they can run us out—kill us. They've shown you they can put you on a spot. Anyhow, they've shown me. I'm convinced. I say: Take this jack and clear out. You'll have your ten thousand back and fifty thousand more. You can go back home, put your dad on easy street, and still have enough left to set yourself up in business. You've played in big luck so far. But you don't know this country. There's an old Siamese sayin', 'If you want to go fast, go the old road.'"

McCOY GAZED darkly at Dolores. "But where do you come in, Sam? Half of this money and half of the sapphires we've mined are yours. I want to go you fifty-fifty."

"I'll make you a dicker," Sam said. "When I left to follow de Silva, I left you my bank roll—twelve hundred ticals. Pay me that and let me have the sapphires we've mined as my share. How many sapphires have we mined?"

"Six hundred and twenty carats."

"They'll fetch," Singapore estimated, "about fifty dollars a cart, when they're sorted and graded. Call it thirty thousand dollars. That's enough for me."

"It isn't fair," McCoy protested. "If it hadn't been for you, I'd be a beach comber this minute. You rawhided me into reopening this mine. You put up the money for it. You certainly deserve half of everything. Give me half the sapphires—three hundred carats—and split the sales money."

But Singapore would not consider this proposition. He argued that he didn't want anything but the six hundred carats of sapphires. It represented, approximately, a third interest, and he was entitled to no more than that.

McCoy wavered and, in the end, reluctantly accepted these terms. Then Singapore said to Dolores:

"Now, sister, let's have a look-see at that jack. I've got a low-down, suspicious nature, and I wanna make sure it ain't funny money."

She surrendered the canvas bag to him. It contained bundles of Hongkong dollars, bundles of Javanese guilders, bundles of Siamese ticals, bundles of Straits dollars, Indian rupees, Burmese rupees, Indo-Chinese piastres, and twenty rolls of United States gold double-eagles.

Singapore sorted out the money, carefully inspected it, counted it and reckoned its value in Siamese ticals at prevailing rates of exchange. It amounted to slightly more than two hundred thousand ticals—approximately sixty-four thousand dollars in American gold.

He subtracted from it the twelve hundred ticals he had lent McCoy and gave the balance to him.

McCoy protested that it wasn't fair; that Singapore deserved more. Singapore grunted these protests aside.

"Haven't I got six hundred carats of sapphires plus the hundred carats I got from de Silva? We forgot to count them in. That makes a grand total of seven hundred carats, don't it, at fifty bucks a carat? Thirty-five thousand bucks! Boy, that's more jack than I ever saw in my life! Now, sis, how do you want the bill of sale made out?"

"It's to be made out to William Shay and Roderigo de Silva."

Singapore looked at her shrewdly for some time. He said, "O.K., sister. I guess my old man has put over another swift one on me, but I guess I'll have to grin and bear it."

When McCoy had written out the bill of sale, he was still protesting.

"Sam, I hate to quit. At the rate we were going, I'd be worth a million dollars inside of a year. I hate to think of those two getting all that money."

"There's an old Siamese saying," Singapore answered: " 'Past events are as clear as a mirror; future events are as dark as lacquer.' "

CHAPTER VIII

DEATH-MARKED

WHEN DOLORES WAS gone with the bill of sale, Singapore said:

"Blondy, we're still in a spot. We don't dare move out of Chantaboun until the Laughin' Lady puts in. We can't use elephants because my old man and de Silva would follow us sure as hell and kill us for this money.

"Now, here is my plan: You move our stuff out of here right away. Take it down to the *sala*. Wear your revolver and have your rifle loaded and ready. I'm goin' off on a little private business errand, and I'll meet you at the *sala* later.

"We'll stock up the *sala* with food and water, and keep all visitors out until the Laughin' Lady calls. If Lucky Jones shows up with the *Blue Goose*, we'll sail with him. I wonder what's keepin' that guy. He should have been here a week ago. The Laughin'

Lady is due in day after to-morrow. If Lucky doesn't show up by then, we'll take her."

He buckled on his revolver and went down to the river. His intentions were to follow Dolores, to be near by when she handed over the bill of sale to her father and Bill Shay. He was certain Bill Shay would be somewhere in the neighborhood, because Bill Shay was sly and would not trust de Silva.

Singapore selected a canoe and poled rapidly down river. At the second bend, he sighted Dolores's canoe. He went ashore a hundred yards above the clearing where the de Silva house stood. Concealing himself behind a mahogany tree, he watched her step out of her canoe. De Silva clambered down the ladder from the house and ran to meet her. But he was alone. Bill Shay was not in evidence.

Singapore waited expectantly. He was certain his father was not far away. The pair moved leisurely toward the house. They were talking excitedly. He heard scraps of their conversation. They were discussing the sale of the mine. He overheard no reference to his father. Perhaps he was waiting in the house. If so, he would come to the doorway when they started up the ladder.

But no one came to the doorway. Dolores and her father went up the ladder and vanished into the house. Their voices came to him clearly on the still air. There was no other voice.

Singapore concluded that Bill Shay was not there. And he realized fully the difficulties which would beset any attempt he made to find Bill Shay. Bill Shay was like a wise old leopard. You might trail such a leopard for months without capturing him. The only way to catch him was by surprise. It was too late for that now.

But Singapore did not give up. He returned to the village and asked careful questions of the lapidaries and the mat makers. He went to the caravansary. And he realized that the answers given to all his questions were carefully guarded. He knew that these natives were lying; that they were against him, perhaps because his father dressed as a Buddhist priest.

Siam is the greatest remaining stronghold of Buddhism. These people looked upon Bill Shay as a holy man. Religious zealots, fanatics, they would promptly resent any harm Singapore did to him. More than that, it was quite likely that they would waylay Sammy; actually murder him, if his father gave the word.

Having exhausted all possibilities, Sammy abandoned the search and joined McCoy in the *sala*. Now, a *sala* is a unique Siamese institution. Every Siamese village, however small, has at least one *sala*. It is a small house built for the benefit of travelers. Any visitor to a Siamese village is welcome to use the *sala*.

The *sala* in Chantaboun was on the bank of the river, a few hundred feet below the dock. It chanced, in the event of an attack, to be strategically situated. It occupied the center of a small clearing. Its ladder ran almost into the river.

SAMMY FOUND McCoy arranging the provisions he had purchased. He had bought a dozen large earthen jars and had filled these with fresh boiled water. There was enough food and water to last them a week. McCoy had bought a half dozen boxes of revolver ammunition in the bazaar. Singapore asked him where his money was.

"I'm wearing it next to my skin. And I'm beginning to think we can't get out of here any too soon. I wish that steamer was coming in to-night, or that pal of yours would show up with his schooner. Where are your sapphires?"

"I'm goin' up river for 'em now. I'll be back in an hour."

He returned with exciting news. De Silva and Dolores had taken possession of the bungalow at the mine. The sluiceway had been reërected. Forty coolies were digging in the pit and carrying up buckets of white sand.

"Was your father there?"

"No."

McCoy looked at him curiously. "You look pale, Sam, and you act mighty nervous. Anything wrong?"

"I wish we were out of here," Singapore said. "There's gonna be trouble. I can feel it in my bones."

His hand flew to his revolver when, a few minutes later, a voice called from the compound. He went to the doorway. A brown boy of ten or twelve was looking up. When he saw Sam, he waved a piece of paper.

Singapore told him to come up. What had looked like a piece of paper was a sealed envelope. It was addressed simply to Sam Shay.

He tore it open, extracted a folded sheet of paper. It contained a penciled message. He read it aloud to McCoy.

> My dear son:
>
> How much longer are you going to be a sucker? As I have informed you before, I don't want to see you and I'm not going to let you see me. Take my advice and stop horning into my affairs. Get yourself and your friend out of here as fast as you know how or you are going to be sorry. I have an idea your sapphire mine is going to make me a rich man. It's too bad I had to take candy out of babies' mouths, but babies don't belong in tough countries.
>
> A dry finger does not lick up salt.
>
> Your loving father,
> Bill Shay.

Sammy, finishing the letter, looked about for the boy who had brought it. He had vanished.

McCoy asked: "What does he mean by, 'A dry finger does not lick up salt'?"

"It's an old Siamese sayin'," Sammy answered. "It means, we are a couple of suckers. It means we aren't properly equipped to deal with clever guys like him and de Silva."

"I wish we hadn't sold the mine."

"I wish," Sammy said nervously, "we were out of here. We will take turns sleepin' to-night, the way we did last night. Don't move around much when it's your trick. Don't stand near windows or door. I mean, don't make a target of yourself."

"Don't you think," McCoy asked, "you're letting all this get your goat?"

"Sure, it's got my goat, blondy! I'm scared! I'm scared stiff! We are in one tough spot, and don't you forget it. If my old man wants this money and these sapphires bad enough, he will work on these people until they swarm in here after us like ants. Don't forget they're religious fanatics, and that he wears the robes of a Buddhist priest."

"We can hold them off until the steamer comes."

"I only wish Lucky was here!"

THAT NIGHT passed without incident. Singapore slept hardly at all. He was nervous, jumpy. When dawn came, he pulled up a chair at the window which faced down river, and he spent most of that day in the chair, looking toward the Gulf; frowning, as if with concentration—as though with sheer will power he would compel Lucky Jones's schooner to come sailing up the river.

But the *Blue Goose* did not come. And the Laughing Lady was overdue. She should have been alongside the dock at noon.

At dusk a half-dozen natives came into the compound and stared up at the *sala*. When they drifted away, after an hour of apparently aimless staring, Singapore grunted.

"Something is brewin'. Hell is gettin' ready to pop."

McCoy was losing his patience. Penned up in the small room with Singapore for twenty-four hours had worn his nerves thin.

He growled, "Aw, stop beefing, Sam."

"Kid, I tell you, we're on a spot."

"What in the devil has got into you, Sam? I never saw you this way before."

"If Lucky would only show up! If that steamer would only come!"

"I don't see anything to get so hot and bothered about. Stop worrying,"

"I wish I could."

He turned back to the window. There was no moon to-night,

and there would be no moon; but the stars afforded him sufficient illumination to see the river.

He began mistaking fireflies for misty starboard lights swinging around bends. But even if the steamer or the schooner came up the river, it would not be until almost midnight, because high tide at the bar was not until ten o'clock.

There was a stiff breeze from the gulf, plenty of breeze to bring the schooner up river under her jibs. This same breeze caused rustlings and rattlings in the palm trees behind the *sala*, and these added to Sammy's jumpiness.

Said McCoy: "Listen, Sam. Even if Lucky Jones should get across the bar at high water to-night, he would anchor in the mouth of the river for daylight. So would the steamer. Look here. Are you holdin' out on me?"

"Huh?"

"You've got somethin' on your mind that you haven't let me in on. Now what is it?"

"How do you figger that out?"

"The way you've been acting. I don't see why we are in the slightest danger."

"Any guy with sixty thousand bucks in cash money pinned to his B.V.D.s is in danger."

"Stop tryin' to kid me, Sam. What your father said in that letter is true. He and de Silva, when they bought that mine for sixty thousand bucks, were takin' candy away from babies. We practically gave them that mine. They're too busy forking out sapphires to bother with chicken feed like sixty thousand berries, and you know it."

"Yeah."

"Then what's eating you?"

"They're a coupla tough eggs, blondy."

"Uh-huh. And maybe you're soft-boiled. Quit worrying."

"O.K."

But Singapore, with plenty to worry about, disregarded his friend's advice and kept on worrying.

MIDNIGHT CAME and went. At about two o'clock Singapore saw a pale glow far in the distance toward the gulf. It vanished. His spirits went up. Maybe it was the schooner! Maybe it was the steamer! A little later he heard some one moving about in the compound. He gripped the butt of his revolver and tensely waited. A whisper floated out of the night:

"Singapore!"

It came from below. McCoy was asleep, softly snoring. Sam went to the door. Below him flowed the river. He had reasoned that, in case of dire necessity, he could probably take a running dive from this doorway, do a belly-smasher, and swim to the dubious safety of the farther shore. The water lapped the shore on this side not a yard from the foot of the ladder.

In the starlight he saw a small, pale face uplifted.

Another whisper: "It's Dolores, Sam. I must see you."

"What about?"

"You know what about!"

"Yeah? What's that you've got in your hands?"

"My Mannlicher. You're going to need it."

"I can still shoot pretty good with my forty-five."

"I'm coming up. Give me your hand."

Singapore's heart was thumping in his throat. Sweat formed a clammy film on his face and forehead.

She handed up the rifle, butt foremost. He pulled it up and stood it against a roof post. Then he reached down for her hand. It was like ice. He pulled her up beside him. She clung to his hand. She was shivering. In the semi-darkness he could hear her teeth chattering. And he could hear her breath coming in little gasps.

"They're going to kill you and Bruce!"

A sleepy voice inquired: "Who the hell's that?"

Sammy said: "Pipe down. It's Dolores."

He heard McCoy's feet thump on the floor. A match scratched, flamed.

"Put that light out!" Dolores whispered.

"What are you doing here?"

"They're wise," she said, when he had extinguished the light. "Sam, they have had forty men working in the pit since yesterday noon. From dawn till dark to-day. They haven't found a solitary sapphire."

"That's their tough luck," said McCoy.

"It's your death warrant!" Dolores snapped.

McCOY STOOD up and walked toward her. He asked in a growl: "How do you figure that out?"

"How," she retorted, "do you suppose they figure it?"

"Look here, Miss de Silva," McCoy said; "we sold you that mine in good faith. If it happened to peter out the day we sold it, that's no fault of ours. We got over six hundred carats of sapphires out of that pit. There ought to be sixty thousand carats more."

"Are you trying to kid me?" Dolores inquired coldly.

"Listen," Sam said; "he ain't in on it. You talk to me."

"Haven't I told you enough? Why didn't you two clear out of here immediately? Why did you have to wait?"

"Never mind that," Singapore said. "How come you're takin' all this trouble? Have you switched camps?"

"Yes."

"Why?"

"You can ask yourself that question."

"Sister, let's can the riddles. What is your racket this time? Are you still workin' for the blue pearl?"

"No, I'll tell you why I'm here. And I'll tell you why I've ditched my father forever." She hesitated. "Sam, I love you. That's why I'm here."

McCoy laughed. "Your father kicked you out. That's why you're here!"

She said, huskily: "Sam, you believe me, don't you?"

"Sister, your brain is too fast for me. What do you aim to do?"

"Stay here and help. Some time between now and daylight my father and a gang of armed natives will try to kill you and Bruce McCoy. If I'm here, they may not shoot. That's logical, isn't it?"

"Everything you've ever said, sister, is logical. That's just the trouble."

"I came here only because I love you. I don't care what happens to me now, as long as I can be with you. Don't you believe me?"

"No!" McCoy snapped.

Sam laid his hand on her shoulder gently. He had always been sorry for her, and he was sorrier for her now than he had ever been. He could not reconcile himself to the demonstrated fact that a girl so beautiful and so innocent-looking could have such a twisted brain.

Dolores bent her head until her cheek was lying on his palm.

"I love you so much!" she whispered. Her arms flew about his neck. She kissed his mouth and fiercely clung to him.

Singapore removed her arms; made sure that the copper wire about his neck had not been tampered with.

"Sister, let's have some more dope on this assassination we're on the receivin' end of. Blondy, you go back to bed. I'll handle this."

McCoy said something under his breath about female snakes.

"Wait," Singapore whispered to the girl. He heard, in the darkness, the groaning of McCoy's cot as he lowered his weight onto it. He whispered into Dolores's ear: "He doesn't know. He thinks all this is a false alarm. He will be asleep in a minute. Stand by, sister."

He pushed her onto a bench and sat down beside her. Dolores fumbled for his hand, found it and clung to it. She laid her head on his shoulder and sighed. Singapore sighed, too.

He waited until McCoy began to snore, then said:

"Say what you feel like sayin' about the sapphire business, sister, and I'll do the same."

"Doesn't he know you salted the mine?"

"Sister, he does not. He thinks six hundred and twenty carats came out of that pit. Well, so they did. But he doesn't know that the original hundred carats I stole off your old man went back into the white sand as fast as he sluiced 'em out. I didn't want him to know. I still don't want him to know. It might hurt his conscience. Me—I haven't any conscience."

"I suspected it from the beginning," the girl whispered. "Every night you took all the sapphires he had sluiced out during the day and threw them back into the pit."

"That's right, sister."

"I don't blame you," Dolores said. "You put over a very clever deal on those two old crooks. It served them right."

Nestling her head on his shoulder, she sighed again. Sam wondered what her game was now. He didn't believe she loved him. It pleased his vanity to think that she might, but he was too hard-boiled; he had seen her in action too many times. Her father and his father had been outfoxed. He and McCoy had the hundred carats of sapphires and the two hundred thousand ticals. Also, he still had the Malobar pearl. She was playing for big stakes now.

"Sam, I love you so much."

He got up. "Sister, if you will stand watch at the window at that end, I'll keep an eye on this one. Is your rifle loaded?"

"Yes, Sam. You haven't said you like me. You might at least say that, you forgive me and that you like me. You think I'm a rather dreadful girl. Perhaps I am. But you'll admit I haven't had much of a chance to be otherwise. I don't care whether you're a saint or a devil. You could be the lowest kind of thief, and I'd still love you. I loved you the night I met you. I knew, whatever else you were, that you're strong. You're the only man I'd ever known I've ever wanted. You've got to say you love me. Say it!"

Her arms went around his neck again. Sam kissed her lightly on the lips and got up.

"Take your post, soldier," he growled. It occurred to him that she might have come up deliberately to kill him and McCoy. He could not say why he was so sure that she had not come up on such an errand.

He was more than half convinced that she was telling the truth.

CHAPTER IX

SUCKERS

SAMMY PULLED IN the ladder and awaited developments. The wind from the gulf blew fresher. The palms behind the *sala* rattled and clicked and created the illusion of falling rain, as palms do when they are attacked by a strong wind.

Shortly before dawn, there was a hail from below. Singapore, springing to attentiveness, recognized the harsh voice as Roderigo de Silva's.

"Dolores!"

She did not answer.

"Dolores, I know you are up there. I warn you it will do absolutely no good. This place is surrounded by armed men. I know that you three cannot have many days' food and water supply. It is difficult to hold these men back. I cannot even promise to hold them back until you are forced out by hunger and thirst. Will you come?"

"I will not!" she cried.

De Silva now addressed himself to Singapore.

"Shay," he said, "you haven't a chance, and you know it. Throw down the sapphires and the money and you can go. I will give you ten minutes to decide."

"He doesn't need ten seconds," Dolores cried. "You don't dare shoot because I'm up here."

That was the end of the parley. Dolores whispered to Singapore: "We can certainly hold out until the steamer comes. Then we can make a dash for it."

But Singapore wasn't so optimistic. He was thinking of his father's influence on these fanatical natives. It required very little to set them off. A howling mob of them might attack at any moment.

HOURS DRAGGED by. The Laughing Lady came steaming up the river and tied up to the dock. Making a dash for the dock would have been sheer folly. Through chinks in the walls, Singapore could see brown men not far away; men with knives and rifles.

Dusk brought the situation to its climax. A bullet crashed through the thatch roof. McCoy was kneeling, looking down with his revolver in his hand, ready. He returned the shot. A man between two palms fell limply—a brown man.

Angry murmurings reached the three in the *sala*. Some one fired from the other side.

Then it was that Singapore, standing back from the down-river window so that he could not be seen, saw the snow-white sails of a schooner bellying before the breeze. He would have known that little ship amidst any amount of shipping. Some men can give their hearts to a ship more easily than to a woman. It was so with Singapore Sammy and the *Blue Goose*.

Even at this distance she showed evidences of the loving care her owner bestowed upon her. Such a princess of the sea was certainly deserving of the best. Her deck was holystoned to the whiteness of parchment. Her bright work gleamed in the failing tropical light. You knew that her standing and running rigging were in perfect condition. Her steel-blue hull gleamed like new metal.

He yelled, "Ahoy, there, Lucky!" But she was a full quarter mile away.

A bullet clipped a roof post close to him.

The besieged three crouched and watched the schooner. She came along swiftly, on the port tack, with water foaming whitely at her bows. But the *Blue Goose* did not make for the dock. She stood off, came sharply into the wind when halfway across the river—still well beyond hail. Her jibs fluttered down, then her foresail and mainsail as the anchor splashed.

Singapore waited. If Lucky did not come ashore now, he would in all probability wait for morning. Darkness swiftly closed down, and no small boat left the schooner.

McCoy groaned: "We may be dead by morning!"

"Not us," Singapore said. "I'm gonna swim out to her!"

"What good will it do?" Dolores wailed.

"Sam," McCoy growled, "you know this river is alive with alligators."

"You'd be shot," Dolores added, "before you got a dozen feet."

"You'd be swept down with the current," McCoy argued. "What can the little handful of men he has aboard do against this mob?"

"Plenty," Singapore said. In the darkness, he had been slipping off his clothing. "Stand away from that doorway!"

He ran back to the opposite wall; braced himself, sprang forward at a run, and vanished out the doorway. McCoy and Dolores heard him splash. They saw the spurts of red flame as rifles blazed.

Singapore executed that dive as he had earlier planned. He fairly crashed onto the water; then he dived down and swam a dozen lengths before coming back to the surface. He heard the rifles on shore, but none of the bullets struck close enough to worry him.

With a powerful trudgeon stroke, he struck out for the *Blue Goose*. When he was within fifty feet of the schooner, he yelled: "Lucky, ahoy! Don't shoot!"

The hard voice of his old friend emerged from the darkness

of the poop, bellowing orders in Malay to his crew. Then a laugh and:

"What in hell are you doin' out there?"

"Haul me in—quick!"

THEY HAULED him in. Sammy outlined the situation in the fewest possible words while the Chinese steward went below for a dry shirt and dungarees. Lucky profanely wanted to know what Sam wanted him to do.

"Run up alongside that bank, under the *sala*. Take the kid and the girl aboard."

"You know what that means, red-head?"

"Sure! Your decks will be pumped full of lead. We both may get shot. I thought you liked a fight!"

"Yeah. But I like to pick my fights. I don't like 'em shoved down my gullet." He began roaring orders in Malay. "Up anchor! Get those sails up!"

The *Blue Goose* became, in a matter of seconds, a living thing again. Singapore took the wheel while Lucky went below to break out arms for his handful of men. *Parangs* and pistols for the Malays. A rifle for himself, another for Singapore, and a sawed-off shotgun for the Chinese steward.

The land loomed close. Singapore kept the lights of the Laughing Lady over his port quarter as a landmark until he saw that the steamer was moving ahead. She was pulling out. Then he steered by guesswork, or it may have been by excellent memory coupled with experienced judgment.

The *sala* was clearly outlined soon against the light of stars. Lucky came aft and took the wheel.

"You go for'ard," he said, "and run this show. It's your show, redhead. And may God have pity on you if we get stuck in the mud!"

That was what was worrying Sam—the depth of the river close under the bank. But the schooner slipped along; came in closer.

He softly called: "Blondy! Dolores! Get ready to jump! Jump when she's under you! Jump in the mainsail, Dolores!"

Rifles began to blaze now. They set up a twinkling along the shore like red fireflies. Sam returned this fire; heard the reports of the Malays' pistols, and the tremendous discharge of the steward's shotgun.

Some one had thrown a torch on the roof of the *sala*. The dry thatch began to burn fiercely. In the ruddy luminance of this, Sammy saw two half-naked brown men clamber aboard from the bank. Simultaneously he saw a flash of white. Dolores had jumped.

Then he saw de Silva coming aboard. Singapore brought up his rifle and pulled the trigger, aiming from the hip. The hammer clicked on an empty cartridge chamber.

De Silva, his yellow face contorting, lifted the revolver clutched in his hand. Sammy was too far away to use his rifle as a club.

Something dark and rod-like flashed past him. He learned later that it was an iron belaying pin. He saw it thud into the shadow between de Silva's eyes, heard the crunch of cracking bone, and saw de Silva, limp, lifeless, slide down the mud into the water. Lucky Jones's aim with belaying pins had always been excellent.

A bullet stung across Sam's shoulder. Then a heavy body thumped down onto the deck beside him. A man went to his knees. It was McCoy. Blood dripped down his face from a gash over his left eye.

LUCKY SHOUTED: "All hands below. Watch out now!"

He had thrown the tiller hard over; the *Blue Goose* was drifting out into the river. Her sails swung over with a crash as she gybed. Sammy saw the bo's'n pick up a lifeless brown man and hurl him far out into the water. A bullet gashed the deck at his feet.

Sam dropped below the bulwarks and crawled forward. He wondered where his father was. He called Dolores. Her frightened voice answered from the windward side. He slid on his belly between two cabins and found her huddled down in the lee of the after one.

"Hurt, sister?"

"No. I saw my father die."

"It was tough, sister; but it was him or me."

She came close to him. Automatically, Sam reached up and touched the copper wire at his neck. The famous Malobar pearl was still safe.

She said lifelessly, "You don't love me."

"That's my tough break," Singapore said.

"But I love you. You are the only man I have ever loved. You believe me. Oh, you must believe me!"

"You aren't playin' fair, sister. Look back, will you? Just look back to all the times you double-crossed me. I couldn't trust you. The first night you met me—"

"I tried to drug and stab you—for that pearl. But I love you now. What is to happen to me? My father is dead. What will become of me?"

"Sister, quit worryin'. You'll never starve. You'll always have pretty clothes. You're too smart. You're too good-lookin'."

She did not answer. He took out of his hip pocket the buckskin bag of sapphires—the one hundred carats of uncut stones which had deceived several credulous men. He laid the bag in her lap.

"You need these sapphires more than I do, sister. They're all yours."

"Sam, I love you so much!" Her heart was breaking in her throat; but Singapore observed that her hands closed greedily about the precious buckskin bag.

Lucky called: "Where-away? Down river, red-head?"

"Get alongside that steamer. We've got a passenger for her."

"The lady?"

"Yep. The lady."

Lucky hailed the steamer. Its engines stopped. The schooner came alongside. As Sam helped Dolores up onto the deck, she said:

"I will love you all my life—and I will never forgive you!"

SOME HOURS later, when Singapore had concluded his recital of his latest adventure to his old shipmate, Lucky said:

"You are the world's biggest sucker. You spend weeks, you risk your life to make suckers out of a sapphire racket—and what have you got out of it? Tell me, willya? You got soft-hearted and gave that kid all the money. You tossed five thousand dollars' worth of sapphires away on a skirt who would as soon carve your heart out as look at you! You think you're hard-boiled. You think you're tough. You think you're smart. You think you made suckers out of everybody. You big lunk, you are the biggest sucker out of the lot! Tell me, what did you get out of it?"

"A nice souvenir," Sam said resentfully. "A nice sapphire-handled dagger."

"Oh, boloney!"

"All that aside," Sam said, "what is this red-hot deal you got on that calls for my slick methods?"

"Pearls!"

"Where?"

"In the Gulf of Tomini! An old guy whom I lent a hundred dollars to in Singapore gave me the low-down out of thankfulness. He says the pearls there are so thick you can scoop 'em up in your hands!"

Sammy bellowed with laughter. "And you think I'm softboiled! You call me a sucker!"

THE PYTHON PIT

Whether it held fabulous pearls, or cannibals,
Singapore Sammy was going to that
forbidden South Seas isle—to kill a man

CHAPTER I

BATTLE ROYAL

IT WAS NEW Year's Eve in the Sailors Delight, and Singapore Sammy was going to be rolled. He knew he was going to be rolled. And he suspected that he was going to be murdered. And he was reasonably sure that his partner Lucifer—"Lucky"—Jones was about to lose his luck and become vulture fodder unless something was speedily done about it.

Singapore Sammy saw the blue bottle spinning lazily through the air toward Lucky Jones's head, spilling its white contents as it came. Lucky was so occupied that he did not see the bottle. With his eyes gleaming with the love of battle, his wild black hair flying, his big jaw out-thrust, he was driving his fists into the face of a Japanese sailor. The Jap went down.

Lucky evidently saw the bottle now but was unable to move—like a man in a nightmare rooted to a railroad track down which a train is thundering.

"Duck!" Singapore Sammy roared.

But Lucky Jones was incapable of ducking. As if he were hypnotized, he stood there and let the half-empty *arrack* bottle go twirling to its destination, which was a spot on his forehead just above the left eye. He sagged from sight—and the brawl went on.

With the best of intentions, Singapore Sammy had started it, when a Malay with one eye reached up and snatched at the copper wire encircling his neck. He had swiftly closed the Malay's other eye, and had recognized in the Malay's fat, brown,

*Lucky stayed
where Singapore
propped him.*

oily companion a man he was extremely anxious to have speech with.

But the oily one had evaded him. And every man in the room had wolfishly fallen upon the two Americans, proving that it does not pay to be an American in a foreign port these days when a brawl starts.

Singapore Sammy, who hated brawls, had acted promptly, however, upon experience. He wrenched a leg from a table and, using it as a club, battered every head that came within reach. And in the forty or fifty seconds which elapsed from the brawl's beginning to Lucky's terminating the flight of the blue bottle, Singapore Sammy had accounted for three Malays, two Japanese sailors, two Chinese coolies and a tall unknown white man who now sat on the floor in a corner mourning a broken nose.

Tobacco smoke hung in creamy layers under the ceiling. Mingling upward were the sour fumes of alcohol from broken glasses and overturned bottles. Shrill curses and yells in many tongues rounded off an impression of great confusion.

Singapore Sammy deftly knocked a gun out of one hand and a gleaming *parang* out of another. The police would be here any moment. What would the judge say?

"Ah-ha!" the judge would say. "So you're back again, Mr. Shay! I thought you were told to keep out of Singapore."

And Singapore Sammy—otherwise, Samuel Larkin Shay, American born but at present citizen of the world—would enjoy the doubtful hospitality of Singapore Town for thirty or, maybe, sixty days.

One of the red-headed American's eyes was turning purple. Blood trickled in a thick red stream from a cut under the other one. His carrot-colored eyebrows moved in agitated jumps. When he was angry, they always did that—wriggling around on his sun-baked forehead like dancing red mice.

A Chinese, biding his time, leaped up unexpectedly and tried to snatch the soft copper wire from Singapore Sammy's neck. Some one else locked arms around his knees. He felt hands pawing at his hip pockets. That was where he carried his bankroll. And the Jap sailor was rushing at him with a three-legged stool in his hands.

Sammy saw that fat, oily, little Malay sliding along the wall toward a door. He couldn't reach him. But he must reach him. He laid about him with the table leg. The Chinese sat down and began to moan. The unseen enemy who had tackled his knees now sank his teeth into the calf of Sammy's left leg. Sammy bounced his club off the Jap's head, and the Jap also went into a flat spin.

But Sammy couldn't wield that club much longer. His throat was as dry as gunsmoke. His heart had become a throbbing ache. His muscles were striking for a five-hour day. He brought the club crunching down on an upturned ear above his left foot, and the teeth disengaged themselves from his calf.

A woman screamed. Her voice penetrated the uproar thinly, like the voice of a locust in a noisy jungle. There was a sudden hush, a sudden cessation of hostilities. And through the doorway surged a dozen—or a score—of Japanese sailors, looking very businesslike and anti-American in their trim blue uniforms.

Sammy saw the dark head of Lucky Jones rise up as if from the dead and waver like a windblown poppy. He shouted, "Out the back door!" But Lucky apparently heard nothing but birds.

The oily one was running for the door. Singapore overtook him, drove a sledgehammer fist into the brown jaw, and hooked his hand under his belt as the Malay dropped. He grabbed Lucky by the elbow with his free hand and, carrying the Malay as if he were a scuttle of coal, managed to escape as the Japanese invaders turned the Sailors Delight into another Manchuria.

He even managed, handicapped as he was, to break into a trot in the narrow alley at the far end of which the lights of the roadstead twinkled.

A COOL breeze blew refreshingly into his hot face. With his burdens, Singapore Sammy trotted down the alley, never pausing, in spite of bursting lungs, until he reached the breeze-swept park that is known as Raffle's Reclamation. Here, a dog of war might pause to lick his wounds.

It seemed to him that he could still hear the clamor of the Sailors Delight, could still smell the fumes of alcohol. He was exhausted and still disgruntled.

With a faint grunt, Lucifer Jones slid to the ground and back into unconsciousness. Singapore arranged him on a bench under a date palm, then propped up his captive in a sitting position beside it and waited for him to come around. While waiting, he took inventory.

His disgust was violently intensified by the discovery that he had, in spite of his efforts, been robbed of $1200 in American banknotes. A quick inspection of the soft copper wire encircling his tough brown neck left him slightly comforted. The little chamois sack dangling at the end of the copper loop had not been looted. The blue fire pearl was still there.

But his money, his share in the proceeds of four months of sweat, toil and haggle with Chinos and Malays and black-skinned savages under broiling tropical suns, was lost forever. Some clever hand had plucked it out of his pocket, back there in that hell hole. An investigation of Lucky's pockets revealed that he, too, had been relieved of his personal fortune.

All gone! And it remained for this fat, oily, unconscious Malay to say whether it had gone in a good cause. Would he talk, or would he refuse to talk?

He presently opened his eyes and blinked at the red-haired man. Sammy gave him a decent interval in which to pull himself together, then said, curtly, "Stand up, scum!"

The Malay groaned again. His hand swiftly went to where his knife had been. His eyes narrowed. The white man lifted one foot. The Malay, squealing, sprang up.

Hitching up his belt in a businesslike manner, the red-headed man growled, "Are you gonna tell me where my old man is, or do I have to shove your nose down between your shoulder blades?"

The Malay, with terror in his eyes, backed against the rough bole of the date palm. He was panting. His mouth hung ajar in an awful grimace, revealing his betel-blackened gums. His teeth were red.

The American shot a hand to the oily brown throat and held him rigidly against the tree.

"Spit it out!"

"*Tuan*, I do not know!"

Singapore banged the frizzly black head against the tree. The Malay repeated that he did not know until a muscular thumb was applied to his Adam's apple. Then he whimpered, "He will keel me, *tuan,* if I tell!"

"I'll kill you quicker if you don't! Where is he?"

He accented each word with increased pressure on the Malay's Adam's apple. The brown man's eyes were bulging.

"He is not in Singapore, *tuan!*"

"Ah!" Sammy breathed. "Where is he?"

"I do not know, *tuan.* I swear to you—" He gasped for breath now. He wriggled and kicked out with his feet. But the relentless hand of the white man held his head immovable.

"Konga!" he gasped.

Singapore Sammy relaxed the pressure. "What's that?"

"Konga!"

"Where is Konga?"

"East of Celebes! Please, *tuan,* let me go."

"When did he leave?"

"Last night, *tuan,* on the bark Bangalore. She sailed on the ebb-tide!"

CHAPTER II

THE GIRL

SINGAPORE SAMMY STARED at him with the aid of a remote arc light; saw the terror which made the Malay's eyes look sick, and dropped his hand. "Lam," he growled.

The Malay lammed. At a safe distance he panted threats and curses, then dived into the shrubbery.

For the past two weeks, since his return to the Straits Settlements, it had been Singapore Sammy's regular habit to prowl among the water front dives, either alone or with Lucky, and to browse through the Chinese and Burmese districts, where pearl and elephant men foregathered, peering into bright shop windows, peering into faces, searching, always searching for an old man who might or might not be wearing the yellow rag's of a Buddhist begging priest.

This man was Sammy's stepfather, and for seven years Sammy had been trailing him. When Sammy was a child of two, Bill Shay had deserted him and Sammy's mother, to answer the siren call of the Orient, taking with him all of Sammy's mother's savings and the will of Sammy's grandfather, which bequeathed to Sammy a fortune upward of a million dollars. Without the will, Sammy could not claim that fortune. And he could not secure the will until he had found his father.

The chase had taken him up and down and back and forth across Asia from Vladivostok to the Red Sea, from Darjeeling to Papeete. Always, that old rogue was one jump ahead of him. For Bill Shay was as clever as he was unscrupulous. He was a thief, a murderer, and, on occasions, a polished man of the world.

This time the trail had led from Bangkok to Singapore. And if Sammy had not encountered that Malay, whom a friendly bartender had informed him was Bill Shay's Number One boy, the trail would have vanished again.

Now it led to Konga. Why Konga? Pearls, no doubt. Well, he would follow the trail to Konga. He must have that will. With the money to which it rightfully entitled him, he and Lucky could buy a small fleet of coasting steamers, now available at a rock-bottom figure. They reasoned that the depression would soon be over. And with business on the upgrade, that small fleet of steamers would make them a fortune.

Lucky Jones was groaning. His eyes presently opened. He sat up and clapped both hands to the seat of his pants.

"They got my roll!" he cried hoarsely.

"Happy New Year," Singapore said. "We've both been rolled. We're clean. But I've picked up the old man's trail again."

Lucifer Jones came, swaying, to his feet. He emitted a trumpet-like yell. "Come on!" he panted. "Back we go!"

"Cool down," Singapore said. "It's all over. It's a closed book. We start to-day with a brand-new calendar."

A heated argument began. Lucifer wasn't going to let that gang walk off with his fortune. Singapore argued that the Japs had taken possession of the Sailors Delight and would give them a welcome they would never forget.

"Listen," he said. "Listen, I've picked up the old man's trail."

Lucky eventually listened. "He's on his way," Singapore explained, "to Konga. It's an island eastward of Celebes, and it must be in the Arafura Sea. Did you ever hear of Konga?"

THE REITERATION of the word brought Lucky Jones completely, sharply, to his senses. He ran the fingers of both hands through his wild black hair. His gleaming dark eyes, one open wide, the other partly obscured by a mouse, gave him the look of a rampant buccaneer. With his hawk's nose, his sun-blackened skin, his sledgehammer jaw, he looked dangerous. He smacked one fist into the palm of the other hand.

"Konga!" he echoed. "How do you get that way, Redhead? I wouldn't put foot on that island for a million bucks! It's haunted!"

"Yeah?" Singapore growled.

"I mean haunted," the buccaneer said, almost savagely. "No man who goes ashore there is ever seen again."

"There you go!" the redhead said, with a deep sigh. "Always seein' spooks. Always throwin' salt over your left shoulder. Always gettin' goose pimples when you see a black cat. Always havin' hysterics when you see a rat swimmin' away from the ship. We're goin' to Konga!"

"And be et by them cannibals?"

"A minute ago they were ghosts."

"They're the Kongans. They might as well be ghosts. Nobody ever sees 'em. When these Kongans catch you, they lop off your head and scoop out your brains. Oh, no; you won't catch me goin' to Konga. In all the years I've been sailin' these waters I've heard of just two men who put foot on that island and lived to tell about it!"

"Yeah? What do they tell about it?"

"Just what I'm tellin' you! They call it the Island o' Dark Figures because, moonlight nights, you can sail in close and see their shadows jumpin' and dancin' on a bleached sandstone cliff inland. These shadows are seventy-five to a hundred feet high!"

Singapore grunted skeptically and said, with sarcasm, "Must be a race of pygmies. What do people go there for if these headache eaters are so hostile?"

"Pearls! A lagoon full of 'em! Lousy with pearls. Big pearls! Fancy numbers!"

"It's all clear now," Singapore interrupted.

"What's all clear now?"

"Why my old man's headin' for there."

"A fat chance he has of gettin' them pearls! That lagoon lays under a cliff five hundred foot sheer up. The Kongans stand up there and throw spears and rocks. If your old man's goin' to Konga, he's dumber than I thought."

"He left on the bark Bangalore last night. And we're followin' him. We can outsail that old boneyard easy."

The buccaneer vigorously shook his head. "I ain't goin' to Konga. I've got a better use for my brains."

STILL ARGUING, they limped through streets graying with the new year's dawn toward Tanjong Pagar, toward the pier off which their schooner the *Blue Goose,* was anchored, taking back streets and alleys to avoid the police, for they were a sorry-looking pair indeed. Each of them possessed a black eye, and numerous cuts and bruises. Their shore-going whites were ruined. One sleeve was missing from Lucifer's white duck coat. One leg of the redhead's pants dangled from the knee by a thread or two. Their faces were bruised, swollen and streaked with blood. There was a goose-egg over Lucky's left temple so large that the mouse under the eye looked like a shadow. They were stiff, sore and quarrelsome. Lucifer steadily and stubbornly refused to entertain any idea bearing remotely upon the suggestion of a trip to Konga, to "smoke out that old rat."

"Just to look at it, sailin' past, is plenty," he said. "It lays there lookin' like one of these prehistoric monsters, all hunched up and scaly and ready to jump. It's all mountains and jungles, and the mountain tops are always full of black clouds. I sailed around it once, a mile offshore. That was enough for me!"

"Who does it belong to?"

"The Dutch, but they don't bother. They sent an expedition in thirty years ago, account of a Dutch trader who went ashore there and got gobbled up, and not a man came out. They found one body floatin' in the lagoon, with the top of his head lopped clean off. They figure it ain't worth the trouble. And if the Dutch don't want it, we don't want it."

"Maybe the old man has figured out a way."

"He'll get his head lopped off!"

"No," Singapore said. "Bill Shay is too foxy. If he's goin' there, he knows it's safe to go there. He's got some dope. The trouble with you is, you believe in witches and bat's milk."

"No," Lucky said, with the air of a man weighing himself judicially, "I ain't superstitious. I'm just sensible. I don't want my brains dished up."

"You're goin' to Konga," Singapore said grimly, "and like it!"

"Is zat so?" the buccaneer inquired.

They limped along in silence. Twin sighs were unawarely released when the schooner they jointly owned hove into view. She was like a phantom riding in the mist rising from the water in the first coral-hued rays of the sun. Her slim blue hull might have been carved from the mist itself. But her spars, snowy white, were sharp and clean against the deep mysterious blue of the night sky. Sunlight glittered on bright-work. And then a miracle happened. The mist in which the *Blue Goose* rode was suddenly shot with gold, and the schooner became a gilded ship with spars of amethyst.

Neither of the men put into words the thoughts that this vision provoked. She was, even without those sunrise trimmings, the prettiest thing afloat on the Pacific. Faithful and fleet, she had borne them gallantly through the dirtiest kinds of weather. In light or heavy winds, she was as fast as she was practical, as staunch as she was beautiful. They don't build them like that any more. Her auxiliary kicked her along at an easy ten knots. Trim and glistening as a millionaire's yacht, she was the envy of every sailing man's eye.

"That little schooner ain't for sale, by any chance, is she, mister?"

Some one was bound to put that question to them in almost every port. Even in these hard times.

AS THEY walked out on the pier they perceived that the outshore end of it was stacked with a miscellany of crates and boxes.

On one of the crates sat a girl in a pale-green dress, golden silk stockings, white shoes. She was softly weeping into a wisp of green chiffon.

Singapore Sammy's eyes suddenly narrowed and turned to jade.

Lucky said cheerfully, "Oh, lady!"

The girl looked up from her woeful occupation as the two battered seafarers approached. They hesitated. A young and lovely girl, attired as if for a tea party, is not a familiar sight on the Singapore water front at dawn.

She looked about nineteen. Large brown eyes in a flushed face contemplated them with forlorn misery and doubt.

The rising sun etched out the soft, alluring line of her chin. Yes, she was very young and as forlorn as a lost kitten, perched there on that large crate.

As if tacitly agreeing that something ought to be done about it, the two young men stopped and uncomfortably waited.

Green chiffon fluttered in her hand. She cleared her throat, looked wonderingly from one bruised, blood-streaked face to the other, and said in a meek little voice, stammering: "Wh-which one of you is the cap-captain of that sc-sc-schooner?"

"The handsome one," Singapore Sammy gravely replied, jabbing his thumb in the direction of his partner's swollen, discolored face.

"Is—is she for charter?" the girl asked with wistful eagerness. The tip of her cute nose seemed to twitch. She softly, plaintively sniffled.

The joint owners of the *Blue Goose* ran speculative eyes over the assortment of boxes, crates and bundles.

"Who wants to charter?" the redhead briskly inquired.

"I do."

"You—yourself—personally?"

"Y-yes!" without warning, the lovely unknown caught the six-inch square of chiffon to her mouth and burst into fresh weeping.

Eying her, Singapore Sammy said calmly, "Why the rainy season, sister?"

She looked up again, this time with hurt and defiance.

"Because you won't charter!" she wailed. "Because nobody wants to charter! I've been trying for five days to charter a ship, and nobody will charter."

"Yeah?" Captain Jones said incredulously. "If I got a dollar for every ship I could charter before noon, I could retire on the interest. There must be a catch in it somewhere. What is this— nitroglycerin?"

"It's because of where it's going," the girl cried. "My father's sick. He was mauled by a tiger. He's there all alone. I must get back to him!"

"Where?" Singapore said softly.

"Konga!"

CHAPTER III

MISSING

TEARS MADE A blur of her eyes. Her nose was pink and shiny. Her mouth was making little gulping grimaces. Her grief was as shameless as a child's. Here, if one could rely on his senses, was a girl all at odds with the designs of fate, a girl upon whom last straws had been relentlessly piled.

"Sure," Lucky said. "We're goin' to Konga."

"Since when?" Singapore inquired.

"Since now. Sister, if you'll just step up to the ticket office and buy your ticket, we'll be gettin' right under way. The *Blue Goose* has every modern convenience—hot and cold running doorknobs, courteous elevator boys, dancing from nine every evening until seven the next morning by our eleven-piece stringed orchestra—"

"Stow it," Singapore growled.

The girl looked bewildered.

"Don't mind him," the redhead went on. "He hit a bottle and a bottle hit him. Let's get this straight, sister. You mean you and your dad live on Konga?"

"Yes!"

"How long you been livin' there?"

"Almost a year."

"And you got out alive," Lucky cried, "to tell about it?"

"I'm not superstitious," the girl said.

"Neither are we," Lucky said promptly. "But we've changed our minds. We ain't for charter. You see, we're pearlers."

"But there are pearls there!" the girl cried. "The most wonderful lagoon of pearls in the archipelago!"

"You heard me wrong, sister. We're whalers."

"Aw, pipe down!" Singapore growled.

But it was too late. The girl slipped down and indignantly faced them. She was smaller than she looked; a half-pint of a girl, not more than five feet, high heels and all. Her eyes were wrathful. Glaring at Lucky, then at Singapore, she said, "You two big hulking brutes ought to be ashamed of yourselves! You're traders. I looked you up. If my father hadn't been mauled by that tiger, I wouldn't be in such a hurry. I'd wait till I found somebody who wasn't yellow!"

"You sure," Singapore drawled, "it was a tiger? Sure it wasn't one of them brain-scoopers?"

She looked at him unflinchingly. "I said tiger."

"Yellow," he said, "is a pretty safe color, though. I'm sorry, sister," he said firmly. "We ain't for charter. Come on, Lucky."

The two young men started on toward the end of the pier.

"I'll make it very well worth your while," the girl called after them. "I'll give you a thousand dollars for the freight and my passage."

Without turning, Singapore called, "Not to-day!"

The two young men exchanged a long glance and walked on toward the pierhead. But they said nothing. At the pierhead, Lucky placed his fingers between his lips and gave utterance to a whistle that resembled a siren's shriek.

No response from the *Blue Goose*.

There was, or should have been, a Malay *serang* and a deck-hand out there. A Malay in a sampan, attracted by the whistling, came alongside the small boat landing stage below the pierhead. The two young men engaged him to ferry them out to the schooner.

SEATED IN the sampan's stern, they exchanged another long, puzzled look before either spoke.

"What's goin' on?" Lucky asked.

"I'd like to know," Singapore said.

"She's phony as hell."

"Sure! And where's our *serang?*"

"She sure looked sweet, though," Lucky said.

The sampan had reached the schooner. Singapore paid off the Malay, and the two young men climbed aboard. They went forward and looked into the fo'cs'le. No one was there. They called. No one answered. The *serang's* and the island boy's belongings had not been disturbed. A tour of the ship disclosed nothing missing. They were about to abandon the search when Singapore noticed a spot on the holystoned deck about two feet abaft the wheel.

It was a faintly pink spot about eight inches in diameter, with a faint but darker ring around it. The discovery sent them looking for similar spots, which they found—a trail of them about eighteen inches apart, leading to the rail amidships on the port side.

The two men, reaching the rail, exchanged a long, probing look and each gave a grunt. Comment was hardly necessary. They knew that those pink spots were washed-up blood spots. Scratches in the recently varnished rail at the spot where the trail ended furthered the theory that they must obviously accept.

The *serang* or deckhand—or both—had been killed or fatally injured and thrown overboard. Those were fingernail scratches on the rail. Some one had clawed desperately at that rail.

Had the *serang* killed the island boy and thrown him to the harbor sharks? Or was it the other way around? No—in each case. Both were too amiable, and they had got along like brothers.

The spots where the blood had been washed up were not damp. Sometime last night, then, some one had come aboard the schooner and killed the two men. Who? Why?

Sammy started forward with the evident intention of making a more thorough investigation, but thought better of it. Reason informed him that it was useless to look for further evidence. Killers who mopped up blood spots did not leave clews.

"We'll ship a new crew," Lucky said quietly, "as soon as we know what our plans are."

These two young men knew their East amazingly well. They had glimpsed a few of its hair-stirring mysteries. They knew that any attempt to track down the killers would be as futile as trying to find an original hair of Buddha. This mystery, like so many they had glimpsed, had neither beginning, middle, nor end. Two men about whom they knew little or nothing had vanished forever. They would never know who had killed the *serang* and the island boy, or why they had been killed. They knew only that something—some chain of darkly obscured events—had come to an end. It was as if they had glimpsed a vague, malignant face receding swiftly into a fog-

It did not occur to them that the ending of an Oriental mystery often cannot be distinguished from the beginning.

CHAPTER IV

DOROTHY BORDEN'S TALE

THEY SEARCHED THEIR cabins and the gun lockers and the galley. Nothing had been taken. Nothing was disturbed. A handful of silver and small gold coins on the desk in Lucky's cabin had not been touched. The mystery was complete.

The two young men, having shaved and showered and applied court plaster patches where they were most needed, were in their respective cabins getting into clean white clothes when their ship was hailed. A girl's clear voice cried, *"Blue Goose*—ahoy!"

Singapore looked out of the porthole and soberly answered, "Ahoy yourself, sister."

She was seated in the stern of the same sampan in which they had been ferried out, and her eye's were large and forlorn. She reminded him more than ever of a lost kitten.

"May I come aboard?"

"Sure! But you're wastin' your time."

When he went on deck, she was seated in a Bombay chair

under a gently waving khaki canopy, with her hands clasped about her knees. He had never seen eyes so large, so tragic. It was as if all the woes, all the unhappiness in the large unhappy world shone out of them. He observed that she had trim little feet and trim pretty ankles. There was a fresh young loveliness about her which, combined with her wistful smile and the hopelessness in her eyes, gave her a terrific appeal. Automatically, Singapore Sammy steeled himself against it. She was as innocent as a rose drenched with morning dew. That kind was the most dangerous, Singapore reflected.

He more than half suspected that she and his father were somehow in league against him. It wouldn't be the first conspiracy that old rogue had rigged up for him, for, according to the terms of that will, in the event of Sammy's death Bill Shay would inherit the money. Wherefore, Sammy was wary of this girl.

Lucky was talking to her when he went on deck, and he was evidently in a similar frame of mind. Lucky's one useful eye was no longer playful; it was hard and unfriendly. He curtly introduced her to Singapore as Miss Dorothy Borden.

"And I just told her," Lucky said, "that she was wastin' her time comin' out here. This schooner ain't for charter."

Miss Borden was quite pale. Her eyes looked as though they might cry again at any moment, and her mouth was tremulous.

She said huskily, "After all, I'm an American. You can't very well let down one of your countrywomen who is in trouble, can you? You must give me a chance. You'll listen to me, won't you?"

"We won't throw you overboard," Singapore said dryly. "Sure, we'll listen to you."

"But it won't do any good," Lucky said with a flash of his wolfish teeth.

The girl's eyes had grown desperate again.

"My father and I have lived on Konga nearly a year," she said in a breathless rush of words. "None of those stories about Konga are true. I know they aren't true. Why won't you believe me? Why should I lie to you? If those stories were true, I'd be dead. There's nobody on Konga except my father and me."

"Yeah?" Lucky said.

"But if there were cannibals there, I'd know about it. I'd have to know about it," Miss Borden said helplessly.

"If it's so safe," Singapore put in, "why hasn't somebody gone after those pearls?"

"Pearl divers are the most superstitious men in the world!"

"What's your old man doin' there?" Lucky asked.

MISS BORDEN'S eyes were miserable. Her hands were clenched in her lap in desperation. She was obviously trying very hard to get herself under control. She nipped her lower lip between her small white teeth, and Singapore saw that her lip was raw and bleeding.

"The only way I can show you how untrue all those old legends are is to tell you the whole story. Will you let me?"

"Shoot the works," Singapore said lazily.

"But I'm warnin' you," Lucky added, "you're wastin' your time."

Miss Borden seemed to pull herself together. She gripped her hands in her lap, drew a deep, resolute breath.

"You men are Americans. Nobody who isn't an American could possibly understand. That's why I've been counting so on you two men to help me. Because you've got to help me. You've got to take this shipment to Konga—and me, too!"

It suddenly occurred to Sam Shay that she might be telling the truth. His father had left Singapore for Konga last night on the bark Bangalore. Was he headed for Konga because there were pearls in Konga—or because he had some diabolical scheme in mind with this girl and her father as his prospective victims? Or both?

Looking at Miss Borden, he felt suddenly uncomfortable. He could see now that the poor kid was worried pink, but he sensed, under her trembling dismay, a fighting determination to convince them of her sincerity. He was anxious to hear her story, and he wondered if her eyes always looked so tragic.

"My father is Daniel Borden. You've heard of him, haven't you?" she asked.

"The name's familiar," Singapore encouraged her. "What's his business?"

"He was the chairman of the board of the American Rod and Wire Corporation—the wire trust. They called him the Wire King. He lost practically his entire fortune—almost a hundred million—in the panic. The bankers called his notes and forced him to resign. They stripped him almost clean. He managed to salvage about a million. It almost killed him. I suppose you think that's terribly funny—a man almost dying because his fortune shrinks to a million dollars!"

"Nope," Sammy soberly denied. "Our fortune shrank down about the same proportion in the past two hours, and we know just how he would feel about it."

"He'd worked," Miss Borden went on, "all his life to accumulate that hundred million. He said a man needed a new philosophy to face the world these days. He was going to devote the rest of his life to enjoying himself. He had always had the dream of living in the South Seas. He asked me to go with him, and I did, because he was practically a nervous wreck. In Surabaya he heard of Konga from a drunken beachcomber."

"What did this beachcomber look like?" Lucky interrupted.

"I don't know. I didn't meet him. But dad talked to him for hours. The beachcomber told him all about Konga. He called it the Haunted Island. He said no white man had ever come out of there alive except himself. Dad checked him up, and substantiated some of what he had said. He decided that we were going there to live."

"In spite of the brain-scoopers?" Lucky demanded.

"You don't know my father!" Miss Borden replied.

SAMMY SAID, "How about you?"

"I was afraid to go. But the minute he began planning he changed so that I didn't have the heart to say I didn't want to go. He was happy for the first time since the stock market crash."

"How did you get there?" Lucky asked.

"At first no one would take us. Government officials tried to dissuade us from going. He had almost decided to buy a schooner when an old Chinese offered to charter him one at a fabulous rate on the condition that the schooner would anchor well offshore and that dad would arrange to land the stuff."

"Wait a minute," Lucky interrupted. "What was this Chink's name?"

"Wan Gow Sung."

"What was the schooner's name?"

"The Lotus."

"Okay. Go on." For the first time since she had begun her amazing narrative, Lucky seemed to believe that there might be a germ of truth in what Miss Borden was saying.

"So we went to Konga," she continued. Her voice still shook a little. "We anchored offshore, and dad took every box and bag and crate and plank and keg ashore in a small boat."

"How far?" Singapore wanted to know.

"A half mile row in and a half mile row back. I went in with the first load with my rifle and some ammunition. I stood guard all day long."

"What side of the island did you land on?" Lucky asked.

"The north side. It's the only side where the cliffs don't drop off sheer to the sea. It's a sandy table land, or plateau, with a few scattered palms, beefwood, jackfruit and mahogany trees—not jungle."

"Big?" Lucky asked.

"It's about two miles long and a half mile wide. A stream comes down from the mountains and runs along the edge of it into a small cove. Back up that ravine, where the stream flows down, is thick jungle. But the flat place was quite open—an ideal place to build a house."

SINGAPORE SAMMY darted a glance at Lucky. That young man was nodding his approval of the girl's description.

"One of the conditions Wan Gow Sung had made before we left Surabaya was that the schooner be unloaded by dark. I mean, he wouldn't lie off Konga longer than from dawn to dark. When darkness came, he would sail out to sea and stand off and on eight or ten miles offshore until the next morning. But dad was so enthusiastic over what he'd seen of Konga that he was determined to get everything ashore by nightfall. I lost count of the number of trips he made. Back and forth—back and forth all day long under that horrible sun. His hands were almost solid water blisters from the oars, and he was a physical wreck. He made the last trip just at dusk."

"With you," Singapore Sammy said, "watchin' for brain-scoopers!"

She nodded. "Yes. I thought any minute they'd come swooping down on us. I was petrified."

"What happened?"

"Nothing. I didn't see a living soul. And in all the months I've been there, I haven't seen a human being. There's nothing but birds and animals. Those stories of head hunters on Konga belong to South Seas folklore. There aren't any savages there, or I'd know about it. I've been over practically every square foot of that island." Her eyes pleaded with them to believe her.

Lucky Jones shook his head somewhat dubiously, but he didn't interrupt.

Sammy said, "What are you living in?"

"We built a little house and put up shelves and made tables and chairs."

"How about food?"

"We brought along crates and crates of canned goods. We

had some vegetable seeds. I planted a garden. We have loads of fresh things."

"Wasn't it pretty lonesome?"

"I didn't mind, because dad was so contented. He looked years younger."

"Didn't it ever strike him," Singapore asked, "that it was pretty selfish of him, pennin' you up in a place like that?"

"It wasn't," she answered, "very hard to convince him that I was perfectly happy there. And I got used to it."

Singapore, watching her soft lips, was trying unsuccessfully to visualize a girl as delicately feminine as Miss Borden living such a life.

"How," Lucky said, "about this row you said your old man had with a tiger?"

"It was terrible," Miss Borden said. She shivered, and her lips trembled a little. "We had arranged with Wan Gow Sung to come back to Konga in six months with mail and supplies. One of the items was hunting dogs—the black skinny kind that are used for game hunting in Sumatra.

"He was absolutely punctual, but he said he hadn't expected to see us alive. He'd brought everything—books and mail and magazines and supplies and dogs."

"What were the dogs for?" Sammy asked. "Cats?"

"No; deer. But dad didn't know how to train them. They'd start off on a deer trail, but when a cat trail crossed it, they'd go off after the cat. We didn't want cats. We wanted deer. It was the only meat we had. One day about six weeks ago he took the dogs hunting. They started off on a deer trail, but they found tiger tracks. They trailed the tiger up a narrow box cañon.

"It was in a cave six or eight feet up the side of the cañon. Dad could smell the tiger, but he didn't realize it was so close."

Miss Borden's face was white.

"The first warning he had that it was so near was when it came rushing out of the cave. Dad backed down the cañon and fired as the tiger rushed, and when he pulled the trigger, nothing happened. The firing pin was jammed."

MISS BORDEN gulped a little and went on in a shaky voice, "He scrambled up the side of the cañon. The tiger reached up and raked his left leg below the knee with its claws. It would have killed him if the dogs hadn't distracted it. Dad hooked his feet around a rock and worked away at the bolt until it worked. But the tiger had killed one dog and wounded another before he could start pumping bullets into it.

"Dad fainted from loss of blood about a mile from the house. I heard the dogs barking and found him lying there with his leg practically in ribbons.

"He ran a temperature of a hundred and five for almost a week. And not a single ship passed by.

"But he pulled through. And when I left him, about two weeks ago, he was able to hobble around and get his own meals. But one of the gouges isn't healed yet. We were running short of antiseptics. I wanted him to come up to Singapore or Surabaya and have proper medical attention, but he wouldn't. So I came."

"How'd you come?" Singapore asked quickly.

"I waited for the weekly steamer from Darwin to Singapore, rowed out and waited for it to pass. I got here about a week ago. I spent one day getting supplies, and the past five days I've been trying to charter a ship. And when I mention Konga, people say they don't want to charter. Last night I heard about you two men. When I heard you were Americans, I almost cried. I was so sure you'd help!"

She paused. Her hopeful young eyes went from Lucky Jones's face to Singapore Sammy's.

Singapore stole a glance at Lucky, and wondered if Lucky was actually listening to what she was saying. His one useful eye was moist and glowing.

It wasn't difficult to understand. Singapore was inclined to feel that way himself. He had been, he realized, seeing himself as the third inhabitant of that island paradise, and there was no room in the picture for Lucifer Jones. He was being swayed by pity. He mustn't, he grimly advised himself, let his seasoned judgment be warped by a foolish desire to take Miss Borden on his lap and comfort her.

He said harshly, "What makes you sure there are pearls in that lagoon? Maybe that's just another old beachcomber yarn, too."

Her answer was to open her small green suede handbag. From it she removed a lipstick, a tiny gold mirror, a gold compact, a gold pencil, a jade cigarette holder and three hairpins.

She extricated a wad of white tissue paper. Carefully, she removed the wrapping, and rolled into the palm of one hand a pale pink, spherical object, which gleamed with a satiny sheen. It was the size of a small pea.

The two young men bent close and peered at that fine pink pearl.

"Did this," Singapore asked, suppressing his excitement, "come out of that lagoon?"

"Yes."

"Any others?"

She seemed to hesitate. "N-no," she said reluctantly.

"You don't mean," Sammy said, "you found this and didn't look for others?"

"I didn't dare. It's a sharks' nest. Thousands of them. And they're absolutely savage."

CHAPTER V

SINGAPORE AGREES

THE RED-HEADED AMERICAN, looking at the pearl, thought of a lagoon infested with tiger sharks.

"Sharks!" Lucky said softly.

"The first time I rowed around into the lagoon," Miss Borden said, "I dropped anchor in about the middle of it. A half dozen giant sharks struck at the anchor as it dropped. I've never seen sharks so savage. I hate them. I've stood on the beach and shot them until my rifle was too hot to hold. I've thrown meat in, and they come rolling up, and when they roll, I shoot. The other sharks pounce on the wounded one, and tear him to shreds. Fights start. They're nothing but cannibals. I've seen that lagoon so pink with blood you couldn't see bottom. And when it cleared, there'd be more sharks than ever!"

"Any octopuses?" Lucky grunted.

She hesitated. "Yes. Big ones. And I've seen fights between sharks and octopuses that sent shivers down my spine. You can see the shells down there so plainly. Big ones! It must be one of the richest beds in the archipelago."

Both Singapore and Lucky were unaware that their expressions had subtly changed. Here was an eye witness to the existence of that fabled lagoon. And here was a pearl from it!

Pearls! A virgin bed of them!

With careful carelessness, Singapore Sammy said, "Why hasn't your old man done anything about those sharks?"

"I don't think he ever gave them a thought," the girl answered. "He isn't interested in the pearls—in making money in any way. The million he saved from the panic he put into a trust company. It pays him around forty thousand a year, and he doesn't need that. He isn't interested in pearling."

Sammy quietly said, "Has anybody been ashore on Konga since you and your father have been there?"

Miss Borden shook her head.

"Didn't Wan Gow Sung come ashore?"

"No, he wouldn't. We see ships pass, from Java to New Guinea and between Darwin and Singapore—five miles or so offshore. But no one has put a foot on Konga since we came."

She paused again and bit her lip.

"Why are you so doubtful about what I say? Why is every one so doubtful? Do I look like a liar or a thief?"

"You get us wrong," Singapore said gently. "Out here in this part of the world you learn to be hard boiled."

"Perhaps you're too hard boiled."

"Yeah. Perhaps we are."

"But it's so queer," Miss Borden said. "What object could I have in lying to you?" Her eyes flitted from one dark, bruised face to the other. Singapore learned now that her eyes did not always have that tragic look. They were sparkling with indignation.

"All I'm asking you to do is to take this shipment and me to Konga. And all you have to do is to say that you will and I'll go get the thousand dollars at the bank this very minute. Isn't it a fair proposition?"

SHE WENT on: "I looked you up. I went to the harbormaster and made inquiries about you. He said you were a pair of very adventurous young men. You're the first men I've really tried hard to convince that Konga isn't what the rumors say it is." Her voice was suddenly pleading. "If you aren't interested in the money—aren't you interested in those pearls?"

"We haven't turned down your proposition yet," Lucky said. "But supposin' we went after those pearls, just for the sake of the argument. Your dad has a prior claim on that bed. What would he do?"

"He isn't interested in them."

"It must be funny to be that rich. But wouldn't he step in and say we were poachin'?"

"I'll guarantee he won't. If you can find a way to beat the sharks, he'd like to have you there just for the company."

Singapore and Lucky exchanged glances that gleamed with excitement.

"We'll find a way to beat the sharks," the redhead said. "How big is that lagoon?"

"About three quarters of a mile in diameter."

"How wide," Lucky barked, "is the inlet?"

"About five hundred feet—at high tide."

"How deep," Singapore wanted to know, "is the water in it at low tide?"

"Not more than a foot or so."

"What's the bottom like?"

"It's a sort of clay-like sand."

"Do you get it?" Singapore said to Lucky.

"Bottle it up?"

"Sure! Bottle it up! We go out there at low tide and drive stakes close together across the inlet."

"Then," Lucky took him up, "we string eight or nine rows of barbed wire along the stakes to keep the sharks out at high tide!"

"Check! Then we dynamite the lagoon. Forty or fifty sticks will send every shark and octopus to the top belly-up. How are we hooked for dynamite?"

"We've got plenty in the lazaret. And all the divin' suit needs is a little patchin'."

Singapore got up. "Okay. We want to be pullin' out of here by four this afternoon."

Miss Borden said hesitantly, "Am I—am I going, too?"

"Can you cook?" Lucky said sharply.

"Of course I can! Do I have to cook?"

"Can you scrub decks? Can you heave an anchor? Can you shinny up a mast?"

She didn't know whether to take him seriously or not.

"Do I have to do all those things?"

"Don't pay any attention to him," Singapore said. "His brain is all crippled up from that bottle. It was lame enough before. Sure, you can go along. Maybe you'll bring us luck. We need plenty. You can use my cabin and I'll bunk in with Cap'n Jones. Let's go!"

They arranged that Lucky and Miss Borden were to go ashore while Singapore stayed aboard and warped the *Blue Goose* alongside the pier. While Miss Borden went to the bank and checked out of her hotel, Lucky would attend to clearance papers, supplies and signing up a new deckhand and *serang*.

CHAPTER VI

SINGAPORE'S PEARL

CONSIDERING THEIR NATURES, it was remarkable that Singapore Sammy and Lucky Jones got along so well. They had been shipmates for upwards of two years, and had never had a serious disagreement. Perhaps it was because they were birds of a feather. Tough birds. Their histories were strangely alike. Neither knew what a home was. Each had been on the go since he was a youngster. Each had fought, begged, stolen and bummed his way all over the world. And each was as hard as flint.

Having no means of measuring his own hardness, Singapore was convinced that Lucky Jones was the hardest individual in the Far East. And the longer he knew him, the surer of this he became. It was not merely that he looked hard; Lucky was hard clean through. But this was, to Singapore, the right kind of hardness. It was the hardness of a diamond, clear and fine and honest.

He privately admired Lucky for looking so hard. With his thick bristling black hair, his eagle's eyes, his leathery complexion, his thin mouth, his sledgehammer jaw and his big muscular frame, Lucky looked his hardness. Singapore had never seen him in a situation, aboard ship or ashore, above water or below, in which Lucky had betrayed the slightest fear. You could depend on Lucky Jones to meet trouble with courage and decision, with all his brawn and all his brains.

It was accordingly painful to the point of being sickening when Lucky Jones started falling in love with Dorothy Borden. It was the first time Singapore had ever seen him betray softness in any degree. And the softness he was betraying over Dorothy was of the consistency of custard.

Almost from the moment he met her, Lucky became a different man. It reminded Sam of a character in Biblical times he had been told about as a kid—some strong man who was softened up because he fell in love with a woman.

While the *Blue Goose* slipped southward over the equator, through the Rhio Archipelago, and into the blazing blue of the Karimata Sea, Singapore Sammy had that painful experience of seeing a good tough man fall hopelessly in love.

There was no question, of course, that Dorothy would have tempted almost any man. Her seagoing togs consisted of snug-fitting Antibe sweaters and snug-fitting white duck sailor pants, both sweaters and pants more or less innocently betraying the fact that she had a perfect little figure.

Lucky would follow her around the deck or sit and gaze at her with love-struck eyes. He sighed frequently. He lost his appetite. He couldn't sleep. He began to take the most elaborate pains with his personal appearance. He shaved every day, sometimes twice. He kept his boots lustrous. He even trimmed his shaggy black eyebrows. It would have been sidesplittingly funny if it had stopped there. But it didn't stop there.

He began to talk about getting married, settling down and giving up the sea. He appealed to Singapore. Wasn't she wonderful? Wasn't she a little honey?

Singapore disgustedly advised him to snap out of it. "Take a look at yourself in the mirror," he urged.

Singapore could, of course, understand Dorothy's falling for Lucky. Plenty of them had, but never before had Lucifer given any girl a tumble. At first it was something of a question whether or not Dorothy was meeting him half-way, or any part of the way. She had seemed to Singapore to be a collected, level-headed young woman. She had seemed to bestow as many glances and smiles on him as on Lucky.

THEN SINGAPORE came upon them one moonlit night. They were seated on a hatch cover. They were clasped in each

*His cutthroat
captors seemed
to be Mexicans.*

other's arms. Their mouths were joined in what appeared to be an eternal kiss. Separating, they each said one word.

"Sweetness!" said Dorothy.

"Booful!" said Lucky.

Unseen, unheard, Singapore departed. There were twitchings in the vicinity of his stomach. He retired to the stateroom which he and Lucky shared. He took the pillow off Lucky's bunk and kicked it until it burst. Feathers exploded and, floating, settled upon everything in the room.

When Lucky came in, an hour or two later and glimpsed the scene, he grunted, "What's this?"

"Horsefeathers—booful!" Singapore jeered.

"You can lay off that," the buccaneer said, projecting his lower jaw and planting his fists on his hips. "This is serious. Get it?"

Singapore, lying on his back stark naked in his bunk, with the ashes from half a dozen cigarettes strewn over his hairy chest, leered and said, "Sure I get it—booful. You're hooked."

He ate his breakfast the following morning in the galley, because he didn't want to see the two of them at the table. He avoided Dorothy the rest of the morning. He was in the bows, smoking and watching porpoises playing when Dorothy came forward and settled down beside him.

She said bluntly, "You don't like me, do you, Sam?"

He grinned at her. "Kid," he said, "I haven't much use for women, no. But I haven't anything personal against you. You've got a good bean, you're a good-looker, and you've got class. A man would have to travel a long way to improve on what you've got."

"Then why are you so opposed to having Lucky like me?"

"A seagoing man who gets married is a sucker," the redhead answered. "Lucky's been at sea since he was old enough to wash behind his own ears. The sea's in his blood. I know that guy, sister. You can't any more take the sea out of his blood than you can out of a shark. If you marry him, what happens? He thinks it'll be easy to give up this life. But sooner or later, he feels the sea tuggin' at him. And then what? He loves you and he loves the sea. If he gives up the sea he'll be sunk. If he gives up you, he'll be sunk."

"Why can't he combine the best features of each?"

"Sister, it's been tried. You can't stay at sea. That means you see him a few days each year. That's the bunk."

Dorothy was smiling mysteriously. "Is that your only objection to marriage, Sam—I mean, where you're concerned?"

"Nope. I am the guy the fellow meant when he said, 'The bird travels fastest who travels alone.'"

"Why do you want to travel so fast? Running away from something?"

"Nope. Lookin' for a guy."

DOROTHY'S EYES sparkled with interest. "Who?"

"My old man," he said. And told her about Bill Shay, about his craftiness, about the will, about that seven-year chase. But he omitted mentioning that Bill Shay was now on his way to Konga, because he knew it would worry her.

"Every time I get ready to close my hands around his neck—

he's gone! Like a puff of smoke. Did you ever try to kill a krait adder by jumpin' on him, sister? The faster you jump, the easier he slips away from you. It's that way with my old man."

"How old are you, Sam?"

"Twenty-five. I've been on his trail since I was eighteen."

"Ever seen him?"

"Just once. In Siam. He was dressed up like an English lord. I talked to him for two hours, never suspectin'. When he got through kiddin' me, he lifted out his monocle and two huskies trussed me up to the post I was leanin' against. It was the first and last time I ever saw him. But I'll get him! And when I get him I'll kill him!"

Dorothy shivered. "It seems horrible to hear any man talk like that about his own father."

"He ain't my father; he's my stepfather."

"But why is your name the same?"

"When my mother married him, I was a year old. She had my name legally changed from Larkin to Shay. The next time I'm in the States I'm gonna have it legally changed back to Larkin."

The girl was looking at the porpoises. When she looked back, the grimness in his face had relaxed. Dorothy dropped her eyes to his powerful brown neck, to the soft copper wire which encircled it.

"Why do you wear that?"

The fingers of one large brown hand fumbled at the copper wire. Singapore quickly lifted the copper loop over his head. Dangling from this strange neckpiece was a small chamois sack. He grinned at Dorothy and loosened the cord at the throat of the sack with his strong white teeth. Then, holding up the bottom of the sack and watching the girl's eyes, he shook down into his palm a blue pearl that gathered fire unto itself from the burning blue sky.

The blue pearl rolled about in his cupped palm, a bubble of magic flame. As blue as a Chantaboun sapphire, as big around as the end of its owner's forefinger, as full of fire as the eye of a charging leopard, that blue pearl was fit to grace the finger or the throat of a princess.

"Notice how it seems to burn?"

"Yes!" she gasped.

"This pearl, sister, is famous. It's the blue fire pearl of Malobar!"

"It's glorious!"

"Yeah. But don't let it hypnotize you. It's hypnotized richer girls than you, sister. It ain't for sale."

"Where'd you get it?"

"I won it in a fight. An up-country Malay sultan put it up for a ten-round go between me and another guy. Winner take all. Loser go to the sultan's black leopards for breakfast."

DOROTHY'S EYES were straining at him; her mouth was like a credulous child's.

"Did he?"

"Did he what?"

"Go to the—the leopards?"

The redhead lazily grinned. "No, sister. We started a riot, and while the riot was on we blew."

Dorothy expelled her breath in a panting sigh.

"It must be worth a fortune!"

"It's worth fifteen thousand in Paris—American gold—as it is. If I could ever find the mate I wouldn't take a hundred thousand for the pair."

"Aren't you afraid of carrying it around like that?"

He shook his head. "Nope. Because I'd die before anybody got it away. That's pretty safe insurance. They've tried to dope me. They've tried to trick me. They've tried to kill me, half a dozen different ways. But they haven't got it yet."

"Who?"

"Just about everybody who sees it."

"May I—hold it?"

Grinning, the redhead dropped the Malobar pearl into the chamois sack, drew the throat cord tight, and dropped the sack inside his shirt. The girl looked blank, as if she had been staring overlong at some dazzlingly bright object in the dark.

"Nobody," Singapore said, "has touched this pearl since I won it in that fight."

"Superstitious?"

"You can call it that."

She shivered. "There's something evil about that pearl. It's like looking at something from another world, something that you never thought existed. I never saw anything so blue or so luminous. It's weird—terrifying."

"Yeah. It gets you."

"It must," she breathed, "if you'd rather part with your life. Don't show it to dad!"

"That's a promise, sister."

She went aft to join Lucky, and the blue fire pearl wasn't mentioned again that day. But the subject wasn't dropped. Singapore woke up that night with the eerie feeling that he wasn't alone. He sat up and lit the gimballed lamp at the head of his bunk. Lucky was not in his bunk. He automatically fumbled at his throat. The copper wire was there. His hand dropped, groping for the chamois skin pouch. *Gone!*

CHAPTER VII

THE PHANTOM

SINGAPORE HAD TURNED in that night in pants and shirt. Without pausing for shoes, he ran out into the corridor. He observed that Dorothy's stateroom door was open, that the light was on in there, but that her bedding was not disturbed.

He ran through the dining room and up the stairs to the deck.

The new *serang* was at the wheel. His eyes were luminous in the ghostly light from the binnacle. His dark body, naked to the waist, glistened in the light of the moon.

Singapore barked, "Where is she?"

"For'd, *tuan.*"

The red-headed man ran forward and found them sitting on their favorite hatch, Dorothy's small curly head close to Lucky's.

Dorothy was holding one hand before her. The fingers were bunched and pointing upward. In the nest formed by their tips lay a fantastic, luminously blue bubble.

Singapore swooped down on them. Panting, he snatched the Malobar pearl out of its nest.

"Somebody," he said harshly, "has a hell of a nerve!"

Lucky slowly stood up.

"Keep your shirt on, Red. She wanted to see it!"

"She saw it this mornin'!"

"Well, she wanted to hold it in her hand."

"Yeah? So you sneaked into my cabin and cut it off this wire!"

Lucky's eagle eyes were level with his. His thin lips were parted slightly. He looked ugly.

Dorothy wailed, "Oh, please, please!"

Lucky said quietly, "You trust me, don't you, Red?"

"You know I don't trust anybody with this pearl."

"Not even me?"

"You heard me!"

The buccaneer drew a deep breath. "Are you sayin' I'd steal your lousy bead?"

"When you're this way, you're not responsible."

He saw Lucky double up his fist, and he saw the fist start toward him. But he did not believe, until it was too late, that Lucky would go through with that punch. He was sure Lucky would pull it at the last moment.

But Lucky didn't pull it.

The punch didn't do much damage. It was a blunt one on the chin, and Singapore had a tough chin. But he wasn't prepared for it. He staggered back, and brought up against the rail, which he gripped hard, one hand on either side of him.

Lucky, with both fists ready, came toward him. He waited. But Singapore, with his tongue wedged against his teeth, held onto the rail. If he didn't hang onto the rail, one of them was going to be killed. His chin burned from the punch, and his forehead felt like ice. His heart was going like a trip-hammer.

He held onto the rail until he was sure he had himself under control. Then, without a word, he turned and walked aft.

He was lying in his bunk smoking a cigarette when Lucky came in. The buccaneer slid a quick glance at him, then skinned off his coat.

He hung up the coat and walked over to the bunk and looked down into Singapore's face.

"Didn't feel like sparrin' to-night," he said, with a rising intonation, but he gave the effect of shoving out the words with his under lip.

Singapore looked up at him with a slightly curling upper lip.

"It would look that way," he answered. "I guess maybe I'm gettin' yellow—or something."

"Nuts. I got you. Red, I want to take that back."

"Go right ahead!"

Lucky lowered his sledgehammer chin. "Sock it."

Singapore reached up with his hamlike hand and dealt him an open-handed blow that sounded like a pistol shot. Lucky stepped back with a grin; rubbing his jaw.

"Okay?" he said.

"Next time, keep your shirt on."

This was the nearest to an apology and an acceptance of the same that these two were capable of. It should have cleared the air. But it didn't. Something was missing.

THIS OCCURRED on the fifth night out of Singapore Town. The *Blue Goose* crossed the Emperor of China reef the next day, and that night, as if bearing out the vague foreboding of disaster with which Singapore Sammy had been visited on sailing day, the phantom stowaway was seen.

It was the kind of night that only the Malayan seas can brew for such occasions. The moon had a green cast to it. There was a thin greasy mist lying on all horizons, and this mist was shot with green. Even the sea, so blazingly blue by daylight, was tinted palely green. A night for ghosts to walk indeed!

Singapore had turned in early. Eight bells—midnight—had been struck perhaps ten minutes previously by the *serang* when Lucky lurched into the stateroom, striking a match along the wall with a sound like ripping cloth.

In the light of it, Singapore, coming fully awake, saw that Lucky's face, ordinarily a rich mahogany, was lemon colored. And the buccaneer's eyes were pale and large. Sweat gleamed on his forehead, nose and cheeks. He was breathing rapidly through loosely parted lips.

"There's something on board!"

With agitated hands, Lucky lighted the gimballed lamp. The chimney danced out of his hand, fell to the floor with a small splintering crash. The flame licked up, orange and smoking.

"Something?"

"I saw it!"

"What the hell are you talkin' about?"

"It was a face. That's all! A white face, but it had a green tinge. Do you remember that dead guy we hauled out of Hongkong harbor? Remember how white and green and glowy his face was from the phosphorus?"

"When did this happen?" Singapore growled.

"Right now, I tell yuh! I was up there on that forward hatch, smokin', when this face came right up over the bows—all white and green and glowy. You couldn't see its eyes. You couldn't see any hands. Nothin' but the face. It floated right up out of the sea!"

"You been hittin' that *arrack* again?"

Lucky said explosively, "Will you listen? I *saw* it! By the time I got for'd it was gone!"

"Where was Dorothy?"

"She turned in a half hour before I saw it."

"You're always seein' things. You saw the deckhand. He's a pale guy."

"How," Lucky cried, "do you think I got this way? The deckhand was asleep in his bunk. The *serang* was right there at the wheel."

"He see anything?"

"How could he when he was 'way aft?"

"Did it look like Biyong?" Biyong was their old *serang*, who had vanished so mysteriously, leaving so little trace, in Singapore.

"No. It was a thin face."

"Like whose?"

"A lifer's. Remember those lifers we saw in the solitary cells at New Hebrides? Moldy-skinned from bein' stir bugs so long? Kind of a green glow to them?"

"Maybe we've got an escaped convict aboard," Singapore said dryly.

"But it wasn't alive!"

"Things can look mighty funny when you're not expectin' them. How good a look did you take for'd?"

"I went over every inch. There wasn't any water. There wasn't any sign of a thing." His eyes dilated. He panted, "You know what it means, don't you, when you can count one more on board than there is? Somebody on board has his number up!"

Singapore said seriously, "If you didn't find it, then there can't be one extra aboard."

"Not findin' it don't mean it ain't aboard!"

"You mean," Singapore said sardonically, "you didn't bother to look below."

"I wanted my gun and a flash light."

"Okay, Take your gun. I'll take the flash light."

SINGAPORE GOT out of his bunk and slipped his pants on.

He was skeptical and a little bored. This wasn't the first ghost Lucky had seen.

The two men went into the corridor. Dorothy was standing in the door of her stateroom. She looked pale and anxious.

"What's happened?" she gasped. "What were you shouting about?"

"Your boy friend says he saw a ghost."

Dorothy said, "Where?"

"Up forward. About half an hour after you turned in."

She seemed relieved. Half smiling, she said, "What did you see, Lucky?"

"A greenish-white face," he said. "It floated up out of the sea."

"With seaweed hanging on it?"

"No."

Singapore, yawning, said that it must have been an optical illusion, perhaps caused by the checkered play of moonlight and shadow on sails or rigging.

Lucky insisted that it had been a human face, a man's face.

"Hair?"

"Tangled dark hair," Lucky said promptly.

"We'll take a look between decks," Singapore said wearily.

"Be careful!" Dorothy wailed.

"Better go in and lock your door," Lucky advised.

Sammy was extremely skeptical of the green-faced apparition, but when your pal has a weakness and you can't cure it, the only thing to do is cater to it. It would make Lucky feel better if they searched the ship, so they would search the ship. Systematically.

Sammy led the way, with the flash light in his hand, down a scuttle hatch into the forward hold. It was empty except for a few scraps of coconut shell—relics of their last copra cargo. The shipment of crates and boxes for which Dorothy had chartered the *Blue Goose* to Konga was stowed in the 'midships hold. The two men entered this hold through a bulkhead door. They looked thoroughly, examining every space where a man might be hiding. They shifted crates and boxes and threw the beam of the flash lights into every crevice. And they found no stowaway.

They next searched the forward end—the chain locker, the paint locker, the fo'c's'le. They searched the galley. They even unlocked and peered into the small closet in which their store of liquor was kept—trade gin, *arrack,* whisky, and beer. They searched the lazarette and the locker in which they stored their deep sea diving gear—suits, pumps, shell baskets.

Singapore prodded with the flash light into the folds of the heavy tarred fishnet which they had picked up cheap in Guam and carried, not for any possible emergency, but in hope that they might some day sell it at a fat profit. There was no stowaway hiding in or under the folds of the heavy net.

They concluded the search by looking into the engine compartment and exploring the spaces about water tanks, oil tanks and gasoline tanks.

At the end of an hour of microscopic search Singapore was still convinced that Lucky had been the victim of an optical illusion. Yet what, Lucky argued, could have caused such an illusion? Both he and the *serang* insisted that none of the sails or rigging had moved for hours. The schooner was ghosting along under the lightest and steadiest of breezes. Unless you looked at the water and saw the passing of an occasional fleck of foam or spark of phosphorescence or clump of seaweed, you would have sworn that the *Blue Goose* was motionless upon a lifeless sea. The water, except in the path of the moon, was as still as glass. Slipping along at no more than two knots on an even keel, the schooner cut through the water with hardly a sound.

YET WHILE Singapore took no stock in Lucky's ghost, he felt suddenly uneasy, and he wondered if this was due to the superstitious fear that had gotten Lucky? Was this ghost Lucky's way of intuitively knowing that something was wrong? For Sam was convinced that something was wrong.

He was not superstitious, but he had developed to a remarkable degree the primitive trait of intuition. When he first came to the Far East, seven years previously, he had been fascinated by the Indian fakirs; had marveled at their ability to walk and dance unharmed on the sharp points of spikes, on knives, on coals of fire; at their ability to go for months without food.

What he had seen turned his point of view topsy-turvy. These things had paved the way to his development of a "sixth sense"— the primitive sense of intuition, particularly his intuition that danger was present when none of his material senses could possibly give him an alarm.

This sense was sounding an alarm now. Something was wrong. Something had been wrong, some danger had been threatening, from the day the *Blue Goose* sailed out of the Singapore roadstead. But he could not localize it.

The next appearance of the "phantom stowaway" occurred two nights later—on the night of the day that they passed the bark Bangalore, some ten miles to starboard, in the northwestern bight of the Banda Sea. The *Blue Goose* would, if these light steady winds held, reach Konga at least a day ahead of the Bangalore, so Lucky estimated.

It was the *serang*, at his post at the wheel, who saw the "phantom stowaway," moving about in the black shadow cast by the mainsail about an hour before dawn. The *serang* hailed him, but the ghostly figure did not answer the hail. It simply vanished. It was, the *serang* babbled, a thin, dark figure, showing no trace of white.

Singapore, Lucky Jones and Dorothy were in their cabins when the *serang* saw the apparition. He hastened below and awakened the men. He was so frightened that he was gibbering. Every one on board was accounted for. The deckhand, a half-caste Malay boy, had been sleeping in the stern, curled up on the deck near the wheel, because the fo'c's'le was so hot that night. Dorothy was asleep in her cabin. It was so quiet that when Singapore went to her door he could hear, through the varnished latticework, her regular breathing.

Singapore and Lucky went to the wheel with the *serang* and heard his stuttering, chattering account of what he had seen. He was looking forward, he said, when suddenly he saw the tall dark figure of a man moving about in the space between foremast and mainmast. The figure looked terrifically tall and thin. It made no sound. It moved about in the great shadow of the mainsail like a blacker shadow.

"Just like a tall black shadow, *tuan!*"

It was Singapore's opinion that the *serang* had seen nothing. He was sure that the *serang*, alone there at the wheel, had let his imagination get the better of him. Doubtless, he had been thinking of the ghost that Lucky had reported, and his imagination had played tricks on him.

But Lucky insisted on searching the ship again, this time thoroughly. Singapore realized that Lucky wanted desperately to prove, for his own peace of mind, that there was a creature of substance, not of uncanny shadow, on the *Blue Goose*.

"We're goin' over this ship," Lucky said grimly, "with a fine tooth comb. This time we'll organize."

Brani, the *serang*, and Rochor, the deckhand, were to go aloft, Brani up the foremast, Rochor up the mainmast. Singapore and Lucky undertook to search the hull. They covered identically the territory they had gone over last night, but with greater thoroughness.

Singapore said to Lucky, "We're not going to find anything. There isn't any stowaway."

Lucky's face was a yellow-white. "I know it," he said hoarsely. But he would not stop searching.

They went over the *Blue Goose*, inch by inch. The sun was up to aid their search by the time Lucky admitted defeat. There was no stowaway!

CHAPTER VIII

AMBUSH

LOUNGING IN A Bombay chair later that day, Singapore was angered over the elusiveness of a hunch. He had had a hunch right along, but he could not lay a finger on it. It was as elusive as a breath of vapor. His intuition was trying to warn him—but against what? Or was he uneasy because of all this talk of ghosts?

They were passing through islands which were jewels in a jade sea—the tropical isles of men's dreams. Off to the north, bestriding the Equator like a great cat with arched back and fluffed out tail, loomed the island of Celebes, tropical stronghold of mysteries not yet solved by any white man.

They flew, under a fresh wind, over the invisible line that divides the Java Sea from the Arafura Sea. Lucky said that they would reach an anchorage off Konga sometime shortly after sunset.

By two in the afternoon, the island began to rise, a dark and mysterious mass, from the southern horizon. And the closer they approached, the more forbidding Konga became. Even in the glare of the equatorial sun, Konga looked as sinister, as menacing as it was, in those old legends, reported to be. It seemed to crouch there, a dark and waiting monster.

At a little after eight bells in the evening watch, Singapore, still lounging in the Bombay chair, darkly thinking and wondering, heard Lucky's sharp voice issuing orders.

"Stand by to lower your jibs! Lower away! Stand by to let go your anchor! Let go!"

There was a splash, a large greenish explosion as the phosphorescent water was agitated. Sails came fluttering down—ghosts in the starlight. There was no moon. It would not come up for another hour.

The *Blue Goose* was no more than a quarter of a mile offshore. The night was warm and sticky. Singapore smelled the odors of frangipani and pepper trees in blossom. They swept out from the land on an almost visible vapor. The effect was an illusion. It was as if cobwebs were stretching across his face. He went so far as to wipe his face with one hand, to get rid of the sensation. He didn't like it at all. Something, something, something was wrong.

He could see the white gleam of the beach, and the dark sinister loom of the mysterious island against the sparkling fat white stars. The Island of Dark Figures!

Dorothy came up from below, garrulous with excitement, like a girl preparing to go to her first dance. He couldn't see her, but he knew how bright her eyes, how flushed her cheeks must be.

She came and stood close to him. "Can you see the light of the bungalow?"

"No," he said. He had seen no lights. He wondered if Lucky planned to stay on this island. Lucky was a little dubious about his reception by her father. What would this millionaire say to his daughter—the apple of his eye—marrying a man who looked like a buccaneer all of the time and acted like one on the slightest provocation? Yet any man but a fool would know that Lucky was solid gold; would be tickled stiff to get him for a son-in-law.

But it was a great mistake. Dorothy was cute and young and pretty. She was smart, too. Just the same, it was a great mistake. Lucky wasn't the marrying kind. You might shore up a ship on dry land, but it was wrong. That ship belonged in the water. Its job was to travel. Singapore knew Lucky well enough to predict that he was paving the way to lifelong discontent and unhappiness. He would never get the sea and the lust for adventure out of his blood. On top of all this, it grieved Singapore more than he would have admitted under torture to see their friendship headed for the rocks.

LUCKY CAME over. Singapore heard the sound of a kiss in the dark.

He stirred uncomfortably.

Dorothy said, excitedly, "When are we going ashore?"

"In the morning," Singapore answered.

"Oh," she wailed. "Not till then? Oh, please, please, please let's go ashore now. Look! There's the bungalow! Through those trees!"

Singapore looked and saw a lone light gleaming.

"I'm going to fire a salute," Dorothy said. She stepped to the rail. A random ray of light from the cabin picked bright glints from the weapon in her hand—a little pearl-handled twenty-five automatic which she wore in a snakeskin holster attached to a snakeskin belt.

Dorothy fired three shots, paused, fired two more. She said: "It's our private signal. It means 'All's well.'"

Singapore, watching the dark loom of the shore, first saw, then heard, the five shots in answer—five little spurts of blue-red fire, then the reports, which some cañon, far away, picked up and sent rattling off until the stuttering echoes subsided to a purr.

"Lucky!" the girl cried. "Sam! Oh, come on! Let's go. Dad'll have fits if we don't come. He'll be worried green. I know!" she said. "You're afraid, Lucky. You're afraid to look my father in the eye. And I thought you were so brave!"

"It isn't that," Lucky murmured.

"What is it?" she demanded.

"I'll tell you," Singapore said. "We're funny that way, kid. We've been cruisin' and tradin' among these islands for a long time. We like to see our noses in front of our faces. That's all."

It didn't seem, to Dorothy, to stand up as an argument. She pleaded with them. She bullied. She wheedled. She grew impatient.

Singapore knew it was ridiculous of him to feel as he felt. It was like a vague bristling, an unreasoning aversion to landing on that infamous island in the darkness. But it was two to one now; Lucky had decided to side with Dorothy.

"I'll just take my toilet things," she said. "The rest can wait until morning."

The *serang* and the deckhand lowered a boat. They were, Lucky said, to stay aboard.

"We may not be back until morning. Keep a good watch."

"Aie, tuan!"

Singapore rowed, with Lucky and Dorothy in the stern seat, holding hands and whispering. Occasionally he caught a word. But he wasn't much interested. He felt pretty sick about it. He was trying to decide what he would do. He would sell his half interest in the *Blue Goose*. He would make that dangerous journey, long-postponed, through jungles and swamps and mountains, into the northern part of Siam, where, he had been reliably informed, lived a Karen chieftain who possessed a mate to the blue fire pearl. He would, of course, wait here on Konga for the Bangalore—and Bill Shay. Then on to Siam!

The skeg of the dinghy grated on sand. He got out and pulled the bow up on the beach, then gave Dorothy a hand out onto the sand. He could just see the pale blur of her face in the starlight. Behind her, Lucky loomed tall and mysterious.

"There's a path through these trees," Dorothy said, and led the way across the beach to a grove. They were scrub palms. Their fronds hung motionless in the still air. Looking above them, Singapore saw the evening star like a dazzlingly bright incandescent light poised on the rim of the mountain. It gave the illusion of being so close that he could almost pick it out of the air.

With Dorothy showing them the way to the path, Singapore followed and Lucky brought up the rear. He was suddenly silent. If Singapore knew anything about it, Lucky was dreading this meeting with Dorothy's father.

"This way." She was walking rapidly. She disappeared into the shadows fifty feet ahead of Singapore.

SINGAPORE WISHED he knew why he felt so uneasy. There was something in the air, an inaudible rhythm, like that of very distant drums to which the skin may be sensitive but the ears are not yet responsive.

The feeling persisted. His uneasiness grew. Something was wrong. He did not know why he wished they had waited until morning, but he did. The queer sense of a rhythm in the air persisted; in fact, became more pronounced. Was it in his imagination? It was, or seemed to be, beating in three-point time, like the blood-drums of the voodoos, like the sacrifice and death drums of savage tribes the world over.

He was certain that it was in his imagination. But the hair at the base of his head stirred a little.

Tumpatum—tump! Tumpatum—tump!

His skin tingled to the remote—or imagined—vibration. His ears strained. Nothing there. Or—not yet? A ghost of breeze, cool as fog, slid through the palm grove. His nerves were jiggling. Behind him, Lucky sighed heavily. Love-drunk!

Once you heard that measured beat, you kept on hearing it. An hour of it was enough to keep it beating in your brain for days. It could come back years later at the rustling of a dry leaf.

Tumpatum—tump! Tumpatum—tump!

A saddle in the hills was silvered with the rising moon. It was as if the saddle along its edges were magically white-hot. Vapors were even rising, as if from a demon's caldron. Singapore saw them with astonishment. Vapors or smoke? Or steam from jungles? No. Too high up for jungles, and the vapor was centered in one spot. Why one spot?

An edge of the moon jumped up, and suddenly illuminated a high wall, a cliff or mountainside, of bleached stone. Bleached sandstone. He stumbled over a root, gathered himself together. The ghostly little breeze carried strongly to his nostrils the sweet pungence of pepper tree blossoms.

He looked back at the mountainside—and suddenly saw something else. The chalky surface glowed not only with the stainless silver of the moon, but there were red-glowing patches, too. They shivered over the silvered wall. Incredulously staring, he saw the shadows of two human giants, crouching. Those shadows must have been hundreds of feet tall.

And seeing them, his ears distinctly heard, for the first time, the rhythm that faintly tapped against his skin.

Instantly, the uneasiness that had been weighing on him since the *Blue Goose* left Singapore sharply focused. His hunch became clear. His intuition, picking at his consciousness, showed him in shocking clarity a pattern formed of seemingly unrelated events.

The girl was perhaps fifty feet ahead of him, hurrying. He could hear the thump of her feet on the packed dark sand. He ran to her, clapped a hand on her shoulder and spun her around. He snatched the pistol out of her holster, and said through his teeth, "You dirty, double-crossing little—"

The girl screamed: "Alvarado! Martinez!"

He closed his hand about her neck, throttling her voice. He panted, "Lucky! Beat it!"

The girl struck at his face, kicked his shins and screamed.

The grove was swarming with giants. They must have been flattened against every palm bole, waiting to pounce.

CHAPTER IX

"WELCOME TO KONGA!"

TWO OF THESE giants fell savagely on Singapore, one from either side. A fist smashed into his left cheek, sending him spinning into a fist that came thumping up into his jaw. This jarred him back on his heels. He had lost the girl's pistol and his own. He straightened up; lashed out into reeling blackness. His knuckles buried themselves in bare flesh.

He fought with the fury of a surprised wild cat, yet he knew he had no chance. There seemed to be dozens of them. A man who must have been a head taller than Sammy threw himself on him and bore him, kicking and struggling, to the ground.

Feet thumped into his ribs. A heel ground into the back of his hand. Fists were rising and falling, beating his face into a pulp.

With a superhuman effort, Singapore twisted his body, threw off the giant who lay on him. He writhed free. He was on his knees when a fist exploded on his chin like a bomb. He collapsed. He struggled up again. He struck out in every direction. Men, dimly seen, panted and grunted and closed in on him again.

Again he went down under the sheer weight of their hurtling bodies. He fought until he had no strength left, until he could hardly suck in his breath.

Then they kicked him to his feet. He threw his arms about a palm bole and clung to it, gasping for breath. Blows fell on his head, his shoulders. His legs were kicked.

It was as unreal as the awful visions of a drowning man. He could not move but fists and feet thudded into him. He fell again and was again kicked to his feet. He struck a man in the face. An oath in Spanish was spat at him. Another man, in the same tongue, demanded to know where "the other one" was. And a third man gave, in Spanish—the Spanish of Mexico—the answer, "Back there."

Through a brain haze, Singapore wondered what Spaniards—Mexicans—were doing here. Spaniards—or Mexicans—on Konga! Stars reeled. He glimpsed, far away, those giant figures dancing crazily against the pink-and-silver glow on the white mountain and panted, "Lucky! Where are you?"

The answer, from a dozen feet behind him, was a coughing, spluttering series of oaths. Then came the distinct crashing of fist upon bone. A softer crash. Lucky was down again.

A hand applied between his shoulder blades gave Singapore a shove. He stumbled and spat out, "Who the hell are you?"

The harsh answer, in English, "You'll find out soon enough!"

So furious that he shook, he muttered, "That dirty, double crossing little—" A fist smashed into his jaw.

"Move along!" A machete was waved threateningly before his face—yet no steel had been used in the fight!

He moved along, and the stars jiggled in their places. Blood was running out of his nose and mouth. One leg felt paralyzed—it hardly supported his weight. He could hardly see, because both eyes were almost swollen shut already. He was beaten—and sick with rage.

"Damn him—damn him!" It was all so clear. That lying Malay he had grabbed in the Sailors Delight. Behind him, that lying bartender. How far back did it go, all fixed, all ribbed?

"Damn him—damn him!"

The murder of the *serang* and the island boy. That mysterious stowaway! Why, Singapore wrathfully asked himself, hadn't he opened those crates in the 'midships cargo hold? He'd have put white-hot pokers against that phantom's feet until he shrieked the whole truth!

He should have suspected the girl from the moment he saw her, wiping off crocodile tears with that green handkerchief.

"Move along, you rat!"

HE STUMBLED on. Oh, it was all so clear now. Why hadn't it been just as clear days ago? But how convincingly the bartender had lied! How convincingly that Malay had lied! And that girl! She had clouded the whole situation just as an octopus clouds up the water to fool an enemy, a victim. Smoother than silk, the way she'd played up to Lucky, luring him, hypnotizing him, throwing their minds off the track!

The light through the trees came nearer. And the moon was up over the mountain now, drenching the little plateau with silver brightness. He was so bruised, so breathless, so sick he could hardly stand. At intervals, a hand in the small of his back gave him a shove. They were laughing about it, babbling in Spanish, flourishing weapons. Now and then a man kicked the calves of his legs.

He tried to pull himself together. It was a time for fast, clear thinking. What were Mexicans doing on Konga? Six thousand miles from Mexico. The tropical moon showed their faces plainly enough. He had, in all his life, never seen such a collection of brutal, villainous faces. There was a man with only one eye. There was a man with a livid scar, as if a horse had kicked him, curving under his mouth—a man with a double grin!

They swaggered and lurched along behind him. They kicked up sand with their shoes. They laughed and roared and cursed. It was like a procession of madmen.

The door of the bungalow was open. He was still under the spell of that clever delusion. Not a bungalow. It was the roughest of rough shacks, roofed with ragged nipa—nothing but a shelter against the rains.

There was a rough plank table inside, and on this table burned the stump of a candle. Its orange flame licked up and fell back.

A thin-faced man with clipped gray hair, a man of perhaps fifty-one or two, with keen blue eyes, sat behind the table. His complexion was beef-red from myriads of tiny ruptured veins and the tip of his large nose was faintly a telltale purple. It was a hard face, a brutal face, and the eyes were those of a predatory bird.

Singapore's heart was thumping. His face was suddenly wet with sweat.

The man at the table watched him with a mockingly grave and sympathetic interest. His mouth began to twitch. Suddenly he laughed; great booming laughter.

The laughter stopped. Old Bill Shay, elephant man, pearler, Buddhist priest, master of trickery, robber, murderer, vagabond extraordinary, bent forward and regarded his stepson with shimmering blue eyes.

"Welcome to Konga!" he chuckled. And added, with mocking sentimentality, "Sonny boy!"

CHAPTER X

BILL SHAY LAUGHS

THERE WAS A dirty old khaki sun helmet on the table before him. And at his hand lay a Lüger automatic pistol.

The two captives were pushed roughly into the shanty.

Old Bill Shay looked very well pleased with himself. As the result of the most ingenious trickery, he had lured his red-headed stepson into a trap from which there was no escape.

He said amiably, "Well, Alvarado, we seem to have done a nice clean job."

The giant who had first leaped on Singapore stood just beside him, with arms folded on massive chest. He looked like a cutthroat, a murderer, a pirate. He must have been six feet eight inches tall.

His face was so brown it was almost black. He had a hawklike beak. His teeth were bared in a wolfish grin.

" '*Sta bueno!*" he said. And launched into profane Spanish. Singapore gathered that Alvarado and his men had found the task a very pleasant one. When the two unsuspecting Americanos had come along that path, they had simply slapped them down.

"It was child's play. A little love tap—like this—and we had them."

In an excess of good humor, he slapped Singapore lightly on the jaw. The redhead brought up his fist swiftly to Alvarado's mouth. The Mexican staggered and roared. Men fell upon Singapore; punched and kicked him. His arms were held. Alvarado rubbed blood from his mouth, then spat into Singapore's face.

Old Bill Shay sat at the table with his chin cushioned on a palm, contemplating Sammy with an amiable grin.

He said now, judicially, "That's the trouble with you, Sammy.

You don't use your nut. You're a born sucker. You think you're a wise guy. You're nothing but a sap. Alvarado, you'd better get your gang on board that hooker. I have some business to discuss with these two sea wolves. Vamose!"

Glaring at him and cursing himself, the redhead tried to put his thoughts in order. It was all his fault. He should have seen through that lying bartender and lying Malay. He should have known that that little siren who called herself Dorothy Borden was a double-crossing liar. He should have opened up every box and crate in the 'midships hold and found that "phantom stowaway."

He had, through carelessness, fallen into the trap they had sprung, and dragged Lucky in with him.

Bill Shay picked up the automatic pistol. He released the safety catch and placed the pistol on the table again. His blue eyes were bright with good humor.

"We are going to have a little talk, sucker. But don't forget yourself again. I want my son to behave himself like a perfect little gentleman. If he doesn't, he gets spanked. Just keep in mind, Sam, that your dear old dad isn't dumb. It would break my heart to have to hurt you, Sam, but business is business. And that goes for your pal, too."

He took out of a pocket of his tunic a white Burmese cheroot. This he lighted at the candle flame, watching them over it with alert blue eyes. He puffed comfortably and said, "Do you remember what I told you in that letter when you were in the Singapore hospital a couple of years ago? 'The hand is faster than the naked eye. A wise man knows the aim of a bottle.' I guess you didn't get what daddy meant. That's the trouble with me. I give you credit for some intelligence. Well, I used to. But you're not smart. You're just a boob."

"You louse!" Sammy panted.

His stepfather gazed at him with a look of hurt surprise.

"That's right," Sammy snarled. "Grab yourself an eyeful of the guy who's some day gonna make you drink your own blood and like it! You wife beater! You baby robber! You lousy thief! I'll do it! I've sworn to do it. And I will."

HIS STEPFATHER lifted one eyebrow.

"Sammy, I'm surprised at you. I'm hurt, Sammy. Don't you remember what Confucius said? 'When early dawn unseals my eyes, before my mind my dad does rise.' Does a nice boy call his daddy names? And I've tried so hard to be proud of you. I've wanted to see you smart—like I am. And once or twice I kidded myself into thinking you were on the right track.

"I thought so that time when you fought your way out of the Maharaja of Malobar's jail—and got away with that fine blue fire pearl. I thought so again when you threw the live cobra into that crooked jeweler's cage in Singapore—and got away with the jack he'd stolen from you. And when you swam through that nest of sharks in Pemanngil Passage and outsmarted Big Nick Stark, the toughest crook south of Shanghai, I thought your brain was beginning to develop a little."

Bill Shay sighed and shook his head. "I admit, Sammy, that I was a little bit irritated at the way you stole the pink pig away from me in Siam, and I was mildly annoyed when you sneaked that sunken treasure out from under my nose up there in Sapahalu Strait. And there was another time when you got a lucky break, when you tricked me out of that salted sapphire mine, up on the Chantaboun River. I was just a mite provoked—I confess it freely, Sam. But I was pleased, too, because I thought you were working and studying hard to become, in time, and with breaks, a half-wit. But I was wrong again. Once a lamebrain, always a lamebrain."

"Listen, tough guy," Sammy interrupted. "I don't like the way your nose grows. I don't like the way you brush your hair. Let's stop slicing boloney and get places. You've got that will of my grandfather's, and you've got me where you want me. You're going to knock me off and get that million. What are we waiting for?"

His stepfather slowly shook his head. "Sammy," he said sadly, "don't you realize that when you say things like that it brings big pearly tears into my eyes? Why should I kill you? Why should I rob myself of the only real fun I have in life? You don't seem to get my point. Of course, you don't get most points. But couldn't you, if you banged your head against a wall, get your brain to working just a little? Can't you grasp that the thing that makes life worth while for me is the laughs I get out of you?

"If I knocked you off, what would be left? Nothing but pearls and elephants It's laughing that keeps a man young, Sammy. And the reason I don't look my age is the laughs I get out of you. Of course, I ought to be ashamed for picking on such a mental cripple, but I'm human, Sammy, and the temptation is too great."

"You rat!" Sammy said.

His stepfather contemplated him with mocking reproach. There was a little pucker between his eyes, as if he were thought-fully turning that epithet over in his mind.

"Perhaps you've never heard the old Siamese saying, 'Rats know the ways of rats.' Why don't you take lessons from me, Sammy? Of course, you wouldn't grasp the fine points, but if you really applied yourself we might filter a little useful light into that dim, echoing corridor between your ears."

Sammy, breathing hard, involuntarily took a step forward. The pistol was instantly in his stepfather's hand. And Singapore knew that Bill Shay would not hesitate to use that pistol, if the issue were forced. He knew that Bill Shay didn't want to use that pistol unless he was compelled to. He wanted to see Sammy squirm.

And Sammy was certain that, sometime to-night, he was going to be killed. Somehow this man was going to put him to death. How? By turning him over to the Kongans? It didn't really matter. Bill Shay was playing with him now as a cat plays with a captured sparrow. The kill would occur when Bill Shay tired of playing.

CHAPTER XI

SHANGHAI SALLY

THE BEAT OF the Kongan drums, up there on the hilltop, created a mad rhythm in Singapore Sammy's nerves. *Tumpa-tum-tump! Tumpatum-tump!* The flame of the candle on the rough plank table licked up. Smoke from the point of it was a black string reaching up to the palm-thatched roof of the shack. There was no wind. He heard the ticking sound of a scorpion crawling in the thatch. The odor of pepper tree blossoms was sickeningly sweet. Mingled with it was the acrid smell of old Bill Shay's white Burmese cheroot.

From the corner of his eye he saw Lucky Jones, beside him, sway a little. How long would the buccaneer preserve his self-control? Only that Lüger in Bill Shay's hand was holding him back. But how long would it hold him back?

Careful, Lucky! Hold onto yourself.

Singapore's heart was beating heavily. He had that desperate feeling of helplessness enjoyed, perhaps, by an insect on a pin. He knew that the sweat of desperation was streaming off his forehead and running with the blood down his face, because he could feel it dribbling off his chin.

His stepfather tilted his head a little and lifted his eyes, as if he were weighing the meaning of the Kongan drums. Then he lowered the pistol. He was amiably smiling again and his eyes were twinkling.

"A father's duty," he said, "is to prepare his son to cope with life. The question is, are you too dumb to learn how? My opinion is that you are. Yet I owe it to you to make you learn a few things, no matter how painful it may be to that poor pulpy mass of confusion back of your eyes.

"We will take the present situation, and how it came about,

as the first lesson. It was a neat trick, and it was smart. I know I ought to illustrate this lesson with diagrams and crayon drawings, so that that last year's bird nest inside your skull will grasp the points, but I'll do my best.

"First of all, Sammy, I kept in mind that I was dealing with a very low order of intelligence. So I said to myself, 'Bill,' I said, 'keep your tricks simple and childish. The simpler they are, the quicker that poor sap will fall for them.' So I primed that bartender, and I primed that Malay so that you would, being so simple-minded, go hot-footing it down my trail. Then I put a pretty girl into the picture, knowing, of course, how big dumb punks like you fall for any line a pretty girl hands out.

"It's going to be hard for you to get the purpose of these simple little gags, but I'll try hard and I'll promise to be patient, knowing how backward you are. The purpose, Sammy, was to get hold of your schooner. These friends of mine needed a good fast schooner and your schooner is good and fast."

Bill Shay paused, his eyes shimmering at the moonlit night behind Sammy and Lucky. Singapore glanced quickly at Lucky. The buccaneer looked dazed. He was in a semi-stupor—out on his feet from the beating he'd taken and the realization that that girl was a lying little cheat, the lowest kind of hypocrite. When Lucky came out of that daze, he was very apt to start wrecking things.

A GIRL'S sweet, clear voice behind him said, "Well, here I am, Bill!"

And the girl who called herself Dorothy Borden serenely walked in with her hand lightly resting on the little pistol in her holster. Singapore had snatched it out of that holster, and the Mexicans, in their rush, had knocked it out of his hand. He supposed she had been all this time looking for it.

She bent down and kissed old Bill Shay lightly on the mouth. Straightening up, she turned toward the two men she had so thoroughly hoodwinked, and her eyes were softly aglow. She was even smiling. It was a sweet, rather gay little smile.

Glaring at her, Singapore found it hard to believe, even now, that she was not what she had professed to be. Her loveliness, her air of fresh innocence, would have deceived any man. It was utterly incredible that a girl who looked so innocent, so sweet, could be what this girl had proved herself to be.

He sent another glance in Lucky's direction, and saw that the buccaneer's jaw muscles were bulging, that that sledge-hammer jaw was outthrust, that every muscle and tendon of Lucky's big frame was straining forward with an almost irre-sistible inclination to destroy her.

The smile the girl wore was, to Singapore, as fantastic as if she had suddenly changed color. How many times had she smiled at him in just that way? So sweet, so innocent, so lovable! It would have been easy to understand, now that her deception was revealed, if she had somehow changed, had turned hard-boiled. But she hadn't changed in the least.

Old Bill Shay asked, "Did these two tough eggs give you any trouble, Sally?"

"Oh, no," she said in her clear, sweet voice. "They were very nice."

"Say," Lucky burst out harshly, "who is this snake?"

Singapore said bitterly, "And that's a compliment."

Bill Shay slowly, with an air of defeat, shook his head. "Is this polite?" he said. "Haven't you even any manners? Don't you know that nice little gentlemen don't call ladies naughty names? I'm shocked. Talking like that about the smartest and loveliest girl in Asia!"

"I'll say this for her," Sammy said grimly. "She makes a cork-screw look straighter than a fishline with a shark on it." And he said to himself, "Keep cool!" But he wasn't keeping cool. A few more of these insults, and he'd ram a fist down that old crook's throat. It would almost be worth getting shot to do it.

Controlling himself with a great effort, he said, "She ought to have quite a reputation."

Old Bill Shay was fondling the girl's hand. "Why?" he said.

"Because she made suckers of you two mental midgets? But you're right, Sammy. She has a reputation. She has the reputation of being the most beautiful, the cleverest and the most dangerous woman in the Far East. Sally Lavender—the girl from Shanghai! She turned Shanghai business and diplomatic circles into a pinwheel. You really started the Chino-Japanese war, didn't you, baby?"

Sally Lavender laughed softly. "Did I?"

"You see?" old Bill Shay cried. "Sally's modest. That's why I'm going to marry her. With her brains and my beauty, we expect to own Asia in about six months. Am I right, baby?"

"Aren't you always?"

"Spoken like a pal!" he chuckled. Then his face became grave. He solemnly regarded his red-headed stepson. His left eyebrow twitched. Then one corner of his mouth twitched. Then the other comer twitched. And he burst into roars of laughter.

"How," he asked, "are you going to like baby for a stepmother, Sam? Of course, it's a shame you can't come to the wedding. You and your pal would make a couple of cute flower girls. How about it, baby?"

MISS LAVENDER smiled. Her large beautiful eyes shimmered at Sammy. He was still finding her incredible. The fact of her was still so fantastic, so difficult to accept, that his face must have betrayed it. For his stepfather again burst into roars of laughter.

"Shanghai Sally!" he gurgled. "It almost rhymes with Singapore Sammy, doesn't it? Said Singapore Sam to Shanghai Sal, 'Momma, you are quite a gal.' Said Shanghai Sal to Singapore Sam, 'You bet your half-baked brain I am!'"

The girl said quietly, "Alvarado's men are on the schooner now. They took most of their things, and they're coming right back for the rest. I waited."

"Attababy! Did they take the gold?"

She laughed. "Did you think they'd give us a chance at it?"

"We'll get it," he said. "I like nice raw gold nuggets. I was just telling the boys, Sally, how to be smart like we are. Not that it will do any good, because there seem to be natural laws which prevent any one from driving nails with sponges. I was telling them about Alvarado's *caballeros*. I want Sammy to learn how things are done. Where was I? I was telling you why Alvarado's *caballeros* needed a good fast schooner.

"I realize, Sammy, that you are far too busy being the dumbest guy in the Far East to read the newspapers. If you were abreast of the times, you would know that, about five months ago, nineteen convicts, mostly murderers, made a break from a Mexican island penitentiary. It's in the Pacific, off San Bias. What's the name of it, baby?"

"Las Tres Marias," the girl said.

"That's it. They got away on a raft. A forty-foot sloop picked them up, thinking they were shipwrecked sailors. They killed off the crew of the sloop and sailed west. Two were drowned or eaten on the way. Three more were killed when the sloop cracked up on the reef out there. They've been here a couple of months. Sheer, downright providence—the same kind of providence that works for seagoing gnat brains like yours—got them this far without capture. There were two full moons, weren't there, baby?"

The girl from Shanghai nodded. She was gazing, with her wistful smile, at the copper wire encircling Singapore's neck.

"It seems that these cannibals," Bill Shay went on, "hold a festival every full moon. Like to-night. They dance themselves nutty. Then, if there are any strange brains around, they come down these hills and eat 'em." He chuckled. "It's just and old Konga custom."

He puffed leisurely at his white cheroot. And Singapore wondered if his stepfather was in league with these savages. He had an amazing way with the natives of all countries. It would not have surprised him to hear that Bill Shay was on good terms with the chieftain of the tribe.

"**EACH MOON** festival," Bill continued, "while these convicts have been here, the Kongans have come down and grabbed themselves a Mex. The convicts got pretty desperate. They got busy and carved a canoe out of a breadfruit log, and Pete Lopez, the most respectable looking one of the lot—it happens he speaks several languages—was picked to go to Singapore and somehow get hold of a boat big enough to take them all off. Lopez paddled all the way to Timor Laut and took passage on a trading schooner. He inquired around for the smartest man in the Far East. That's how he came to find me. He wanted a good, fast schooner. Naturally, I thought of your schooner.

"Do you see, Sammy, how nicely it all dovetails? Are you learning this lesson? Try hard! Wrinkle your brow if it will help. Would you like to gnaw your thumb? Keep on trying to concentrate. Do you begin to see, through the fog, how smart your daddy is? For delivering them your schooner, I get all the money they found on the sloop when they pirated it, and, before I'm through, I'll get all the gold they found here.

"Did I mention the gold? They've been placer mining, Sammy, and they have a box of big shiny nuggets which they think they're going to keep. But they aren't going to keep them, Sammy. Because they are half-wits, just like you and your pal. Before I'm through with them, I'll have all the nuggets they mined. See how nicely it all fits together, Sammy? You simply play all the ends on the middle. They get a schooner. I get all their money and I get all your money. And Sally gets the Malobar pearl. That was the price she put on her services, and that's the price she gets. Is it clear to you now how a pair of smart brains work? Or is it completely over that genuine ivory ball you carry on the end of your neck? Don't you want to ask any questions? Teacher will gladly answer any questions. Don't be ashamed of being curious. Even rabbits are curious."

"Who killed my *serang* and deckhand?" Lucky hoarsely asked.

"I don't know. Who killed 'em, baby?"

"Lopez."

"And Lopez stowed away," Lucky snarled. "And when that cargo came aboard, he hid in an empty crate."

Bill Shay nodded indulgently. "That was my idea, too. He goes to the head of the class, doesn't he, baby? That cargo was also my idea, Sammy. In case you didn't investigate, it contains enough food to last the *caballeros* six months, or at least until they reach Madagascar."

Sally Lavender said quietly, "Bill, aren't those drums closer?"

Bill Shay leisurely stood up, with the Lüger in his hand. He walked around the table with his eyes on Sammy.

"Yes," he said, "they're pretty close. Sammy, it's taken me some time to get around to the point of this talk, but I've had to explain myself in language that that crock of liverwurst under your hair could grasp. The point is, as Confucius says, 'The superior man will gladly lay down his life for his father.' Of course, you's not a superior man, but you'll do. Comfort yourself with the reflection that you aren't fit to spend your own money anyway. You can go to hell happy, knowing that your grandfather's money is going to be spent by a clever man."

"You lousy, cold-blooded murderer!"

HIS STEPFATHER clicked his tongue in gentle reproof, then he smiled indulgently.

"I understand," he said. "You're joking with daddy. Where would you be, Sammy, without your sense of humor? It's nice to have a sense of humor, isn't it, baby? It takes a good, practical sense of humor to laugh when you learn you're going to have the top of your head lopped off and your brains scooped out and eaten like beans within the next few hours!"

"You rat!" Lucky rasped through puffed and bleeding lips.

"So that's how we get it?" Singapore said.

His stepfather seemed amazed. His eyes were large and round. He softly exclaimed, "Did you think I was going to kill you unless you forced me to? Don't you know, Sammy, that it's against the law to kill a man? I'm not going to kill you. I'm going to let the snakes or the Kongans do it. Then I'm going to take what's left of you to Surabaya as fast as I can—before it spoils—for purposes of identification. The law compels that, and I wouldn't dream of violating the law.

"Easy, Sammy! Don't lose your temper! Maybe a Konga queen will fall in love with your red hair and marry you. Being a queen's husband is a job that doesn't require any intelligence. Or maybe you'll get an idea and save yourself. I don't know what your brain would do with an idea if one got lost and strayed in there, but mistakes do happen. While there's life, isn't there always hope? Or, as Confucius says, 'The superior man has neither fear nor anxiety.'"

Singapore's eyes flicked to the girl. Her face was calm, not alarmed. Her eyes were large, round and watchful. The little pistol was in her hand. He heard Lucky groan with suppressed fury.

"Will you two men," the girl said in her deceptively sweet, gentle voice, "move over to the wall, facing it, with your hands above your heads?"

The two adventurers hesitated. But Singapore was more in fear of what she might do if he hesitated too long than he was of Bill Shay's coldblooded ruthlessness. This girl, he knew, would not hesitate to shoot him in the back. So he raised his hands above his head and moved to the wall, facing it. And Lucky Jones did likewise.

Singapore felt fingers fumbling at the copper loop, felt the wire slip over his head.

Then the girl softly exclaimed, "Bill! It's gone! It was there when we came ashore. I made sure—felt it in the pouch when he helped me out of the dinghy; The pearl and the pouch are gone!"

CHAPTER XII

INTO THE PIT

SINGAPORE FELT HIS stepfather's hot breath on the back of his neck. Then Bill Shay prodded him in the backbone with the muzzle of a Lüger.

"Sonny boy," he said softly, "where's Sally's pearl?"

"That's funny," Singapore jeered. "You two are so smart. You're the smartest pair of thieves in the Far East. Two people as smart as you are shouldn't have any trouble findin' Sally's pearl."

Old Bill Shay said sadly, "Sammy, I'm afraid I'm going to have to hurt you a little."

And Sammy answered, "Go to it."

"Search them both," Miss Lavender suggested.

"Okay. Keep them covered." Very thoroughly and systematically the old elephant man conducted that search. The pearl was, very evidently, not concealed on either man.

"He got rid of it," the girl said, "when the Mexicans attacked. He couldn't have hidden it very well. He didn't have time."

The Lüger gently prodded Singapore in the backbone again.

"Sam," Bill Shay said, "that pearl is your wedding present to your stepmother. Am I going to have to be rough?"

"I was figurin'," Singapore said grimly, "on givin' it to her at the weddin'."

The pistol jabbed him in the spine again. This time it hurt so that he winced.

"I'll give you just ten seconds, sucker."

"It's in the ocean," Sam said.

"That's a lie."

"I can't get away with anything with you, can I, big shot? Sure it's a lie. I buried it in the sand while I was rasslin' with your boy friends."

"That's another lie!"

"Sure it is! When I'm in Rome, I go Roman all over!"

Bill Shay laid a powerful hand on his neck. With his other he jammed the muzzle of the Lüger once again into Sammy's sore backbone. A fury that he could not control swept in a kindling wave through the redhead. He could restrain his urge to fight back no longer.

Within a space of time immeasurable, so swiftly did he go into action, he spun about. By some trick of mental telepathy, some electrically-transferred nerve impulse, Lucky Jones went into action at the same split-second.

Both men whirled simultaneously. The pistol's muzzle raked along Sammy's ribs as he whirled. His right fist, on a crooked stiff arm, smashed into Bill Shay's face at a spot along the jaw midway between point of chin and ear. Lucky's left-handed punch brushed the pistol out of the girl's hand in passing and thumped into Bill Shay as his head rebounded from Singapore's punch.

The old elephant man was caught, as it were, between two hurricanes of bone and flesh. For a moment, his large red face remained stationary, a target like a half moon. Before it could waver, Singapore's fist struck one eye, the nose and the mouth with savage and beautifully timed precision. Bill Shay fell back with such violence against Sally Lavender that she sprawled backward, bringing up against the opposite wall. She slid down to the dirt floor. A shower of palm leaf splinters rattled down.

Bill Shay, continuing his precipitate backward flight, struck the table. It disintegrated. The elephant man went down noisily in its collapse. The candle flame vanished. The Lüger sent three stabbing red-blue flames toward the roof in the immediate darkness.

There was silence, disturbed only by the distant beat of the drums.

THE SUCCESS of their unpremeditated attack was so startling that neither the redhead nor the buccaneer could, for a
moment, speak.

Then: "Lucky!" Singapore croaked.

"Right here!"

"Hit?"

"No! You?"

"No! Breeze!"

They breezed, going through the narrow door shoulder to
shoulder. Through the trees, they saw the gleam of the moon on
wavelets. This was the shortest way to the ocean, and the ocean
was their objective.

A path led from the shanty to the beach in a direct line—half
again shorter than the way they had come.

They started down this path at a hard run, side by side. What
their plan was, Heaven only knew. An uproar of men's voices
over the water told them that the convicts had taken possession of the *Blue Goose*. Behind them, up on the hill, the Kongan
drums sent down their pagan rhythm. *Tumpatum-tump! Tumpatum-tump!*

And suddenly, as he raced for the beach, Singapore realized
that the drums had stopped; that his ears, so attuned to the beat,
were merely repeating the rhythm. He guessed this meant that the
Kongans were on their way.

"We should have grabbed them guns," Lucky panted, as he
ran.

"What good would guns do?" Singapore answered.

"What do you figure we're gonna do?"

"Swim!"

"Where?"

"Anywhere! We'll find heavy enough driftwood on the beach
to hang onto. We'll kick out and wait for a ship to pass."

"And get et by sharks!"

"Better than havin' our brains et like beans!"

They plunged through a scraggly grove of beefwood trees. One of two dark oblong patches, set close together, each perhaps ten feet wide by twenty in length, lay in their path. Nothing about those patches suggested treachery. They were such patches as fallen leaves might make.

The two sprinting fugitives dashed out upon the oblong patch directly in the path. The oblong patch gave way. It simply collapsed. The two men, in mid-stride, went down with it. Down, down and down. A rectangular pit ten feet wide and twenty feet long, and perhaps fifteen feet deep. It might have been a grave dug for a giant's burial.

The bottom as soft wet clay. Striking it, the two adventurers skidded and fell, splashing.

"What the hell is this?" Lucky panted as he struggled up.

SINGAPORE DID not answer at once. He had fallen on his back, and the wind was knocked out of him.

He gasped, "Help me up!" And the buccaneer yanked him to his feet.

The moon rode high overhead and sent sufficient light into the pit to illuminate it perfectly. It plainly showed the stratified earth into which the pit had been dug. The upper stratum was white sand. Below that was a gray layer, of darker sand. Under that for five or six feet stretched black earth. Then came clay—slippery, slimy gray clay.

"Did they," Lucky panted, "expect us to fall into this if we made a getaway?"

Singapore didn't know. He was busy looking for a way out. He leaped up, tried to dig fingers and toes into the wall and claw up the side. But the sides were perpendicular. He fell back, with lumps of black dirt raining down upon him.

They both tried. But the top of the pit was a full nine feet above their heads. It was almost impossible to maintain a footing in the watery clay. It was like a mixture of lubricating oil and grease, strewn with the light branches and leaves which had camouflaged the pit. There was no strength in these branches. They broke like straw stems.

"There's only one way out of here." Singapore said. "We've got to kick down enough clay to make a ramp up to where we can claw out the dirt. Got a knife?"

"Nope. They took it."

"Let's get busy and kick. Look here!"

He indicated, with his foot, a square dark patch of earth on the side of the pit, perhaps two feet square, and about a foot from the bottom.

"What do you suppose that's for?"

"It blocks a tunnel!" Lucky cried. "It's the way out!'

This seemed logical—so logical, indeed, that Singapore disregarded the sudden sharp warning of his intuition. He had, in the excitement, forgotten about the pits dug in Malaysia and Sumatra for the trapping of wild animals; forgotten that these pits were dug side by side with only a thin layer of earth between the two, so that, with the animal in one pit, a cage could be lowered into the other, and the animal transferred from the one pit to the cage, merely by knocking out the thin separating wall of earth.

When Lucky kicked the square dark patch, his foot went cleanly through. That blow loosened all the earth, and a two-foot square aperture was revealed.

Lucky cried jubilantly, "It's a tunnel all right! Hey! Hold on! Maybe the Kongans use this tunnel! Maybe this is how they snuck up on them greasers!"

Singapore was staring suspiciously at the square, black hole.

Suddenly, he shouted, "Plug up that hole! Quick!"

He picked up clumps of clay in his hands, tearing them from the walls, hurling these heavy clumps at the opening. He had glimpsed two pairs of luminous, cold green eyes shining like emeralds in the blackness of the adjoining pit. They danced from side to side. They advanced. They retreated.

A sickening stench poured out of the hole.

"Pythons!" he yelled.

HOARSELY SUCKING in his breath with the sound of a sob, Lucky clawed out a lump of clay and hurled it at the hole. The lump struck the wall perhaps six inches above the hole. The force of it dislodged a thin slab of clay eighteen inches square, enlarging the aperture to that extent.

"Lower!" Singapore shouted.

"Why," Lucky panted, "didn't you let me get them guns?"

The two adventurers were working furiously, scooping up handfuls of clay and hurling them at the hole, raking it down from the sides in great wads with hooked fingers.

The head of the largest snake Singapore had ever seen suddenly darted out of the hole. The scaly dark body attached to the head was as thick as his forearm.

He hurled a ball of clay at it. The head darted aside, and the body behind it came sliding out of the adjoining pit, writhing and twisting like a huge and horrible cable of black steel.

Unawarely, the two men were shouting and cursing in the frenzied panic that this monster provoked. Sammy clearly understood now old Bill Shay's reference to snakes—the alternative to being bound to trees for the Kongans to capture. Bill Shay had planned to cast them into this pit! And Singapore Sammy knew that these pythons must be starved.

A large loop of the snake, cold and wet and slimy, went around him. The head of the reptile plunged down to within an inch of his eyes. Its eyes were green and coldly murderous. The loop settled about his shoulders, slipped down until it encircled his waist.

He struck at the head with his clenched fist. The emerald eyes slid away. A forked tongue darted out at him. The loop was tightening about him just above his hip bones; closing down, preparing to crush the life out of him.

He struck and clawed and pulled at the cable-like loop across his stomach; saw Lucky go stumbling past him, with a fold of the other python entwined three times about his chest and middle. A twitching black tail, blunt as the end of a club, caught at first one leg, then the other. It was pulling Sammy off his feet. He could not stand up. His hand went blindly out. He was lifted into the air, half-way to the top of the pit. He clawed at the side. He was filled with a desperate futility. The exertion of his utmost strength made absolutely no impression on the python.

He could hardly breathe now. The great black loop about his waist was tightening, tightening. He could feel the mad thumping of his heart against the awful irresistible pressure of it. He knew that his eyes were bulging from their sockets.

And now that they had subdued their victims, the two pythons proceeded more slowly. Another fold of the slimy black body slowly slipped over Singapore's head. For many seconds his nose was pressed flat by the white belly of the snake, and his nostrils were full of the awful stench of it. Then the coil slipped down to his neck, slid over his shoulders and joined the other convolution, tightening, always tightening.

He felt the pressure of blood against the sides of his head, pounding in his throat and ears, as the constriction about his chest and stomach increased. He was so weak now he could hardly struggle. He tried to speak. He knew this was the last act—curtains! He wanted to say so-long to Lucky. But the breath was squeezed out of him, and the coils of the python prevented him from swelling the walls of his chest to inhale. He felt ribs beginning to buckle, to crack. The pain where they joined his backbone was unbearable.

He was helpless. He knew he was going to die. This hideous pressure would continue to increase until death came, until he was crushed to a pulp. Then the huge jaws of the python would dislocate, and he would be forced into the monster's stomach.

His ears were full of a roaring, like that of a torrent of water. But there was no sound in the pit, except the sharp, short gasps of the doomed men and the slithering sound of the pythons settling down to their destruction.

His eyes, blinded by pain and blood, did not see a rope fall into the pit; nor was he aware of a small, slim figure sliding down the rope.

Perhaps his tortured senses registered flashes of blue-red; crashes of pistol fire. Next moment he was unconscious.

CHAPTER XIII

SALLY LAVENDER ACTS

SINGAPORE SAMMY'S RETURN to this life was signalized by a faint glow before his eyes and the sensation of fresh air being sucked into aching, fiery lungs.

He lay on his side, with his back to a wall of the pit. Close to his face lay a black thick loop of the python. It was quivering.

Sammy could not move. Intelligence informed him that the python must be quivering in its death agonies. The pit was very quiet. Some distance away, at the opposite end, he heard a faint gasping and gurgling. He managed to sit up.

Lucky was sitting at the far end, feebly wiping blood from his face.

Singapore said, weakly, "What—happened?"

A girl's clear voice answered, "I killed them. I shot them both through the head. They nearly killed you in their death struggles. I had to take the chance. There wasn't any choice."

He looked around. Sally Lavender was standing over him with her automatic pistol in one hand, a *parang* dripping with blood in the other.

"After I shot them," she said, "I hacked their heads off. Can you stand up? You'd better try."

Singapore tried. It called for all the strength he possessed to lift and push himself up. Then he had to cling to the slimy clay wall to keep himself erect. His legs were numb. His head whirled. His lungs burned and ached. But the bones of neither arms nor legs were broken. There was, however, a sharp, persistent pain where his ribs joined his backbone.

Dazed, he wondered why this girl had risked her life to save his and Lucky's. He staggered across the slippery clay to Lucky Jones and pulled him up.

"Where's the old man?" Singapore asked.

"He flew," the girl told him. "We've got to get out of here. Can you make it?"

"I can try."

She said breathlessly, "The other end of this rope is tied to a tree. Pull yourself up, then get us out."

"Okay. But I don't think I can make it."

He grasped the rope and tried. His bruised and torn muscles rebelled. He sank his teeth into his lower lip, breathed deep and tried again. Digging into the slippery wall with his toes, he kicked and pulled himself up to within four feet of the top. There he hung. Sweat oozed out on his forehead, ran into his eyes. Lucky, under him, was trying to help.

"Stand on my shoulders."

Sammy's feet found the buccaneer's wide shoulders. He took another deep breath and reached up on the rope. His mouth tasted salty with blood from his lip. He put all his strength into it. Slowly, slowly, his head rose up until his eyes were level with the gray stratum. Up! On up! The gray layer inched past his eyes, turned white. His eyes came level with the ground. He kicked, clawed, heaved; swung his body up over the edge. He rolled over and lay on his back, feebly gasping, utterly exhausted.

A VOICE said, "Hurry! Oh, hurry!"

He could not hurry. He could not move. He tried to get his breath. He tried to command his worn-out muscles to further effort.

Sammy succeeded in rolling over. A man was lying beside him. The man was Alvarado. His eyes, not two inches away, stared coldly into Singapore's. There was a wolfish grin at his lips.

Sammy was whirled into the air.

Singapore grunted with dismay, then sucked in his breath with horror. The eyes of the Mexican were cold indeed—cold in death. Something was wrong with his face—worse than mere death. Above his thick, bristling black eyebrows, it ceased entirely to be.

"Hurry!" the girl's voice said.

Sammy got up on his elbows. Alvarado's head had been cut off cleanly just above the eyebrows, so cleanly that there was only a little blood smeared along the edge of the bone.

Singapore looked closer. Alvarado's head was as empty as an eggshell! The brains had been cleanly removed!

Had this, Sammy frantically wondered, happened while he and Lucky were in the pit? Or had Alvarado been lying here, in this shadow, when they ran down the path?

Struggling to his knees, panting for breath, more than half sick, the redhead looked about him. Each tree, it seemed to him, was thicker than it should normally be. Distorted imagination— or did every tree shield a silent, blood-thirsty savage?

There was no sound, except, distantly, the uproar from the schooner. Cold waves of horror squirmed down Sammy's spine. He sweated with the realization that he could not move.

"Hurry!" The girl's voice was a thin wail.

He felt his flesh tingling, tightening, with an awful terror. But he forced himself to move. He crawled to the edge of the pit, with his head hanging drunkenly. He looked down.

Moonlight flooded the upturned faces of Lucky and the girl from Shanghai.

"Pull her up!" Lucky panted.

Singapore automatically spat on his hands and grasped the rope. His actions, the response of protesting muscles, were as automatic as the beating of a heart. His body was a pulse of pain. His brain was sick—chaotic with fear of the unseen dark figures which he thought hysterically must be all about him, creeping toward him.

But he hauled on the rope. The girl slid up into view, pawed at the white sand and pulled herself up the rest of the way. She had fastened the rope about herself, under her arms. She untied it and dropped it back into the pit. With herself and Singapore pulling, Lucky was brought up.

His breath whistled with a horrid sound in his lungs. He tottered, saw Alvarado, and fell to hands and knees. He looked at the dead man's empty skull and groaned.

"How long—" he began thickly.

The girl cried softly, "Hurry! Oh, hurry!"

Lucky clawed feebly at the air; got to his feet and staggered.

"What's that?"—a thin whisper. Sally Lavender was pointing a shaking hand toward the thicket nearest the dark shack. Singapore, staring, was sure he saw a shadowy figure flit from one tree to another. He could not be sure enough. His eyes were playing tricks. First the moonlight was green-tinged, then it was red-tinged. No one ever had seen a Kongan and lived to tell about it!

Were there dark figures behind all these trees? The very air seemed alive with the imperceptible rustlings they made, with their breathing, with the beating of their hearts, with the very heat of their naked black bodies.

Lucky seemed too sick to grasp the danger. The girl seemed paralyzed. Sammy heard her whisper, like a faint echo, "Oh, hurry!" He would hear her saying that in his dreams, he believed, forever. Hurry! Oh, hurry!

HE CLUTCHED Lucky by the arm. He made himself move and dragged Lucky with him. They stumbled along. Lucky lurched out of the path like a drunken man. Sammy tottered with him, fought for balance, pulled him back into the path. Sally Lavender was trying to run. She tripped and almost fell. Sammy heard her frightened sobs. He looked back. His scalp prickled. Were those shadows moving?

They plunged from the palm thicket onto the beach. "There!" the girl panted. The dinghy had been left high and dry on the white coral beach.

Staggering and stumbling, the two men pulled, lifted, pushed. They inched the boat into the water. The girl scrambled into the stern. Gasping, they tumbled in after her. Lucky dragged himself to the forward seat. Singapore snatched up the oars, dropped one, grabbed it as it slid into the water, began frantically to row. His lungs felt white-hot. The muscles of his back were a gnawing ache.

"Oh, hurry!" Sally whispered. Her eyes, enormous with fright, were on the black mass of trees.

With burning back and agonized lungs, Sammy bent forward and strained back. Forward, dip, pull. Forward, dip, pull. He rowed, it seemed, forever, keeping on a line midway between the schooner and the shore. He did this automatically, obeying his intuitions. Cannibals on the shore—murderers on the ship! Forward—dip—pull! Forward—dip—*pull!*

The beach blurred. The trees jigged. A million white-hot suns swam across his vision.

Sally's voice seemed to float to him from a great distance.

"Maskee! We're out of range."

He dropped the oars, crumpled forward until his head thumped down on his drawn-up knees. Presently he sat up and wiped his hand across his eyes. He stared at the shore. He stared at the girl's face. There was something uncanny, unreal about their being here.

"Where were they?" he said.

She whispered, "Why did they let us go?"

Their eyes were fixed hypnotically on each other's.

"Because you're a woman."

"Because you have red hair. Perhaps they've never—"

"Oh, no," Sammy said. "Oh, no." He paused. "Alvarado—"He stopped again. "Maybe they're still—"

She shivered; determinedly made the effort to pull herself together. Sighing, she said, "But, we're safe, Sam; we're safe."

He turned and looked out at the schooner, then back at her slim hand, resting on the pistol in her holster. Raucous laughter came in bursts from the *Blue Goose*. There was a soft, peaceful gurgling under the stern of the dinghy. Moonlight made crinkling silk of the sea. Singapore was suddenly conscious of a feeling of relief. He and Lucky were out of that trap. Or were they?

HE LOOKED back at her hand on the pistol. He knew that she was as cold-blooded, as ruthless as those pythons. And he wondered if this was another trap into which she was leading them. Was she still acting under Bill Shay's orders, or was she carrying on an enterprise of her own? Yet if Bill Shay had wished them killed, why had she risked her life, leaping into that pit?

"Yeah," he said sourly. "Yeah, we're safe, all right."

"But they're bound to go ashore! On account of Alvarado."

"And what makes you think they won't spot us?"

"I don't think they can see us from the schooner. Aren't we in the reflection of the mountains and those trees? We've got to take that chance. When they go ashore, we go aboard."

Sammy glanced at her hand again. Still on the pistol.

"Suppose," he said, "they decide to double cross Alvarado. They've got that gold on board, haven't they?"

"Yes," she said,. "but they'll go ashore. They want your blue pearl. They'll be sure Bill has it by now—they'd know he was going to double cross me. They'll try to double cross him for the pearl just as he planned to double cross them for their gold."

"And you're bettin' they'll all go ashore."

"I am."

"Not leavin' a single man on guard?"

"I know them, Sam. They wouldn't leave one man aboard—he'd double cross them and run off with the ship and the gold. And they'll all want to be on hand to get the pearl from your stepfather. And they planned to watch the pythons eat you. They wouldn't miss that."

"Maybe Alvarado was gonna double cross them and get the pearl off the old man."

"No. He was going to be talking to him when they came and ganged him."

"Yeah. Listen, sister. You want to watch out you don't get balled up and double cross yourself."

"I've managed," she said serenely, "to think fairly clear so far."

Singapore pondered that. "Yeah," he said, and wondered what she was thinking now.

The dinghy rose and fell gently with an almost imperceptible ground swell. The waves, breaking on the beach, made a soft whisper occasionally blotted out by the tumult from the schooner.

Sally Lavender said, "It's our only hope of escape. We three can handle the schooner—can't we, Lucky?"

The buccaneer answered in a thick, gritty voice, "I haven't a thing to say to you."

There were savage undercurrents in his voice. A sound of dull thumping floated from the *Blue Goose*.

"Red," he panted, "we've got to get aboard. You hear what they're doin'?"

"Yes, but we've gotta wait."

"The lousy scum're tearin' her apart!"

Sally said, "Don't you see, Lucky, if we're going to outwit those cutthroats and get away alive, we must pull together?"

"You heard me," Lucky said.

The girl made no answer. Her expression was serene. Sammy knew she didn't regret what she'd done to Lucky. She was like platinum. Nothing evidently touched her emotions. She was as impervious and as cold as that moonlike metal. Singapore had encountered her kind before, but never one so clever, so finished. He knew she was still after the blue fire pearl. But what was her scheme?

He drawled, "Where's your sweetie now?"

"You don't mean Bill Shay!"

"Why don't I?"

"I told you. You knocked him unconscious. The instant he came around, he left. He was almost strangling with rage. When I told him the drums had stopped, he simply flew."

SAMMY GAZED at her with a pucker between his puffed and swollen eyes. In the moonlight, her face was like new ivory— softly white and somehow luminous. Her eyes were enormous. Her mouth was a shadow. It was a tragic and a beautiful face. It was like a deadly flower of the jungles. It was as mysterious as a whisper heard in the night. As long as he lived, he would never answer her riddle. He was utterly fascinated by her contradictory blending of beauty and evil, of girlish innocence and diabolical cleverness. The devil disguised as a virgin!

"It beats me," he said, "how you fell for an old cobra like him."

"I wouldn't trust that man any farther than I can see around a corner!"

"Yeah? And he trusts you as far as he could throw that schooner by the bowsprit. How's he gettin' off the island?"

"He had a whaleboat hidden in some mangroves around on the south side. If the natives haven't grabbed him, he's well at sea by this time, cursing. How he must be cursing!"

Sammy smiled for the first time in hours. "He ran out on you!"

He had picked up the oars again, was slowly rowing. He wanted to be on the seaward side of the schooner when the Mexicans went ashore—if they went ashore. He wondered how long it would take them to drink up the contents of the liquor chest.

"No," the girl said. "I had three possible choices of getting away. With him. With Alvarado's men. And with you. I knew your chances were better than either his or theirs. You're resourceful and you're absolutely unafraid."

"You mean, you take us for a pair of suckers. What makes you think we'll save you? What makes you think we won't toss you to the sharks?"

She waited for the echoes of a splintering crash aboard the schooner to die away.

Lucky growled, "Those lousy wreckers—"

The girl said, "Neither of you would hurt a woman."

"Then why keep your hand on that gun?"

"I'm taking no chances."

Contemplating this false madonna with the most intense curiosity, Sammy slowly, with a baffled air, shook his head.

"How did you get to Konga in the first place?"

"Your stepfather and Lopez and I sailed from Timor Laut in the whale-boat."

"Why Lopez?"

"We had to have a pilot."

"You mean, you didn't trust Bill Shay?"

"I don't trust anybody but you, Sam."

"Boloney. Isn't Lopez the real brains of that outfit?"

She hesitated. "Yes."

"Who is Lopez?"

"He's the assassin of President Ortiba, but the Mexican authorities didn't find it out until after his escape from Las Tres Marias."

"How much reward they offerin'?"

"Twenty-five thousand pesos."

Sammy softly whistled. "Ten thousand gold! I thought you were a smart girl. When you were both in Singapore, why didn't you turn him in and collect that ten grand?"

"Because I'd given my word to help."

"Horse feathers! You figured the blue pearl was worth five thousand more than he was. You haven't stopped thinkin' about that pearl once!"

She said, "I'm thinking exclusively about our get-away. What are we going to do if those cutthroats come back aboard before we can get under way?"

"We've got plenty guns aboard," Sammy said. "We can start the kicker. She makes ten knots under power."

He was staring across the water at the *Blue Goose*. Men were swarming over the deck. One fell overboard. There were shouts of drunken laughter, then a sudden commotion alongside. They had lowered the longboat and were tumbling into it. The man in the water climbed in.

The longboat moved away from the side of the schooner. Oars flashed silver in the moonlight. The longboat moved toward the beach.

"How many do you count?" Sally whispered.

"Eleven," Sammy said.

"They're all there! Hurry!"

CHAPTER XIV

THE NET

WHEN THE DINGHY reached the schooner, the longboat was just reaching shore. The girl from Shanghai seized the rail and swung herself up on deck. Lucky climbed up and Singapore, making the painter fast to a shroud, followed.

He slipped and almost fell in a pool of blood. Lucky was standing, with one hand grasping a shroud, staring down at the *serang*. The Malay was dead. His throat had been slit.

"God!" Lucky said.

The girl had gone aft. She called, "Hurry!" It was, to Sammy, like the beat of those drums. Hurry! Oh, hurry!

The two men went aft. On the deck, just forward of the wheel, the deckhand lay, crumpled, with his face pillowed in the crook of his elbow, his legs drawn up under him. His head had been crushed in. His *parang* was lying beside his lifeless hand.

Lucky groaned, then slowly turned away. He sat down heavily and dropped his face in his hands. He lifted his head and said tonelessly to the girl, "You did this. You might as well have done it with your own hands."

She said evenly, "Do you realize that if we don't get out of here, or make some preparations, they'll kill all of us? Aren't you going to start the engine?"

"Don't talk to me," Lucky said hoarsely. "For God's sake, don't talk to me."

"Sam!" she cried. "They're coming back!"

He looked at the beach. The uproar of the eleven men came,

loudly across the quarter mile of water. It was too far to see
them clearly, but what he saw indicated that the Mexicans were
launching their boat, and that the greatest confusion prevailed.

The longboat was moving slowly out from shore. Oars
appeared to be in a tangle. And as he looked he saw a flash of
phosphorescence streak through the water alongside the boat.
There was another flash. Then another.

The girl cried, "They're throwing spears at them!"

Sammy saw more phosphorescent streaks, but he could see
no one ashore. The Kongans, in the black shadows under the
trees, were hurling spears but, true to those legendary accounts,
were remaining invisible.

Some sort of order, however, had been established in the longboat. Those nearest the stern were blazing away at the trees with
pistols and rifles. The others were working the oars with greater
unison, but they were still obviously panic stricken. Singapore
could now occasionally see the flash of moonlight on a spear
before it struck the boat or the water beside it. One oar suddenly
ceased to move and slipped overboard.

The convicts were firing steadily and rowing furiously, and
the gap between them and the shore was perceptibly widening.

There was now not time enough to get the schooner under
way. Time only to drive off the returning convicts. With the
same inspiration, Sammy and Lucky rushed for the cabin. Lucky
reached it first.

It was in the wildest disorder. Furniture was overturned and
smashed. Charts, letters, papers, empty bottles and broken
glasses were strewn over the floor. The nara-wood panelling
was splintered and scratched and dented where bottles and other
objects had been hurled at it.

And the firearms were gone. The locker in which rifles and
side arms were kept was empty except for some cleaning rods,
some gun oil and a tube of gun grease.

The girl, waiting on deck, cried, "They're almost here! Hurry!"

The two men returned to the deck. The longboat was within two hundred yards of the schooner.

Sally wailed, "Where are the guns?"

"Gone!"

She stared at them in sudden terror. "What are we going to do? I've only two bullets left in my pistol—and the rest of my ammunition's ashore. They'll kill us all!"

"Lucky!" Singapore barked. "Dynamite! Come on!"

THEY RAN and stumbled back to the cabin. Singapore opened the little door into the lazarette, where their dynamite was stored. But other things were stored here, too. Coils of rope. Bales of oakum. Spare sails. Oars. Odds and ends.

The dynamite, fuses and percussion caps were hidden under sails. They frantically removed the sails. Singapore pried off the top of a box of dynamite and snatched out several sticks.

Lucky cursed and said, "Red! There's only one cap! We were gonna get more caps in Singapore and forgot!"

"Come on!" Sammy snapped.

When they returned to the deck, the longboat was less than two hundred feet away. The Mexicans, still unaware that the schooner was occupied, were staring at the shore, still blazing away at the trees.

Singapore snatched up the dead deckhand's *parang* and swiftly cut a short length of fuse. He fitted the cap to a stick of dynamite, and the fuse to the cap. Bending low, he struck a match and lighted the fuse.

Sally Lavender's serenity had completely deserted her. Watching him, she beat her hands together and whispered hysterically, "Throw it!"

But Singapore gravely watched the fuse burn and Lucky, familiar with the habits of fuses and dynamite, gravely watched, too. He stepped back. At that moment, Singapore stood up and threw the dynamite.

It left a filmy thread of cream-colored smoke, an arc, as it rose and fell. One of the Mexicans saw it; shouted a warning.

The stick of dynamite fell short of its target. It struck the water five feet ahead of the oncoming longboat.

Sally burst out, "Oh, you fool! Why didn't you throw it harder?"

Sammy drawled, "It's waterproof fuse, sister."

The men in the longboat, suddenly aware of their danger, were in an uproar again. A rifle cracked. The bullet ploughed across the rail, ricocheted, screaming. Splinters flew. Another bullet went past within inches of Singapore's left ear with a sound like savagely ripping canvas.

Then, just under the bows of the longboat, there was a terrific turbulence. No more than three seconds had actually elapsed since that stick of explosive had struck the water. A mass of water ten feet in diameter surged up from the ocean's surface to the accompaniment of a brief red flash, a tremendous muffled detonation.

The longboat vanished in spray. The girl from Shanghai staggered across the deck, clutched frantically at a spoke of the wheel as she went past, and fell into a Bombay chair. The two men had dropped to their knees.

Sammy watched the mass of water spring into the air, solid and green, and calmly waited for it to tumble back.

When it did, what remained of the longboat became visible. It had been shattered to a point half way aft. The stern was down. Men were kicking and struggling. One of them sank. Two must have preceded him to the bottom, for only eight remained. These eight were in the water, swimming confusedly, evidently stunned.

The shattered longboat was slowly drifting aft with a litter of oars and splintered strakes. The eight survivors, in a cluster a hundred feet away, were now swimming toward the schooner. The shock of their immersion, coupled with the awareness of their danger, seemed to restore their strength. They came floundering through the water.

The girl screamed, "Stop them! Do something!"

Singapore panted, "Lucky! Come on! That fishnet!"

"What?"

"Come on!"

They dived into the cabin and ran to the locker where their diving gear was stored. They pulled and yanked and cursed at the heavy fishnet. But they succeeded in dragging it out of the locker, through the cabin, and up on deck. It had seemed to take ten minutes, yet only seconds had been consumed, and the eight swimmers were still twenty feet away.

They had spread out, were swimming in a line toward the schooner. Evidently they had agreed on a plan—to swarm up over the side as one man. Three of them had knives in their teeth.

Sally Lavender had her pistol in her hand. Two bullets! A disengaged corner of Sammy's mind wondered if she intended to shoot herself with the second one.

WORKING SWIFTLY, the two men spread the heavy, tarred net along the deck. When completely unfolded, it was about a hundred feet long by fifty in width. But they did not require all of it. They unfolded and stretched out only half of it.

With Lucky at one end and Singapore at the other, they lifted it clear of the deck and started to swing it like a giant hammock.

Singapore panted, "Let go at three! One!"

"Okay!"

"—Two!—Three!"

The eight swimmers snarled and shrieked curses in Spanish. Some of these were as picturesque as they were blood-chilling. They would nail the Americanos by their tongues to the mainmast! They would hold them in the water for sharks to devour!

One snatched the knife from his teeth and hurled it. The knife skittered across the deck.

The heavy net swung outward and down upon their heads.

And the water under the net was quickly white with the efforts of the trapped eight to escape. Hands frantically pushed up against the net. Fingers clawed at it. Faces appeared momentarily to gasp; rolled over, disappeared, came up again. One man with a knife hacked desperately at the thick web. But the net sank upon him before he could hack a hole large enough.

Two of them dived down in an attempt to swim under and beyond the net. The outer fringe of it had sunk deep. There was a sudden churning phosphorescence where one of them was trapped.

But the other dived and swam deeper. He came up, gasping, free of the net. He spat out water and curses and struck out for the schooner.

Sally Lavender breathed, "Lopez!"

Lucky snatched up a boathook. Lopez saw the galvanized iron end of it sweeping down on him and began to babble.

Lucky thrust the hook under the half-drowned Mexican's belt, and, "Gimme a hand, Red," he said.

Singapore laid hold of the handle, and they hauled Lopez aboard. Before Lucky could disengage himself from the clumsy handle, Lopez sprang at him. From a sheath at his hip he snatched a knife.

The redhead rushed at him as the knife went up; struck Lopez stiff-armed in the jaw. The knife rattled to the deck and rolled into a scupper. Lopez staggered back. One foot descended on the gleaming blade. The foot slipped. In a frantic effort to right himself, Lopez caught his other foot in a bight of the main sheet. In another instant his precipitate backward flight had taken up all the slack in the rope, and it brought him to a violent halt. He plunged, twisting, to the desk. There was a sharp, brief snapping sound, a yelp of agony.

The Mexican rolled over and moaned with the pain of that broken leg. Singapore looked over the side, to where the net had been. He saw nothing at first but green luminous bubbles.

Then, deep down, he saw a large formless mass like a shadow slowly, slowly sinking.

His recent strenuous demands on muscles already overtaxed had left him faint and cold and sick. The glimpse of that dark formless mass slowly sinking sent an icy chill up his spine.

He said huskily, "Come on, bozo. Let's get that anchor up. Let's get to hell out of this place."

"Okay."

Behind them, the clear, sweet voice of the girl from Shanghai said, "Both of you—stand where you are. Put your hands up."

CHAPTER XV

"COME AND GET IT!"

THE TWO ADVENTURERS slowly turned. With small feet planted apart, with automatic pistol in hand, the girl from Shanghai resembled, in her snug blue-and-white striped sweater, her mud-spattered sailor pants, a small boy playing pirate. Her expression was calm.

"Sam," she said, "I want—"

"Yeah," he interrupted. "You want the pearl."

"And I'm going to get it."

"Sure," he said. "Sure, you're gonna get it, baby. Step right up and take it."

"It's no use, Sam," she said sweetly. "I've got you on a spot. I know that pearl isn't on the island. It's handy. I want it and I'm going to have it. If I don't get it there is going to be one dead man on this ship—perhaps two. Now—just a moment. You don't have to tell me that pearl is insured with your life. I know you're stubborn enough to let yourself be killed before you'll give it up. If you don't give me the pearl I'm not going to kill you. No! I'm going to kill your pal! If either of you takes one step toward me you're both going to get it. I've got two bullets. And I'm a good shot."

Sammy, contemplating her, so innocent looking in that boyish get-up, felt cold sweat prickling out on his forehead. He heard Lopez thinly moaning.

"I know you won't sacrifice Lucky's life," she went on. "And you know I mean what I'm saying. You know I'm utterly ruthless. You know I haven't a heart. You know I'll kill him—or you:—without an instant's hesitation. I will count five. If that pearl isn't lying at my feet by then, I will kill Lucky. *One!*"

"You can stop counting," Singapore said. "You're dead wrong, sister. I ain't on a spot. It's you that's on the spot."

"Two!"

"If you kill Lucky," Sam went on, in the same steady voice, "who gets you out of here? Who sails this ship? Lopez—with that broken leg?"

"Three!"

"If you kill Lucky, it leaves you and me alone on this ship. You can't kill me with any twenty-five calibre bullet. Not unless you shoot me straight through the heart or brain. And I'll be on you like a hawk the minute you pull that trigger on Lucky!"

"Four!" But it wasn't certain. Her voice wavered.

"If you kill Lucky, two minutes from now you'll have a broken back. Three minutes from now you'll be where those Mexicans are. Give me that gun."

He walked toward her with his hand outstretched, as if he were about to shake her hand. He took the pistol. She offered not the slightest resistance. Her fingers were limp. She all but dropped the pistol into his hand.

She said wearily, "It was empty. I used the last bullets in the clip to kill those pythons. And you aren't going to hurt me." She was looking up unflinchingly, but without a trace of defiance, into his eyes. "Because I saved your life."

SINGAPORE DROPPED the pistol into his pocket and drew a long breath of relief.

"You're smart," he said slowly, in a marveling voice. "You're the smartest woman I ever met. I guess I've given you a lot of laughs. Now I'm gonna give you another laugh. When those greasers jumped us tonight, the first thing that struck me was how smart you are. I knew you were so smart that you always manage to land butter-side up. I knew you were so smart that, no matter what happened, you would wiggle out of this with a whole skin. I knew that, and I had a hunch you were gonna keep after me till you got that pearl."

Sally Lavender was looking up at his eyes steadily.

"I don't know what you're getting at," she said.

"No," he said, "you don't. That's why I'm givin' you this explanation. When we went ashore and I saw those big shadows dancin' on the cliff, I knew you had double crossed us plenty. So I ran to you and grabbed your gun out of your holster."

"Yes," she said. "Alvarado knocked it out of your hand. What are you driving at?"

He reached for her holster, tilted it up. A small dark object slid out of the holster and into his palm. It was the little chamois skin pouch. He opened it and rolled out into his hand a glittering blue bubble which seemed to absorb the cold white light of the moon and give it back in a fiery iridescence.

The girl from Shanghai stared at it. She sucked in her breath through tight lips. For a moment, Sammy believed he saw stark murder in her eyes, but perhaps he imagined that; for she was sweetly smiling.

"Sammy," she said, "you're a smarter man than I am."

"Thank you, Sally," he replied, "for takin' such good care of my luck piece. Well, Lucky," he said, "what are we gonna do with this little cobra? You've taken the beatin'. What do we do with her? It's up to you."

Lucky turned away and started forward, as if he did not intend to answer. He paused and partly turned his head.

"No," he said. "It's your job. As far as I care, she don't exist and she never did exist. I don't want to see her again, dead or alive. I don't want to hear her again."

He walked away, limping.

Sally Lavender's eyes were large as they stared up into the battered mask that was Singapore Sammy's face. She was taking little quick breaths. One hand was pressed up under her heart, as if she were trying to subdue its tumult. Her slim, small figure was rigid with terror.

She whispered, "What are you going to do with me?" Then, in a panic: "Don't look at me like that!"

He grinned at her. "Sister, you were dead right. That guy and I are a pair of soft-hearted suckers when it comes to hurtin' any woman. But, sister—how I wish you were a man!"

Sammy folded his arms on his chest and tightened his mouth.

"Sometime to-morrow," he went on, "we'll be droppin' anchor off the *kampong* at Timor Laut. That's where we say so long. Until then—stay in your cabin."

The girl walked slowly to the cabin door. Reaching it, she slowly turned and looked at him. Her lips were smiling. Her eyes sparkled with tears, as they had that morning when Sammy first saw her, as forlorn as a lost kitten, perched on a crate on the Tanjong Pagar dock.

Her mouth suddenly made a little gulping grimace. The fingers of one small white hand were still outspread against the blue and white stripes across her left breast. She looked like a little girl, a heartbroken little girl who wanted to be assured and comforted. She looked delicate and fragile and hopelessly innocent. There was something childlike about her shameless grief. It was pathetic and appealing. She sniffled.

"Sammy," she said softly. "Oh—Sammy!"

"Listen, sister," Sammy said, "if you pull any fast ones, like tryin' to sink this ship, I'm gonna wring your doggoned little neck! Get into your cabin. Scram!"

A shout from Lucky hailed him forward, The buccaneer

was on hands and knees before an opened box near the anchor winch. Other objects—machetes and piles of men's clothing were nearby.

A match flame sputtered in Lucky's hand. He was staring into the box, which was about ten inches square and of about the same depth.

The match flame was dancing.

"Red!" he yelled. "Look! Gold!"

Singapore looked, just for an instant, before the flame expired, into the boxful of glowing yellow metal. He caught the expression, in the same fleeting instant, on Lucky's face. The match went out, leaving the expression sharp and clear in Sammy's mind. It was excited and jubilant.

"Four thousand dollars' worth o' nuggets!" Lucky said enthusiastically. "And listen, bo. That cargo down there is ours, too. Say, boy, we haven't done so bad for a pair o' suckers. A thousand cash for the charter. Four thousand for the gold. Another two thousand, anyhow, for the cargo. And ten thousand more when we turn Lopez over to the cops in Singapore! That's seventeen thousand bucks, Red! We sure cleared a pretty profit on this cruise. We're set, fella! We start tradin' again!"

"We sure do," Singapore said. "S'posin' you get this anchor chain up and down while I start up the engine."

He went aft and opened the engine hatch. He didn't quite share Lucky's enthusiasm. He couldn't get the picture of Sally Lavender out of his mind, standing there in the cabin doorway, shamelessly crying like a little girl. And he didn't have his grandfather's will. He'd been outsmarted once again by old Bill Shay. But if the Kongans hadn't killed Bill Shay they'd meet again, sometime, somewhere. And it was a great relief to know that Lucky's heart was on the road to convalescence.

ISLE OF THE METEOR

In that ball of fire that skimmed the southern
seas was gold, so the story was told to
Singapore Sammy—gold from the skies

FOREWORD

SHORTLY BEFORE MIDNIGHT on the night of August 7th, 1856, a meteor entered the earth's atmosphere above the Banda Sea—approximately in 130° east longitude, 5° south latitude. This celestial body came flaming across the starry heavens like a small and terrible sun, passing high above the masts of a clipper ship, the *Jade Lady,* then en route from the Spice Islands to San Francisco.

The officer on watch, one Zachary Teakdale, reported that a ball of fire a thousand feet in diameter was traveling in a southwesterly direction at tremendous speed and at a height of perhaps a mile. Soon after it had roared past, the ship was showered with globules of hot metal. The sails were torn to shreds. Hunks of metal were buried in the deck. One chunk struck Mr. Teakdale in the left arm, above the elbow, gouging out a gobbet of flesh, and leaving a scar which he would exhibit proudly until the day of his death. Another chunk struck the man in the crow's-nest in the head and knocked him unconscious. Ira Sand, the man at the wheel, leaped under an overhang of the cabin roof in time to be spared injury.

Mr. Teakdale reported that a great swishing sound was set up as this rain of meteorites swept southwestward along the sea.

Their passage through the air from the molten parent body had cooled the pellets somewhat. It was fortunate that they were not in a molten state when they came showering down on the

175

Jade Lady, or she would no doubt have gone up in flames. But they were still too hot for naked fingers to handle.

Aroused by the uproar, the captain rushed on deck. In the midst of the confusion, some one discovered that some of the pellets had the yellow look of gold. All hands were piped on deck, and the crew was set to work bending new sails. When the *Jade Lady* was once again navigable, all hands were ordered to gather up the pellets and stow them in canvas bags made from remnants of the old sails by the sailmaker. Some of the pellets were embedded deeply in the deck. Some had drilled their way through cabin roofs. Some were even found embedded in the masts.

On reaching San Francisco, the captain dutifully turned over the stuff to his owners, who promptly had it assayed. Most of the pellets proved to be nothing more than the usual mixture of iron and copper, but there was a quantity of pellets of almost pure gold. That midnight shower on the Banda Sea netted the owners about $2,600.

It was Mr. Teakdale's belief that the meteor plunged into the Banda Sea which is, at that point, about twelve hundred feet deep. In later years, as he recounted his remarkable experience, Mr. Teakdale was wont to exaggerate a little, as sailors will—to

"One false move and you'll get a load of buckshot!"

embroider his tale. He would declare that the meteor plunged with a most venomous and terrible hissing into the sea before his very eyes, with clouds of spray and steam rising up and the great ball turning a dark and angry red just before it sank crackling beneath the surface.

"There lies the golden meteor in two hundred fathoms," Mr. Teakdale would say, with a smacking of his lips, "and there she'll lie till the crack o' doom!"

But Zachary Teakdale was wrong.

CHAPTER I
THE DYING MAN

ON A NIGHT some seventy-seven years after that momentous night on the Banda Sea—to be exact, on a night in April, in the year 1933—a red-headed young man angrily walked out of the American consulate in Saigon, French Indo-China, and angrily strode toward the waterfront. With the smoke from a cigarette spurting out tugboat style over his wide shoulders, he made his way down Rue Lagrandiere to Rue Catinat and thence to the Quai Francois Garnier off which, in the Saigon River, his schooner, the *Blue Goose,* was anchored.

A self-important American consul had been inquisitive about the kind of traffic the *Blue Goose* was engaged in, and had summarily called the redheaded owner to the carpet. The American consul had heard a rumor that the *Blue Goose* was running opium.

The schooner's owner, Samuel Larkin Shay—otherwise, Singapore Sammy—had indignantly denied this aspersion on his honor.

"Then you've been running guns," the consul said, "to the Javanese rebels."

"Horsefeathers," said Singapore Sam. "Can't a guy drop his hook in this river without—"

"You've been up to something!" the consul snapped.

Singapore Sammy looked at him with sunburned blue eyes and slowly shook his head, a comment on the stupidity of all officialdom.

"Sure!" he drawled. "I've been lookin' for my old man. I'll tell you the story, mister. Years ago my old man used to be an elephant man with Bartrom and Bradley's circus. He ran out on my mother and me when I was two years old, and he took all her savin's and a will of my grandfather's that leaves me a cold million. I can't get the million without that will. I heard in Bangkok he was up this way, so I sailed up for a look-see."

"I've been hearing that story for seven years," the consul said freezingly. "It's nothing but a smoke-screen. You're a thieving scoundrel. Maybe you can tell me why you've done time in every jail in the Far East!"

"Sure!" said the redhead. "It's a case of mistaken identity."

"You're a disgrace to your country!" the consul cried. "Don't hang around Saigon or I'll have you clapped in jail! Now clear out of here!"

It was enough to make a man's blood boil. But Singapore

Sam's blood had been kept fairly close to boiling pitch by the unsympathetic attitude of American consuls these past seven years.

HE THREW away his cigarette and drew in lungfuls of fragrance released by the surrounding jungle. It was a hot night, with a moon in the first half. Not a breath of wind was stirring. Behind a red-lac door a woman softly laughed. Down on the river, mother of waters, some one was beating out barbaric music on bamboo sticks.

Singapore Sammy was unaware of these things. Anger stopped boiling. He was suddenly as alert as a panther on the prowl.

By quickly, unexpectedly, jerking his head around he saw, from the tail of his eye, the shadow flit into the doorway of a darkened jade shop. It was a habit you learned in the Far East, that quick and unexpected head twist, if you went in for dangerous business and didn't want knives in your back.

For three days—since the day after his arrival in the French jungle capital—Singapore Sammy had been aware of this dark and furtive pursuer. Another twist of the head informed him that the shadow had left the jade shop doorway and was darting down Rue Vannier to Bond Point, no doubt with the intention of waylaying him among the dark warehouses on the quai.

Singapore Sammy made sure that the flap on his hip pocket was unbuttoned and went briskly on his way.

It was dark among the warehouses. The full moon fingered out interesting possibilities. Among bales and crates, whole armies of assassins might readily lurk!

Warily he approached the dock off which lay his two-masted schooner, slim and staunch and beautiful, a dream-ship in the flood of moonlight.

A patch of inky blackness between crates of ancient pottery from the great wat at Angkor gave forth a faint whisper.

"*Birahi*—master!"

Singapore Sammy stopped. Automatically his left hand went

to the copper wire encircling his neck, while the right dropped to his hip pocket. He turned and took a quick step toward the whisper. The shadow, he assumed, was about to give up its secret.

But at that instant a native policeman emerged from the doorway of the adjoining warehouse and flashed on an electric pocket light. Without a word to Sammy he ran down the aisle formed by the stacks of crates and bales, and Sammy saw a thin, small man in black with the frizzled black hair of a Malay dart from a hiding place and vanish inland.

The white man waited, but neither the shadow nor the policeman returned. Both had seemingly been swallowed by the night.

Baffled and intrigued, Singapore Sammy waited a little longer, then went to the edge of the dock and down a ladder to a platform. A sampan was tied up there, with its coolie curled up asleep in the stern.

Sammy cast off the line, woke up the coolie, settled down in the stern, and was presently being transported across the swirling muddy water to his schooner.

The *Blue Goose* wasn't, properly, his schooner. He owned only a half interest in her, his partner, Lucifer—Lucky—Jones, a buccaneering, black-haired young fellow, owning the other half. Lucky Jones was at this moment off on a gold-hunting trip on the island of Sumatra, an adventure which Singapore Sammy had chosen not to join.

Astern of the *Blue Goose*, perhaps two hundred yards, another schooner lay at anchor; a black and ugly hulk with stumpy masts and dirty upper-work; an island trader. She had nosed up the river on a making tide and dropped anchor astern of the *Blue Goose* an hour before sunset. Other than her riding light, there was only one glimpse of illumination aboard—an oblong of orange at a window, aft.

SINGAPORE PAID off the sampan boy, boarded his schooner and, stopping at the rail near the stern, scrutinized the palm-fringed shoreline. Gilded temple spires gleamed under the moon. He was very curious about that Malay. An outrigger canoe with a brown man at the sweep drifted past on the current. Then, suddenly, Sammy heard the creaking of oarlocks.

Some distance astern a pair of dripping oars was making whirls of quicksilver in the lane of moonlight that stretched from the black schooner to the *Blue Goose*. A man in a dinghy was making his way up this moonlit lane.

The dinghy came up under the stern of the *Blue Goose* and a wizened old Chinese face was turned up to Sammy.

A respectful voice whispered, "Can catchum that Masta Sammy Shay?"

"I'm Sam Shay."

"Hi-yah! That Cappum Cobbledick wanchee catchum chin-chin alongside you that side—chop-chop!" All of which meant that Captain Cobbledick wanted to have a talk with Sammy aboard the black schooner at once.

To which Sammy replied with quick interest, "Captain Ralph Cobbledick?"

"Yes, masta."

"Is that the Island Queen?"

"Yes, masta."

"What thing your master wanchee?"

"Cappum Cobbledick velly sick. Plitty soon b'long dead. You come along that side?"

"Not so fast! What thing Captain Cobbledick hab got?"

"No savvy, masta. Velly quick b'long dead. Plenty bhobbery this side." The ancient Chinese placed one hand over his heart. "Docta man come. Docta man look-see. Docta man talkee plitty quick dead. You come along?"

"Can do," Sammy answered. "Stand by." He was puzzled and suspicious. He had never met Captain Ralph Cobbledick, but he was familiar with the Cobbledick reputation, which was written mostly in blood in the annals of the South Seas. Captain Cobbledick was a trader; an old rogue. He was a man who would trade your eye teeth out of your mouth if you didn't look sharp.

He had engaged in every variety of nefarious trade known to these cynical seas. He was a sea-going fox, a pirate, a two-fisted drinker, and a man very handy with a gun.

Before visiting Captain Cobbledick, Sammy wanted to be, to a certain degree, prepared. He went below, entered his cabin and removed from around his neck the copper wire. A great many people had attempted, in one way and another, to get possession of the small chamois-skin sack which dangled at the end of the wire, and Sammy did not trust Captain Cobbledick.

He lifted a corner of the mattress in his bunk and inserted the wire and the sack in a little slit there. Then, patting the automatic pistol on his hip, he returned to the deck and climbed into the stern seat of the dinghy.

He wondered, as he boarded the Island Queen, what variety of ax Captain Cobbledick was planning to grind. Anticipating a trap, he went warily.

The hull, the deck, the masts and the rigging of the schooner all showed evidence of scandalous neglect. Sammy, who took a seaman's proper pride in keeping the *Blue Goose* shipshape, was oppressed by these indications of a good little ship so mistreated.

HE DESCENDED a steep stairway into a dining room lighted by an oil lamp in gimbals which found greasy gleams in plates, knives and forks, empty bottles and glasses on the untidy table. The bottle had contained trade gin—the rotgut of the islands.

"This way," a voice boomed.

Sammy tracked down the voice. In quarters adjoining he found, in a large untidy bunk, propped up on many pillows in a welter of bedclothes, this old rascal of whom he had heard such hair-raising stories.

Captain Cobbledick was reputed to be seventy-five years old. He looked a hundred. An enormous old man, his body, under the dirty cotton sheet, was a mountain range. His face was a mango moon, capped with snow. Beside him on a chair sat a drinking glass and a half-full bottle of *gin-bijt*.

A glance at the old fellow's eyes and lips was sufficient. But even the glance was unnecessary. The room was rank with the death smell. It lay in the air like a heavy, intangible mist.

But the old trader did not seem in the least depressed. His eyes were somewhat bleary, but at sight of his visitor they lighted up and he grinned.

"So you're the guy they call Singapore Sam," he said, jeeringly. "The guy with hair like a bonfire and eyebrows that crawl around his forehead like red mice when he gets mad!"

"I never take a good look at my eyebrows when I get mad," Sammy said.

Captain Cobbledick held out a shaking, horribly swollen white hand, as cold, as moist, as lifeless as fresh clay, and shook Sammy's.

"Set down," he bellowed. "Have a drink. Is it true you've been lookin' all over the Far East for seven years, tryin' to find your old man?"

"Yeah, it's true."

"And the only clews you got is that he's nuts about pigs and nuts about pearls?"

"That's right," Sammy answered.

"And is it true you carry a big blue pearl on a copper wire you wear around your neck?"

"Sometimes," Singapore said, and his eyes became more alert.

"Is it true," Captain Cobbledick asked, "that the Maharaja of Malobar put up that pearl as a prize for a fist-fight between you and a slugger named Burke, and you knocked out Burke and got the pearl?"

"Yeah. That's how I got it."

Captain Cobbledick pushed himself up on his elbows. His sunken eyes stared glassily at Sammy. "You're the lad I'm lookin' for, Singapore. Shut that door and shoot the bolt."

When Sammy had complied, the old trader said, "A doctor was just aboard, and he said there's no hope. Any time now, I'm apt to start for that place they don't sell round trip tickets for. I've got a responsibility. I've heard plenty about you. I know you're a square shooter. So I'm goin' to trust you. And I'm goin' to give you a chance to make a fortune—I'm goin' to hand it to you on a silver platter for doin' me a little favor!"

CHAPTER II

A STRANGE TALE

THE DYING MAN'S eyes, luminous with moisture, studied Singapore Sammy's weatherbeaten young face. Captain Cobbledick reached for the trade-gin bottle, spilled a three-inch drink into the glass and lifted it to his mouth. He swallowed the awful stuff in one gulp. He made grunting and gurgling sounds.

"You're smart," he said. "You're a smart lad. But you don't know anything. If I hadn't spent every dollar I earned as fast as I made it, on liquor, cards and women, I'd be the smartest man in the Far East. You know what my business is?"

Sammy nodded. "Sure. You're a trader."

"You bet I'm a trader. And I'm the smartest trader that ever hit these islands! There's one island alone that makes me a fortune every year. And I'll bet you never heard of it! Simarong Island. Ever hear of it?"

"No."

"No! And there isn't another man in the Far East who's ever heard of it! And I make a fortune out of it every year!"

Captain Cobbledick's eyes became crafty. His air was confidential. "Do you know the Jalap Archipelago?"

"It lies somewhere east of Celebes."

"It lies where the Banda Sea joins the Arafura Sea. You thought they were uninhabited islands. You thought there wasn't anything there but rocks, sea gulls and jungle. That's what everybody thinks."

Captain Cobbledick was grinning. "And the natives say

they're haunted. Did you ever try to make a native go ashore on any of those islands? Now, listen close, Singapore. Simarong Island is the center island of the group. And every six months I carry a cargo of supplies to Simarong. Nobody but me in the whole wide world knows that Simarong is inhabited. Nobody but my crew—and they know better than to open their mouths! There's a colony of white people there, Americans, who went to Simarong durin' the World War. Since then not a man, woman or child has left that island—or set foot on it and lived to tell about it! Except me! I am the only man in the world who knows that colony is in existence!"

The dying man paused again to stare at Singapore Sammy. His eyes were steady and shrewd.

"Don't think I'm havin' the katzenjammers," he said. "Don't think I'm out o' my head with the fever. I'm lettin' you in on a secret that's goin' to make your fortune—if you play it smart. Shall I shoot the works?"

The redhead nodded. "Shoot."

"This colony, when they went there," Captain Cobbledick went on, "totaled upwards of three hundred men, women and children. They've died off and been killed until now there's less than a hundred. But let me begin at the beginning. One night, durin' the war, a feller named Alexander Zorin came out to my anchorage in Singapore in a sampan. Said he wanted to make me a proposition. Said he had to trust somebody up to the hilt, and he heard I was a close-mouthed man.

"Here was his proposition—and when I tell you this, Singapore, I break a vow of silence I've kept sacred for sixteen years. Zorin had an old chart showin' where Simarong is, and he wanted me to take him and his crowd there. Said he'd heard it was a deserted island, and that's just what he wanted. It seems that Zorin and his bunch were all opposed to war and to everything else in civilization. They wanted to start a new civilization. If I would take him and his bunch to Simarong, he would pay well—and give me the exclusive tradin' concession to the island.

"I took him up. And I took him and his crowd down there— includin' a handful of Malays to do the field work—and they started their new civilization. If you ask me, it's a crazy idea. Somethin' like communism. Everybody free and equal. No bosses. No government at all. Just a big happy family!"

SINGAPORE INTERRUPTED. "How do the Malays fit in?"

"They're slaves. You see, Zorin's idea is that, while white people should be free and equal, they should rule the world. Every other race should be slaves to the white race. And, as I was sayin', they wanted to stay untainted by the old, outworn civilization, so in all these years not one scrap o' news has gone into Simarong. No newspapers. No magazines. No books.

"As far as they know, the war may still be on. They never heard of the depression. They don't know who's livin' or who's dead in the outside world. When I drop anchor off Simarong, in the little cove there, twice a year, they set a guard to watch me. No one's allowed to ask me a question. I see a curious look in your eyes, Singapore. What is it?"

"What," the red-headed young man wanted to know, "do they use for money?"

Captain Cobbledick chuckled. "Gold—pure bar gold! They dig it out of the ground and smelt it down. They've got a fine battery of smelters there. For years I've been bringin' them the most up-to-date minin' and smeltin' machinery. You see, there were a few things Zorin didn't tell me. He didn't tell me, for instance, that this old map was a treasure chart. Even if he had, I'd have laughed in his face. I've heard too many treasure stories in my time. But that chart was on the level. The gold was there. Copper, too. Copper, silver and nickel. Twice a year I go to Simarong with machinery and supplies and get my pay in pure bar gold."

The dying man looked furtively about him, as if the Island Queen were swarming with eavesdroppers.

"At war prices!" he whispered. "Everything! Machinery, oil, food, clothing—all supplies! That's the trick, Singapore. Prices have gone down and up since the war days, but they've never touched war prices. So, at the bottom of the depression, I'm chargin' that crowd twice, three times what the stuff is worth. Why not? I'm a smart trader. They don't want news, so they don't get news."

Singapore Sammy was staring at him with fascination. It was a fantastic story, but he believed that Captain Cobbledick, for once in his life, was telling the truth.

"How," he asked, "about their exports?"

"They don't export anything!" the old man cried. "They're stackin' up a fortune in copper, silver, nickel and gold. Storin' it in their treasure house! The only metal that leaves the island is the bar gold they pay me for the things I take them."

"What are they goin' to do with the rest of it?" Singapore asked.

"I don't ask questions. I let well enough alone. At the prices I charge them I'd be the richest man in the Far East to-day, if only I'd kept away from women and whisky, cards and dice. Look at me! Dead broke and three-quarters dead! Look at the shape this ship is in! A derelict! I was headin' south from Hongkong, where I got this cargo together. My heart went bad and I ducked in here for a doctor. He says I'm done."

THE OLD man stopped again. He poured himself another stiff drink and tossed it down.

"I'm due at Simarong in about two weeks," he went on. "Under my hatch covers I've got the usual six months' supplies— machinery, tools, food, clothing and knick-knacks. The total cost to me was under thirty thousand, American gold. The price of this cargo C.I.F. Simarong is ninety thousand! Do you get it, Singapore? A clear, clean profit of better than sixty thousand bucks! Sixty thousand bucks profit out of that island—twice a year! Add sixty thousand and sixty thousand together, and you get my average yearly income—and what yours will be if you play the game my way! Now, here's my proposition:

"Warp your schooner alongside and transfer this cargo. When

you've collected your gold from Zorin, keep ten thousand of it for your trouble and hold the balance for my granddaughter in New Zealand. I'm seventy-six years old, and I've never drawn a decent, honest breath in my life. I'm no good. I never was any good. You think you're tough, but I've forgotten more ways of goin' to hell than you'll ever learn.

"But that girl mustn't suffer for it. She's a fine, sweet little girl. Guys like you and me, Singapore, have got to protect the weak and innocent when we get the chance. I want this girl protected against the kind of hell a girl runs into when she's broke. I want you to take that eighty thousand and put it into a trust fund, so she can't touch the principal. But as long as she lives she'll have a good, comfortable income.

"You see, I'm bettin' on you, Singapore. This eighty thousand is all I've got in the world to bequeath to her, and I can't bequeath her that without your help. I'm a dying man, Singapore. And I'm askin' you to do this not for me—for this kid here. Look."

A stubby swollen forefinger was indicating a faded snapshot thumbtacked to the wood panel above the bunk. It showed a girl of about twelve—a sweet-faced, smiling girl with curly dark hair.

"That's her," said Captain Cobbledick. "I ask you, a man can't kick off and leave a granddaughter as sweet as that to shift for herself, now can he? Will you do it, Singapore?"

Singapore took out a cigarette, snapped a match against his thumb nail and smoked. If it had been any other man in the world but Captain Cobbledick, he mightn't have been so suspicious. But he had been too long in the Far East, and he had heard too many authentic accounts of Captain Cobbledick's trickery. And a man with Ralph Cobbledick's past might be planning mischief on his very deathbed.

"What," Singapore asked, "becomes of this schooner?"

"The American consul here will slap an attachment on her in the mornin' to satisfy a Hongkong ship chandler's judgment. I cleared out of Hongkong one jump ahead of an injunction.

If this cargo ain't shifted to the *Blue Goose* by mornin' it'll be grabbed, too."

Still cautious, Sammy asked, "Any guns, ammunition, opium or other contraband in this consignment?"

"Nope! Go ahead and open every crate, case and bale!"

The redhead arose. "Okay," he said. "I'll do it—but I won't take the commission. I'll lay down this cargo in Simarong. I'll take the gold bar to Singapore, sell it and put the proceeds into a trust fund, in your granddaughter's name. What's her name and address?"

"Alice Cobbledick, Sacred Heart Convent, Auckland, New Zealand. Singapore, you're a white man."

The old trader reached for the bottle and the glass.

CHAPTER III

"WELCOME TO SIMARONG!"

SINGAPORE SAMMY RETURNED to the *Blue Goose* and aroused his *serang*.

"We're going alongside the Island Queen," he said, "and transfer her cargo. Pay out anchor chain and drift alongside. Let me know when you're tied up."

Singapore went below to consult charts of the wild and little known section of the East Indies where the Banda and Arafura Seas join. He found the Jalap Archipelago, but none of its member islands were named on even his largest charts.

He was comparing charts when he heard, in a lull in the rumbling of the anchor chain, a faint splashing alongside, then a gasp and a grunt. Following this was a swishing sound, then the patter of water dripping on deck, and more heavy breathing. The renewed rumbling of the anchor chain blotted out these alien sounds.

It was reasonably obvious that some one had swum up to the *Blue Goose* and come aboard; was now on deck. A visitor!

Cautiously, Singapore slipped up the stairway to the deck. On the starboard side, almost amidships, he was sure he saw a darker shadow in the lee of a cabin. The rumbling of the anchor chain continued. The *Blue Goose* was now not more than fifty feet ahead of the Island Queen.

The shadow moved. Sammy leaped. His arms enfolded a skinny man, naked to the waist. His skin was cold and wet. The stranger backed away, tried to wriggle free, but caught his heel in an eyebolt set in the deck.

The visitor went crashing to the deck with Singapore straddling him. The face of the man underneath was now well lighted by the moon. It was a thin dark face topped by frizzly black hair. A Malay. It was, Singapore was certain, the Malay who had whispered to him on the quai.

The breath was now knocked out of him. Liquid dark eyes implored for mercy. Then a gasping whisper came, "*Birahi*—master! I mean no harm."

He was so thin that his ribs under his brown skin made ridges and hollows. He was hardly more than the skeleton of a man.

Singapore removed his weight and the Malay sat up.

In Malay, the white man said sternly, "What are you doing on this ship? Why have you been following me around for the past three days? Who the hell are you?"

"My name is Sidin, *birahi*. I have followed you, not three days, but four months."

Still breathless, the Malay stopped to gasp. He went on: "Please do not kill me, master. For four months I have tried to find you. Always, when I reached the place where they said you were, you were gone on. I have followed you from Hai-Phong to Pemmangil, from Pemmangil to Borneo, from Borneo to Belawan Deli, from Belawan Deli to Singapore, from Singapore to Bangkok, and from Bangkok to Saigon. Always, you left just before I arrived. Look at me, *birahi*—a thing of skin and bones. Have mercy! Do not kill me!"

Singapore growled, "Get up off that deck. Why are you following me?"

"I have a most important message from my master, the Sultan Proknam Lat Chou Chuggore. He wishes to buy a precious gem that you possess. A pearl. A blue pearl."

Sammy said grimly, "I have never heard of Sultan Proknam Lat Chou Chuggore. Where is his sultanate?"

"It is the island of Simarong, in the Jalap Archipelago, *birahi*."

SAMMY'S FACE looked very thoughtful. The *Blue Goose*, slipping imperceptibly downriver, was now almost abreast of the Island Queen. Out of the softness of his heart, he had, only a few minutes ago, agreed to take a mixed cargo to the island of Simarong, in the Jalap Archipelago, to a colony of civilization-hating white men.

He stared for a long time into Sidin's luminous dark eyes.

"My master, the sultan," Sidin went on, "has heard that you possess this rare pearl. In his possession is the duplicate of this pearl. He wishes to buy yours. He entreats you to come swiftly to Simarong and negotiate with him. He will pay you richly. Even if you do not wish to sell your pearl, he entreats you to come to Simarong, so that he may see these two brilliant pearls side by side."

"You are a *pamboung*," Singapore said.

"*Birahi*, by the sacred forehead of Buddha, I am talking true. It is my master's devout wish and hope—"

"You want me to sail my ship down there. Is that the idea?"

"Yes, master," A sly look came into Sidin's brown eyes. "It is my hope, *birahi*, that I may receive a little *cumshaw* from you if this transaction is successful. Will you go?"

"Sure, I'll go!"

"You are not making a joke, *birahi*?"

"Not me. This is not my night for joking. We will go to Simarong. We will either steal the sultan's pearl, or we will sell him mine. Is that your idea?"

"Master, you have pierced my poor mind as sunlight pierces the pool of clear water in the forest. I am your slave."

"Okay," Sammy said. "We will go to Simarong and you will help me steal the sultan's pearl."

"*Birahi!*" the Malay boy wailed. "You do not believe me!"

"Sure, I believe you. Senga!"

His *serang* answered, and came trotting—a middle-aged, gray-haired Malay.

"Yes, master?"

"Get a rope over to that ship. Ahoy, there!"

The old Chinese, evidently the sole remaining member of the Island Queen's crew, popped out of a hatch.

Sammy said to Sidin: "Do you know the captain of this schooner—Captain Cobbledick?"

He saw momentary amazement in the Malay's face, then came the tremulous answer, "No, *birahi*."

"Catchum this line," Sammy said to the Chinese. "We're coming aboard for a chin-chin with the captain." It was his plan to place Sidin and Captain Cobbledick together and let them compare stories.

"Allatime too late," said the old Chinese. "Cappum b'long dead."

"When did it happen?"

"You go. Fi' minute go. Then velly quick—cappum go angel side. *Maskee!*"

"That's tough. Make this line fast, Senga. Sidin is goin' to help us move that cargo. Hey! Where the hell is he?"

The mysterious Malay was no longer standing near by. Where he had stood was a small puddle of river water. A trail of wet footprints led forward, and out onto the bowsprit. It was evident that Sidin had taken advantage of his first opportunity to slip away, was even now in the river, swimming.

But the mystery of him remained. After a brief survey of the Island Queen's cargo, Singapore was convinced that Sidin was a liar, that Captain Cobbledick had died virtually with the truth on his lips.

Then who had coached Sidin to attempt to lure him to Simarong? Certainly it was some one who knew him, his habits, his weaknesses, fairly well. Some one knew him well enough to realize that the threat of danger in the adventure would add to his eagerness to meet a sultan who owned the mate to the Malobar pearl!

The question was tantalizing. In light of Captain Cobbledick's account of the island, no one living there could possibly know of the existence of the blue fire pearl—or of Sammy, either; for no one was permitted to land on the island or to leave it.

Sidin had, perhaps, been a slave on Simarong—one of the field workers. But what had his scheme been—and who had inspired it?

THE WORK of transferring the cargo was begun at once. Bales, crates and boxes came out of the hold and were stowed aboard the *Blue Goose*. Each box, each crate, each bale was carefully inspected by Sammy before it went into his holds. He was determined to leave no stone unturned. The more dubious boxes he opened. He had run contraband himself and he knew the tricks.

But every item of that cargo was innocent; every item bore out Captain Cobbledick's assertions. Mining machinery and tools. Electric light bulbs and equipment. Drums of oil and gasoline. Clothing, food, innocent odds and ends. No guns. No ammunition, except a case of shotgun shells. No opium. No contraband of any description.

But who was behind the Malay's fantastic invitation? It was an unsolved riddle. On the voyage down the China Sea, through the straits, across the Java Sea and the Banda Sea, Sammy gave the riddle his attention, but it remained, when he cast anchor at last in the little cove on the northern side of Simarong Island, a riddle.

They made the landfall early in the afternoon. It was midnight when the *Blue Goose* anchored. The waning moon showed Sammy the through a narrow but deep little inlet, past sand spits into a cove that was almost a perfect saucer. Nipa palms grew thickly along the shore. Beyond was a narrow coastal plain, thick with palms. Where the plain ended, rolling hills began. Beyond them were mountains, black against the deep velvet blue of the night sky.

Skirting the northern shoreline, with binoculars to his eyes most of the way, he had searched for and failed to find any sign of human habitation.

He was on deck in the morning in time to see the sun rise. With the sun a mild offshore breeze sprang up. It carried on its breath the fragrance of pepper trees and jungle blossoms, and it also carried the faint but decisive tang of smoke—*coal* smoke. He could not see the smoke, but he could smell it.

Singapore Sammy had breakfast and waited. The tropical sun rose higher. He watched the shore. The dawn breeze subsided. The heat increased. The sun struck hot glints from almost motionless water.

And Simarong Island lay inert, apparently lifeless, in the sun. By noon he grew impatient. Certainly the queer colony on this island—the civilization haters—must keep lookouts posted. If Captain Cobbledick's story was true, the *Blue Goose* had doubtless been under close scrutiny since the previous afternoon.

He presently realized that there was a definite reason behind this appearance of lifelessness. The denizens of Simarong were accustomed to the semi-annual visits of the Island Queen. Naturally they would look upon any strange vessel with suspicion.

He would go ashore at once, explain himself, deliver his cargo, and collect the money—$90,000 in gold bars!

HE SLIPPED his automatic pistol into his hip pocket and rowed ashore in the dinghy. Hauling the little boat up onto the beach beyond reach of the incoming tide, he struck inland. Not more than twenty yards from the beach he came upon a faint path. He followed this through a grove of gnarled beefwood trees and on toward a box canyon a half mile away.

The path was little used, but it certainly had been made by human feet.

He was about to enter the box canyon when two men stepped suddenly into view from bushes bordering the path ahead. White men. Both were young, in their early twenties. Both were dressed alike—khaki sun helmets, blue denim work shirts, khaki shorts. They wore no footgear.

One was unarmed. The other carried a double-barreled shotgun, hugging it against his side by his elbow. His fingers were on the triggers. He did not point the gun at Singapore, but he had the air of a man who might with little provocation.

Grim looking young men, these were. And even before they spoke, Singapore was aware of tension in their faces, their very manner—a nervous tension as of great irritability.

The man with the gun said, in a voice and with an air of belligerency, "Where the hell do you think you're going?"

Singapore, believing he understood their antagonism, set about explaining himself.

"I'm lookin' for a man named Alexander Zorin. He—"

"Who," the man with the shotgun interrupted, "told you you could find him here?"

"Captain Cobbledick. He died in Saigon a couple of weeks ago. Before he died he asked me to transfer his consignment for you to my schooner, deliver it to Alexander Zorin, and collect the money."

The unarmed man said in a throaty voice, "Expect us to believe that cock-and-bull story?"

Singapore's smile vanished. "Not if it's against your religion, brother," he answered. "Suppose we can this argument and go look up the big shot."

"Wait a minute," Shotgun said. "Search him for weapons, Mike."

Mike searched him, relieved him of the automatic pistol and said in that tense, throaty voice, "Walk!"

"Ahead of us," Shotgun said. "One false move and you'll get a load of buckshot in the back."

"What you mean," Singapore said dryly, "is, welcome to Simarong! Okay, boys."

CHAPTER IV

TREASURE HOUSE

SINGAPORE STARTED DOWN the path, with the two hostile young men following. Nothing more was said. Singapore was not worried; was not even concerned. These were understrappers. He would make himself clear to the big shot. He would deliver his cargo, collect his money, and blow.

He was, indeed, glad of this opportunity to see something of the island—perhaps to see something of the way this queer outfit lived. He was very curious to inspect, at close hand, this tribe of white Americans who had given up civilization to found one of their own. He was most anxious to see what kind of civilization it was.

And—somewhere in this colony lay the answer to the riddle of the Malay who had told him of the Sultan of Simarong and the mate to the blue fire pearl!

The box canyon narrowed and came to a dead end. Off to the left, up a sheer rock wall, the trail zig-zagged. In some places it was necessary to use hands and feet.

Singapore climbed. After fifteen minutes of strenuous climbing he reached a cut which marked the innermost crevice of the canyon's end. A pair of hot blue eyes was regarding him along the barrel of a machine gun.

"Halt!"

"Advance, friend," Singapore said amiably, "and give the countersign."

The hot blue eyes narrowed. Thin red lips tightened. For a moment Singapore believed that the sentry was going to press the trigger.

Then one of the men behind him called, "Let him pass, Jake."

Singapore looked beyond the sentry. The hill fell sharply away into a rounded valley about half a mile across. In the distance he saw a village of nipa-roofed shacks. Beyond them were two thin iron smokestacks, from one of which pale green vapor climbed in a long stem into the motionless heat of the equatorial noon.

It was a perfect hiding place for a village on this supposedly uninhabited island. And he saw that this eminence on which he stood commanded a view of the sea in all directions. Far below him, in the saucer-shaped cove, the *Blue Goose* lay like a miniature model of a schooner.

"Keep walking," the throaty man said.

Singapore walked past the sentry and started down the grade. Across the valley a cataract of water, a bridal veil falls, splashed down the red hillside into a pool. From this pool it ran through irrigation ditches into green fields. These were to the left of the village. Singapore saw men working in the fields; saw clusters of men in the streets of the village. He saw no women.

Beyond the hundred-odd nipa-thatched cottages, or bungalows, were more pretentious buildings, of stone and sheet iron. From these the two iron smokestacks arose. These were, presumably, the smelters. Beyond this cluster of buildings was another building which stood alone—a building of stone with a row of barred windows. It looked like a jail. And perhaps a quarter mile beyond, this was a great circular depression in the dark red earth. It might have been the crater of an extinct volcano. And was probably the source of their gold. An open pit mine.

Beyond this crater the valley came abruptly to an end. It was, Singapore thought, an interesting layout. Here a colony of men had come and founded a brand-new civilization; had built their houses, made their fields, created their industries.

It was interesting, and, in a way, amazing. It was amazing that this colony had carried on their experiment for sixteen years without having had a stranger, a man from the outside world, intrude on them. He was reasonably certain that—if Captain Cobbledick hadn't been lying—he was the first man from the outside world to step foot inside this forbidden valley. Captain Cobbledick had not been admitted here, or he would have mentioned it.

Singapore was close to the village now, looking about him with the liveliest curiosity. And he saw now that many of the people he had believed to be men were actually women, for men and women were dressed identically—sun helmets, shirts, and khaki shorts. No shoes or stockings.

Women and children were gathered in small knots along the street and in the doorways as he passed. They stared at him as if he were, indeed, a creature from some strange world. Two girls of seventeen stepped out of his way and stared with avid curiosity. He was presumably the first strange man these girls had seen in all their lives.

And it suddenly occurred to him that, having been shut off from the world and from all news of the world, these people, if they should return to civilization, would be so many Rip Van Winkles.

HE RETURNED their stares with a curiosity no less bold. He had decided, at first glance, that they were homely girls. But he revised that estimate. They would have been beautiful if their faces hadn't been so dull, so sullen. Their interest in him was, it appeared, a resentful sort of interest; it did not dismiss the dullness from their eyes, or the set, sullen look about their mouths. No lipstick, no rouge or powder here! These girls had never heard of a talking picture, or listened to a radio!

Here, it was obvious, were young women bitterly resentful. Of what? Their frustrated lives? Their fate? And about them, too, in their very movements, he detected once again that strange tension. It seemed to affect every one here. As he passed the two girls and looked about him at other men and women, he continued to sense it—a tension as if nerves were at the cracking point.

He realized that he was on the fringe of a human volcano. And he wondered if this was the result of sixteen years of isolation, or whether it sprang from some recent irritation.

He had reached the end of the village. Beyond were the smelters, side by side; a small one and a large one. Once, at a low ebb in his fortunes, Singapore had worked in an Australian copper smelter. The larger of these two furnaces was, he guessed, for reducing copper; the smaller, a "muffle" for melting gold. Behind the furnaces were coke ovens, a small mill for concentrating the copper, and a battery of cyanide tanks for extracting gold. A complete milling, cyaniding and smelting plant!

The two furnaces, built solidly side by side, faced a compound or enclosure, about two hundred feet square. Across from the furnaces was a windowless stone building with a copper slab for a door. The third side of the enclosure consisted of a high stone wall which ran from the farther end of the windowless stone structure to the farther end of the copper furnace. The fourth and nearest side of the enclosure consisted of a high fence of thick copper bars with a wide gate, now open, at which a red-haired man stood.

Within the enclosure, Singapore saw great mounds of copper ingots beside the machine in which they were cast. Tons of copper ingots! But he saw no gold.

The guardian of the gate was a red-haired blue-eyed man of perhaps thirty-five—a stocky, freckled man, with carrot-colored fur on his massive arms. He was the first individual Singapore had so far seen who had not glared at him. His eyes were intensely curious, but amiable. A faint grin even appeared at his hard thin mouth. He and Singapore Sammy might almost have been brothers.

Singapore passed inside the compound. Through peep-holes

in iron aprons over the front of the large furnaces he caught the iridescent gleam and shimmer of white-hot copper. The smaller furnace was cold.

The copper door of the small stone building opened. A man stood in the doorway, staring out. Sunlight, falling past him, burst into a soft yellow glare. Gold! Stacks of pure ingot gold!

Singapore caught only a glimpse of it before the man closed the copper door. But that glimpse set his heart to thumping. That stack he had seen was at least four feet in height by five in width. Gold stacked up in bars like cordwood!

Then the man closed the door and came toward him. Singapore did not have to inquire who this man was. He knew that the man who had come out of that house of gold was Alexander Zorin. Upon him was the unmistakable mark of leadership.

CHAPTER V

PRISON

ALTHOUGH HE WAS dressed as were all the others—khaki shorts, a blue work shirt, soiled and battered khaki *sala* topee— he was one of the most striking men Sammy had ever seen. At least six feet four inches in height, with tremendous shoulders and mighty arms, there was about him an air of relentless strength and power.

His face, in spite of the furnacelike tropical sun to which it had been exposed so many years, was dead white. His thin, leathery lips were brownish in color—masterful in expression. His eyes, it suddenly occurred to Singapore, were as fiery, as inscrutable as the Malobar pearl. But they were not blue. They were a deep, glowing black. And it struck Singapore with some force that these eyes were not quite rational. In them, however, was no dullness, no resentment, no evidence of the crackling nervous strain Singapore had seen elsewhere. They were the gleaming, rather terrible eyes of the fanatic.

Singapore's heart beat dully as his own eyes encountered them. He had seen such eyes before. He had seen them in religious fanatics. And he knew there was no reasoning with any man who had such eyes.

In a deep, clanging voice, this man said, "Who are you? What are you doing on this island?"

"I am looking for a man named Alexander Zorin," Singapore answered steadily. His heart was pumping more rapidly. Here was red danger. He must think fast, talk with care, and not let this man see that he was afraid of him.

Thin-lipped, the man with fanatic eyes said, "I am Alexander Zorin."

"That's fine," Singapore said airily. "You're the man I'm lookin' for. I'm here in place of Captain Cobbledick. Captain Cobbledick died two weeks ago in Saigon. A few minutes before he died he sent for me and asked me to transfer his cargo from the Island Queen to my schooner, the *Blue Goose,* and deliver it here to you. I've done just that. Your consignment is aboard my schooner, lyin' out there. I've been anchored since midnight, waitin' for somebody to come out and claim it. We can begin unloadin' any time you say. The sooner the better."

Toward the end, Singapore was talking, not with care, but with speed. His words were having no more apparent effect on Alexander Zorin than have machine gun bullets on an armored cruiser. The gleaming black eyes stared intently into his, without expression, without wavering. So hard, so inscrutable was this stare that Singapore felt himself flushing, as if he were lying, as if this man penetrated through his lies to an amazing, terrible truth.

"You are lying," said Alexander Zorin.

"You don't have to believe me," Singapore said. "Come aboard my schooner and you'll find your stuff. Let's go."

Alexander Zorin had not once blinked his eyes. They were as steady as the glass eyes of a stuffed panther.

"You say that Captain Cobbledick died two weeks ago in Saigon. Who killed him?"

"He died," Singapore said, "tryin' to drink all the trade gin in the East Indies. His heart went out like a light. He knew he was goin' to cash in. He told me about this place, asked me to deliver the cargo, and died inside of an hour."

ALEXANDER ZORIN clamped his lips still tighter. After a moment, he said in his harsh, deep voice, "That's your story. How do I know you are telling the truth? How do I know you did not murder Captain Cobbledick and rob him of his cargo? How do I know that you are not a pirate?"

"The easiest way to check up on me," Singapore said, "is to check over the cargo. If I was lyin', if I had pirated the Island Queen, why should I bother bringin' the cargo here? How would I even know you were here? It's a secret, isn't it? I am carryin' out the last wishes of a dyin' man."

Zorin snapped, "Does the name Sidin sound familiar to you?"

Sammy started, and stared at Zorin. He had forgotten the Malay boy who had trailed him to Saigon.

"Sidin—" he began.

Zorin's black eyes were flaming.

"Yes, Sidin!" he boomed. "I see the name is known to you. Sidin is a Malay boy who escaped from this island several months ago. And it was from him you heard of us—and of Captain Cobbledick. So you murdered the captain and stole his cargo!"

It was perhaps unfortunate that, at this point, Singapore's red hair began to do the talking. Red-haired, Irish-eyed, he could not remain diplomatic for very long in the face of such rank injustice.

"You rat-eyed punk," he said, "I came down here to do you and a dyin' man a favor. What would happen to you, you saw-toothed baboon, if I hadn't done it? What would happen to this colony of nuts if I'd refused to come?"

Zorin said: "Take this man to jail! We will have a meeting of The Ten later, to decide what is to be done with him."

Singapore spun about. He would have begun using his fists, but a glance at the circle of tense faces with their resentful eyes was enough to check this primitive impulse.

He let his arms relax at his sides. "Okay," he said. He might just as well be philosophical about it. This jail was one of the few in the Far East in which he had not spent some time, and he might as well get acquainted with it; learn how to break out of it as soon as possible. But he was, in spite of this philosophy, alarmed. He was on a tough spot. He had never been on a tougher spot. Fanatics like Zorin killed men for less reason than this.

His two original captors took him to the jail. It was the stone building near the crater—the building with the row of barred windows.

There was a jailer seated on a small porch at the entrance—a typical jailer: a black-haired, pig-eyed, lantern-jawed man, who glared at Singapore with something more than the typical resentment.

The young man with the shotgun said, "Lock this fellow up, Harry."

Harry licked his lips and arose. He opened the door and jabbed inward with a thumb.

Singapore entered what appeared at first to be blind darkness. The truth was, after the equatorial glare of outdoors, his eyes were temporarily blind to such diminished illumination.

He was pushed along a corridor. He heard a heavy lock click. Again he was pushed. He was familiar with this sensation, too. It meant that he was now in a cell.

A metallic clang at his back verified this guess. The footsteps of the jailer retreated.

A girl with a sweet musical voice exclaimed, "Great heavens!"

He turned around. He dimly began to see things. One of the first impressions to take form was that of a pale oval at bars across the way—a face. A girl's face.

"Sam!" she cried. "Oh, Sam; you're here at last!"

NO ROOM for doubt could remain in Singapore's mind. It was Sally Lavender—Shanghai Sal—the most beautiful woman he had ever seen in the Far East, and, by long odds, the most dangerous, the most unscrupulous.

His heart was banging. When last seen, Sally Lavender and Singapore's father had been working as a team. They had lured him, with diabolical ingenuity, into a trap from which he had escaped by the narrowest of margins.

His eyes grew used to the semi-darkness, and he could see that she hadn't changed. It was the same beautiful, innocent face, with eyes of a young madonna—the eyes of virginal innocence. All her charm was that of lovely, unspoiled innocence. She fooled experts. She had fooled Singapore Sammy, who was as hard-boiled as they come. She had only to raise those long sweeping dark lashes from those large, dusky, trusting eyes, and you would sell your soul. Singapore almost had.

She was wearing the familiar Simarong costume—a blue denim work shirt and khaki shorts. She had slim, long, beautiful legs; small hands and feet.

Rather than detracting from it, that masculine attire emphasized the slender alluring perfection of her body.

Sammy felt the old familiar thrill at the sight of her—and the old familiar feeling of stealthy danger lurking. Here was a girl as beautiful as a dream and as dangerous as a black leopard.

Sammy remembered her as he had last seen her—tears in her lovely eyes and a promise to go straight, on her lips. And he had known as she promised that she was lying with every word she spoke!

"So it was you who sent that Malay," he said.

"Sammy, I'm sorry. I'm dreadfully sorry. But it was my only chance. I sent him away from here with that message more than four months ago. I thought he was dead. I thought you hadn't believed him and weren't coming. I've died a thousand deaths waiting for you to come. And you didn't get here a day too soon. Sometime to-night they're going to kill me. They're going to put me into that copper furnace alive!"

Singapore could see her clearly now. No; Sally hadn't changed. No matter how shrewdly you looked at Sally Lavender, you could see no trace of the ruthless black thing that was her soul.

"Yeah?" Sammy said skeptically. It all sounded wild and fantastic to him.

"I'm not lying. And I didn't do it for myself. I did it for the man I'm in love with—the man I'll marry if we can only get out of this hell-hole alive!"

Singapore had become aware by this time that the cell to the right of hers contained an occupant—a darkly-browned, sandy-haired young man who was scrutinizing Singapore through the bars.

"This guy?" Sammy asked.

"His name," she said, "is Cosmo Sand."

SINGAPORE LOOKED again at Cosmo Sand and the brown young man grinned at him. He guessed Mr. Sand's age at twenty-four. There was a look of leathery hardness about him that Sammy approved of. He looked back at Sally. Her eyes were shining like stars.

"What have they got you two in for?" he asked.

"I'm taking the rap for your father. He heard there was a fortune in gold bars here, and the double-crossing old—"

"Where did he hear that?" Sammy snapped.

"From an old island trader named Cobbledick. Your father met him in Kuala Lumpur. This man, this Cobbledick, had been on a black smoke jag. He was drinking trade gin, trying to straighten himself out, when your father met him. Cobbledick talked. He told your father all about this island."

"Where were you?"

"In Shanghai. He cabled me to join him in Singapore. He said he had a chance to make both our fortunes. Do you remember I promised you I was going to go straight? Well, I was. I was trying. I had a job as a stenographer in Shanghai. I was fired. I was broke. I thought if I could just clean up a fortune, it would be easy to stop being crooked then."

"Yeah," Sammy said. "Smarter crooks than you have landed right where you are by thinkin' just that. So what happened?"

"I met him in Singapore and we made our plans. It was to be a pretended shipwreck. I was to be cast away on this island and found wandering around. Our yacht had struck a reef and sunk. I was to pretend to be his daughter. Next day he was to be washed ashore—after I'd had time to arouse their sympathy. We pictured how tickled they'd be to see me and my dear old father reunited, after each had thought the other had drowned."

"But it didn't work out that way," put in Cosmo Sand.

"No," Sally said. "They found me lying on the beach, soaking wet. They brought me before this human demon named Zorin. He questioned me for ten hours. It was like torture. They locked me up in this jail. Next day, when your father was washed ashore, Zorin gave him a real third-degree. He threatened to pour molten copper into his veins if your father didn't tell the truth.

"Your father said he was an old, old man, under my diabolical influence—that it was true that I was his daughter, but that I was a fiend; that I had thought up this whole scheme. By the time he'd got through talking, he had Zorin convinced."

"But Zorin tortured him just the same," the sandy-haired young man broke in. "They cut off his ear-lobes with tinsnips. They were going to burn his toes off when the old fellow got away. Grabbed somebody's gun and shot down two men. In the confusion, he escaped."

"Off this island?"

"Yes."

"Over that pass?"

"Perhaps. There are several paths up the sides of these hills."

"If he did it—" Sammy grimly began.

"Cosmo," Sally Lavender cried, "Sam Shay is the smartest white man you ever met. He has got himself out of practically every jail between Bangalore and Tientsin. He's really a perfect Houdini. And if he can get us out of here, you can get us to the beach. And this time there won't be a slip-up."

"Yes," Cosmo Sand agreed without enthusiasm; "they can only burn us alive once."

CHAPTER VI

SAMMY'S TRICK

BY PRESSING HIS cheek close against the bars, Sammy could see the length of the corridor; could see their jailer perched on a bench on the little porch, too far away to overhear, provided they pitched their voices low.

"Let's have the rest of this story," Singapore said. "After the old man made his getaway, what happened to you, Sal?"

Her eyes became stars again. "Cosmo used to come down to the jail to see me—secretly," she answered. "You see, one of their rules is that no news of the outer world can come into Simarong. And, of course, I had all the latest news. They had dozens of debates about what was to be done with me. Each time Cosmo took my part. He finally settled it by saying that he would make himself personally responsible for me. He said: 'Keep her in jail for two years. In those two years let her communicate with no one. By that time anything she can say will no longer be news.' And they agreed."

"But I ruined it," Mr. Sand said ruefully. "By that time I was in love with her. I couldn't keep away from here. I used to sneak in every night when the jailer was off at supper. I made love to her through the bars. One night I overstayed my time. The jailer caught me. I've been in here ever since. They'd have killed me months before this, but my father was one of the founders of the colony. It was he who had the chart showing where the meteor might be found."

Singapore said, "What meteor?"

"In the year 1856," the young man answered, "a meteor fell into this island. It was reported by the first mate of an old clipper ship at the time. The *Jade Lady*. He thought it had fallen into the Banda Sea. It showered gold on the deck of his ship, so it became known as the golden meteor. But the wheelsman on watch had seen, just before it fell, the outlines of an island. He kept his mouth shut, looked up the location of the island on a chart, and a number of years later came back looking for it.

"I don't believe he lived to reach the island. Perhaps he reached here and died. No one knows. But when he started out, he left, among his papers, a sealed envelope containing a copy of the chart and an explanation of what he was going to do. His name was Ira Sand. He was my great-grandfather."

Sammy softly whistled. This, then, was the explanation of that craterlike depression beyond the village.

"I suppose, in those days," Cosmo Sand went on, "people were just as skeptical of buried treasure stories as they are to-day. Anyway, nothing was done about the golden meteor until those old papers were found by my father in a trunk in the attic of our ranch house in Wyoming, sixty years later. They'd been carted out there with other heirlooms.

"About that time my father met this fanatic, Zorin. They organized and financed this colony, and came out here with that old chart. I think they found the crater the meteor had made within a month. It wasn't solid gold, but it was rich in gold. It had plunged through ten feet of topsoil, through a false bedrock and exploded into great hunks, some of them buried a hundred feet deep in a volcanic, sulphurous substratum.

"All through here there are strong formations of almost pure sulphur. The white-hot meteor struck this sulphur substratum, and must have burned for years. But there are still big areas of unburned sulphur all about the surface, where it was kicked up. Great mounds of it.

"Where the meteor fell is now a honeycomb of shafts, cross-cuts and drifts. We've found most of the gold in chutes—flour gold. My father was killed in the collapse of a tunnel about four years ago. He had charge of these workings. I think, toward the end, he was pretty disgusted with Zorin's Utopian ideas. He often told me it was a great mistake. I don't remember much of the first years. I was only eight when we landed here."

HE STOPPED. Singapore asked him how much gold was stacked up in the treasure house.

"Nearly six million."

"What's it goin' to be used for?"

"Lord knows—now. Zorin's original plan was to accumulate a large fortune—ten or twenty millions; then go out into the world and start a tremendous advertising and propaganda campaign—to sell his idea of civilization to the rest of the world. But that plan miscarried. Everything has miscarried—because his civilization is no good. It doesn't work. The colony has always been a failure. The last of our morale has crumbled. The experiment is at an end, but they won't admit it.

"Anyway, Zorin won't admit it, and he still has enough of a following to back up what he says.

"It was to have been an experiment in pure socialism. Everybody was to be free and equal. There were to be no restraints, no laws, no religion. I believe everything ran smoothly for a year. Then some of the people got tired of the isolation—wanted to go back to America. Zorin refused to let them go. Then he announced that death was to be the penalty of attempted escape. One night twenty of them tried. This happened after the colony had been here about two and a half years.

"They were recaptured, brought back, lined up against the wall of the treasure house—and shot. Fifteen men and five women! That was the beginning of the end. There were suicides and more attempts at escape. Finally Zorin passed the law that any one who attempted to escape was to be tied to a pole and put into the copper furnace—roasted alive!

"He thought that would stop them. But it didn't. In spite of that law, more than thirty people have tried, singly or in groups, to get away. I've seen old women roped to poles and put into that furnace. I saw my own cousin—a sixteen-year-old girl—put into that furnace. There were three hundred and twenty in the original colony. There are less than seventy left.

"I tell you it's been like growing up in hell. Yet it wasn't so bad for us youngsters, or the children born here, as for the older people who remembered America and were so homesick that they would risk that horrible death, trying to escape. I'd never thought seriously of escape until Sally came here. When I fell in love with her, and learned something about the outside world, I wanted to clear out.

"But that wasn't all. Instead of a free and equal social state, what we have always had was a dictatorship—Zorin. Under him is a group of old men known as The Ten, or the Council of Ten. This group runs everything, has the final say. These old men, with their arbitrary powers, have taken all the young women for themselves. The young men have no say about it. What The Ten wants to do, it does. A young man might fall in love with a girl, and she with him; but if one of The Ten wants her, he has her."

Singapore recalled the bitter resentment he had seen in the faces of the two seventeen-year-old girls he had passed in the village.

"The real trouble about Sally," Cosmo Sand went on, "began when Zorin decided he wanted her. It developed that two of the Council of Ten also wanted her. At the end of two years, if we weren't going to be killed to-night, one of them would get her—not I!"

Sammy was wisely, slowly nodding. "I get it," he said. "You two have pulled off an escape that went haywire."

"Last night," Sally affirmed. "We were in cells farther down the corridor. For two solid months Cosmo hacked away at the window bars with his pocket-knife. They're copper, you know. Last night he cut them through. He got out, slipped around in front and overpowered the jailer. He got the keys and let me out.

"We knew that Cobbledick would reach here to-day, because he's always here exactly on schedule. We were going to swim out to the schooner just before it pulled out. But we were caught on the other side of the mountain, brought back here and sentenced to death in the furnaces for attempted escape from the island. I had given up hope of your ever arriving, because the Malay had been gone four months, and I supposed he had failed."

SINGAPORE OBSERVED that the sun was setting. In the pink suffusion of light at the end of the corridor he could see Sally Lavender's face as clearly as if it were illuminated by foot-lights. It was the drawn face of a girl who had been suffering.

She was staring soberly at him.

"Do you blame me," she said, "for sending that Malay to trick you here? He used to sweep out the cells. It took me a month to persuade him to go. You see, Sam, I've changed. I'm not what I was. I've learned my lesson. If Cosmo and I can get out of here, we're going to Wyoming—to the family ranch. For the first time in my life, I'm really in love."

Singapore said nothing. Not long ago she had said the same thing to him. But perhaps, this time, she meant it. Perhaps Cosmo Sand was the man who could handle her.

She said urgently, "You do believe me, don't you, Sam?"

"Sure. Sure, I believe you."

"Then you will help us try to escape—for his sake?" She plunged a hand into the bosom of her blue denim shirt and brought out a little nickel-plated automatic pistol.

"If they come for me, I'm going to shoot myself. Do you believe that?"

"Yeah," he said. Maybe she was cured of being a menace to law and order, and maybe she wasn't. But there was no question of her desperation. The trouble with Sally Lavender was that she was too smart. She would always be too smart. She was perfectly aware that his only hope was in helping her and Cosmo Sand.

Sally dropped the pistol back into her bosom and continued to stare at him with large, childlike eyes of tragedy.

"Do you forgive me for tricking you down here?"

"Forget it," he growled. "You might as well know I didn't fall for that Malay's chatter."

"You didn't?"

"No. Captain Cobbledick died in Saigon." And he gave her an account of that eventful night on the Saigon River. "The *Blue Goose* is in the cove now, if they haven't scuttled her."

"They won't sink her," the sandy-haired young man said firmly. "I'm certain that Zorin is planning his own getaway. I know he realizes he can't sit on this human volcano much longer. My hunch is that he was waiting for Cobbledick to get here. At least, that's the general belief—that he was going aboard Cobbledick's schooner with all the gold he could carry—and get away. No, he won't have your ship scuttled. The reason he didn't believe your story was that it didn't suit his plans. He'll kill you and take your ship."

Sally said, "Sam! There's so little time! You've broken out of every jail in the Far East. If any man in the world can get us out in time, you're the man. What can you do?"

"I'll look around."

He looked about the cell. The copper bars at his window were fully an inch thick, and about five inches apart, as were those of the door. He gave his attention to the lock. It was not the type that a hairpin would unlock from the inside. There was a steel plate a foot square covering the back of it, and a coarse-mesh wire grille surrounding that.

No, it was impossible to get at that lock with a hairpin.

Sally called softly, "Any hope?"

"Not yet. I could get a tunnel started if I had any kind of tool. This floor's pretty easy. But it would take a couple of nights.

Look here, Mr. Sand. Once we get out o' here—if it can be done—where do we go from here?"

"Up over the south hill," the young man said. "It's a jungle on the other side for about a mile, but I know the path. And there's a moon to-night. That path brings us out on a long mesa, or plateau. We go down the west side of it, and come out on the beach on the west—about five miles from the cove. The rest of the way is easy going—we just follow the beach. But how are we going to get out?"

Singapore didn't answer. For a moment he forgot plans of escape. It had occurred to him that he was not going to make good on his promise to Captain Cobbledick. He had made this trip for the sole purpose of securing for Cobbledick's grand-daughter a sum of money sufficient to insure her against want.

Almost the last words of the old trader were, "It's guys like you and me, Singapore, that have got to protect innocent kids like her." He had made this disastrous voyage purely for that sentimental reason. And it struck him now as a great pity to leave Simarong without attempting to get some of that gold. And even if they could make good their escape, which was very unlikely, it would likewise be a shame for Cosmo Sand to depart without his legitimate share of that gold. And, for that matter, Singapore's hands were itching for a share of that bright yellow metal.

THE DAYLIGHT was now almost gone. He lit a cigarette and paced from the door to the window of his cell—forth and back, turning over in his mind plans of escape. He would use, he finally decided, the scheme which had worked so well in the tight little jail at Penang.

He called softly to the girl in the darkness across the way, "I'm goin' to pull the dummy-chucker stunt. Have you got any soap over there?"

"Yes." A moment later there was a soft thud against one of the bars. He saw the gleam of it in the corridor; reached out and picked up a half-worn white cake.

Electric lights came on along the corridor just as he withdrew his hand.

Sammy bit off a corner of the soap cake and began to chew it. He put the remainder of the cake in his pocket, stretched out on the floor of his cell and said, "Okay—scream!"

Sally Lavender began to scream. And these were the screams of a woman in the grips of a sudden and awful terror. Heavy footsteps came pounding down the corridor. Singapore Sammy was now writhing about and foaming freely at the mouth.

The lantern-jawed man said angrily, "What the hell's goin' on here?"

"Look!" Sally shrieked. "Look at him! He's dying! Do something! Call a doctor! Get him out of there!"

The jailer came over to Sammy's cell and looked. He said impatiently, "What's the matter with you?"

Singapore did not answer. He groaned and writhed about. It was as if he were having a convulsion. Nothing of his eyes was visible but the white areas. His legs twitched. A white lather gurgled from his convulsing lips.

The jailer whipped a key-ring from his pocket, unlocked the cell door and came in. He bent over Sammy.

As he did so Sammy came to his feet with a sudden spring—and found himself being coldly stared at by the muzzle of a revolver!

The lantern-jawed man said wearily, "I've had that one pulled on me before, Red."

Sammy spat out the soap, wiped out his mouth with a handkerchief and grinned ruefully.

"I figured you were dumb," he said. "I figured I could get away with it. But I was wrong."

"Yeah," the jailer agreed, "and I figured you for one of these wise guys, and I was right."

"Sure," Singapore said, still with that crestfallen air. "You figured me, but I didn't figure you. Well, we all make mistakes.

But I'll bet I can show you something you never saw before in your life."

"A trick," the jailer said. "You can't show me a new trick. I know every one in the deck. Any more of your tricks and you don't get any supper."

"This isn't a trick," Singapore said.

"All right. Show it to me from the other side of this door."

The lantern-jawed man backed out and sent the door shut with a clang. He restored the keys to his pocket and the revolver to its holster.

Singapore was slowly pulling the copper wire over his head.

"Watch me close, Harry," he said, almost in a whisper. "Beautiful women sob and strong men get headaches when they see this."

"I suppose," the jailer said, "you'd like me to step close up to the bars to see this trick."

"Nope. Stand wherever you want to." He was opening the little chamois-skin sack. "But watch close. Keep your eyes on the little bag, Harry. You're going to get a shock. Ready!" Now he was untying the red cord at the throat of the little bag. "Look, Harry, look!" he whispered.

HE ROLLED the blue fire pearl out of the sack and onto the tips of four bunched fingers. It was as if a round ball of blue fire had magically sprung into being and perched there. In the cold hard gleam of the naked tungstens overhead, the pearl was a living bubble of blue flame.

It seemed to tremble, to shiver, it seemed to sing. It might have been a ball formed of fiery blue tropical sky, or a bubble of valley mist lacquered satiny blue by an Oriental magician. As blue as a Chantaboun sapphire, that amazing pearl was fit to grace the finger, or the throat, of a princess. No wonder Singapore Sammy had refused more than twenty thousand dollars, American gold, for that pearl. No wonder it was his passion.

Shimmering, blazing with its mysterious inner fire, it seemed to dance on his fingertips.

The lantern-jawed man was staring at it. Across the way, Sally Lavender emitted a little gasp, then a long sigh. Once she had all but murdered him to possess that pearl. Others had tried, had failed. Singapore Sammy would part with his life before he would part with this incredible fiery blue gem.

"Look at it, Harry," he whispered. "It's a pearl. It's the blue fire pearl of Malobar. There ain't another one like it in the world. Did you ever see the equal of it? Would you like to hold it in your hand?"

Harry's small black eyes, as if borrowing from the curious luster of the pearl, had become fiery, too. He licked his red lips.

With a sudden snatching gesture, he shot his hand through the bars, his fingers crooked hard like claws.

And in the shade of an eyewink, Singapore Sammy popped the pearl into his mouth and clamped down with both hands on the jailer's wrist. He sent both feet against the bars—a foothold—and gave the wrist a tremendous pull. Unprepared, the greedy one came smashing into the bars, head down, striking them with such terrific force that it appeared, for a moment, that his head was wedged between two of them.

That awful impact might have felled an ox. It felled the jailer. Unconscious or dead, he slid head foremost to the floor.

Sally Lavender softly cried, "Good work, Sammy! Oh, hurry, hurry!"

Cosmo Sand was gently, jubilantly cursing.

Singapore worked swiftly. Each moment might now be well worth its weight in blue fire pearls. He restored the pearl to its pouch, the wire to his neck. He reached through the bars and pulled the limp body of their former captor close. He pulled and pushed and rolled it about until he had secured keys and revolver. The revolver he dropped into his vacant hip pocket. He reached around the wire grille and tried the keys. The third one worked. He opened the door, dragged the unconscious man into the cell, went out and sent the door clanging shut upon him.

He crossed the corridor and quickly unlocked the doors of Sally's and Cosmo Sand's cells.

There was the sound of a foot grating on the stairs which led to the porch.

Singapore sped on tiptoes down the corridor. He flattened himself against the wall inside the door as these footfalls grew louder.

The door opened. Sammy briefly recognized the blond young man who had been one of the two who had apprehended him on the path from the cove. He drove packed knuckles into the newcomer's face; stood back to let him fall, seized the collar of his shirt and dragged him down the corridor and into Cosmo Sand's cell. Cosmo Sand kicked the door shut.

Sally whimpered, "Hurry! Oh, hurry!"

CHAPTER VII

SALLY SNARLS

A COOL SPICED wind fanned Singapore's heated face as he followed Cosmo Sand and Sally Lavender into the darkness of a dubious freedom.

He saw the twinkling of lights in the village, the red glare of the copper furnace on men in the square enclosure and on the face of the little treasure house.

Then a man's voice, near by in the darkness: "Who's that?"

The three fugitives started to run. Cosmo Sand led the way down the valley toward the loom that was the south mountain. The voice behind them shouted, "Stop!"

There was excitement in the village now. Voices were calling. The three jail-breakers reached the foot of the mountain and started scrambling up a rough path. Sally fell, cut her knee on a rock, gasped that she was all right, and they ran on.

Behind them lights were darting to and fro. Pistols were being fired—the alarm! A growing uproar of voices from the direction of the village indicated that a pursuit was being organized.

Singapore, scrambling up the path behind Sally, wished that he knew something of the lay of the land. A jungle, a mesa, Sand had said, then the beach. Then what? If the *Blue Goose* was under guard, as she undoubtedly was, how were they to board her and take possession?

He could hear men, not far behind him, panting on the trail. Farther away a voice shouted in explanation: "They've broken out of jail—all three!"

The fugitives reached the pass, started down into the jungle. The moon would be up soon. Its palely glowing promise was on the eastern horizon. Singapore caught the toe of his boot under a root, tripped, sprawled and cut his hands on the flintlike pebbles. He arose and plunged on.

They reached the jungle. Here, progress was necessarily slow. The jungle was totally black, and none of them had a light of any kind; not even a match among them. Singapore had used his last to light a cigarette in the cell while he pondered the first step in their escape.

Lights flickered behind them. It was impossible for a man without lights of any kind to run through such dangerous territory; but the men behind them could run. They had flashlights.

The three reached the mesa, ran the length of it, and descended with the gleam of the beach and the surf ahead.

Cosmo Sand, panting, called back softly: "Watch out for an ambush here. They can cut around ahead of us."

And now the scene was palely flooded with a green-white glow. The moon was up.

They stopped, perhaps a hundred feet from the beach. They listened, but heard no sound of the pursuit except directly behind them. Then they started at a run along the beach toward the cove where the *Blue Goose* was anchored.

THEY RAN until they were breathless; paused only long enough to gain second wind, then ran on. They no longer heard the sounds of the pursuit. They saw no one, heard no one, until they finally reached the cove.

A whaleboat, loaded almost to the waterline, was pulling away from the schooner. Two men stood on the deck of the *Blue Goose*. Several men were on the beach. It was impossible to say how many there were, because of the palms and the bushes this side of them.

The three fugitives stopped again, in the shelter of a bush. And at this juncture occurred a most unexpected revelation in the waywardness of human nature. Singapore should have been prepared for it, but he wasn't. He was too intent on a plan for boarding the *Blue Goose*, making his getaway from this fantastic island.

It was Sally Lavender who provided the surprise. Before he could guess her intentions, she had swiftly removed from his hip pocket the revolver he had taken from their jailer.

As he whirled about, she was leveling the gun at his chest.

"Put your hands up," she said. "You, too, Cosmo. I want that pearl."

"You little double crossing sap," Singapore growled, "you're goin' to wreck everything."

"Everything is wrecked," said Shanghai Sally. "There's just one chance in fifty of getting off this island—and it isn't by way of that schooner."

Cosmo Sand, automatically putting his hands into the air, was staring at her with incredulity.

"Sally," he whispered. "My God, you can't do this."

"I'm doing it."

"But you—you love me."

"A dead woman can't love a dead man. I'm serious. I'm desperate. There's a way for just one of us to get off this island—and I'm taking it. And I'm taking that pearl with me. I've wanted that pearl for years. I'm going to have it."

"You're cracked," Singapore said. "You can't get off this island."

"I'm going to take the chance."

"Sally," her lover said, "you're hysterical. You don't mean this. How are you going to get off the island?"

"Swim!"

"Through these sharks and over the octopus caves? Sally, listen. I've got a hunch I'm coming through this with a whole skin. If you do this thing, by God, I'll find you. I'll spank you. I'm going to make a woman of you if I have to half-kill you!"

"You're an optimist," Singapore said.

Sally came slowly toward him, holding the gun with a steady hand. There was black desperation in her eyes. It was possible that Cosmo Sand was right; that Sally didn't know what she was doing. But Singapore did know that this girl, with these blackly ominous eyes, would shoot him if he made one wrong gesture. Shoot him through the chest. He had always declared that he would part with his life before he would part with the Malobar pearl. But he did not move when she reached up and snatched the copper wire over his head and looped it over her own, stuffing the little chamois sack into her bosom.

As she backed away, she said, "Stand just where you are. The man who follows me gets shot."

And she blew them a kiss from her fingertips.

COSMO SAND muttered, "I ought to hate her, but I don't. And I hope she makes it."

"How," Singapore growled, "can she get away?"

"I'm sure," the other answered, "she has a boat hidden—the boat she came ashore in the night she told her phony shipwreck story. But I'll catch her. We'll get off this island. I'll catch her if it takes the rest of my life. I suppose you think I'm crazy."

"No," Singapore drawled. "I felt that way about her myself

once. I was goin' to make a good woman of her—with the flat of my hand. And maybe you're the man to do it."

Sally's voice called from a distance: "I mean it—I'll shoot the man who follows me."

The two young men saw her emerge from the shadows into the moonlight. She vanished around a bush. There was a pistol shot, a scream. Then more screams.

Sand gasped, "They've got her!"

Singapore seized him by the shoulders as he started off.

"Hold it, fellow," he said. "You can't do anything for her that way."

The other young man snarled, "Hands off!" He spun out of reach and would have plunged on down to where Sally still screamed if the redhead had not hooked an arm about his neck and dragged him back.

Panting, Sand struck at him. The punch caromed from the side of Singapore's head.

He ducked his head, walked close and slugged the over-excited young man in the jaw.

Sand dropped on his side at Sammy's feet. The screams retreated; became muffled.

Perhaps fifteen seconds elapsed before Cosmo Sand opened one eye, then the other.

He rubbed the back of one hand across his mouth, spat out blood.

Sammy, helping him to his feet, held firmly to one elbow and said, "I'm sorry, kid, but it had to be done. We'll backtrack. If you insist on savin' this double crossin' little brat, we'll be of more help to her and ourselves if we keep out of the hands of this gang. Let's use our noodles. Where will they take her? Back to the village?"

"To the furnace!" Cosmo Sand panted. "They'll lash her to a pole and shove her into the furnace!"

"Steady, fellow! Keep your shirt on."

"Will you help?"

"Sure, I'll help. I want that pearl back. And I want some of that gold. And I'm goin' to get some of that gold—all I can carry!"

He suddenly heard the furtive movements of some one close at hand; seized Cosmo Sand's arm and pulled him back and down. After a few seconds three men with rifles went tiptoeing past.

When they were gone the two young men crept out from under their bush. Cautiously they made their way back to the higher sand, where the undergrowth was thicker. From this rise they could see the beach and schooner more clearly. They saw a knot of men moving down to where the whaleboat was pulled up on the beach. The nucleus of this group was Sally Lavender.

CLOSER AT hand men were shouting back and forth, searching, beating the bushes for Sally Lavender's two companions. But the hunt was presently abandoned. From their new hiding place the two young men, listening to calls and answering calls, gathered that there was little hope of their escaping. Their only chance lay in boarding the schooner, and two men had been left on guard there. All the others, the pursuers as well as those who had been engaged in the work of unloading, were returning to the village.

When it was evident that the pursuit had been temporarily abandoned, the two fugitives started back along the way they had come. It was longer, Sand explained, but safer. He was white and shaking.

"If Zorin hurts that girl I'm going to kill him!"

"Forget Zorin," Sammy said. "You want your girl, I want my pearl, and we all want some of that gold. We'll get 'em all."

"How?"

"I'll get ideas. Are you sure they're goin' to shove that double crossin' little rat into the furnace?"

"Unless we can stop them."

"What happens? Give me a picture."

"Only that. The men attend to it. The women never watch it. The women lock themselves up in their houses."

"And if the women see us, they'll likely take pot shots at us."

"It isn't likely."

"No, and it wasn't likely that Sally would grab that pearl. Is the enclosure gate locked?"

"Yes. What are you planning to do?"

"On an island as crazy as this, anything can happen. We've got to find a way to get into that enclosure."

"It's impossible."

"Sandy, we are going to walk into the enclosure, grab your girl and my pearl—and walk out loaded down with gold."

"It can't be done."

"Says you. How do we get inside the enclosure? Think hard, fellow."

They were half running, half walking now along the beach, retracing their steps.

Cosmo Sand said suddenly, "The muffle!"

"What?"

"The little furnace they melt the gold down in! It's been shut down a month. It's cold. They're relining it. We can get in through the back or outer end. There's a hole broken there. We can crawl through—out the mouth—into the enclosure. There will be upwards of forty men in there, all armed. One sight of us and we're goners. If you get any ideas," he said bitterly, "let me know."

"I've got the idea," Singapore said. "It's goin' to take nerve. We're goin' to have to work fast—almost too fast for the naked eye to follow. We may get shot. Will you risk it?"

"Certainly! What's your scheme?"

"You said something about sulphur outcroppings around the crater. Is it good yellow sulphur?"

"Yes. As yellow as lemon."

"Okay. What we want is a chunk of sulphur as big as your head."

CHAPTER VIII

INTO THE FURNACE

WHEN THE TWO young men came down into the valley, a sullen roar of angry voices reached them. This persistent roar of sound originated in the pinkly glowing enclosure. The heavy iron shields had been drawn aside from the mouth of the copper furnace and the great pool of white hot molten copper it contained lighted the scene glaringly.

As the two young men drew closer they saw that Alexander Zorin was the central figure in a large group of angrily talking and gesticulating men. It appeared that a number of the men were violently opposed to the execution of Sally Lavender.

A man shouted: "While we're wasting all this time, those two are getting away."

Another cried: "There's been enough of this killing. I'm sick of it. This whole damned—"

His voice was drowned by the rising clamor. But it was evident that Zorin still had the situation under his control.

And Singapore could now see that the preparations for Shanghai Sally's execution were complete.

It was hard for his practical mind to grasp—that this crowd of white men intended to kill this girl by thrusting her body into a lake of molten copper. He had seen strange, cruel, fantastic things in the Far East in these seven years. He had managed to understand most of them, but this was beyond his grasp.

Here was a crowd of supposedly civilized men wrangling as to whether or not a girl was to be burned alive in a lake of copper! She was lying on the ground near them. Singapore could see her eyes—eyes glassy with terror. Her mouth was gagged. Her hands were lashed behind her. Her shoulders, waist and feet were lashed along one end of a thirty-foot pole. Strong men would presently seize that pole and thrust Sally Lavender into that pink lake of molten copper!

Until this moment, Sammy's hard young mind had refused to deal with a situation so grotesque, so barbarous. To him it was more incredible than the bizarre creeds of India. These forty men, with their sixteen years of isolation, were not sane.

Fanatics to start with, they were madmen now.

He hugged the great skull-sized lump of yellow sulphur to his chest and slipped on behind the muffle, followed by Cosmo Sand.

The back, or outer end of the muffle was a hole approximately sixteen inches in diameter. To Singapore's exploring fingers the surfaces of the bricks felt like talcum. They were burned out. He and Cosmo Sand must go carefully through the muffle or it might collapse on them.

Singapore went first. The long square tunnel, once he was inside, afforded him just enough room in which to crawl. The front end of the muffle was blanked off by a large sheet of iron— an apron, similar to the aprons which hooded the mouth of the copper furnace.

He heard Cosmo Sand softly cursing, panting, behind him. And in the enclosure ahead a sudden silence fell, disturbed only by the hissing of the gas in the adjoining furnace, the "working" sounds of the molten copper.

This sudden silence startled him. He wondered if he and Sand had been watched, were about to be seized. His heart was trip-hammering in his throat. Sweat dripped from his face.

Then a man said scornfully, "All right! One more murder, Zorin!"

And another said, "Let's get this over with."

Singapore slipped out of the furnace to the ground. The iron sheet gave off a deep ringing sound as he struck it. It tipped outward and would have fallen if he had not grabbed the upper edge.

He waited with sweat streaming from his forehead into his eyes. Seconds passed. Evidently no one had heard the deep clang of the apron.

He peered out the side. The pink glare from the mouth of the copper furnace fell like a great spotlight on the figures of the men. They had moved back. Zorin, in the center, was facing the furnace with arms folded on chest. In that pink glare, with his jaw outthrust, he might have been a god of vengeance. His black eyes glowed, deep and wild and a little mad. But several of the men had their backs turned to that glare.

SIX MEN, in three pairs, were standing beside the pole to which the girl was lashed, watching Zorin, waiting apparently for an order from him to carry through this hideous, monstrous ceremony. They wore leather gloves. The faces of five of them were set and expressionless. One stood with little streams of moisture sparkling down bis cheeks from his temples. His mouth writhed terribly.

Cosmo Sand crawled out of the muffle. His eyes, in the pink glare, were strained and bloodshot. His lower lip was raw from gnawing.

"Get behind that other apron," Singapore whispered. He stuffed the sulphur skull inside his shirt, picked up the make-shift shield and started for the furnace adjoining.

He moved swiftly, keeping the shield turned toward the massed men. With the glare in their eyes, he hoped that they would not see the iron apron sidling through the shadow.

He glanced behind him. Cosmo Sand, similarly shielded, was closely following him.

A voice cried, "What the hell is that?"

Singapore ran the rest of the way—stopped when he could not endure approaching any nearer the hellish heat.

He pulled the sulphur skull exit of his shirt and pushed it up so that the upper rim of it would be seen above the shield.

Then he shouted: "Stand back, you guys!"

A voice from the crowd bellowed: "Keep that sulphur away from that copper. What the hell are you doing? Who are you?"

"Stand back," Singapore shouted, "or this sulphur goes in there! Any one of you make one move this way—any one of you shoot a gun—and in goes this sulphur! If you don't know what happens, I'm gonna tell you. But maybe you guys know about runaway copper. The minute this sulphur hits that copper—up she blows! And out that copper comes like Niagara Falls! It'll fill this enclosure a foot deep in melted copper. And, that's what I'll do if any one of you maniacs makes one phony move! I'm tellin' you! Stand back and don't shoot or in she goes!"

He had found a rivet hole in the apron. To this he placed an eye. The crowd of men had not moved. They were standing just as they had been before, apparently struck motionless by surprise.

The red-headed gateman cried: "It's the guy off that schooner!"

"Get that man!" Zorin bellowed with an imperious gesture.

"And in goes this sulphur!" Singapore snapped. "And I mean it, Zorin. I'm a lunatic, too. We'll burn up in a river of copper together, Zorin. Stay where you are, all of you. And do what I say. First, toss your guns in a pile and stand back. I'm gonna count five. *One!*"

A nickeled revolver fell with a thud. A black automatic pistol joined it.

"*Two!*" shouted Singapore. "And it better begin rainin' guns!"

Another pistol and two revolvers fell to the ground. Zorin, as if suddenly recovering from a paralysis, snatched a revolver from his hip pocket. He brought it up and down, but before he could pull the trigger, the red-headed gateman struck it out of his hand.

"You damned fool," he snarled, "you'd kill all of us!"

"*Three!*" Singapore snapped.

The pistols and revolvers stopped falling.

Singapore barked: "Turn your backs, put up your hands and form a line. You, too, Zorin. Snap into it!"

When the forty dazed men had complied, Singapore said, "Okay, Mr. Sand."

The young man dropped his shield. Grim lipped, he went to the pile of guns and selected a pair.

Zorin stood rigid, motionless, black eyes smoldering in his dead-white face.

Thus, step by step, Singapore Sammy's mad scheme worked out. Cosmo Sand went down the line, searching for weapons. He secured Zorin's keys. He presently announced that every man was unarmed.

With the situation now under control, Sammy tossed aside the sulphur skull and selected a pair of revolvers from the pile.

COSMO SAND was bending over Sally. He removed the gag and untwisted the wires which bound her to the pole. He lifted her up. With a sob the terrified girl clasped his neck with her arms. Firmly Cosmo pushed her away. She staggered, might have fallen if Singapore had not caught an arm. She stared at him; tried to speak. Only a faint gasping sound came from lips which were swollen and cracked.

Sammy plucked the copper wire from her neck and opened the little chamois skin pouch. The blue fire pearl was safe. He slipped the wire over his head and tucked the sack inside his shirt.

"Sammy—" the girl began in a shaking voice.

"Grab a couple of guns," he said, "and try to be useful for once in your life."

Sally Lavender stared at Cosmo Sand, and he glared in return.

She bent down to pick up a pair of guns. As she did so there was a sudden movement in the line of men. Zorin had spun about and so, simultaneously, had the red-headed gateman. The white-faced giant leaped toward the pile of firearms. He reached it just as Sally bent over it. He swept her hands out of his way. But before Singapore could act, the red-headed gateman leaped on Zorin. The two men rolled over and over in the fine red dust toward the mouth of the furnace, into the belt of its terrific, withering heat, sending up clouds of smoky dust in their struggle.

It was impossible to see just what was happening, because of that dust screen. A sound like a sigh rose from the line of men. In the dust one figure suddenly reappeared, as red as fire, as red as blood, in the awful glare from the lake of molten metal.

It was the red-headed gateman. Sweat streamed from his hard square face. Blood oozed from a gash beneath one eye.

He disappeared again into the dust cloud. Again he became visible. But this time the giant Zorin was in his arms. Perhaps he was unconscious. Perhaps he was dead even then. It would be more merciful to believe so.

The squat, powerful red-head lifted him as if he were a log. And in silence broken only by the bubbling of the copper in its great vat and the hissing of the gas flames, he ran to the oblong mouth of the furnace and threw the fanatic Zorin into that iridescent lake.

Sally Lavender screamed once.

The gateman ran back from that awful blast of heat. His eyes were bulging and bloodshot and the grin at his raw, bruised mouth was more than a little mad. He put his hands into the air. His hands and arms were badly blistered.

Puffing, with blistered hands in air, he strode to Singapore.

"All right," he panted. "That's done. For years I've been itchin' to do that. Now it's done. It's where he belonged. Right where he shoved all the others. Roastin' in hell!"

Gasping, he stopped. "I guess we can talk business now, eh? I guess you know which way the wind is blowin'."

Sammy drew a deep breath, and relaxed. A little chill ran down his spine and he shook himself.

"Get back in that line," he said, "before I drill you. Sally, pick up these guns. Now, you guys, forward march, and the next one of you who runs amok gets messed up plenty. March!"

THE FORTY dazed men were marched to the jail, divided into groups and locked into cells. Their dazed astonishment at their amazing capture, at the horrible, grotesque death of their fanatical leader, vanished as, with hands in air, they trudged toward the jail. They pleaded with Sammy to listen to reason. The red-headed gateman shouted that they wanted to play ball with him. And when he remained vigilantly silent, they cursed. And when they were safe behind cell doors, they clamored again for fair play.

The red-headed gateman said, "Name your price, Red. All most of us want is to get off this island."

"Here," Singapore said, "take this and use it." And he pushed through the bars a rusty old file he had picked up in the enclosure. "With luck you can file your way out of here by mornin'."

"Listen, Red," said the other redhead, "it's worth an even million bucks to you to let us out of here right now."

"Any man," Singapore answered, "who would stand by and let a girl be shoved into a furnace of hot metal is too crazy for me to deal with. File your way out. I'll come back here in a couple of weeks. You can talk business then. Come on, Sandy."

Followed by curses, pleas and threats, the victors left the jail. Outside, Singapore said, "Sandy, round up your Malays. How many are there?"

"Seven."

"Okay. Send 'em down to the treasure house. I'll be there countin' out the gold. When you've rounded 'em up, go to the cove and tell those two guys on the schooner if they don't surrender, we'll come down there with a machine gun and blow their heads off. Sally, you trot down to the village and have a talk with the ladies. Tell them they're safe.

"Tell them to keep away from the jail and the treasure house. Tell them to stay indoors."

The sandy-haired young man said, "How much gold are you going to take? All of it?"

"Nope. The Malays get ten thousand apiece for what they've been through. I'm gonna drop 'em off in Singapore. Myself, I take a hundred and fifty thousand—ninety for my cargo, and sixty for the wear and tear on my carcass. How much do you figure is your fair share?"

"I've been thinking about it," Sand answered. "These people here, after all, are the only friends I have. I won't rob them. All I want is what I'm entitled to—say, a fiftieth, or a hundred and twenty thousand dollars. That makes a total of three hundred and forty thousand."

A few minutes later, at the treasure house, Singapore figured it out with a nail and a bar of gold, because he couldn't find pencil and paper. Gold was $20 an ounce. Twelve ounces of gold made a pound. In terms of weight, $340,000 proved to be 1,458 pounds of gold. More than half a ton of gold.

He put down a selfish impulse. The sight of these great stacks of beautiful soft yellow metal made his heart thump.

He might be, as the consul at Saigon had said, a disgrace to his country, a thieving scoundrel—but he didn't steal from lunatics or women!

CHAPTER IX

WITH THE RIGHT HAND

THE MOON WAS setting when the *Blue Goose*, with 1,458 pounds of gold bars beneath her hatch covers, and Singapore Sammy at the wheel, slipped out of the cove. Up forward, seven dazed and deliriously happy Malays were squatting, staring aft at this amazing red-headed white man who had miraculously delivered them from slavery, and had, by his generosity, made it possible for them to be head men in their *kampongs*.

Cosmo Sand was lounging against the stern rail, staring gloomily at the receding island. Sally Lavender was below.

Sammy glanced up at the snowy, filling sails, then around at the despondent young man. Cosmo Sand's face was white. His lips were hardened against his teeth. There was a gleam of fury in his eyes.

Singapore looked back at the sails with another kind of gleam. He believed that Cosmo Sand had come to a decision in the matter of one Sally Lavender, and that the results would bear watching.

He heard the girl's foot on the stairway. Then he heard a sound like a faint snort from the vicinity of Cosmo Sand.

Shanghai Sal came up into the moonlight. She had taken a shower and arranged her hair. Once again she was lovely. She paused. Her beautiful eyes swept past Singapore as if he did not exist.

"Cosmo," she said.

"Come here," Cosmo said.

With a little gasp she went over to him. There was a stool near where Cosmo stood. As Sally approached him he seated himself firmly on the stool.

He grasped her hand. Singapore observed the grim set to the young man's mouth.

Before Sally quite realized what was happening, Cosmo Sand had taken her on his lap. But not in the conventional way. His powerful hands turned the astonished girl over as if she were a small child. He held her face down across his lap. Her legs began to kick, and she began to shriek when she realized what the purpose of these maneuvers was.

Holding her firmly, Cosmo waited patiently for the kicking and shrieking to stop.

Then, in a furious voice, he said: "I told you back there on the beach there were two things I was going to do to you. Spank you, then take you back to Wyoming and make something out of you!"

The flat of his large brown hand came down.

"One for me," Singapore said. "One hot one for me. Attaboy!" Sally wailed.

The spanking came to an end. Cosmo got up and gripped the sobbing girl by the shoulders. He shook her just a little.

"The next time temptation gets too strong," he said, "keep my right hand in mind."

Sniffling, Sally crept into his arms. "Darling," she whimpered, "I'll be a good girl. I promise. I'll do whatever you say. Kiss me."

"Senga!" Singapore shouted. His *serang* answered briskly from forward.

"Trim that jib," Captain Singapore called, "then go down in my cabin and get the prayer book."

BUDDHA'S WHISKER

*Singapore Sammy and his pal knew they'd collect
either a fortune or a coffin from their temple raid*

CHAPTER I

A JOB OFFERED

THE RED-HEADED MAN gave a long low growl of surprise. He pushed himself into a sitting position. He dug his fists into his eyes and gave each fist a savage twist. Having thus aided his powers of vision, he lifted his sunburned lids all the way and peered ferociously about him.

The glare of tropical sunlight on water the color of stale mustard stung his aching eyeballs like so many white-hot needles. He shut his eyes again. But he had seen enough to know that he had no business being there.

Evidence of eyes, nose and ears indicated that he was, in the Far Eastern meaning of the words, on the beach. The stench of mudflats and moribund seafood indicated that he was on the tidal reach of a river. He was lying in the mud, underneath a wharf of rotting planks. The lazy current of a tropical river gurgled and lapped at the barnacled piles of the wharf, and oozed downward to the sea.

What sea? What river? The Rangoon? The Irriwaddi? The Menam-Chow-Phya?

It was probably the Rangoon, flowing lazily down to the Bay of Bengal. A mile away, across the muddy stream, he saw palms and thatched huts on stilts, all tinted coral by the last rays of the setting sun. Outrigger canoes, loaded with fruit, flowers and vegetables, floated down the river.

It was all very mystifying. Just how he came to be lying in the mud under a rotting wharf, on the bank of a tropical river, with

the pulses in his head imitating Brunei war gongs, was a question which only time and painful investigation could answer.

More urgent was the question of just what had happened to his personal fortunes. For some moments, the awakening red-headed man did nothing but wait for the war gongs to stop their damnable banging. But when they did not stop, he realized that one of the most devilish of birds known to mankind—the bird-that-beats-on-gold, or less lyrically, the brain-fever bird—was perched in some tree not far from the wharf, calling its mate, uttering in measured strokes this brazen clanging. And it was a sound not calculated to bring peace to the nerves of a man suffering from a most noble hangover.

The red-headed man opened his aching eyes again. He saw that while his white drill pants were spotted and caked with river bank mud, his white shoes were relatively clean. Evidently, he had not got here under his own power. He had been carried here and left to sleep it off.

His suspicion that he had met with foul treatment became firm conviction when his fumbling hands explored his pockets. His roll was gone. Even his small change was gone. For a moment, he stared dully at the lazy mustard-colored river, with both hands shoved down into his pants pockets. He was trying

*Lucifer Jones was
doing his share.*

to muster enough courage to investigate the piece of soft copper wire which he knew ought to encircle his sun-baked neck.

He sent a hand venturing up to his chin—and gave a grunt of relief. The copper wire was still there. Hopefully, he pulled the loop of soft wire out of his shirt. For almost two years, a little chamois-skin sack with a red silk cord had dangled there, protected against greedy and clever thieves by his quick wits and quicker fists.

His fingers closed on the sack. But the familiar hard, round lump was missing. The blue fire pearl of Malabar was gone! In its place was a soft, irregular lump.

He opened the sack and decanted into his hand a wad of pale green paper. He unfolded the paper. Scrawled upon it in charcoal were two Malayan words—*macam amie.*

"WHAT THE day brings, I take," the red-headed man translated. That's what the two little Malayan words meant.

The brief, jeering message wasn't signed. It didn't have to be signed. The handwriting—and the handiwork—were those of the smartest, cleverest, most unprincipled little rat in the Far East.

The red-headed man said grimly, "What the night brought, you took, you little tramp!"

He refolded the square of pale green paper and restored it to the chamois sack. He dropped the sack back inside his shirt. On hands and knees, he crawled out from under the wharf, stood up, swaying, and looked about him. The world was going around like a pinwheel. The brain-fever bird was still keeping time to the banging of the war gong inside his head.

It was, of course, Rangoon. Upriver and down were rice mills. Farther away were paddy fields. Over the trees in the distance rose sun rays from behind the jungle lighted the upper hundred feet of the thin, golden spire of the Schwe Dagon Pagoda. Burmese fishermen, workmen and paddy field coolies passed him, singing and laughing. The Burmese are a happy race.

An American girl in a rickshaw went by, and stared at him with pretty, wide-eyed alarm. Her perfume lingered a moment. She reminded him so much of the girl who had drugged and robbed him that he almost shouted her name.

The American girl glanced back at him, still wearing that look of alarm. The red-headed man sent a shaking hand to his chin. What wasn't caked mud was stubble. He knew he looked like a bum.

Two Burmese girls passed him, stared curiously up into his haggard, unshaved face. Each of them mysteriously resembled the girl who had doped and robbed him. And because of this illusion, the red-headed man suddenly felt that the world was unreal and menacing.

But he wasn't a bum. As long as he owned a half-interest in the finest little schooner on the Indian Ocean, he wasn't a complete bum.

His throbbing eyes probed here and there about the river. He had left the *Blue Goose* anchored in mid stream, off Sook Challaban's rice mill. The familiar contours of Sook Challaban's rice mill were visible in the dusk. But nowhere in the neighborhood was there a blue schooner with arrogantly raked masts.

In a tangle of shipping at a Chinese boatyard across the river, he believed he saw the *Blue Goose*, the bright glimmer of her hull against the muddy water; the sharp, white masts. But he couldn't be sure. The drug in his veins was still doing tricks to his eyes, and the dusk was turning purple.

The finest little schooner on the Indian Ocean was certainly not where he had anchored her last night. A feeling of dire foreboding possessed him. He had vowed that he would part with his life before he would part with the Malabar pearl. And he loved the blue schooner in a way that one can understand only if he has sometimes given his heart to a small sailing ship. If the *Blue Goose* was gone, he was on the beach, indeed. He was licked.

LIGHTS WERE coming on along the muddy street. Smells of cooking flavored the air. A white balloon with two legs, two arms and a dirty sun helmet cocked at a rakish angle, stopped bouncing along the street and yelled:

"Hey, Singapore!"

The red-headed man stopped, looked across the road, and saw in the fading twilight the florid features of Rincon Deal. The fat man came bouncing over. Piggy eyes surveyed the redhead from mud-caked hair to scuffed white canvas oxfords.

"You look like you're on the bum, Singapore," he said.

"Yeah?" the redhead said.

"You sure look like you been havin' a tough time."

The man addressed as Singapore stared at Rincon Deal from red-rimmed eyes.

"So what?"

The white balloon came closer. His eyes had a crafty look. Cupidity was doing tricks with his sensuous little mouth.

"I got a proposition for you," he whispered.

Singapore said nothing. His eyes looked fiercer:

"It's a pushover," said Rincon Deal. "It's a chance for us to

knock off fifty thousand rupees apiece! You're just the man!—
And it's honest!"

"Nothing you ever laid a finger on was honest, you baby-
killer!" the redheaded man said without heat.

Rincon Deal laughed softly. "Listen, Sam. You got me wrong.
This is hot, and it's easy—one night's work."

Singapore Sam was apparently without curiosity. "No,
thanks!"

"Why not?" Rincon Deal snapped.

"Maybe I don't like the shape of your nose. Maybe I wouldn't
trust you, you jellyfish, any farther than I could swim through a
wall of reinforced concrete."

"Yeah?" the fat man snarled. "You ain't kidding me any,
redhead." He seized Singapore Sam's mudcaked lapel. "And
I'm warnin' you. If you won't come in with me on it—don't go
messin' around on your own. Or "—his pendulous underlip
jutted out grimly—"I'll—get—you!"

He walked away, leaving Singapore Sam aware of a sinister
feeling in the air!—Danger!—What was going on?

The Brunei war gong in Singapore Sam's head had stopped
beating. A steady humming, as if his head were full of angry flies,
had taken its place. He put his feet down carefully. He might
have been walking on eggs or thin ice. The ground felt unsteady
and uncertain, as if it might fly out from under him with the
least encouragement. And he wondered if it could be the dope
which the little rat had slipped into his beer that made the world
seem like a mysterious illusion. Nothing was real; he was a man
lost in a fog, or dreaming.

Even the cooking smells were unreal. He wasn't hungry, but
he had a powerful thirst. What he needed was gin.

In the next block, a familiar scared, brown face flitted past
light streaming from a chink.

Sam shouted, "Senga!"

THE MALAY slipped into a doorway. In the darkness here,

the redhead's big powerful hands found his naked shoulders and dragged him back into the streak of light.

Senga was the Malay *serang* on the *Blue Goose.*

"What the hell's goin' on, Senga? What's she doing over there?"

The *serang* answered, "Lin Chang kicked me off, *birahi.*"

"Who is Lin Chang?"

"The new owner of the *Blue Goose, birahi.* The boatyard man."

"Since when has he been owner?"

"This morning, *birahi.*"

"Is Captain Jones in Rangoon?"

"I know not, *birahi.*"

"Who sold her to this Lin Chang?"

"The lady with brown eyes!"

"The—?" Singapore began profanely.

He became calm.

"Senga, go back to your ship. There has been a mistake. She has not been sold to Lin Chang or anybody else. I am still the master."

"Aie, birahi!"

He let the Malay go, caught gleams of light on the muscular, oily, brown shoulders as Senga vanished like a snake. There was still no reality in the world. Everything was a dream. And his thirst was terrific.

There was a grogshop not far from Sook Challaban's rice mill. It was called, in poetical Burmese, the Happiest Blue Elephant. The Happiest Blue Elephant was Singapore Sammy's objective. And the Happiest Blue Elephant was the last scene he could recall of the previous night's drama. He had been saying good-bye forever to the most beautiful little crook in the Far East when the universe went into a tailspin. He was tempted to lay the Happiest Blue Elephant in ruins.

HE BECAME aware that a tall Chinese coolie, with a Peninsular & Occidental warehouse chop on his jerkin, was walking beside him, keeping step, grinning in a sinister manner. Singapore Sam continued to put his feet down with the utmost care upon a lurching earth. He hoped Lucky Jones was in town. Lucky was his pal. Lucky was, or had been, co-owner of the *Blue Goose*. Lucky had been in Sumatra the past four months, hunting for gold; and Lucky Jones, according to a cablegram which Singapore Sam had received in Penang, had made a good placer strike. If he could only find Lucky Jones!

The coolie said thinly, "Joe Fong wanchee hab chin-chin."

"What's he want?"

"No savee. Him talkee my, him wanchee you that side chop-chop."

Sam considered. Joe Fong was the greatest full-grown yellow rascal in southern Asia.—Life, the red-headed man reflected, was like this. Once you got down, the world was full of nothing but rats.

"No can do," he said. "No wanchee catchee chin-chin with Joe Fong."

Then he saw the glitter of a nickeled revolver in the coolie's hand. The coolie had stopped grinning; his eyes were a killer's.

"You come along," he said. "Walkee chop-chop!"

Singapore Sam went along—chop-chop. He knew Joe Fong's bazaar. Five years ago, an innocent in Far Eastern matters, he had wandered into Joe Fong's.—But Sam was no longer an innocent.

He walked through the bazaar, which smelled of camphor-wood, and climbed a flight of teak stairs into a cubicle rancid with smoke from coolie cigarette tobacco and coolie grade *chandoo*, the lowest known grade of opium.

Joe Fong, yellow, fat and greasy, was seated at an American rolltop desk. He had learned most of his tricks in San Francisco.

He spun about in a Grand Rapids desk chair and smirked. One of his eyes was cocked. He looked like a Chinese pirate.

He wheezed, "Hola, Sammy! Down and out, huh?"

The red-headed man drawled, "Who the hell says I am?"

"You got the look, Sammy. I saw you talkin' to Rincon Deal. Any guy who gives Rincon Deal more than two seconds of his time is on the bum."

In Joe Fong's eyes and manner was the contempt of the Oriental for a white man "on the beach."

"I hear they got your ship and your roll," he wheezed. "Where's the Malabar pearl?"

"Who wants to know?"

"So they got that, too, huh?"

Joe Fong studied the red-headed man with amused contempt. The smoky little room was beginning to revolve for Singapore Sammy, and he grasped a chair back.

"Sammy, I got a job for you."

"Yeah? I must be on the bum, all right."

"This is a nice, easy job, Sam—a night's work. There's a hundred thousand rupees in it. We split it fifty-fifty."

"I heard about that job," Singapore Sammy said. "Every yellow-bellied hophead and every white gin blossom in Rangoon knows all about that nice, easy job. You can take that job and—"

The rest was drowned in the heavy, slow thumping of his feet as he walked down the stairs. At the bottom he paused and called back:

"Next time you send your hatchet man with an invitation for me, I'll make him eat his tin gun."

He was only faintly curious about the 100,000-rupee job. It must be a crooked job, or Joe Fong and Rincon Deal wouldn't be in on it.

HE LIMPED on down the road toward the Happiest Blue Elephant, still unable to shake off the feeling that these were the events of a dream; that all of this had happened to him somewhere before. His brain simply wasn't clicking. If he could only find Lucky Jones! Lucky would get between him and this cockeyed world until the drug wore off.

As he limped along, a coolie with a gray hood covering his

face slipped out of Joe Fong's bazaar and loitered along behind him.

Another Burmese girl who looked like Sally Lavender passed him, stared into his face in the dusk, and giggled.

Now he knew that all this was a dream. A hundred feet on, staring into the window of a jade shop, stood a tall elderly white man—lean and gray-haired. The man was Sammy's father. But it was too good to be true. For six years, Sammy had pursued will-o'-the-wisp rumors all over the Far East—wherever pearls were fished for, wherever elephants foregathered—in an attempt to lay his hands on that elusive father of his.

Old Bill Shay, an elephant man with Bartrom & Bradley's circus, had long ago deserted Singapore Sam's mother, taking all of her savings. Sam was about two years old at that time; but that wasn't Sam's only reason for wanting to lay hands on the old rascal. Bill Shay had in his possession the last will and testament of Sam's grandfather, which made Sam the heir to an estate valued at upward of a million dollars—if he could only secure and probate the will! But old Bill Shay was wise and wily; he had plans of his own.

Sam quickened his pace. He broke into a run. He expected that Bill Shay, staring in at the window, would take alarm and run like hell. But Bill Shay didn't move. He stood there—and was magically transformed into an old Burmese, staring wistfully at a jade image of the Gautama Buddha!

With angry disgust, Singapore Sam limped on.

The establishment known as the Happiest Blue Elephant was a nipa-thatched shanty with a galvanized iron roof. It contained a mahogany bar salvaged from the wreck of a ship, a half-dozen round tables, and a bench.

An oil lamp in gimbals picked out glints on bottles behind the bar, and turned into a dark buccaneer of a white man who stood with one foot on the brass rail, arguing confidentially with the brown man behind the bar.

The light also gleamed on the handle of a dirk sticking in the bar. That dirk was familiar. The handle was carved gold.

As if hypnotized by the golden gleam of the knife handle Singapore Sammy limped toward the bar. The buccaneer roared: "Hey! You red-headed ape!"

Singapore Sammy seized the edge of the bar, and it started to slide to leeward.

"You lousy bum!" he panted.

Here, at last, was reality. His troubles were over! For the man at the bar was Captain Lucifer Jones!

CHAPTER II

TO BE PERSUADED

STEADYING HIMSELF, GRINNING with delight, Singapore stared at this tried and true friend. Lucky Jones's face was somewhat blurred. He was pale, and his eagle's eyes were bloodshot.

The redhead glanced back at the gold-handled dirk. It was no longer sticking in the bar. Where it had been now stood a squat dark green bottle. *Gin-bijt*—raw trade gin. It would eat barnacles. It would reach a man's stomach with a result similar to that of swallowing a lighted skyrocket. And it was exactly what Sam needed to jolt him back to his senses.

He had no interest in the miracle itself. It wouldn't have surprised him, in the present state of his brain, if the dirk had transformed itself into a pair of dancing elephants.

He grasped the squat bottle in both hands, upended it, and let the liquid fire gurgle down his gullet. He set the bottle down and smacked his lips.

His companion of a thousand and one wild adventures now repeated the ritual. With deep gargling sounds, he dispatched a half pint of the fluid dynamite.

Both men smacked their lips.

"Boy," Lucky Jones said, focusing those keen blue eyes on his pal, "you sure look like the wrath of God! Look at them clothes! Look at that mud! Whose pig sty you been sleepin' in?"

Sam's vision was rapidly returning to normal. Lucky didn't look so hot himself, but he let it pass. He had too much to say.

"She got the pearl," he announced.

The buccaneer's head ducked down.

"Not Sally Lavender!"

"Yeah. And my roll—And Sidin' says she sold the Goose."

"Let's hear it, Red."

"There ain't much," Sammy said. "This tells the story."

He pulled the little chamois pouch out of his shirt, unknotted the red silk cord at its throat, took out the wad of pale green paper, and unfolded it for Lucky to read.

"What the day brings, she takes," the redhead repeated sourly. "What the night brings, she takes. What sunup and sundown brings, she takes. You can't name a time of day or night that ain't her office hours!"

"So," Lucky Jones jeered, "she made a sucker out of the big wise guy?"

"Let me tell you," Sammy growled. "I was doin' her a favor. I saved her lousy life. I took her off Simarong Island with a guy named Cosmo Sand, You don't know Simarong Island. Nobody knows Simarong Island. It's in the Tamil Sea, near Timor Laut. There's been a colony of political nuts living there since the war. They had a gold mine. And Sally went down there on a hot tip with my old man, to get some of the gold. They had her in the jug when I got there. So I managed to get her and this guy Cosmo Sand—a good guy—out of the jug and aboard the Goose."

"Yeah!" Lucky jeered. "You was always nuts over that dame."

"Don't say it again," Sammy said quietly, "if you don't want me to mop up on you. This guy Sand was nuts about her, too.

He wanted to take her back to America and reform her. And she says she was nuts about him, too.—And would I marry 'em?"

"How could a slab-sided ape like you marry 'em?"

"I was skipperin' the Goose, wasn't I?"

"You ain't got your skipper's ticket."

"WELL, IT would have been a good enough marriage for that little rat. But just as I was reading the service, she backs down. She starts to bawl, and says she can't go through with it. She says she's got to be free. She says she don't love Cosmo Sand, after all. So I drop him off, and I kick her off in Penang.—I got your cable, and I also picked up the old man's trail, headin' this way. So I put to sea again, and I wasn't hardly out into the straits, sittin' there at the wheel and smokin' my pipe, when she comes walkin' aft."

"Stowed away, eh?"

"Yeah. She says she knows I hate her like a shark, but please let her go as far as Rangoon. She says she's got friends here. So I says, 'Okay, baby. Just keep away from me and mind your own business; and if you pull any fast ones you are going overboard!'"

"Just the same, you're nuts about her—and you always will be."

Singapore Sammy balled his fists and snapped his teeth.

"Who the hell wants to say that again?"

"All right, all right!—Let's have the rest of it."

"I anchored here, off Sook Challaban's rice mill, about eight bells last night. Sally says, 'I hate to part with you like this, Sam—hatin' me the way you do. For crying in the foothills,' she says, 'let's let bygones be bygones! We will never see each other again. Let's have a farewell drink, and part friends.'

"So we come here and sit down at that table. That table, right there! I ordered a bottle of beer and she ordered a bottle of charged water. She started to cry. She told me I was the only friend she'd ever had, and that she could murder herself for all the fast ones she'd tried to pull."

"Did you mention the time she tricked us into that trench where the pythons were?" the buccaneer interrupted.

"No. I let her talk. She kept snifflin' away. She told me she loved me dearly and that I was really a fool not to team up with her and write a missus on her ticket.—'But I know how you feel about me,' she says. 'Drink your beer,' she says, 'and kiss me goodbye, and we will go our separate ways.'—I took a swig of the beer, and she looked at me with those big, starry eyes of hers. And ten seconds later I went out like a light."

"Yeah? I thought you was so smart!"

"I woke up an hour ago, in the mud," Sammy said in conclusion. "My roll was gone. The pearl was gone. She even took my small change. And somehow or other, she sold the Goose to a yellow-belly. Go ahead! Call me a sap! Call me a sucker! She's been after that pearl for two years. Well, she got it.—But I'll get it back! And when I do, there won't be a square inch on her that ain't black and blue!"

The coolie with the gray hood partly covering his face slipped into the Happiest Blue Elephant and sat down on the bench, with his back to the bar.

Sammy reached for the bottle of *gin-bijt.* But he did not lift the bottle to his mouth immediately. With his hairy red hand grasping it, he looked at Lucky Jones with an affectionate grin.

"ALL I got to be thankful for," Sam said, "is that one of us ain't such a sap. With that placer stake of yours, we can get started again. We can hire a lawyer to get the Goose back. And as long as we have the Goose under our heels, what the hell!"

"Yeah," Captain Jones said bitterly. "It's a good thing that only one of us is a sucker."

"How much gold did you find down there?"

"Close to eight thousand bucks."

"That's fine!" Sam said. "That's wonderful.—Here's to you!"

Lucifer Jones reached impulsively for the bottle, as it left

Sammy's mouth. He took a generous swig, and set the bottle down.

"About what time was it," he asked, "when she got through with you, last night?"

"Nine o'clock. Maybe nine-thirty."

"I met her at ten."

"You met who at ten?"

"I met Sally Lavender at ten."

"Yeah?—Go on."

"I was just comin' ashore from the pearlin' lugger that brought me up from Padang. She was walkin' past. We saw each other under a street light. It was a quincidence. She lets out a little yell, and then she flings both arms around me and kisses me."

"You always was nuts about her," Sammy said.

"If you're lookin' for trouble, say that again!"

"Nemmind. Then what?"

"She says she was never so glad to see a living mortal in her life. She says she was reformed. She says she had a job here, doin' stenographer work in a government office. She says she didn't have a friend in the world—and oh, how nice it was to see my face again!"

"Did she mention me?"

"Not till I brought you up. I said I was here lookin' for you, and she says she hasn't laid an eye on you in years. She says, 'Let's do somethin'—let's have some fun. I'm just dyin' for a little excitement!' she says.—So we went to Foy Toy's gamblin' house. We got to drinkin' and rollin' the bones."

"Just you and her?"

"That's all. Not against the house; just against each other. By the time we was through, she had my gold belt."

"The whole eight thousand?"

"The whole eight thousand. She began cryin'. She hated to take all that money away from a guy she liked so much. She says she wanted to give me a chance to win it all back—in one roll.

She says, 'Do you still own a half interest in that schooner?' And I says, 'Yes.' And she says, 'Where is she?' And I says, 'You're on the way here from somewhere.' And she says, 'Well, I'll tell you, Lucifer; I will roll you one roll for your interest in the *Blue Goose*, against this eight thousand in dust and nuggets.' So we rolled."

Lucky Jones fell silent. Singapore Sam said nothing.

"I went over to Lin Chang's boatyard this afternoon, when I'd sobered up. She had sold the Goose to Lin Chang for thirty thousand rupees."

"How could she?" Sam asked. "How could she sell my half interest?"

"She had a bill of sale, signed by you, for your half."

"She forged it—the dirty, double-crossing little—!"

"Well, Lin Chang took it—and she got the dough."

BOTH YOUNG men reached simultaneously for the gin bottle. After dividing what remained in it, Singapore said: "We're a pair of suckers! But we'll catch up with that dame if it takes us to our dying day. You are on the beach. I am on the beach. I think she came her to join up with my old man again. We are gonna catch the two of 'em, and we're gonna take them apart with our bare hands!"

"Sure!" Lucifer agreed with gravity. "And after that, we're gonna go to the Island of Balataboo. Ever hear of Balataboo?"

"Ixnay."

"Well, we're goin' there next. It's haunted. They say there's a thing that comes crawlin' up out of the sea, and wraps itself around its victims, all soft and slimy, and cracks their bones and sucks 'em dry—like an octopus. An old pearler used to live there. He's got a fortune in pearls buried there. This thing crawled out o' the sea and squeezed the juice out o' him—but the pearls are right there! The natives are scared of Balataboo. I got this straight from an old Dutchman in Palembang. To get there, though, we'll need some dough."

"Why?" Sammy answered. "It's only a three-thousand-mile swim—and we can eat air."

"To get to Balataboo," Lucky continued, "we'll need dough. And I've got an idea for raisin' the dough. Up in the jungles, about a hundred miles from here, there's a town called Bangwar. In this town there's a golden Buddha in a temple. He has ivory teeth, and in his forehead is a ruby as big as a major league baseball."

"I've been to Bangwar," Sammy interrupted. "I know Bangwar like the palm of my hand. But I know this gag better."

The coolie got up leisurely from the bench and slipped out of the Happiest Blue Elephant. A white man with crinkly-curling gray hair, who was drinking beer alone at a table, looked up sharply at Singapore Sam.

He looked away again.

"This Buddha—" Lucky began.

"This ruby," Sam again interrupted, "is a cinch! All you gotta do is climb up and pry it out—and Tiffany's will lay a hundred grand on the line for it!"

Lucky was looking at him admiringly.

"The only trouble with the gag is that these Fuzzy-Wuzzies don't know the meaning of distance or time or trouble, when it comes to trailin' down the saps who steal forehead jewels."

"Who said anything about stealin' a ruby?" the buccaneer interrupted. "This is better than any ruby. Between his teeth there's a little gold box—a kinda casket—"

"It wasn't there when I saw it two years ago."

"No. It didn't get there till lately."

"What's inside this gold casket?"

"A little lapis lazuli box."

"Yeah? What's inside that?"

"A little ivory box."

SINGAPORE SAM leaned heavily against the bar and waited.

"And inside the little ivory box there's a tube of red obsidian, covered with old Sanscrit writing carved into it. The inside of the tube is so small you can hardly insert a pin. It's stoppered at both ends; a diamond plug is at one end, an emerald plug at the other."

"And what's inside the tube?"

"A genuine whisker of the Great God Buddha!"

"Yeah?"

"Yeah."

"And what do we do with a lousy whisker?"

"We give it back to the guys it was stole from—and collect one hundred thousand rupees! It was stolen from up river. It belongs to a temple in the village of Lak Chan."

Singapore Sammy's green-blue eyes had turned dreamy with speculation.

"So that's their gag," he growled.

"Whose gag?"

"A few minutes ago two different guys braced me on this same proposition," Sam answered. "Anyhow, it sounds like the same proposition. A nice, easy night's work—a hundred-thousand-rupee split. Every mug in the Far East seems to know about this hundred-thousand-rupee whisker. Unless I'm cockeyed, the biggest crook convention in years is gonna meet in Bangwar. Where did you hear about it?"

"From a little Burmese girl named Ma Kwe Yo."

"That means Miss Dog's Bone. Where'd you meet her?"

"She was standin', lookin' up at the Big Pagoda. Well, you know how pretty these Shan girls can get. We got into a conversation. I could see she'd been cryin'. It seems she's from Lak Shan. She's dedicated her life to the job of gettin' that whisker back for her village, but she don't know how to go about it. And she don't want any of the jack, either. She says she has a scheme—a good one—but it'll take a coupla guys. I told her I expected my pal in port any minute, and if I found him, we'd talk it over."

"Why don't she want any of the jack?"

"All she wants is the honor of takin' the whisker back to Lak Shan. It'll give her a lot of merit."

"What else did she tell you?"

"She says, if we're interested, to meet her in the big teak yard, up the river.—And she told me something about this whisker. It's the only genuine whisker of Buddha in the world, she says. She says it's worth a million rupees, anyhow. But her village is starvin' poor, and all they can scrape up for a reward is a hundred thousand."

"How did Bangwar get the whisker?"

"Some tough mug—a Bangwarese who wanted to be a big shot stole it out of the Lak Chan Temple. The Lak Chans are peaceable people, and they won't go to war to get it back unless everything else flops. Well, that's the lay. It's a chance to knock off a nice little pile of jack. What do you think about it?"

"I think you're nuts!"

"Okay," Lucifer Jones said angrily. "If you know a better way to knock off a hundred thousand rupees as easy as takin' pennies off a dead man's eyes, let's hear about it!"

SINGAPORE SAMMY looked dreamily at the gin bottle for a number of seconds. He furrowed his brow. But no ideas came tumbling out.

"What's the matter with the idea?" Lucky persisted.

"Nothing. Only it's lousy. There's too much competition. We would be up against killers like Rincon Deal and Joe Fong. They're on this job, too. They've got well-trained gangs. They'll all be in Bangwar as soon as we are, or sooner. If any of these guys spot me up there—I'm cooked! And if any of these fanatic priests smell us out, we're fried in oil! Any way I look at it, Bangwar ain't a health resort."

"The trouble is," Lucky argued, "you've lost your confidence. And you're overlookin' a bet. If all the smart crooks are headin' for this job, why won't Sally Lavender and your old man be in the procession? What makes you think that little tomato, Sally, didn't get word about this whisker while you were in Penang—word from your old man to meet up with him here? They'll be there."

"Maybe," Sam said. "And maybe they're like me—too smart to be there. Any time you get mixed up with anything that's been copped out of one of these Fuzzy-Wuzzy temples, you're sayin', 'Howdy, Trouble!'"

"Look at it this way," his pal said, with the patience of one trying to reason with a stubborn child. "First of all, we're on the beach. You may think we ain't, just because you're full of gin at the present moment."

"What dice-throwin' sucker says I'm full of gin?"

Lucifer Jones hitched up his belt. "No sap who lets the fast-est-working skirt in the Far East put knock-out drops in his beer can call me a sucker!"

"Yeah?" Sammy snarled. "And what name do you give a guy who lets the same skirt take his roll and his schooner *without* puttin' K.O. drops in his beer?"

"Who says she didn't put knockout drops in my gin?"

"You didn't say she did!"

"Did I say she didn't?"

"Did she?"

"She did!"

The two pals held their fighting postures for a moment.

"Where was we?" Lucky inquired.

"On the beach. Just a coupla lousy beach combers."

"You're my pal," Lucky said. "Don't ever forget that."

He wiped a tear from his eye with the back of one hairy hand.

"I won't forget it," Sammy said. "If I live to be older than the pyramids of Egypt, I'll never forget it."

"If we could just get to Balataboo Island, where them pearls are," Jones took up the broken threads of his discourse, "we could carve off some wonderful excitement for ourselves. But where do we get the jack?"

Singapore Sam made an airy gesture with his hand. "I'm open to any suggestion," he said.

"Then we'll grab the whisker and collect a hundred thousand rupees. It's our chance to get back on our feet, get back on our ship, and get our bank rolls back on our hips. What do you say?"

"I say, you're nuts!"

"Is it gonna cost you anything to chew some fat with this Shan girl?"

Sammy pushed himself away from the bar, flecked a flake of dried mud from the lapel of his white coat.

"Okay," he said. "We'll chew some fat with the Shan girl—and the scheme will still be lousy."

As they left the bar, the man with the crinkly-curling gray hair finished his beer, got up and sauntered out. He watched them with a grim, evil smile as they walked unsteadily away.

CHAPTER III

UNCOOKED SCHEME

IT WAS A five-mile hike to the big teakyard, the last part of the way through mud up to their ankles, because there was no light to reveal the meanderings of the narrow plank walk. Reeling slightly, as they left the Happiest Blue Elephant, they were nevertheless sober enough when they arrived at the teakyard.

In the head *mahout's* hut, near the elephant sheds, they found Miss Dog's Bone. She was drinking *lehpet,* or pickled tea, and eating an appetizing mess of purple rice, fried red ants, iguanas' eggs and fish paste when the two weary adventurers climbed the ladder to the doorway of the little thatched dwelling.

Sammy surveyed her skeptically as she arose from her cross-legged position on the floor and laid her lacquered bowl and chopsticks on the mat beside the brazier.

A brass lamp shed soft golden rays on her pretty brown face, and the rainbow hues of the *tamein* wound tightly over her ripe young breasts. It fell in soft, bright folds below her knees. Sammy saw that she had dainty ankles and naked little feet. Bright, fragrant malla flowers from the jungle were like colored stars in her blue-black hair, which was arranged in an elaborate coiffure glistening with coconut oil.

She carried no cheroots through holes in her ears, as do most Burmese beauties. She would have been beautiful, according to American standards, if her teeth had not been darkened by betel chewing since she was a child.

Sammy guessed her age at sixteen. He could understand Lucky's interest.

Miss Dog's Bone greeted the two American beach combers with the gayety of her kind. She laughed excitedly and clapped her little brown hands. Her eyes became shimmering stars, but her mouth was grave as she uttered the accustomed greeting:

"May Buddha bless the stranger within our humble walls!"

Singapore Sammy, who spoke the Burmese tongue almost as fluently as he did his own, gave the accustomed answer:

"Let us hope to be preserved from the Three Calamities, from the Four States of Punishment, and from the Five Enemies!"

The head *mahout*, a skinny old man with fuzzy white hair worn in a topknot, bleated devoutly:

"The sun may rise in the West; the summit of Mount Meru may be bent like a bow; the fires of hell may languish and die out, the lotus may spring on the tops of the mountains, but the words of Truth and Wisdom are always the same."

"You have come to help my people!" Miss Dog's Bone declared.

"We have come to talk the matter over," Singapore corrected her. "Do you speak our language, Ma Kwe Yo?"

"A tiny leetle," she answered.

"Is Burmese okay for you, Lucky?" asked Sam, turning to his companion.

"I know it like a duck knows water. Shoot!"

In Burmese, then, Sammy said to Miss Dog's Bone, "Talk, sister."

Ma Kwe Yo began animatedly to talk. The sacred whisker of Buddha, she said, had been under the personal guardianship of her father, who was one of the head men of Lak Chan—an honor which had been handed down from father to son for hundreds of years.

"The disgrace has almost killed my poor father," the Shan girl said. "It has sickened all the people of my village. And it has filled us full of a great fear. For all these centuries, we have worshiped the sacred whisker. Now that it is gone, it is as if the life had run out of Lak Chan. And we live in daily fear of a great catastrophe."

Miss Dog's Bone's small brown face was fascinating in its liveliness. Her eyebrows were in perpetual motion. She registered sadness, fear, happiness, and other emotions, with animated hands and features. And animation heightened her soft appeal.

"A guy could fall for a dame like this," Sammy said in an English aside to Lucifer Jones.

"Yeah!" Captain Jones affirmed. "And don't forget who saw her first!"

MISS DOG'S BONE was ardently explaining that she did not believe that a man from Bangwar had stolen the whisker from the Lak Chan temple. It was her father's belief that the unforgivable theft had been the inspiration of Japanese spies, who were doing everything in their power to start trouble in Burma—to distract attention from the Japanese campaign in Manchuria.

"Yet the Bangwarese have always been a warlike, greedy people," Ma Kwe Yo said. "The golden Buddha in the Temple of the Golden Buddha, in Bangwar, was made of gold ornaments stolen from temples all over Burma, six hundred years ago. These ornaments were melted and cast into the big golden Buddha. The teeth are of elephant ivory, beautifully shaped and carved. The teeth are parted. And in this space between the teeth there now rests the golden casket containing the sacred whisker."

Miss Dog's Bone clasped her little brown hands over her heart.

"The sacred whisker must be returned to my people—or we are doomed. My people will pay a hundred thousand rupees for its return. It is an undertaking for a pair of strong, brave men like yourselves. I am only my father's emissary."

"Where would we collect this money?" Sammy asked.

"From Mr. Beyond Comparison—Maung San Nyun."

She indicated the old *mahout,* who bobbed his fuzzy topknot in affirmation.

"What's this scheme of yours, sister?"

Ma Kwe Yo removed from the folds of her *engyi* a small green silk pouch, of the size and shape of an ordinary tobacco pouch. She opened it with great care, saying:

"This is very dangerous."

Sammy peered into the green pouch and saw a mass of blue powder, soft and light as dust.

"This is a magic powder," the Shan girl said. "It is sleeping powder—very swift and deadly. If you were to breathe into your lungs the amount of it that I can pinch between my two fingers, you would fall asleep instantly! Yet there are other ways of using it, and this is my plan. The temple of the Golden Buddha has only two doors. But it is guarded day and night by twelve powerful young priests. Not only that, but if they saw any one attempting to climb the Buddha and steal the sacred whisker, they would make outcries, and a thousand men would answer!"

"I get it," Sammy said. "You go into the temple and blow this stuff into the priests' faces."

He shook his head firmly.

"Sister, you couldn't get away with it." And to Lucky, "The scheme is still lousy. From the minute we went into Bangwar until the minute we pulled out, we would be on a hot spot. If they spotted us, they would carve our hearts out."

"But that is not how I have planned it," Ma Kwe Yo said. "If this powder is dropped into the incense pots, it will swiftly fill the air with fumes which cannot be seen or smelled—and these fumes are as deadly as if the powder were blown into one's face!"

"What's the rest of it, sister?"

"One of you stands at either of the two temple doors, to prevent any one from coming in while I sprinkle the powder in the incense pots—and get the sacred whisker!"

"Wait a minute. A whale could swim through the loopholes in that scheme. How can Captain Jones and I, standing in each doorway, stop people from shoving past us into the temple? And what's to prevent this powder from putting you to sleep, along with the priests?"

MA KWE YO laughed gayly. "Did I not say it is a magic powder? It will not affect me!"

Singapore grunted, "I don't believe in black magic or blue magic, either, sister."

She giggled excitedly.

"But it is so simple!" Miss Dog's Bone cried. "I carry with me a little piece of silk. So." She produced it—a little square of white hand-loomed Irriwaddi silk. "I hold it to my nose. So." She placed it against her dainty nostrils. "I pour some of the magic blue powder into the braziers—the incense pots. I breathe through the magic handkerchief. I do not go to sleep!"

She laughed excitedly.

Sammy reached out and took the handkerchief.

"If this gag is on the level," he said to Lucky, "this hunka cloth is soaked with some chemical that filters out the blue smoke, the same way the chemicals in a gas mask filter out poison gas."

He held the silk to his nose and sniffed. He detected a pungent aroma, a certain spiciness.

The Shan girl merrily added, "I hold it to my little nose—and all the blue magic ever brewed in Mandalay cannot make me fall asleep!"

"You dead sure?" Sammy asked, dubiously.

"It is all part of the magic!"

"All right, sister. We will grant that this stuff will do what you say. But what's to prevent anybody from slipping past us while you're putting the priests to sleep and getting the whisker?"

"Mr. Beyond Comparison will show you!"

The old *mahout* opened a teakwood chest which stood against a thatched wall.

Out of it he spirited bolts of yellow silk and other objects.

"Your costumes!" Miss Dog's Bone cried. "You go to Bangwar dressed as Buddhist begging priests. Here is the *dugot!*" She held up the two bolts of yellow silk. "Your robes! Here is the *kowut* and here the *thabeit.*"

The *thabeit*, or begging pot, looked like a soup tureen, only it had a long leather thong by which it was intended to hang from the mendicant's neck.

"And here is the *kaban*, the *pekot*, the *at*, and the *yesit.*" She displayed, in turn, a leather girdle, a small ax, a needle and a water strainer. "And here is a little bottle of stain for your skin."

Lucky said admiringly, "Is she hot—or is she hot?"

Sammy was carefully inspecting the robes and the equipment. He presently laid them aside and pondered. His red eyebrows were a flat line which met above his nose. His forehead was corrugated.

Impatiently, Lucky snapped, "Well, how do you like the scheme? It sounds good to me."

"Yeah? Well, it still sounds lousy to me."

"Louse-see?" Ma Kwe Yo repeated, with a bewildered air.

"Let me think a moment, sister," said Sammy.

Mr. Beyond Comparison nodded his fuzzy white topknot in eager affirmation.

"The beauty of women and the sweetness of sugarcane bring satiety," he pronounced judicially, "but the words of wisdom never pall. Let this man think, my daughter."

Miss Dog's Bone nodded. From a little lacquered box beside her she removed a golden betel case. Opening this, she took out a bright green ceri-leaf on which she dabbed lime paste of a vermilion color. Adding a pinch of powdered tobacco, she rolled the leaf into a wad, popped it into her mouth, and began to chew.

Her starry eyes watched Sammy dreamily. From time to time she gave him a demure little smile. She was flirting with Sammy.

"**THERE MAY** be a better way," he said presently. "But I've got to think it over."

"The more you know," Mr. Beyond Comparison said sagely, "the more luck you have. This man is no dunce."

"When do you figure," Sammy asked, "on pulling this stunt?"

"To-day is the Day of the Tiger," Miss Dog's Bone answered. "It is not my lucky day. But to-morrow is the Day of the Lion—a very lucky day indeed for me. However, to-morrow there will be a great mob in Bangwar. Had we not better wait until the following day—the Day of the Elephant With Tusks?"

"What's going on to-morrow?"

"There will be a sacrifice to the Balancing Buddha."

Sammy pondered. He said to Lucky:

"If we're gonna be a pair of saps and help this baby, it will have to be to-morrow. We've gotta act quick—before every crook in the Far East gets there."

He turned back to Miss Dog's Bone, "How well do you know Bangwar, sister?"

"I know it well. Do you?"

"Like a book. Do you know where the big rest *sala* is, down by the river?"

She nodded brightly.

"Can you be there by to-morrow morning?"

The *mahout* said, "I will provide her with my fastest elephant. She will be there well before the dawn."

"Then you will help?" Miss Dog's Bone asked with eagerness.

"Not so fast, sister! If we get the whisker, where do we collect the hundred thousand rupees?"

"From Mr. Beyond Comparison."

Firmly Sammy said, "All right, Maung San Nytin; let's see the color of those rupees."

His jaw was firmly set.

The old *mahout* said ironically, "Thou art undoubtedly a *yahanda*, fit for Ne'ban, possessed of the Six Kinds of Wisdom."

Nevertheless, he reopened the teakwood chest and brought forth a fat roll of rupee notes. And when Sammy had assured himself that this not stage money, and that the roll contained approximately the amount stated, Sammy and Lucifer Jones took their departure, taking with them the begging robes and equipment.

The little brown girl came to the doorway and ejected into the darkness from her lips a stream of bright vermilion juice.

"Do not forget, brave one," she cautioned Sammy, "that the begging monk fixes his eyes unwaveringly on the ground, six paces ahead, with hands clasped beneath the begging bowl, and solemnly meditating on his own unworthiness and the vileness of all human beings!"

"It will be easy, sister. Besides, I've worn this get-up before."

"Thou art a prince!" the little Burmese girl laughed.

WADING BACK through the mud toward the center of Rangoon, Singapore said:

"It's dynamite! These Fuzzy-Wuzzies have a saying, 'When luck stops smiling, tickling does no good.' We are down on our luck. We gotta be careful. We don't want eight inches of curved steel in our backs. That scheme of hers leaves too much to chance."

"Have you got a better one?"

"I certainly have—but it isn't all cooked yet. Let it stew a while. I am interested in this sacrifice to the Balancing Buddha."

"What's it all about?"

"It's a racket that makes any American big-city racket you ever heard about sound like tinhorn stuff. Every year, they make a human sacrifice to this Balancing Buddha. He's a squatting

Buddha on top of a big pyramid. One of his hands has mechan-ical fingers, worked from inside. They put the sucker to be sacri-ficed into this hand, and the guys inside pull levers or turn wheels that make the fingers close down on the sucker."

"Where's the racket?"

"It's a honey! Every year, long before the big day, the Bang-war priests go around visiting people who have sons about the right age. The right age is twelve. They tell these people that the stars in their courses looked pretty good for their boy. They tell 'em that it looks as if the star gods are gonna pick their boy. And every family that has a son around that age gets a visit from this strong-arm squad.

"When they tell 'em how good things look for their boy to have the honor of getting squashed by the mechanical hand, the parents cough up. If you cough up enough, your boy isn't honored by being squashed. Naturally, the boy they elect every year always comes from poor parents."

"Why don't the British do something about it?" Lucifer Jones asked indignantly.

"Because the Bangwarese are too powerful and too danger-ous. The British just don't happen to be lookin' that way when it happens.—The resident goes down river to visit his mother-in-law, and the other white officials decide that it's a fine day for a tiger hunt. Not a white man stays in Bangwar on the day of the sacrifice. The natives go nuts. They work themselves into a frenzy. A white man caught in Bangwar to-morrow is just outa luck.

"When we go to Bangwar tomorrow it'll be like walkin' into a powder magazine smokin' Pittsburgh stogies. I mean—danger-ous. My scheme ain't ready yet. I'm foolin' with an idea for killin' two birds with one stone."

They were passing the Rangoon gymkhana grounds. Sammy said: "I got to see an American architect. While I'm seein' him, you get us a speed boat. I'll meet you at the yacht club."

CHAPTER IV

THE TEST

WITHOUT QUESTIONS, LUCKY went on toward the river. Sammy turned into the compound of the Minto Mansions Hotel. At the desk he inquired for Mr. Stanley Rysdale. A Chinese boy appeared presently and conducted him to Mr. Rysdale's suite—perhaps the most amazing hotel suite in all Burma, if not in the entire Far East. The rooms were filled with Oriental treasures of a beauty and rarity which would have entitled them to prominent space in any great museum. In one room was the finest private collection of images of Buddhas in existence. On the walls were rare tapestries. On the floors were rare rugs. And on tables and taborets about the rooms were knick-knack objects of jade and gold and silver; braziers, shrines and obscure Oriental gods; carved inlaid tusks, sacred plaques—treasures beyond cataloging.

Stanley Rysdale enjoyed the unique distinction of being the only Occidental architect in this exotic land who had ever succeeded in winning the confidence and trust of these pagan peoples. How he had won it was a mystery. The fact remained that he was called upon to design and supervise the construction of temples for Chitties, Hindus, and Buddhists alike.

Stanley Rysdale was a slender, scholarly man of about fifty with shining silver hair and twinkling eyes. At the moment, the architect was bending over a drawing table littered with blueprints and a draughtsman's paraphernalia.

Mr. Rysdale got up and grasped Sammy's hand.

"Sam Shay!" he cried. "You old pirate, you're just the man I'm looking for! You must have come in answer to my prayers. I'm leaving for Tibet next week, and I want you to take charge of the expedition. You're it!"

"I'm out," Sammy said. "I got a date with an island next week."

"Buried treasure?" the architect asked softly.

"Who told you about it?"

Mr. Rysdale chuckled. "There hasn't been a time since I've known you when you haven't been hunting buried treasure. What can I do for you to-night?"

"I'm thinking of going up to Bangwar to see the sacrifice to-morrow. I was wondering how much you knew about Bangwar."

"I've spent some time in Bangwar."

"How much did you have to do with the architecting of those Buddhist temples?"

"I built the temple of the Sapphire Buddha. I re-designed several others which were about to collapse of old age. You know how these Buddhists are, Sam. They acquire merit only in the building of a temple or a shrine. Doing repair work doesn't give them an ounce of merit. So they let their temples go to pieces. When I get a Buddhist temple to do, I invariably try to sell them on the idea of strengthening and repairing the old temples. But it's a thankless job."

"What do you know about the Balancing Buddha at Bangwar?"

Mr. Rysdale eyed Sammy narrowly and gave him a brief, hard grin.

"That's a horse of a slightly different color!" he answered. "It wasn't originally a balancing Buddha at all. It got that way through erosion—sun, rains, the general ravages of time. I inspected it pretty thoroughly. And I went away from there pretty rapidly! There it sits, ready to go crashing down that pyramid at the first earthquake. A hundred-mile wind could start it down. I told the head priests at Bangwar that it might kill a lot of people some day.

"But they don't want it changed. Its balancing stunt is, they say, a symbol. For the past seventy years, they've called it the Buddha of Life. They fancy the notion that, because of its precarious balance, it symbolizes life. Perhaps they're right. I myself have found life fairly precarious. If I wanted to walk into the very jaws of death, I should visit Bangwar—to-morrow! Why are you interested in the Balancing Buddha?"

"I was just wonderin'," Sammy answered.

The architect, wise in the wisdom of the East, asked no further questions. He said, as Sammy started to go: "If you should change your mind about Tibet, let me know."

"Okay, Mr. Rysdale."

SAMMY LEFT the Minto Mansions Hotel in a thoughtful frame of mind. He secured his begging robe and paraphernalia from under the dwarf tamarind where he had left them, and proceeded toward the river.

But he did not go directly to the Rangoon Yacht Club. He had one more little errand to do. Almost in the shadow of the great, golden pagoda he came to a road which was under construction. Beside a steam shovel he saw a small shanty, and in the lee of this the glow of a red spark. A moment later he detected the sour, acrid fumes of a cheap cheroot.

A British watchman rose up from the darkness. This was, Sammy reflected, as good a time as any to try the sample of blue powder he had filched from Miss Dog's Bone's silk pouch. He placed it in the palm of his hand and folded his fingers tightly over it.

"Hi, brother!" he called amiably, as he approached the watchman.

"Keep right on rollin' along, you," the watchman replied, with a strong cockney accent.

Sammy opened his palm, placed it close to his mouth—and blew hard in the watchman's face.

The cockney uttered some fearful oaths. He sputtered and heavily sat down. With a soft groan he rolled over on his side.

Sammy knelt beside him, felt his pulse and listened to his breathing.

"Brother," he said, "with any kind of luck, except the kind I've been havin' lately, you'll be awake in time to save your job."

A gentle snore was his answer. Sammy marveled. He'd have to get a supply of this blue powder. There had been times in the past when he would have gladly paid a thousand dollars for a pinch of it. It was truly magical stuff.

He went to the shanty and entered it. He selected three sticks of sixty per cent powder, a six-foot length of fuse, and three percussion caps. These he distributed about his person. Then, warily, he started toward the Rangoon Yacht Club.

Lucifer Jones was waiting under a bush near the entrance. He conducted Sammy to the river front and silently indicated a long, low racy mahogany speedboat.

"Gassed up?" Sammy asked.

"Yeah. And she's the fastest thing on the river."

"Okay, buddy. Crank 'er up."

Forty seconds later the two thieves were skimming over the dark and silent waters of the Rangoon River at forty miles an hour.

IT WAS a little after four o'clock in the morning when they ran the Lotus Land under the overhanging mahogany trees on the left bank of the Rangoon, about a mile below the city of Bangwar. Ashore with their disguises, they pushed the Lotus Land out into the stream, where, presumably, it would be carried down past Rangoon in due course, and perhaps be recognized by its surprised owner.

By the discreet light of candles, the two adventurers painted each other with walnut stain and shaved each other's heads, staining even their scalps walnut.

Singapore Sammy's blue-green eyes were a dangerous feature about which nothing could be done. But with his eyes downcast, according to ritual, he might escape attention. He *must* escape attention—or never leave here alive!

The sun was coming up over the jungle across the river, when they set forth with packs on back, eyes downcast, begging bowls held in steady hands, but with thumping hearts and tingling nerves.

They made their first stop at a little rest *sala* where a family of upcountry pilgrims were preparing breakfast. The two begging priests were received with respect, if not with enthusiasm. The Far East is ridden with beggars, and begging priests are only a shade superior to ordinary beggars. But their yellow robes got them a meal. They drank pickled tea, and ate bowls of boiled rice and curry. They hadn't been suspected!

Breakfast over, the two adventurers followed an old elephant trail along the river to the large rest *sala,* and their rendezvous with the Burmese maiden. With the admirable patience of the East, Miss Dog's Bone was waiting under a banyan tree, leisurely smoking a whacking white cheroot. She stood up respectfully when the two monks in yellow robes stopped and saluted her with flowery Burmese good-mornings. This was nervous work.

"Your presence, my daughter," said the more talkative of the two holy men in a voice loud enough for bystanders to hear, "is as soothing as shade after heat. Your form is as grace-ful as a young tree. The palms of your hands are like lotus blossoms. Madi, the wife of Mahawthata, was famed for her charity. We holy men crave an after-breakfast smoke. One glance assured us that you are as generous as you are beau-tiful."

The Burmese maiden gravely produced a pair of white cheroots ten inches in length by an inch in diameter. She lighted them.

The holy men accepted them and puffed. Lucifer Jones began to cough, but somehow suppressed it. Sam's heart stopped beat-ing for a moment.

They strolled on, and Ma Kwe Yo, after an interval, strolled after them. The two men waited near a palm tree. Temple gongs were beginning to ring. The fragrance of fine incense slowly perfumed the morning air. The feeling of tension increased, also.

"Brave ones," Miss Dog's Bone whispered, "what is our plan?"

Sammy, in detail, described the plan which had been hatching in his head. Ma Kwe Yo listened with large, starry eyes of alarm and excitement. Sammy wondered if she was as nervous as he was.

"We shall not see you again," Sammy concluded, "until it is all over. Where shall we meet?"

"At the north gate," Miss Dog's. Bone said decisively. "There are bushes there where I can hide. I will hide with the sacred whisker, there in those bushes, until you come. And do not delay, my brave ones. I shall be in a state of terror. I shall need your courage."

"The north gate," Sammy verified. "We will all meet in the bushes at the north gate."

"Go thou with Buddha, my king!" the little Burmese maiden said huskily.

Lucky was growling under his breath when they left her.

"Last night you were her prince, and now you're her king. You're goin' up in the world!—Where the hell do I come in? It's always like this. I go out and find me a nifty little doll—and you ain't happy till you cop her!"

"I got something they can't resist."

"Horseradish!"

"There's the Balancing Buddha," Sammy said, and shivered.

The image occupied the peak of a black stone pyramid of four sides—a stern gray mass against the early morning sky. And the pyramid occupied the center of a plateau known as the Plain of the Thousand and One Buddhas.

At the base of the pyramid were numerous shrines, some of marble, some of stone, some of bronze. In each shrine was an image of Buddha.

CHAPTER V

THE WHISPERER

AS THE TWO young men climbed up the winding road which led to the Plain of the Thousand and One Buddhas, Sammy pointed out various objects of interest; tried to stop feeling so jumpy.

"Over yonder," he said, "the temple with the blue roof—that's the Temple of the Golden Buddha. That's where the whisker is."

Lucky glanced in the direction of the cobalt roof, but his eyes, as if fascinated, strayed back to the great gray god atop the black pyramid. The image was evidently carved of stone—a Buddha of the usual seated type. The head must have been at least fifteen feet in diameter. This Buddha sat there with its great stone arms folded upon its great stone chest. The fingers of the left hand were distended.

"That," Sammy said, "is where they put the victim. Then those fingers curl down on him and squash him. But let's take a look at the golden Buddha. I want to see that casket."

"Okay. But let's walk around some first. I want to get the feel of this place. I was never so nervous in my life."

The two adventurers strolled on toward the great black pyramid, with their eyes piously fixed on the ground, but missing nothing, their begging bowls ready for anything that anybody wished to contribute. Both of them continued to perspire freely.

At the foot of the pyramid there was an open space, perhaps five hundred yards wide. This extended about the entire base of the black pyramid. Flanking this open space were countless small and large shrines where resided reclining Buddhas, laughing Buddhas, starving Buddhas, Buddhas of prosperity, of sorrow, of meditation.

From time to time, the two young men stopped to stare up

the black steps of the pyramid at the famous Balancing Buddha. It seemed to cast a spell over them.

Near the pyramid steps, on the west side, they came upon a gigantic sun dial. It was carved from rock—a finger of gray rock about ten feet tall, with a sharp point. It threw a sun shadow somewhat greater than that length; and on the gray flagging below, a fresh cross had been made with blood-red paint.

"The sacrifice takes place," Sammy explained, "when the shadow reaches that X. It won't be long."

Nearby was a tragic family group—father, mother and son. They sat in a bullock cart, and were the objects of grave curiosity. Yet no one approached them closely. Poverty-stricken farming people they appeared to be; an elderly, toil-bent Burmese, his toil-worn wife, and a son of ten or eleven, all of them lemon-hued with fright. As if enchanted, the three were staring up at the great Balancing Buddha.

SAMMY AND Lucky paused again to look up. The sun was just rising behind the pyramid, silhouetting against an aura of gold the great gray mass at its peak.

The two begging priests approached the bullock cart. The parents of the sacrificial victim stared at them dry-eyed, without betraying their grief. But the boy was sobbing in a frightened way.

Sammy laid his hand on his shoulder, and the boy looked up at him with blurred, reddened eyes.

"Why do you weep, my son?"

"Because, holy father, I am to die to-day."

Sammy's eyes shifted to the boy's mother.

"Take heart, my daughter," he said. "Buddha may yet save the life of this small one. It is the Day of the Lion. It is a day of many miracles."

The woman gave them a heartbroken smile. "Buddha is all-wise, all-seeing, all-hearing," she intoned. "I have made offerings. I have said many prayers. But I have lost hope. The time is so near! In less than an hour, holy father, my little son is to be crushed in The Hand."

Her eyes, suddenly terrified, stared at the sun dial.

"My daughter," Sammy said sternly, "I have told you that this is a day of miracles. You will take your small son home with you to-day—alive and happy. I have spoken!"

The woman seized his hand and kissed it. The father gave each of the holy men a ripe mango. The priests strolled away, eating the juicy tropical fruit.

"Sap!" Lucifer Jones hissed. "You want to tip us off?"

"Who the hell says I tipped us off?"

"All that horseradish about miracles!"

"Listen, gnat-brained. That poor dame needed encouragement. And when we get through with this joint, they'll think a dozen miracles have hit 'em at once!"

"Nuts! She was lookin' right at them green eyes of yours!"

"She was blind from cryin'.—Now let's take a look at this Golden Buddha. I want to check over Miss Dog's Bone's part in this miracle of ours."

"You think she's bit off too much?"

"My luck don't feel right yet."

They passed a Punch-and-Judy show.

Beyond, in a compound, a rich Burmese in royal purple satins was tossing limes for which a hundred half-naked brown children were scrambling. The limes were slit, and each contained a silver coin.

A lime rolled past Lucky's feet. He started after it, but Singapore grabbed his elbow.

"Let it lay, you swab! This is a kid's game."

THE GHOST of a whisper reached them from behind, at that moment. It was a whisper calculated to send shivers along the spine of a bronze image. It was like the wailing whisper of a banshee. Chillingly, it said:

"You guys are gonna get yours!"

The two holy men turned quickly about, with banging hearts. All about them were large and little shrines. Each contained a solemn Buddha. No one was in sight who could possibly have uttered that banshee whisper, that startling warning.

Even as they stared, it came again, like a shiver in the breeze— *"You guys are gonna get yours!"*

"Says who?" Lucky inquired.

"Pipe down," Sammy whispered. "It's a gag. Leave it lay. Come on!"

Freely perspiring, the two yellow-robed mendicants started again toward the temple of the Golden Buddha. From the tails of his eyes, Sammy explored the neighborhood. No one was in sight except the elderly Burmese in royal purple, who continued to toss limes to happy, scrambling urchins. Singapore stared at him for a moment with great interest.

Then, at a quickened pace, the two worried adventurers proceeded to the temple with the blue roof.

This was one of the largest and most imposing temples on the plain. The walls were of blue tile and heavy teakwood timbers. Glass and silver wind bells tinkled under the eaves. In the doorway a black-robed priest thumbed the taut skin of a great drum, sending forth mumbling sounds almost too low in pitch to register upon the human ear.

Lounging near the doorway was a Burmese with a stalk of sugar cane under one arm. He had black eyes. A half-inch of native cigarette was pasted to his lower lip. His shiny little eyes flitted across the faces of the two priests.

Sammy looked at him thoughtfully, and his eyes narrowed. "Trouble!" he whispered to Lucky.

The two priests went into the rich, fragrant darkness of the blue temple. In the distance, gleaming, was gold; and as their eyes grew used to the brown murk, the two Americans saw the famous Buddha in greater detail.

He must have weighed twenty tons—twenty tons of what seemed to be pure gold! He sat, in the usual squatting posture, on a blue stone dais. The dais was six feet from the temple floor, and was enclosed in a brass and ebony fence of about the same height. On either side of the dais, in front of the fence, was a large incense pot which sent lazy coils of scented blue smoke toward the black rafters.

Sammy studied the incense pots, but his eyes quickly returned to the massive golden idol. He glanced at the great ruby burning with deep fire in the idol's placid forehead. Then his eyes descended to the tranquilly smiling mouth.

This was the only Buddha with teeth he had ever seen. They had amazed him before. Each was a tusk of ivory, cleverly carved into a giant's tooth. The teeth were parted about three inches, and lying on the lower row of teeth was a little gold casket—the casket containing the sacred whisker of Buddha. It was beautifully carved, and about four inches long by an inch wide and thick. It gleamed, it twinkled, with precious stones. It was a fitting repository for such a priceless relic—a genuine whisker from the chin of the great god Buddha!

It wasn't worth a hundred thousand rupees. It was worth a hundred million!

THINLY, THE banshee whisper again shivered through the rich gloom of the great blue temple:

"You guys are gonna get yours!"

Singapore remained in an attitude of rigidity, staring up devoutly at the little golden casket. But he had found and was gripping Lucky's elbow fiercely.

"The joint," Sammy whispered, "is crawlin' with 'em! Half the people here are crooks. Those three heavy-shouldered Chinese standing by the *paribawga* are some o' Javanese Jimmy's gang. That guy out front with the sugar cane is an Indo-Chinese. He don't belong here."

He paused, and then his grip on Lucky's elbow tightened. Over the crowd, near the eastern doorway, he had glimpsed a tall, sad-looking man with crinkly, curling gray hair. The man's skin was as brown as Sammy's.

"Pipe the guy with the gray hair," Sammy whispered. "That guy was drinkin' beer in the Blue Elephant last night—but he was a white man then! He's a temple priest now! That's Penang Pete, or I'm screwy!"

The man with crinkly, curling gray hair was looking at Sammy. The expression on his face did not change any more than the expression on the face of a still lake changes when a thin skin of ice suddenly, instantaneously, forms across it. It was simply that its wary expression became set.

Penang Pete—if it was he—lifted one shoulder slightly. Sammy knew that this was a signal, and Sammy's eyes became busy, looking for signs that that signal was being executed. But there was no disturbance.

"He's spotted us," Sammy whispered, and was conscious of a sudden tightening in the atmosphere. You could expect a dirk in the back at any moment now. "We'd better get out of here. We don't belong here anyhow. I figure there's at least five different gangs here, and Lord knows how many ambitious guys on their own!"

"Who the hell's been doin' that whisperin'?"

"If we could only figure it out! It may be my old man. It may be Sally. You know damned well they'll be here. And they're probably here with the smartest scheme of all. If we could only spot 'em!—But we're gonna find out who's doin' that whisperin'—or we're fried!"

Sammy took a final look at the golden Buddha as they started out. He was trying to figure how Miss Dog's Bone, with that spicy handkerchief held to her nose, would be able to scramble up and snatch the golden casket. It was possible, but difficult.

Something fell softly into his begging bowl. It was a folded piece of paper. Sammy palmed it and nudged Lucky. They drifted toward the eastern doorway. A tall, black-robed young priest stared at him suspiciously. Sammy, recognizing the priest as a member of Penang Pete's gang, felt another shiver ripple down his spine.

Just then, from somewhere behind him, the banshee whisper repeated its blood-chilling warning:

"You guys are gonna get yours!"

A thing like that, Sammy reflected, as he darted wary eyes here and there, could get a man down. It was making his heart do tricks; it was making him sweat. Icy winds danced along his spine.

But he saw no one who might have uttered the shivery warning.—Some one disguised, of course.—But how?—Who?

CHAPTER VI

THE THOUSAND STEPS

PRESSING THEIR WAY through the crowd, the two uneasy adventurers sought an unoccupied corner. They found it in the lee of a crumbling sandstone shrine, not far from the sun dial and the bullock cart where the youthful sacrificial victim and his parents crouched and stared up at the monstrous Balancing Buddha.

The tip of the shadow was now within a few centimeters of the red cross on the sun dial flagging. Anxiously, Sammy reflected:

"My luck feels wrong."

He opened the note. It contained a string of sharply square, black capital letters. This was the message:

COME AT ONCE TO THE TEMPLE OF
THE ROSE QUARTZ BUDDHA.

Sammy and Lucky stared breathlessly at this unsigned, mysterious communication. Who had sent it? Friend or foe? In Bangwar to-day, Sammy reasoned, there was no such thing as a friend—unless the message had come from Miss Dog's Bone.

Perhaps it had, of course. Perhaps she had looked over the lay of the land and desired a last minute shift in plans. Perhaps—

"Where the hell is she?" he asked. "We ought to have seen that girl by now. The time's almost here."

"We'd better go look-see this rosy Buddha," Lucky growled.

The temple of the Rose Quartz Buddha was one of the lesser shrines. It was tucked away in a confusion of smaller and larger structures. The young men found it and went in. Within was comparative darkness, scented as usual with incense. There was a glimmer of light from a hole near the black roof, and this glimmer played mysteriously on the small Buddha—a fat little pink god set in its *oddeitha*.

"This don't look so hot to me!" Lucifer Jones breathed.

It didn't to Sammy, either. For one thing, there were two pairs of doors, and both pairs swung shut with weights.

"Who wants what?" Sammy said, experimentally.

A round-looking bulk oozed out from behind the white stone *oddeitha*—the inner shrine enclosure. A picturesque old Chinese with mandarin mustaches hanging straight down beside his mouth, and with a rubby button cap on his head appeared, arms tucked into opposite sleeves of a blue brocade jacket.

"Gentlemen," he whispered, "I welcome you to the shrine of my ancestors."

His English was excellent, almost without accent. He came slowly toward them, his air benign.

"I have pierced your disguises," he whispered. "I know why you are in Bangwar to-day."

There was something hypnotic about this old Chinaman. Perhaps it was his whisper, which issued from him mysteriously, a soft and velvety thread of sound.

"I know," he went on, "that you are possessed of a powerful magic." He was addressing Sammy. "Last night in Rangoon, I saw you puff out your cheeks at the watchman. I saw him fall instantly to sleep. I wish to possess some of this magic. There is no price I am not willing to pay."

"At 'em!" Sammy snarled.

With his left foot he kicked out violently behind him. The heel established violent contact with a shin. A man groaned thinly. Steel clattered on the stone floor.

At that instant, Lucky's left fist went thumpingly into a dim, saffron face.

But Sammy was occupied with his host.

"Joe Fong!" he growled. "You double-crossing rat!"

He sank a fist, wrist-deep, into the opium smuggler's paunch. Joe Fong gave a vast gasp, and clapped both hands to his belly. Bending over, he met the smacking impact of Sammy's right fist, and fell flat to join his ancestors, at least temporarily.

A **WELL-SHARPENED** steel blade whistled under Sammy's chin. He straightened up to hear it clang against the base of the *oddeitha*—and found himself involved with a pair of spidery arms. He promptly slung one over his shoulder, gave a heave and a lurch, and had the satisfaction of hearing three bones snap as one. The object lesson went squealing down into a corner at the same moment that a yellow foot came swiftly toward Sammy's face. That was an old Malay maneuver.

Sammy caught the foot in two hands, jerked it up and over, and paused no longer than a third of a second to hear a skull crack on the solid floor.

Lucifer Jones, meanwhile, was mopping up in his own department. A lover of free-for-alls, a master at close quarters, he was accounting for his fourth and final victim.

Presently, seven men—the attacking party—lay in attitudes of sleep or death about the temple of the Rose Quartz Buddha, and the two adventurers were hastily leaving the scene. They entered the broiling sunlight again. Singapore was unmarred, but his best friend was bleeding freely from the nose. It seemed to be fractured, and it was swelling.

As they started toward the black pyramid, a gong began deeply to boom. It boomed in measured strokes, to the rhythm of a dirge. The sacrificial procession was starting.

A marrow-chilling whisper behind them said, *"You guys are gonna get yours!"*

Sammy spun about. No one was in sight now, except the personage he had seen and thrice suspected before, the elderly Burmese in the royal purple *paso*. Sammy had first seen him in the act of tossing limes to a group of shrieking, scrambling small boys.

"We've gotta give this guy a fast workout," Sammy breathed.

He recognized him now—the balloon of a man who had accosted him when first he emerged from under that wharf yesterday morning—Rincon Deal. Rincon Deal was grinning beneath his clever makeup, as the two holy men swiftly approached. His grin was, however, a little apprehensive.

"You lousy rat!" Sammy began.

"Now—just—a—minute!" Mr. Deal protested, dragging out the words for emphasis. "I seen through you guys like a pair of glass windows. I propositioned you yesterday, Red. My gang is scattered through this mob, all ready to jump you."

"Nuts!" Sam said.

"Nuts right back at you," Mr. Deal said, with assurance. "Do we do business, or do we do business? Take your pick, boys. There ain't much time. Every thug here is set to go, when that ceremony starts; and I know it as well as you do.—Do we talk?"

"Sure, we talk," Sammy said. "But not here, sucker! We want privacy."

"Not me," said Mr. Deal. "Not with a pair o' strong-arm artists like you two."

Sammy's fist moved less than four inches, but its knuckles found Mr. Deal's solar plexus. He would have dropped, if Sammy and Lucky, each to an arm, had not whisked the beautifully costumed white man into the temple and up to the Little Sleeping Buddha which was but a step away.

IN THIS retreat, swiftly, dexterously, Sammy and his companion tore enough royal purple strips from Mr. Deal's *paso* to fashion a gag and bind his hands and feet.

But there was more competition to deal with. They strode through the mobs at the base of the pyramid, saw that the black shadow cast by the great stone finger was just touching the red cross, and made their way to the eastern entrance of the temple of the Golden Buddha.

The throngs were thinner here, but the black-eyed Indo-Chinese with the sugar cane still lounged there.

A Burmese girl drifted near. She had jungle flowers in her hair, and carried a little green silk pouch in one pretty brown hand.

Sammy measured foot-seconds. He approached the Indo-Chinese from the rear. With a sweep of his hand, he spilled the stalk of cane out of his hand and sent it bounding a dozen feet. It fell with a tremendous crash. The cane flew into splinters, and out tumbled a long, thin, slightly curved *parabanga*—a native sword!

Black-robed priests raced out of the temple as Sammy melted back into the crowd, near the spot where Miss Dog's Bone stood. Other priests seemed to spring out of the very ground. They closed in on the Indo-Chinese. Sammy heard him scream—and saw no more of him.

The incident was unnoticed by the crowd.

It was almost time for the sacrificial procession to start. The holiday mood of the mob had passed. They were chanting now, keeping time to the gong, and to the beating of lesser gongs and temple drums. The air was filled with the rhythmic vibrations of voices, some of them shrill with frenzy, and of gongs and temple drums.

The sacrificial procession was forming at the base of the pyramid, preparing to ascend on the northern side. The gongs and drums and yelping voices beat in faster rhythm now.

Sammy bent down until his lips were close to the Shan girl's brown ear and whispered, in her language:

"You must work fast, sister. Get that casket and get out of here like an eel. Every crook in the world is on this job. I've been doing my best to confuse them."

"I do not fear, my king," Miss Dog's Bone answered resolutely. "I will meet you at the north gate, with the casket—or I will not be alive at all. Go thou with Buddha!"

Sammy saw, over her shoulder, a familiar pair of green-black eyes slanting at him. There was a stirring in the crowd. Sammy gripped Lucky's arm and whispered:

"It's half-baked, but we gotta go. Something is cockeyed with my luck. It won't turn. I can't feel it turn. It still points the wrong way.—But let's go!"

As he and Lucky started for the base of the great black pyramid, he saw the stirring in the crowd become a definite movement—as definite as the movement of tall grass when a large, long snake wriggles through it along the ground.

It spelled trouble. It spelled pursuit. Doubtless spelled Penang Pete's gang, thirsting for trouble—Joe Fong's gang, thirsting for revenge—anybody's gang going to any pains to block whatever it was he had up his sleeve.

A five-second advantage was all that Singapore Sammy asked for. He had it—almost. From now on, anything was in order, from knives to poisoned darts.

But he was sweating prematurely. That hard, cold feeling inside still persisted. It was the feeling that his luck wasn't turning; wasn't even ready to turn.

He saw that the shadow of the sun dial pointed squarely at the red cross on the flagging. The gong was booming faster and faster, trying to outrun his heart. The doomed boy's father and mother were still in the cart, staring up in terror at the great, gray blob atop the pyramid. But the boy was gone; the priests had him.

Singapore knew what was wrong. The Malabar pearl! He'd always tried not to be superstitious, but his luck was never as wrong as this when he had the pearl.

HE WAS walking faster and faster, keeping time with the gongs and drums. A cloud of smoke was rising up from the fiftieth step down from the top of the pyramid. Incense. Almost a smoke screen. He could use a good thick smoke screen from now on!

"When do we go up?" Lucky got out through clenched teeth.

"Another six seconds."

That long snake behind them was out of the grass now. There must have been forty men in the crowd. Here, the pilgrims were thinner—all clustered on the northern side, where they could see the most. But he kept up the five-second gap.

Sammy didn't want to lose the snake. He wanted to draw these cutthroats away from the blue temple, to give Ma Kwe Yo the fullest possible freedom.

"Now!" he snapped, and started up the black steps.

The two holy men gathered their robes in their hands and went flying up. Ten seconds later, looking back, Sammy saw the forty thieves strung out, following, staring up, some of them puzzled. He didn't stop climbing, however.

His heart began to thump and climb from these unusual demands. But he kept going—up and up. A thousand steps! He'd once counted them. Up and up and up....

Bangwar, the Plain of a Thousand and One Shrines, was spread out below now like a landscape view from an airplane. He could see the lush green jungle across the river. He could see the outriggers on the river, a milling jumble of them. Sun struck glints from temple roofs of glazed tile. He looked down on a sea of brown and saffron faces, upturned. But the sightseers weren't watching him. They were watching the procession of priests, in the center of which was the Burmese boy who was about to be offered up in sacrifice to the God of Life.

Mr. Stanley Rysdale had said to Sammy last night, "I have found life fairly precarious." Sammy was swiftly coming to the conclusion that for him life had never been more precarious than it was at this moment. It now looked as if the forty cut-throats were going to follow him to the bitter end. And there were fanatics ahead.

His and Lucky's robes should get them by. But the forty trailers would arouse anybody's suspicions.

A priest met the two mendicants at the step where the incense pots were throwing their scented gloom into the blue noon sky.

Sammy panted, "Oh, holy father, we wish to seek a spot near heaven, where we can dwell upon the iniquities of mankind."

He said it with half-lidded eyes, trusting to the priest's evident shortsightedness to prevent discovery of his green-blue eyes.

"Who are these that follow?" the priest asked.

"We know not, holy father."

While the priest stared at the forty who came panting up, Sammy and Lucky slipped past the fateful nine hundred and fiftieth step. They climbed on up, and Sammy did not pause to ponder the fate of the pursuit. If the priest let them through, or did not let them through, it didn't matter.

He was examining the job ahead of him with the eye of a practical engineer. The great stone Buddha—a hundred and fifty tons of it—was at hand now.

Sammy ran around to the north side—saw that the sacrificial procession was about half-way up. They were coming faster now however, in time to the steady booming of the temple gongs below.

Sammy resumed his engineering investigation. The flanks of stone had been eaten away by sun and wind. But most of the weight, as he had believed, was on the east side.

He spirited the three sticks of dynamite, the percussion caps, the fuse from his pack. He opened a pocket knife. Recklessly, he punched a hole in one end of each stick of powder. He cut off four inches of fuse for each stick. He crimped each length of fuse into each percussion cap with his teeth, then rammed each percussion cap into its appointed hole.

HE WAS sweating now. His heart had jumped into his neck, behind his ears, and was thumping there.

It was going to be close work. He had often worked with dynamite, but this time he based his expectations largely upon hope. If he had guessed wrong, if the one hundred and fifty-ton mass of stone went down the wrong slope of the pyramid, it would be mighty tough for the Shan girl. It would be even tougher for the Burmese boy and his parents. And Sammy didn't want to kill any more people than he could help.

On the other hand, the Balancing Buddha might be resting more securely than it seemed to be. Perhaps Stanley Rysdale was wrong. A hundred and fifty tons of stone was a lot of stone. Yet if a hundred-mile wind would start it to going....

"Grab it!" he panted, as he finished with the last stick. "Shove it into that crack!"

Lucky snatched the stick out of his hand. He jammed it into the crack and struck a match. Sammy rammed the other two sticks into strategic cracks. With shaking hands, he struck a clump of matches, wired together especially for this occasion.

As he lit the fuses, five or six priests came surging into view from the opposite side. They saw the white smoke fizzing from the fuses. They shouted.

Lucky, running around, started down the south side of the pyramid. Sammy waited just long enough to make sure that all three fuses were burning well. He hoped the priests would either misunderstand the fizzing of the white smoke, or would be afraid to do anything about it if they did understand.

He started down the black steps, taking them three at a leap. Behind him, the priests yelled. Glancing back over his shoulder, Sammy saw that reinforcements had joined them. Some one had tipped them off! Or perhaps some priest had been suspicious of them as they climbed up. Anyhow, the fat was in the fire now. And it was reasonably certain that he and Lucky wouldn't get out of Bangwar with whole skins—if at all!

He was trying to count the seconds as he bounded down the

steep side of that pyramid after Lucky. Fuse burns at the rate of one foot per minute. The four inches should consume about twenty seconds before it reached the dynamite.

Sammy had estimated that he and Lucky would reach the bottom of the pyramid before the dynamite went off. But the first blast occurred when he was less than two-thirds of the way to the bottom. A terrific detonation shook the air. It was instantly followed by the others, so close together that they sounded like one explosion. He did not dare look behind him until he reached the bottom. A misstep here might mean a cracked skull.

Lucky was springing down ahead of him in great bounds, and when the explosions occurred, he did not hesitate.

REACHING THE bottom-most step, Singapore hesitated only a moment. Lucky paused also. The two men stared up. The Balancing Buddha was still there!—But it was no longer where it had been. It had begun to lean.

Then the great gray mass of stone began to slide. It was leaning to the east, but sliding to the north!

A score of men in black robes were streaming down the face of the pyramid. They were shouting, but their shouts went unheard in the uproar. The gongs and temple drums had either stopped or been drowned out in the greater noise. People were screaming. The air reverberated with the high, frantic voice of a sea of brown humanity in terror.

Sammy and Lucky did not pause to watch the downfall of the Balancing Buddha. But what they heard told the story. Even above the bedlam of voices, they heard the thunder of that great mass of stone as it started down the north slope of the black pyramid. It filled the world with a deep and awful booming, a sound of grinding and crumbling—a sound of earthquakes and eruptions, as if the very world were disintegrating. Minor boomings, crashings and cracklings accompanied the deep reverberation set up as the Balancing Buddha slid and smashed and bounded down the north slope.

By this time, the two American trouble hunters were trying to lose themselves from a score of murderous brown fanatics. They darted down narrow little alleys behind shrines, looking for a way of escape. The priests split up into scouting parties.

Near the temple of the Kingfisher Jade Buddha, four priests cornered them. The two white men armed themselves with stones from a crumbling shrine. The four priests, knives in hands, charged—and a volley of marble fragments checked them. Another volley caused them to retreat long enough for the two white men to scale a wall, gain comparative freedom.

They heard the sounds of pursuit withdraw. They heard the shrieking of the mob subside.

Singapore panted, "I think we're okay now. If all that uproar didn't attract everybody but the priests out o' that temple, then my luck never will turn. I figure Miss Dog's Bone dusted the powder into those pots on schedule. Right this minute, that baby ought to be walkin' out o' that temple with the whisker up her sleeve!"

"Yeah," Lucky said in a shaky voice. "Let's go."

"That ain't the way."

"You're nuts! She said the north gate."

"Sure! That's why we're goin' to the south gate."

"Don't you trust her?"

"I trust nobody!"

"Okay," Lucky said belligerently. "Go to the south gate, then! Me, I'm goin' to the north gate."

"Suit yourself. We're better off separated, anyhow. The word's gonna be out for a coupla beggin' priests.—Mingle with the crowd! Act natural! Keep your eyes down! Whoever gets the whisker goes straight to old Fuzz-Nut, down at the teak yard, and collects.—And we meet aboard the Goose. Okay?"

"Okay," Lucky affirmed, and strode away—in the direction of the north gate.

CHAPTER VII

THE LUCK THAT TURNED

SAMMY DID NOT walk to the south gate; he ran. He bolted down lanes. He vaulted fences. He dashed through compounds. He wanted to outdistance pursuit—and to reach the south gate before Miss Dog's Bone got there.

The wind might have reached the south gate faster, yet others were travelling with as much alacrity. This was the vanguard of fugitives—pilgrims terrified by the explosions in heaven which had sent the fearsome stone Buddha toppling from its pyramid.

In the forefront of these was a familiar trio—the mother, the father, the youthful sacrificial victim.

And their faces were grim with the resolve to escape this blessed but terrific miracle.

They did not see Sammy. They saw no one. But the glow of joy and release was in their eyes.

Sammy reached the south gate and waited in the lee of the great blue marble bulwark. Nearby grew a thicket of bamboo. He darted to this and entered it, regardless of cobras.

Presently he began to doubt his guesswork. Miss Dog's Bone did not come.

People flooded through the south gate in a yelping mob. But Miss Dog's Bone was not among them. Either he had done her a great injustice—or she had lost her life in the attempt to steal the precious whisker.

Then he saw her coming. She was trotting along with the rest of them, and she was looking neither to right nor left. She did not even glance at the bamboo thicket.

With a hard grin, Sammy stepped out and followed. Presently she left the main torrent of humanity and darted off down a path which led straight to the river, then climbed a hill.

Sammy, shielded by trees and bushes, skirted the hill, watching her every movement. He had made a brilliant discovery. But he was a cat playing with a mouse; at least, he fancied he was.

Ma Kwe Yo had hesitated at the top of the hill. She was shading her eyes, staring toward the river. Silhouetted there, like a slim and beautiful Oriental statue, she remained rigid for a moment, then, wildly, she waved both arms above her head.

Sammy stared hard at the river. In the confusion of boats on the river, one somehow stood out. In the stern, manning a sweep, stood a man in yellow—a man in the garb of a Buddhist begging priest. The only difference between Sammy and the man at the sweep was that the man at the sweep had his yellow hood pulled down well over his face.

Watching, Sammy saw this man suddenly waving his hands in a signal identical with that of the girl on the hilltop.

Sammy waited no longer. He knew a shorter cut to the river than the girl would take. He took it, running the full distance at his best speed.

He reached the river bank as the man in the outrigger maneuvered his boat alongside another which had the position of vantage beside the bank.

Sammy's breath was coming in hard, short gasps. But not from the exertion of that stiff sprint. Here was indeed, the end of a long, long trail. For the man in the outrigger was, without question, his father! That mendicant's costume was old Bill Shay's favorite disguise!

SAMMY YANKED the hood down about his own head, stepped aboard the canoe alongside the bank—leaped nimbly into his father's boat.

"Now, you old rat!" Sammy said harshly. "We're gonna settle a few accounts."

The man in the stern peered at him from the folds of his cape. "Sam!" he cried. "Not Sam!"

He lifted the sweep out of the water—no mean feat—and

brought it swinging up and over. It almost took Singapore Sammy by surprise. But he had had dealings with this clever old rogue in the past. He made a flying jump at his father. Old Bill Shay dropped the sweep, laughed, jumped a clean six feet sideways, and landed on his feet in another outrigger. Without hesitating, he vaulted over a canoe loaded with plantains—and vanished into the brown, swirling waters of the Rangoon!

Sammy knew that trick. A man sank down amongst and under a jumble of these outrigger hulls, and he could laugh at pursuit.

He stared at the stop where that wily old rascal had disappeared, took a deep breath, picked up the sweep and with his free hand adjusted his hood so that it almost covered his face.

Old Bill Shay had slipped through his fingers like the human eel he was. But did that mean that luck hadn't turned? What was the main chance, after all? Was it old Bill Shay or was it Miss Dog's Bone?

Sammy waited for the other fish that remained in his sea.

She came trotting along presently, all out of breath. Sammy averted his head slightly.

The lovely little Shan girl climbed into the canoe. She was panting. In English, she said sweetly:

"All right, Bill—step on it!"

Sammy shoved the sweep into the mud, and maneuvered the little craft out into an opening. He watched the water with the eyes of a hawk. He didn't want a surprise that he wouldn't be able to handle adequately. But Bill Shay evidently thought better of a surprise attack. At all events, he made none.

Sammy waggled the sweep. The outrigger scraped other hulls, found its tortuous way into clear water at last.

But Sammy was not satisfied. He continued to work the sweep until the canoe was well on its way toward mid-river.

The girl began to giggle as she panted.

"I got it!" she said, exultantly. "It was a tough assignment,

Bill—And I couldn't have done it without those two suckers. Did you see them blow up that Buddha?"

"Yeah," Sammy said, in his father's deep, slow voice.

"Wasn't it a dandy little gag?"

"Yeah."

"It worked out beautifully, Bill. Sam cleared the track for me very nicely. All I had to do was to go in and pour the blue powder into the incense pots. I held the silk to my nose—and just climbed. Two or three gangs were fighting each other outside. But if it hadn't been for those two prize suckers I never could have done it!"

Sally Lavender began to laugh again.

"I was thinking," she laughed. "Will your cocky son's face be the color of his hair when he guesses the truth!"

SAMMY HAD now driven the little canoe well into mid river. There were no boats of any kind near.

Carefully he hauled the sweep aboard and laid it across the stern. Then, on hands and knees, he crawled toward Sally Lavender. With a puzzled smile, she watched him come. She had been sitting there, relaxed, on the floor of the canoe; but now she sat up.

"Whose face?" Sam asked amiably.

He threw the hood back from his head with one hand. With the other, he seized the nape of Sally Lavender's neck. She screamed.

"You double-crossing—!" she began, but the speech ended in a squeak. "Sam!" she implored. "Sam, for God's sake, be reasonable! I'll split with you!—I'll play ball! I'll be square with you!"

Holding her by the neck, Sammy ripped the *tamein* from her body. Under it she wore a khaki shirt and a pair of khaki shorts.

"You little tramp!" he said.

Methodically he went through her pockets. In a hip pocket he found the blue fire pearl of Malabar. In another hip pocket he found approximately thirty thousand rupees—the purchase price of the *Blue Goose*. And around her slim waist he found Lucifer Jones's gold belt.

He had caught the right fish, after all. That matter of the will would have to wait.

The little golden casket containing the Sacred Whisker he found in a fold of the *tamein*.

He strapped the gold belt about his own waist, under his robe, and in his pack disposed of the thirty thousand rupees and the little golden casket. The Malabar pearl he restored to its pouch at the end of the soft copper wire about his neck.

Sally Lavender, cleverest little thief in the Far East, flattened herself against the floor of the canoe—shrank from him in terror.

Having disposed of the prizes of the hunt, Sammy stared down at her indulgently. Her eyes stared back with terror.

"I got a good mind," he said, "to wring your lousy little neck."

"Sammy!" she bleated. "Listen, Sammy! Don't hurt me! You— you wouldn't hurt me!—You know why I did it. If you don't, you ought to know. Put yourself in my position!"

"Not a chance! You—"

"Listen, Sammy! What would you have done? I've told you, as frankly as a girl possibly could, that I love you. I've always been goofy about you.—And what did you do?"

"Sure! I let you put K.O. drops into my beer!"

"Only because I was furious—humiliated! I've never offered my love to any other man—"

"What were you offerin' to Lucky Jones one hour later?"

"Not my love!—Never!—If he says so, it's a lie! I've always loved you. If—if you'd give a girl a break—if you'd only been nicer—if you'd only said—But you didn't! Why shouldn't I put K.O. drops into your damned beer?"

Sammy, in spite of his best resolves, was interested. Maybe Lucky was right. Maybe he'd always been nuts about this dame.

"YOU'RE SO damned stubborn!" Sally cried. "Why—why—

why won't you team up with me? I'll go straight. I'll eat out of your hand!—You're the only man I've ever known that I've respected. And I do respect you. Listen!…"

"Talk fast, baby; I got a date with an island."

"What island?"

"Nix!—On second thought, it's a small island."

"I know!" she cried. "I know! And you're just a fool! It's another of your wild-goose chases—another of your treasure hunts! It's all you've done ever since I knew you—you treasure-chaser! Why can't you be sensible? With our combined courage and brains, we—we could own all Asia!"

"What would I do, baby, with real estate?"

"Oh! I could shake you!—You've let fortunes dribble through your fingers since I knew you!—Why did you give Cosmo Sand all that gold you took from Simarong Island? It was yours—honestly yours. You'd earned it."

"Sandy needed it worse than I did, kid."

"If you'd say the word—if you'd team up with me, Sam—we'd have your father trapped in no time. We'd get that will. You'd get your inheritance.—And that million would only be the beginning! We could be rich, because we're both smart and because we're both fearless!"

"Why do I want to be rich? If I was rich, I'd have to be respectable."

"You like being a T.T.T.!"

"Sure, I like being a Typical Tropical Tramp. I like bumming. I like the feel of a nice little ship under me. I like the sound of the wind. And I like to go snoopin' into new ports."

Sally Lavender made a gesture of despair.

"Then listen to me, Sam Shay! If you turn this casket over to that *mahout* for a measly hundred thousand rupees, you're the biggest sucker that ever lived! I can sell it to a temple in Mandalay for three hundred thousand rupees—almost a hundred thousand dollars, gold. In fact, I've closed the sale!"

"Nothing stirring! I'm a man of my word."

She sniffed contemptuously.

"You're a sap! Sell it to the Mandalay temple! Are you going to turn me loose in this god forsaken country without a dime? I'm dead broke."

Sammy deliberated. He had never met a girl who appealed to him as Sally Lavender did, nor a girl whose air of sweet young girlish innocence was so utterly deceiving. At any time, within the past twenty-four hours, she would have struck a knife into his heart, if that in any way could have aided her latest cause.

Still, he couldn't help being just a little goofy about the little rat.

He took out the roll of rupees and peeled off a thousand-rupee note, which he tossed to her.

"It's the loser's end, baby!"

She snatched the note and stuffed it into one of her pockets.

"I suppose," she said, scrambling away from him, "you think that entitles you to black my eyes now."

Sammy grinned at her. He hadn't the slightest intention of harming her.

"I was thinkin'," he said, "of givin' you that good-bye kiss and puttin' you ashore—before I weaken."

Sally misconstrued that as sarcasm. She scrambled swiftly into the bow of the canoe and poised there, like a bird about to take flight.

"Wait a minute, baby!" Sammy said. "Don't get so excited."

But she dived cleanly into the water, striking out vigorously for shore, looking back over her shoulder at every stroke. She was no doubt prepared to dive, if he attempted to overtake her.

Sammy didn't attempt to overtake her. Instead he picked up the sweep, leaned lazily against it, and watched her swim.

Her feet, and her legs, as far as her knees, were stained brown. The rest of the way, they were white. She had slim, strong legs. She had a slim, beautiful, strong young body.

"If only you were as good as you look!" Sammy sighed.

He began briskly to work the sweep, and the swift current aided him.

IT STILL lacked an hour of dawn when he reached the teak yard, left the canoe in the mud, and climbed the ladder to the hut of Mr. Beyond Comparison.

The old *mahout* was awake and waiting. He met Sammy with an ancient Mauser rifle, but dropped the gun at sight of the little gold casket.

He cried, "The sun is in the House of the Elephant! Thou art undoubtedly a *yahanda!*"

Mr. Beyond Comparison gave a sob, and dropped to his knees.

He kissed Sammy's muddy toes. He kissed the hem of the yellow gown. He babbled:

"You can hear like a cat and see like a *ngat*—and you have a knowledge of the unfathomable future!"

But he would not produce the hundred thousand rupees until he had made sure that the treasured whisker was intact. He opened the little jeweled casket, and from it he lifted the little sapphire-blue lapis lazuli box, intricately carved and inlaid with gold. And from the little lapis lazuli box, he removed the tiny ivory casket with its dazzling rows of diamonds—themselves worth very close to a hundred thousand rupees!—Then, with shaking hands, he took out of the slender ivory casket what appeared to be a rod of opaque red glass. It was a hollow tube of red obsidian delicately carved, stoppered at one end with a plug carved of emerald and at the other with a plug carved of diamond.

Breathlessly, the old *mahout* shook the tube, and into his hand fell the thinnest sliver of gray. A hair! A whisker! A whisker from the chin of the greatest of all Oriental deities!

"A holy whisker of Buddha!" the old man said devoutly.

And Sammy, pagan though he was, felt stirring within him a feeling of awe, of superstitious respect.

Presently the old man replaced the priceless relic in its tube, reassembling the various little caskets.

"We have both gained merit," said Mr. Beyond Comparison, and he gave Singapore Sammy one hundred thousand rupees.

As Sam returned to the dugout, the rising sun, a red and golden glory above the jungle, saw him sending the canoe downstream like a speeding arrow. The jungle foliage was still sparkling with the overnight dew when he leaped from the canoe to the deck of the blue schooner.

A Chinese watchman in the stern blinked sleepily at him, and sprang to his feet, reaching for the rifle on the deck.

"Go fetch Lin Chang, chop-chop!" the American barked.

"Lin Chang allatime sleepy side," the watchman protested.

"Wake him up!" Sammy roared. "Tell him Singapore Sam is on deck and wants action!"

"My no savee."

Nevertheless the watchman departed.

HE RETURNED presently with a sleepy-looking Oriental who eyed Sammy distrustfully. There ensued a bitter debate. Lin Chang wouldn't talk business. Come back later.

Sammy ended it by running down into the cabin and bringing back a pair of dice.

"I got a feeling, Lin Chang," Sammy said, rattling the bones in his hand, "that my luck has turned. It just hit me, all of a bunch."

"My no savee!"

"Savee this?"

Sam sent the dice bouncing into the scuppers. He yelped. He had rolled a seven. Lin Chang awoke. Being a member of a race that would rather gamble than eat, he became interested.

"What thing wanchee?"

"One roll," Sam said. "One roll for the Goose! High man wins!"

"Against what thing?"

"Fifty thousand rupees! Can do?"

"Can do.—Pay my look see."

Sammy gave him the look-see—slapped fifty thousand rupees on deck.

"Roll!" he roared.

Lin Chang, glinting-eyed, snatched up the dice in his long, yellow fingers. He nursed them to his lips. He spoke an enchantment over them. He clicked them softly against his ear. He rolled—a pair of fives!

He grinned. Maybe the white man could tie that!

Sammy grabbed the dice. He crooned to them.

"Bones," he crooned, "roll with my luck! Roll where my luck is rollin'! Talk to me!"

He snapped the dice out of his fingers and they went dancing down the deck.

Lin Chang went dancing after them; so did Sammy. The spinning cubes came to rest—*a five and a six!*

LUCKY JONES came wearily aboard, shortly before dusk that evening. He had walked all of the way from Bangwar. He came aboard to find that the *Blue Goose* was outfitted for a three-months' cruise, that her decks had been holystoned, that her spars had been repainted, that she was spic and span and shipshape, from stem to stern....

Some hours later, in the light of a crescent moon, the finest little schooner on the Indian Ocean slipped down the Rangoon River and into the Bay of Bengal.

The two friends lounged in Bombay chairs in the stern and smoked their pipes, watching the lights of Burma dwindle into the shore haze. Sidin, their Malay *serang*, was at the wheel.

"What gets me is, why we didn't spot her," Lucky said. "We saw her in broad daylight, and we didn't know her!"

"I've figured that out," Sammy replied. "She was the one dame I've seen in the past twenty-four hours, yellow or brown or white, who *didn't* look like Sally Lavender!"

"Maybe," Lucifer Jones said. "And maybe it was those teeth. Sally's teeth are like pearls. Miss Dog's Bone had teeth reddened by betel."

The two successful adventurers puffed comfortably at their pipes for a while.

"Now, this island," Captain Jones began again, "lies dead south of the Paracels Reef, and due north of Pemanggil. The old Dutchman I talked to in Palembang swears that old guy left a treasure in pearls buried there.—Did I tell you about this spooky thing that comes crawlin' up out o' the lagoon and squashes the juice out of its victims?"

"Yeah," Sammy said dreamily. "And it sure sounds like our meat!"

ABOUT THE AUTHOR

THE DECISION TO become a writer of fiction was made for me by fate. In 1914, in Panama, where I spent a week when I was a wireless operator on a little steamer that creaked up and down the Central American coast, I met an author who painted the joys of free-lancing so vividly that I could not resist the call. We were drunk. I was twenty. Since then, I have been trying to catch up with all of those joys he mentioned.

Starting to write stories in 1914 and, four years later selling my first one, marks up, I suppose, a very poor batting average. But in those years I was getting experience, seeing the world, and acquiring knowledge. I "punched brass" as a wireless operator all over the Pacific. I entered Columbia University in 1915, and one year later left because I didn't believe in higher learning. I still don't believe in it. I became a newspaper reporter, later a magazine editor.

Then came the war, which I won practically single-handed by writing high-pressure publicity to induce patriotic Americans to send books to Washington for camp libraries for soldiers and gobs. Books came by the carload, by the ton: McGuffy's readers, old almanacs, spellers, arithmetics, out-dated novels and just trash. The soldiers and sailors who read those books soon hated the war so bitterly, that they promptly got busy and ended it. That's how I won the war.

After the war, I wanted another look at China, and was sent

to the Far East by *Collier's* to write articles on China, the Philippines, India
and Malaya.

The first story I sold was written
while I was editing a motion picture
trade paper. It was bought by the
Argosy, and it was about a wolf named
Murg. Don't ask me why. In the inter-
vening years I have written millions of
words. Perhaps it is Murg who sits so
patiently at my door!

George F.
Worts

I started writing fiction under the
pen name of Loring Brent, because it would have annoyed the
owner of the motion picture magazine to learn that I was writing fiction out of hours. He thought I fell asleep at my desk
because I was working so hard for him! When my income from
fiction exceeded my salary, I quit the job. Since then I have been
free-lancing exclusively, except for a two-year period when I
lived in a Florida swamp town and added to my writing the
duties of postmaster, game warden and deputy sheriff. Out of
that experience came a long series of stories about a Florida
town I called Vingo.

I have enjoyed most writing stories about certain established
characters. Apparently the most popular of these have been the
Peter the Brazen, the Vingo and the Gillian Hazeltine stories. I
stopped writing about Peter the Brazen (a swashbuckling wireless operator on ships in the China run) about ten years ago.
He was, incidentally, the subject of the only novel I have had
published in America. I am now starting a new series about him.

When I am not traveling I live in Westport, Connecticut. My
interests are horses, sailing and flying. I took up flying about a
year ago to write some articles on how it feels to learn to fly, and
was badly bitten by the bug. I can make a three-point landing
about five times out of ten.

I like New York, but would prefer to live in Honolulu. I smoke sixty cigarettes a day. I like murder trials. I have never mastered the noble game of poker, although I once wrote a book about it. In my spare time I study law and medicine. I have two young sons and a still younger daughter; an able crew for my sailboat— except that there is usually mutiny aboard the lugger!

1. GENIUS JONES by Lester Dent
2. WHEN TIGERS ARE HUNTING: THE COMPLETE ADVENTURES OF CORDIE,
    SOLDIER OF FORTUNE, VOLUME 1 by W. Wirt
3. THE SWORDSMAN OF MARS by Otis Adelbert Kline
4. THE SHERLOCK OF SAGELAND: THE COMPLETE TALES OF SHERIFF HENRY,
    VOLUME 1 by W.C. Tuttle
5. GONE NORTH by Charles Alden Seltzer
6. THE MASKED MASTER MIND by George F. Worts
7. BALATA by Fred MacIsaac
8. BRETWALDA by Philip Ketchum
9. DRAFT OF ETERNITY by Victor Rousseau
10. FOUR CORNERS, VOLUME 1 by Theodore Roscoe
11. CHAMPION OF LOST CAUSES by Max Brand
12. THE SCARLET BLADE: THE RAKEHELLY ADVENTURES OF CLEVE AND
    D'ENTREVILLE, VOLUME 1 by Murray R. Montgomery
13. DOAN AND CARSTAIRS: THEIR COMPLETE CASES by Norbert Davis
14. THE KING WHO CAME BACK by Fred MacIsaac
15. BLOOD RITUAL: THE ADVENTURES OF SCARLET AND BRADSHAW, VOLUME 1
    by Theodore Roscoe
16. THE CITY OF STOLEN LIVES: THE ADVENTURES OF PETER THE BRAZEN, VOLUME
    1 by Loring Brent
17. THE RADIO GUN-RUNNERS by Ralph Milne Farley
18. SABOTAGE by Cleve F. Adams
19. THE COMPLETE CABALISTIC CASES OF SEMI DUAL, THE OCCULT DETECTOR,
    VOLUME 2: 1912–13 by J.U. Giesy and Junius B. Smith
20. SOUTH OF FIFTY-THREE by Jack Bechdolt
21. TARZAN AND THE JEWELS OF OPAR by Edgar Rice Burroughs
22. CLOVELLY by Max Brand
23. WAR LORD OF MANY SWORDSMEN: THE ADVENTURES OF NORCOSS, VOLUME 1
    by W. Wirt
24. ALIAS THE NIGHT WIND by Varick Vanardy
25. THE BLUE FIRE PEARL: THE COMPLETE ADVENTURES OF SINGAPORE SAMMY,
    VOLUME 1 by George F. Worts

26. THE MOON POOL & THE CONQUEST OF THE MOON POOL by Abraham Merritt
27. THE GUN-BRAND by James B. Hendryx
28. JAN OF THE JUNGLE by Otis Adelbert Kline
29. MINIONS OF THE MOON by William Grey Beyer
30. DRINK WE DEEP by Arthur Leo Zagat
31. THE VENGEANCE OF THE WAH FU TONG: THE COMPLETE CASES OF JIGGER MASTERS, VOLUME 1 by Anthony M. Rud
32. THE RUBY OF SURATAN SINGH: THE ADVENTURES OF SCARLET AND BRADSHAW, VOLUME 2 by Theodore Roscoe
33. THE SHERIFF OF TONTO TOWN: THE COMPLETE TALES OF SHERIFF HENRY, VOLUME 2 by W.C. Tuttle
34. THE DARKNESS AT WINDON MANOR by Max Brand
35. THE FLYING LEGION by George Allan England
36. THE GOLDEN CAT: THE ADVENTURES OF PETER THE BRAZEN, VOLUME 3 by Loring Brent
37. THE RADIO MENACE by Ralph Milne Farley
38. THE APES OF DEVIL'S ISLAND by John Cunningham
39. THE OPPOSING VENUS: THE COMPLETE CABALISTIC CASES OF SEMI DUAL, THE OCCULT DETECTOR by J.U. Giesy and Junius B. Smith
40. THE EXPLOITS OF BEAU QUICKSILVER by Florence M. Pettee
41. ERIC OF THE STRONG HEART by Victor Rousseau
42. MURDER ON THE HIGH SEAS AND THE DIAMOND BULLET: THE COMPLETE CASES OF GILLIAN HAZELTINE by George F. Worts
43. THE WOMAN OF THE PYRAMID AND OTHER TALES: THE PERLEY POORE SHEEHAN OMNIBUS, VOLUME 1 by Perley Poore Sheehan
44. A COLUMBUS OF SPACE AND THE MOON METAL: THE GARRETT P. SERVISS OMNIBUS, VOLUME 1 by Garrett P. Serviss
45. THE BLACK TIDE: THE COMPLETE ADVENTURES OF BELLOW BILL WILLIAMS, VOLUME 1 by Ralph R. Perry
46. THE NINE RED GODS DECIDE: THE COMPLETE ADVENTURES OF CORDIE, SOLDIER OF FORTUNE, VOLUME 2 by W. Wirt
47. A GRAVE MUST BE DEEP! by Theodore Roscoe

48. THE AMERICAN by Max Brand
49. THE COMPLETE ADVENTURES OF KOYALA, VOLUME 1 by John Charles Beecham
50. THE CULT MURDERS by Alan Forsyth
51. THE COMPLETE CASES OF THE MONGOOSE by Johnston McCulley
52. THE GIRL AND THE PEOPLE OF THE GOLDEN ATOM by Ray Cummings
53. THE GRAY DRAGON: THE ADVENTURES OF PETER THE BRAZEN, VOLUME 2
    by Loring Brent
54. THE GOLDEN CITY by Ralph Milne Farley
55. THE HOUSE OF INVISIBLE BONDAGE: THE COMPLETE CABALISTIC CASES OF
    SEMI DUAL, THE OCCULT DETECTOR by J.U. Giesy and Junius B. Smith
56. THE SCRAP OF LACE: THE COMPLETE CASES OF MADAME STOREY, VOLUME 1
    by Hulbert Footner
57. TOWER OF DEATH: THE ADVENTURES OF SCARLET AND BRADSHAW, VOLUME 3
    by Theodore Roscoe
58. THE DEVIL-TREE OF EL DORADO by Frank Aubrey
59. THE FIREBRAND: THE COMPLETE ADVENTURES OF TIZZO, VOLUME 1
    by Max Brand
60. MARCHING SANDS AND THE CARAVAN OF THE DEAD: THE HAROLD LAMB
    OMNIBUS by Harold Lamb
61. KINGDOM COME by Martin McCall
62. HENRY RIDES THE DANGER TRAIL: THE COMPLETE TALES OF SHERIFF HENRY,
    VOLUME 3 by W.C. Tuttle
63. Z IS FOR ZOMBIE by Theodore Roscoe
64. THE BAIT AND THE TRAP: THE COMPLETE ADVENTURES OF TIZZO, VOLUME 2
    by Max Brand
65. MINIONS OF MARS by William Gray Beyer
66. SWORDS IN EXILE: THE RAKEHELLY ADVENTURES OF CLEVE AND D'ENTREVILLE,
    VOLUME 2 by Murray R. Montgomery
67. MEN WITH NO MASTER: THE COMPLETE ADVENTURES OF ROBIN THE
    BOMBARDIER by Roy de S. Horn
68. THE TORCH by Jack Bechdolt
69. KING OF CHAOS AND OTHER ADVENTURES: THE JOHNSTON MCCULLEY
    OMNIBUS by Johnston McCulley

70. THE BLIND SPOT by Austin Hall & Homer Eon Flint
71. SATAN'S VENGEANCE by Carroll John Daly
72. THE VIPER: THE COMPLETE CASES OF MADAME STOREY, VOLUME 2
    by Hulbert Footner
73. THE SAPPHIRE SMILE: THE ADVENTURES OF PETER THE BRAZEN, VOLUME 4
    by Loring Brent
74. THE CURSE OF CAPISTRANO AND OTHER ADVENTURES: THE JOHNSTON
    MCCULLEY OMNIBUS, VOLUME 2 by Johnston McCulley
75. THE MAN WHO MASTERED TIME AND OTHER ADVENTURES: THE RAY
    CUMMINGS OMNIBUS by Ray Cummings
76. THE GUNS OF THE AMERICAN: THE ADVENTURES OF NORCROSS, VOLUME 2
    by W. Wirt
77. TRAILIN' by Max Brand
78. WAR DECLARED! by Theodore Roscoe
79. THE RETURN OF THE NIGHT WIND by Varick Vanardy
80. THE FETISH FIGHTERS AND OTHER ADVENTURES: THE F.V.W. MASON FOREIGN
    LEGION STORIES OMNIBUS by F.V.W. Mason
81. THE PYTHON PIT: THE COMPLETE ADVENTURES OF SINGAPORE SAMMY,
    VOLUME 2 by George F. Worts
82. A QUEEN OF ATLANTIS by Frank Aubrey
83. FOUR CORNERS, VOLUME 2 by Theodore Roscoe
84. THE STUFF OF EMPIRE: THE COMPLETE ADVENTURES OF BELLOW BILL
    WILLIAMS, VOLUME 2 by Ralph R. Perry
85. GALLOPING GOLD: THE COMPLETE TALES OF SHERIFF HENRY, VOLUME 4
    by W.C. Tuttle
86. JADES AND AFGHANS: THE COMPLETE ADVENTURES OF CORDIE, SOLDIER OF
    FORTUNE, VOLUME 3 by W. Wirt
87. THE LEDGER OF LIFE: THE COMPLETE CABALISTIC CASES OF SEMI DUAL, THE
    OCCULT DETECTOR by J.U. Giesy and Junius B. Smith
88. MINIONS OF MERCURY by William Gray Beyer
89. WHITE HEATHER WEATHER by John Frederick
90. THE FIRE FLOWER AND OTHER ADVENTURES: THE JACKSON GREGORY
    OMNIBUS by Jackson Gregory

www.ingramcontent.com/pod-product-compliance
Lightning Source LLC
Chambersburg PA
CBHW060425030726
47495CB00003B/747